'SIPPI

'SIPPI

John Oliver Killens

TRIDENT PRESS · NEW YORK · 1967

For PAUL *and* MALCOLM

Library of Congress Catalog Card Number: 67-16400

Published simultaneously in the United States and Canada by Trident Press, a division of Simon & Schuster, Inc., 630 Fifth Avenue, New York, N.Y. 10020.

Printed in the United States of America

PROLOGUE

It was one of those moments all over the world when time caught up with history. From Johannesburg to Birmingham, from Rangoon to Ouagadougou, from Timbuktu to Lenox Avenue, time and history ran a dead heat down the last lap of the human race. Even a sophisticated disenfranchised city like Washington in the District of Columbia in the United States of North America could no longer maintain with dignity its "objective" posture on the sidelines of the main event. And this race was the main event of the entire twentieth century.

It was on a Monday morning, a day not unlike a thousand other days in Washington in the springtime season. And spring came earlier than usual that year. Cherry blossoms already gleamed and glittered along the famous "speedway," that boulevard of feverish lovers, where Romeos and Juliets oohed and aahed and told eternal truths and lied magnificently and swore love everlasting and necked until ungodly hours. And thought that the whole world loved them, save the Capital police.

On Wilburger Street at the corner of 6½ and T in the little alley next to the Howard Theater, some sucker, black and sentimental, played Dusty Fletcher's record all night long that night before the fateful day.

Open the door, Richard

Already a bright and sparkling greenness lay over the land from Capitol Hill to the Washington Monument to the Lincoln Memorial to Mount Vernon in old Virginia, all the way to Mississippi. The sun had risen that fateful morning from a long night's winter sleep and with a giant paintbrush had splashed the stone and concrete of this pure-white-as-the-driven-snow city with dazzling colors of pink and orange and red and blue. Children went to school as they had always done, or played hookey as they sometimes did. The city was white, virginally immaculate, in the downtown governmental section. The august halls of Congress, as per usual, rang to the rafters with memorable

[v]

rhetoric, Southern drawl, Northern brogue, Middle West and Western twang, but drawl, brogue, or Western twang, it was more than likely pretty talk for talk's own sake and seldom led to concrete action. Like art for art's own precious sake. Men and women (civil servants) went dutifully to work that morning mostly in the gleamingly white governmental edifices, or they stayed at home on "sick leave" as they sometimes had a way of doing, devilishly. The Capital Transit buses were as crowded that memorable morning as they always were, as Washingtonians went about their daily business, as if nothing out of the ordinary were about to happen. Notwithstanding, it did happen. And nothing, repeat, absolutely nothing, was ever quite the same again. It was, moreover, time and history in a conspiracy of dastardly subversion.

The man on Wilburger Street said:

> *Open the door, Richard*
> *The man's out here.*

He had knocked on the damn door all of his life, but Richard had never answered. Not to mention Mister Charlie.

On that morning of May 17, 1954, nine highly distinguished Americans, noted for their wisdom and broad vision, grimly lit a fuse to a keg of dynamite upon which a mighty nation had reclined sublimely for more than nine decades. It was indeed a devilish prank for men of such high respectability to engage in; notwithstanding, these wise men set off a chain of reactions that caused explosion after explosion all over this peaceful, democratic, best-of-all-possible worlds. Even down in Mississippi.

Legend has it that when old Jesse Chaney got the word that the Supreme Court had spoken, it was all of two weeks later. Somehow, even with television (he didn't own one anyhow), it took all of two weeks for the word to reach him bending deep in the cotton field on Mister Charles James Richard Wakefield's plantation. Jesse didn't stop running till he reached the Big House more than a mile and a half away. He was in his late fifties, and he had been working cotton since he was seven. Jesse was the best cotton-picking cotton chopper in all of Wakefield County.

He was a tall gangling hulk of brownish-black man. He seemed pure Yoruba stock. Mister Charlie had had no fingers in the pie of his ancestry. He'd tell anybody, and proudly. His skin was smooth and tight, burnished-black, and tender as a newborn baby's backside. You'd have thought a razor had never touched his face. But you could see the years of pain and anguish etched forever in the deep set of his eyes; the years had painstakingly sculptured the contours of his face, had sketched a tender firmness in the corners of his mouth. After he had been running for six or seven minutes, his breathing came in heavy, quick, short gasps. He was too old to run so fast so far. But he had waited so long for this moment. He had bowed and scraped and agreed with his close friend, Mr. Wakefield, so long, so Lord-have-mercy-long, he had begun to walk bent over ever since he was twenty-five years old. But at last the day had come. The day he had hoped for, prayed for, watched for, but had sometimes thought would never happen in his lifetime. The Federal Government was on his side now. Hallelujah! Lift every voice and sing! His bowing and scraping days were over. His heart began to silently sing an old song he had almost forgotten.

> *King Jesus got his arms all around me.*
> *No evil can ever harm me,*
> *For I, thank God, am in His care.*

Against his will his legs slowed down almost to a walk. His heart and soul and mind cried out to his body to keep moving. But his legs felt like he was jumping up and down in forest fire. Can't stop now, his soul entreated him. His chest would burst wide open any minute, and he saw white spots before his face. His head was swimming around and around in a white and swirling river. Can't stop now. He stumbled. He thought the earth was coming up to smack him in the face. But he kept his footing. Can't stop now. His mouth was parched, his throat was scratchy. It was as if he had been running up a long steep hill all the days of his life, and now that he saw the summit in sight, it seemed to move further and further away. Closer—further, closer—further, closer—further. His heart boomed away like thunder. He thought it might leap from his chest. It was frightening, the way he could hear his old heart pounding like the sound of distant drums. Pounding way up in his forehead. But then he got his second wind. He was like an old car going up a mountainside. It reached a high plateau and shifted gears to make the final slope.

Charles James Richard Wakefield (some of his close friends called him "Jimmy Dick," affectionately, as did some of his distant friends and likewise some who were not his friends at all) saw Jesse from his front porch when Jesse was still quite a distance away, still deep, deep in the cotton, chugging like an old freight train, but gaining all the time. Wakefield wondered idly, what in the hell was anybody doing running like that in all this God-forsaken heat? Especially a poor-ass Negro. What in the hell did he have to run for? Wakefield smiled. Must be the Devil chasing him.

Wakefield was an unusual white man for these parts. Ask any black man. "He spoiled the niggers." Any white man would tell you how he spoiled them. A Negro was lucky to work on his plantation. You only had to work sixty hours a week. And Wakefield paid his lowest workers all of fifty cents an hour. Some folk called the Wakefield plantation, "Nigger Heaven." And another thing: He paid his workers

[vii]

wages. He did not believe in cropping shares. He'd tell anybody's body. "Cropping shares is tantamount to slavery."

He was a big, handsome, black-haired man with eyes as blue-green as the ocean's edge. A modernistic Mississippian a world traveler, a true cosmopolitan. Sometimes he felt more contempt for his white contemporaries than for the Negroes who worked for him. After all, the Negro never had had the opportunity to lift himself. But in this land of the free and home of the courageous, what the hell was the poor-ass peckerwood's excuse?

Yes, Wakefield was the gracious lord of the manor and the manor was a vast sprawling Mississippi plantation, where cotton was still king and he was King Cotton. Fields of white fruit, row after row, rolled for miles to and from the river, flowing like the river itself. Rolling like the river. His plantation was seventy-six miles south by southwest of Oxford, Mississippi, the home and the site of another famous Mississippi plantation owner. Oh yes, he and Willie Faulkner had emptied many a bottle of Scotch and bourbon together in their day, and laughed about the poor-ass peckerwoods and commiserated over the poor downtrodden colored people, especially those of the "noble savage" genre. He liked to think of people like himself and Willie Faulkner as being the last proponents of noblesse oblige. And he would be the first to admit that, these days, they were a rare breed indeed in Mississippi and everywhere else throughout his beloved Southland. Some of the more literate peckerwoods referred to him as the "Duke of Wakefield County," and to his good wife as the "Duchess." The manor house of the duchy was modern like his lordship. Well, it was not exactly modern. It was of another century. Tall and wide and awesome and white against a background and a foreground of green shrubbery and white cotton. But it had all of the modern amenities. For example, Wakefield and the Duchess did not sit on the front porch fanning themselves with funeral-parlor fans as old-fashioned, rich white folk did in Tennessee Williams and Willie Faulkner movies. "The Duke" believed in automation. Manual fanning was self-defeating anyhow.

One of his famous Wakefieldisms was: "If it's hot enough to fan yourself, it's certainly too damn hot to engage in the physical exertion required to do the fanning." And even before the Supreme Court decision, he had had the foresight to know that it was not slavery time anymore, and you could not expect Negroes to pretend it was and stand around and do your fanning for you. So Charles James Richard Wakefield had had four electric fans installed in the ceiling of his porch, and they were going every waking hour of the good old summertime (April through October). Not that he spent that much time on the front porch, but Anne Wakefield did, and he did everything in his power to make things comfortable for her.

"Who in the hell is that running so fast in all that God-forsaken heat?" he wondered aloud. It made him sweat just to watch and contemplate. His wife knew the question was not meant for her, so she kept rocking and humming softly to herself some half-remembered hymn.

It was a hot and suffocating day for the first day of June, a hot day even for Mississippi, where summer had an awful habit of coming early and staying late and always wearing out its welcome. Summer was in love with Mississippi. This was the one hour in the day in a workaday week that he allowed himself a momentary respite from his terribly frenetic schedule. He was the busiest businessman in all the county, maybe even in all the state. Sometimes he did not know which way was up. But for one solid hour after noonday dinner every Tuesday he just sat on the porch and sipped his Scotch and branch water and meditated on the sad state of the race. Upon very rare occasions he even read his Holy Bible to the Duchess, who faithfully fell asleep. "Let the Words of my mouth and the meditations of my heart be acceptable in Thy sight, Oh Lord, my strength and my Redeemer." It was his favorite quotation. He was not a fanatically religious man. But he was an avid reader, when he found the time, and he looked upon the Bible as the most beautiful book in all the world. He had a feeling that everything was worked out right here on this earth and therefore he did not really believe in the Hereafter in which his wife believed with unimaginable devotion. But to be on the safe side, just in case she knew something he did not know, he paid the preacher regularly, much more regularly than he went to church. Indeed he was the church's most substantial benefactor. He was the Good Lord's right hand. Financially speaking.

At first sight, as she sat there rocking back and forth and humming a church song for her own entertainment, one would conclude that the Duchess was the Duke's diametrical opposite. And one would be absolutely right. She was, of course, first of all a woman, but a woman who had begun to waste away early in the game of life, and by now the waste as well as the game was just about complete.

"Damn I reckin! That poor black bastard is hauling ass!" Wakefield wiped imaginary perspiration from his brow, as he empathized with the black, long-distance runner.

Wakefield stared sideways at the Duchess. He was filled with a great compassion for her, and he immediately felt better for it. Sometimes he wondered why she did not go to the cemetery and give herself up. He wondered why she persisted in this meaningless camouflage, which was what he pictured her life to be to her. A pitiful charade. There were times when he felt an overwhelming sorrow for this gentle woman, who looked so much older than her fifty-five years. You could tell that she had been a pretty one in her day, maybe even beautiful. But her day had been of a very brief duration, a billionth of a tick-tock of infinity. She was swarthy, tan almost, and dark and wide of eye. Her nose was thin, turned slightly upward toward the heavens. Once upon a time, her hair had been as black as midnight in the colored quarters. But now it was as white as cotton balls at picking time.

He watched her now, rocking back and forth. Her eyes were deep black canyons of nothingness. His own eyes almost filled, but not quite. As a young girl she had been the gentlest woman he had ever known. She'd been too good to be true. She would not have harmed a mosquito had it been biting her on the top of her nose. And in bed she had been completely passive. So gentle and doll-like, he'd felt like a rapist every time he had gone inside her. He would swear on a stack of Bibles she had never known what it was to have an orgasm, except as she had sneaked and read about it in the modernistic novels. That was one of her few vices, probably her only one. She read all the cheap spicy novels when no one was looking. He knew she read them. But she could never live them, except vicariously. He knew this too. That is why, after awhile, he had felt that he was imposing on her with the sexual act. And he was sexual from head to toe. So he had put his queen, his angelic "Duchess," on the pedestal where she belonged and had gone out in his dukedom and planted his seed all over the place, in black earth as well as white. He'd tell you he did not discriminate. He thought satirically of himself sometimes as "the Last of the Great White Planters." Others called him more vulgarly a "whoremonger." Some called him "Jimmy Dick, the pussy chaser."

Sometimes, when he felt lonesome and sorry for himself, he blamed Anne Barkley Wakefield for the fact that he was the lonesomest man in Wakefield County. At his age, still going from pillar to post, with no place permanently to lay his handsome head. He, the wealthiest, the most intelligent, the most important, the most sophisticated, the most powerful, and the most generous man in that section of the state, was the loneliest man in Mississippi. But deep in him he knew she was not to blame. If there ever were a blameless woman in this satanic world it was his Duchess, Anne Barkley Wakefield.

His mind and eyes went back to the runner now. Ain't that something! He got up and walked to the edge of the porch and stared. He could make him out now. Goddamn! How did that man run like that in all this heat with all those years behind him?

Jesse Chaney was one of the closest friends he had in all this world. But what the hell was he running for? Something must have happened to his boy, Chuck Othello. It was the only thing that could make a man that age run like his house was burning down. Jesse's boy, Chuck Othello, had been born around the same time as Wakefield's daughter, Carrie. Their births came less than a week apart. He had kidded Jesse that they must have gone on the same picnic. And

Jesse had named his baby "Charles" after the lord of the manor. In democratic reciprocation and in the spirit of jolly good humor, Charles Wakefield had named his daughter "Carrie" after Jesse Chaney's wife.

Carrie had been a long time coming. Charles and Anne were well into middle age when the blessed miracle occurred. It had been their last clear chance. It had been years since he and Anne had lived together as man and wife. But one evening, after he had come home from the Great War, he had pursued a young, good-looking, buxom, black woman to her shack and she had rebuffed him, the Duke of Wakefield Manor.

"Get the hell outa my house, you old dilapidated peckerwood mother-fucker!" She had to be pulling his leg, so he put his arms around her like a damn fool. She couldn't be serious. She couldn't be rejecting the Duke of Wakefield Manor. "Come on, baby!" Pleading like a little boy for his mother's nipple. And she had to be kidding. He pushed himself up against her. And she backed away from him and spat in his face. He raised his arms to slap her, but his enormous ego would not let him. When he thought about it later, he thought maybe it was his latent democratic chivalry. Because he was a chivalrous man, and he was overly democratic. But Lillie Brown's rejection of him had scared him half to death! Had he actually deteriorated into an old dilapidated peckerwood? It was as if Lillie Brown had sentenced him to hell's fire and eternal castration.

He went home roaring drunk and raped his fragile Duchess and planted the seed of Carrie Louise Mariah Wakefield. It was the last time that he would rape the Duchess. She literally raped him from then on. Sexually, she had been rotting on the vine, dying for want of attention. But now she came suddenly alive and made demands on him. Sexual ones. And she wanted retroactive payment. She wanted all the goodies she had missed before and had never even known she'd missed. And the more pregnant she got, the more sexual and demanding. She took the initiative and wanted to call the shots and lay the ground rules.

In a way, she was pathetic. The fatter she became, the more lipstick and rouge she used. Wakefield was shocked at first. She unnerved him with her greed, with her vulgarity, and vulgarity was one word he had never dreamed of associating with his Duchess. Her lips seemed to grow larger and larger during that season, and she never ever got enough. She even started to flirt with other men. He indulged her and her insatiable appetite at first, but after awhile he fled from her. He had awakened the sleeping animal in her and the animal was out to destroy his manhood, he thought. She started reading books about it. She wanted to experiment. She wanted to be in the saddle and ride astraddle. She wanted to discuss it with him, which was, of course, out of the question as far as a Southern gentleman was concerned.

Yet he was never really sure that she ever had an actual orgasm. With all the screaming and moaning and groaning and swearing she did each time she went for broke, he was never ever sure.

A couple of months after the baby came he turned away from her and went back to his old ways again. After a few futile and pathetic extramarital flirtations on her part, which he knew about and tolerated, she went back to rotting on the vine again, and he to his role of Great White Planter, feeling guiltier than ever before.

Jesse's boy would be close to nine years old now. Time sure did fly. Before you turned around he'd be in high school and out already. Unknown to Jesse, Wakefield generously arranged for the boy's college education the very day the boy was born. He purchased an annuity for him, out of his deep and abiding friendship for the father. Wakefield and Jesse grew up together on Wakefield Farms. Wakefield always said that if other Southerners showed the same attitude toward their Negroes that he showed toward his, there wouldn't be the rigmarole about a Supreme Court decision. He had warned his white colleagues many times everywhere he went, everywhere he spoke, everywhere he drank.

As Jesse came within about a hundred yards of the Big House, Wakefield broke into a great big smile of friendly welcome. Jesse's mere presence always gave him a genuine warm feeling of one human being to another, the kind of feeling that did not come easily these days. It also gave him a feeling of the rightness of his approach to *his* Negroes. But now the smile left his face, unknowingly, as he watched Jesse continue toward the front porch where he stood beneath the electric fan. Instead of his flanking movement to go around to the back door, old Jesse came straight across the yard. In the entire relationship between these lifelong friends, Jesse had never before come straight across the front yard. Never ever. Wakefield did not want to believe what his eyes beheld. But by the time Jesse was ten or fifteen feet away from the porch, it became obvious, even to a friend like Wakefield, that this particular day was different from all the other days in the world. And Jesse was not going to stand on tradition or formality. Wakefield was afflicted with lockjaw, momentarily. As Jesse kept coming toward the porch, he ultimately found his voice again.

He was more flabbergasted than angry with his boyhood friend. "What's the matter with you, Jesse boy? The heat got the best of you?"

"The Supreme Court done spoke!" Jesse shouted, like he had just got that old-time religion and his soul had been converted. "Ain't going around to the back door no more. Coming right up to the front door from now on!"

"What'd you say?" Wakefield asked him, thinking maybe he had not heard properly. It was too hot to get angry with the best friend he had in all this world. Jesse was humility personified. Yet and still—

"And another thing—ain't no more calling you Mister Charlie. You just Charles from here on in. Or Jimmy Dick."

Wakefield's face lost color. The fan blew heat onto his forehead now. "Jesse, you going too damn—"

Jesse turned to saintly Anne Barkley Wakefield who wouldn't harm a mosquito if it were biting the tip of her turned-up nose. "And another thing—no more calling you Missy Anne. You just plain old common Annie from now on."

The sweet angelic woman gasped and put her handkerchief to her mouth. She stopped rocking momentarily. Her world was moving swiftly out from under her. This was too much for Charles Wakefield. Friendship or no friendship. Wakefield was completely out of control, a thing that seldom happened to him. Sweet and painful years of racial understanding and race philosophizing went by the everlasting boards. Even as he told himself, "Keep calm, C. J. R. Wakefield," almost against his will he heard himself shout:

"Nigger, don't you know you're in Mississippi?"

Wakefield immediately wished he could call the words back but they were gone from him forever. He had not meant to call his close friend, "nigger." Yet he felt a kind of cleansing of his heart and soul. He felt whiter, purer, inside. The atmosphere was clearer now. And he was somehow glad he had brought things out in the open, things that had been hidden between them all these many years. Sometimes the "word" had to be used to put things in perspective. Even between the best of friends. It had a therapeutic value for everyone concerned. Jesse would bow his humble head now, ever so slightly, and hide the hurt in his eyes with the noble savage's smile of profound humility. He would put his tail between his legs and go around to the back door, and God would be up in His Heaven again and all would be right with the world. Wakefield would forgive and forget. He was the biggest man in Mississippi. He could afford to be forgiving.

Obviously, Jesse had not read the script. "That's another thing," the noble savage shouted, like he was preaching from a colored Hardshell Baptist pulpit. "Ain' no more Mississippi. Ain' no more Mississippi. It's jes' 'Sippi from now on!"

PART ONE

PART ONE

Chapter
1

They said she was born with a silver spoon in her mouth. Wakefield County people said it proudly and reflectively, as if the expression were original with them. Notwithstanding, almost since birth, she struggled hard to extricate the vaunted spoon. Most likely she had a peculiar feeling it was gagging her to death. This child was Wakefield to the core. The only heir to the Wakefield dynasty. The last clear chance. The more walls the great and revered name of Wakefield constructed between her and people, ordinary people, the more walls were there for her to break down, all over the sprawling plantation. She tackled the job with a chaotic seriousness. She was a one-woman demolition squad, since babyhood. She was Joshua at the Battle of Jericho, David facing big Goliath. She seemed to think that fences, like straw men, were constructed for her to bring to the ground. A kind of therapeutic calisthenics. From birth, the child was some kind of a claustrophobe, whose theme song might very well have been "Don't Fence Me In."

It rained all night long the night this comely child was born, this Princess of Wakefield County. And rained the day before and the night before the day before. It seemed that all the dikes in Heaven had sprung great leaks, as God unleashed His awful thunder and His terrible lightning. Oh my Lord, didn't it rain! Lieutenant-Colonel Charles Wakefield, 48-year-old war hero, was just ten months almost to the day from the battles for the vast Pacific. In his mind's ears he could still hear sound and fury way out on those far-flung islands, where he'd lived two years with fire and brimstone. And folk still sang, "Praise the Lord and Pass the Ammunition," even down in Mississippi. "In the midst of life is death," so the Holy Bible said.

"In the midst of death is life," Colonel Wakefield thought, ironically, as he stared anxiously toward the birth room. He was just two months removed from the bloody worldwide madness, where death and blood and dying were the order of the day. But here was new life in the offing.

Anne Wakefield's water had broken about two-thirty in the morning amidst the crashing of thunder and the flashing of lightning, as if the war had come to Wakefield County. There wasn't time to get her to the hospital. Two doctors and three nurses and four servants were at their proper stations, scurrying on hurried tiptoes to and from the master bedroom, bumping into one another. The raging storm outside was like a thousand-man drum corps beating against the windows in a wild and ritualistic celebration of the blessed of all blessed events. Wakefield watched, fascinated, from a safe distance, seriously wondering how a great little bouncing hunk of human essence could possibly emerge from this organized confusion. It reminded him of the Army and the madness that was World War Two. Somehow, somewhere, sometimes, tiny atoms of sense derived from total nonsense. Out of war, peace ultimately came forth, was man's eternal hope. God was mysterious but good.

She was Carrie Louise Mariah Wakefield, one of those rare species of children who learned to run before she walked. And she ran everywhere her leggy legs would carry her. She was born with a full head of hair the color of newly threshed straw, and she proceeded to pull every strand from her pretty head when she went into her tantrums. By the eighth month she was as free of hair as a desert is of bright green bush. She was like Mr. Clean before his time. But she was beautiful. Bald and beautiful. And she had a way with people. First, she wasn't scared of people, therefore she loved them without inhibitions, reservations, or didn't love them. Therefore they loved her, or they didn't. In any event, she was the Big Man's daughter, she was the Princess, and even if they didn't love her, they had to put up with her. She was her father's glorious obsession.

Chuckie Chaney, born of Jesse and Carrie Chaney, was one of her first playmates, for the simple reason that Carrie Chaney worked in the Big House and used to bring him from the servant quarters with her to work each day. And the two little innocent hell-raisers would romp and tear and turn the Big House upside down and sideways, much to the nervous self-conscious amusement of the grown-ups. Being an only child, Carrie Louise was spoiled to rotting. One of the servants said, "That child so spoiled she smell bad."

[4]

Charlie Wakefield found it near to impossible to deny her anything. So if Jesse Chaney's boy happened to be a toy, a plaything that amused the Princess momentarily, he was a plaything that Wakefield was certain she would someday soon grow weary of and cast aside, as she had done her first dolls, blondes, brunettes, redheads, her electric trains, her construction sets, her this, her that. Chuckie was her first black doll. So why in the name of all that made good Southern sense should he raise the race question with her at the tender uncorrupted age of three and four and five and six? Preposterous. Ridiculous! He was an educated civilized human being and he was not going to allow the stupid prejudices of Mississippi to rob his daughter of a few moments of pure and innocent happiness. She was free now and he would let her keep her freedom for a time until the world moved in on her. It was her prerogative as Princess of the Wakefield duchy. The Wakefields were a privileged class unto themselves.

One day in the copper-golden autumn of her fifth year with the woods afire with autumn garments, her long five-year-old legs took her away from the plantation all by her little fearless lonesome—freckle-faced and blue-eyed and yellow-haired. She just got a notion and took off down the road to find out what the world looked like beyond the fences. Were reddish-brown leaves falling everywhere? Were cotton blossoms blooming all over the wonderful earth? Her mother never told her anything. Her mother was wild with fear, as they looked for her all over the vast plantation in every corner, behind every bush, deep in the corn they looked in panic, all over the sprawling cotton patches. Unearthed a nest of rattlesnakes but no sign of Carrie Louise Mariah Wakefield. Her mother would not go near the river, nor would she mention it to the searchers. She would not allow herself to even think about the river, which ran through Wakefield County like a great snake twisting and turning all the way. She must not think of the river in connection with her missing daughter.

Her father was away at a business conference in Jackson and called her mother long distance and asked to speak to Carrie Louise. Terrified, her mother told her father Carrie Louise was taking her noonday nap, a nap nobody's body had ever been able to get the active child to take. She was not the napping type. There was no time for it. She was growing old each minute and had too many things to do, too many lives to live.

[5]

Three, four, five hours passed and no sign of Carrie Louise Mariah Wakefield, Princess of the Wakefield Manor. They even went into town in search of her. The mother was certain Charles's baby (as she often thought of Carrie Louise) had been kidnapped or bitten by a venomous snake or drowned in the river or raped and killed by a vicious nigger. She envisioned a hundred morbid possibilities. And always with the fear behind it all of how her husband would react should he find out about the incident. This fear was as deep as the fear for her daughter's safety. She swore the servants and the searchers all to secrecy.

About four in the afternoon, two policemen in a squad car saw Carrie Louise walking unperturbed around Wakefield City in a colored neighborhood. She had been playing with some colored children. Naturally they picked her up and drove her home.

When she reached home she got out of the car and walked toward her mother, who was by then in a state of near-shock (which was not much different from her usual condition). Actually, she was closer to hysteria. Carrie Louise, noticing no great difference in her mother, said, nonchalantly, as if what she had done that day were the most normal thing in the world for a girl of five long years to do, as if she had just gone downtown to do a little old shopping, "Hello, Mother, I want you to meet two pals of mine. I hitched a ride with them. Will you please get them some lemonade?"

Once upon a fine summer's afternoon, when life was carefree and hearts were happy and souls were free of life's corruption, she wandered into the servant quarters and came upon a man and woman wrestling seriously and nakedly with each other with an iron bed as the wrestling ring. This child was not only a great demolisher of walls and fences, she was an opener of doors. (And without knocking.) She stood there mesmerized by the sight of these two grown folks wrestling like children, but moaning and groaning as if the world were coming to an end. Then finally the struggling ceased and one lay panting upon the other, both of them breathing deeply into each other's face, their bodies lathered with perspiration.

And—"Lord have mercy! Baby! Baby! Baby! Baby!"

A strange, sharp, sweetish, salty odor made Carrie Louise's nostrils quiver.

[6]

And—"That was so good, sweet Papa!" Like shouting from the amen corner.

The one topside said, "Lord make me truly thankful for what I just receive to nourish." And they both laughed. And the wrestlers kissed each other, long and lovingly. She had watched wrestlers on television but this was altogether different.

The whole performance kicked off a strange excitement in the girl. The odor in her nostrils, the funny taste in her mouth, her throat. When she could contain herself no longer, she shouted: "Who won? Who won?"

The two grown folk leaped from the bed and dove for pieces of clothing to hide their privates which were at that moment very public. But they didn't move fast enough for her not to notice that they were constructed differently. She had quick eyes. The Good Lord had discriminated against one of them, or both.

As they stood before her, hiding their nakedness from her, the one that was built differently growled at her. "Where in the hell did you come from?"

The other wrestler volunteered the information. "She come from the Big House. That's where she come from. She's Mister Jimmy Dick's only child."

"Shit I reckin!" the man exclaimed, and leaped into his trousers and pulled on his shirt, all in one swift motion.

"What kind of game was that you were playing?" Carrie Louise demanded.

"If we tell you, will you promise not to tell anybody else?" the man asked gently. "Not a single living soul?" He smiled so sweetly at the little girl.

"Yeah," she said, "I promise!" Her eyes widened and glowed with excitement. It must be a terrible wicked game.

"Cross your heart and hope to die?" the wrestler insisted.

"Cross my heart and hope to die," she readily agreed. She was so eager she could taste it. She would have promised anything to know this terrible wonderful secret.

"Nobody—not even your father or your mother?"

"Not even your father or your mother," Carrie breathlessly repeated. She raised both hands to the Lord on High.

Her eager mouth hung open with the agony of expected treasures. Her tongue slipped over her lip as if she were licking an ice cream cone. She couldn't wait to know the name of this outrageous game.

[7]

"Not *my* father and mother," he corrected her. "*Your* father and *your* mother."

"I will not tell your father and mother, and I will not tell my father and mother," the little girl assured them. "I will not tell nobody's father and nobody's mother."

"We were playing Mama and Papa," the man said sweetly. "That's what we were doing."

"Yes," the lady said. "We were playing Mama and Papa."

"Do all mamas and all papas play like that?" Carrie Louise asked them, skeptically. What kind of a fool did they take her for?

"Yes," the woman said.

"Every day," the man assured her. "You better believe it."

She stared at them long and hard to see if they were serious. "My mama and papa don't wrestle like that," the girl said. "I guarantee you."

"Oh, but they do," the man insisted. "You better b'lieve it."

"I better b'lieve it?"

"You better b'lieve it. You just better."

And Carrie Louise ran from the quarters out across a green field; she ran and ran and fell and lay on the grass behind a bright green bush and cried and cried, with the gay blades of green grass bitter in her mouth. She cried because she wouldn't believe that her mother and father played like that. She couldn't believe that her mother in her entire life had ever played at anything, and especially with her father. "You better believe it! You better believe it! You better believe it! You better believe it!"

She kept her promise though. For a long long time she didn't tell a single soul, but she thought about it constantly. And she got a funny feeling every time her mind reconstructed the peculiar wrestling match, a match nobody seemed to win, but which left both of the wrestlers happy. How could it be wicked if it made them happy? Oh how could it be wicked? Yet somehow she knew it was.

One day a few months later, she ran into one of the many guest rooms in the Big House and Chuck Chaney ran after her. She shut the door behind them.

And when she turned to face Chuck, she said, "Let's me and you play Mama and Papa."

He said, "All right. I'll be the papa and you be the mama."

She said, "Goody!" And she pulled off her dress.

But he looked around him and said, "You got any dolls up here? What we going to use for children?"

Carrie Louise was arrogantly disgusted with such childish ignorance. "We don't need no children for us to play Mama and Papa." She was breathing hard. "You better believe it."

He laughed at her. "How you going to be a mama or papa if you don't have any children?"

"Don't need no children, *silly!* You better believe it!"

He laughed disdainfully. "Anybody knows you got to be Mama and Papa of something."

That stumped her for a moment. It even made sense—almost. But then the answer came to her. I'll be your mama and you be my papa."

He laughed. It didn't make much sense to him but he didn't argue with her any further. After all, it was only a game.

She stepped unselfconsciously out of her drawers and she was just like she came into the world. He felt a strange sensation coming over him. She commanded him, "Pull off your clothes too, stupid!"

He bristled. "Don't you call me stupid, stupid!"

She remembered how the couple in the servant quarters had spoken to each other. Her voice softened. She said, "I'm sorry, sweet Papa. You better believe it!"

He pulled off his clothes. "Now what?"

"Now let's get on the bed and wrestle," she said excitedly.

And he got on the bed and she got astride and they wrestled up an awful sweat. They whooped and hollered like the Wild West and she murmured, "Sweet Papa," to him, as, with a kind of grim determination, they pretended to enjoy themselves, their faces masked in seriousness and sweat.

Finally he lay perfectly still beneath her, and relaxed his hold around her waist. He said, as a matter of fact, "I don't see any sense in it. What's the fun in you bumping up and down on top of me?"

She had just about reached the same conclusion. Then it came to her suddenly. "We're doing it wrong—we're doing it wrong! You supposed to be on top. You're my papa, I'm your mama."

And so warily he climbed into the saddle and they again went grimly through the motion of this silly grown-folks game of Mama and Papa, of bumping up and down and moaning and

[9]

groaning, and what in the devil was the sense of it? Where was the fun?

They were striving to have a bumping good time, when his mother came into the room. Mama Carrie had a sudden seizure of cold chills all over her body. She was motionless at first, paralyzed with fear. She snatched them apart. She was so scared her voice forsook her temporarily. Her eyes filled up with tears and terror. She made them put on their clothes. She marched her baby to the servant quarters where they lived. She got a switch from a tree in the backyard and she tore the clothes from his body, and she gave him a whipping he would never forget the longest day he lived.

He whimpered pitifully as he scrambled around the floor in front of her like a chicken with his head chopped off. Her helpless baby! Her own, black, flesh-and-blood and painfully-birthed-by-her and helpless baby!

"Mama Carrie! Mama Carrie! I ain't gon do it no more! I ain't gon do it no more, Mama Carrie!" He did not, could not, begin to realize what his great crime was and least of all its magnitude. She had to make him know deep deep down in his black soul.

The more he cried the more she whipped him, because somehow she would not be intimidated by his screaming. At the same time she hated herself for doing what she had to do.

"Shut up! You just dry right up!"

"I can't help it, Mama Carrie! Please don't whip me no more! Please, Mama Carrie! Please don't kill me!"

She had lived in Mississippi all her born days and had given birth to nine black children (six had lived) and he was the last one, Jesus, he was the baby, born on the change, and she had seen and known of too many black men cut short in the springtime of their lives, given up as a sacrifice at the altar of white womanhood in *their* peculiar "Christian" ceremony.

"Carrying that poor little innocent thing up to that room and attacking her like some kind of devilish fiend or something. That's what they say about you black mens. Just waiting for the chance to jump into bed with any old white woman! You ain't knee-high to a hoppergrass and picking on that poor lil innocent child. Fore you grow another inch they'll string you up so high——"

"I ain' no man, Mama Carrie! I ain' no man! I'm just a poor

[10]

lil innocent child my own self!" He looked so pitiful and help-less, his mouth, his eyes, his nakedness.

Her heart overflowed and tears were in flood tide from both of them now, from mother and from son. She sucked the stran-gling tears back up her nostrils. She shouted at him through the fresh tears that spilled from her. "Hush up! You just dry right up! You want the whole plantation to know about it?"

He screamed louder than before. "Don't kill me, Mama! Please don't kill me!"

"The more you scream," she told him quietly, "the more I'm sure gon lay it on you."

But he screamed louder and louder, and finally her arms hung helplessly at her sides. She could whip her boy no more. No more, Jesus. No more! No more!

Later that day, Chuckie came upon Mama Carrie with the white girl crying in her arms. "There—baby—there now—" He softly shouted, "I'm your baby! Not that white gal!" And Mama Carrie would never forget the look on his face, this hurt far deeper than the pain he'd felt from the whipping she had given him.

A couple of evenings later, the boy was taking his Saturday night bath in the tin tub in the kitchen. His father noticed the bruises on his back.

"Come here, boy."

The boy came and stood before his father.

He was a shorter, younger version of Jesse Chaney, Senior—as if they had cut off Jesse's head and sat it on a shorter body. He looked just like his older brother, Jesse Chaney, Junior, had looked when he was Chuckie's age. Folks said Jesse Senior and Jesse Junior and Chuckie Othello looked just like stepladder twins.

"Where you git them things on your back?"

"Sir?"

"You heard me—you ain' deef," the father said impatiently.

"I don't know what things you talkin about."

"Them bruises, you know what I mean."

The boy's lips quivered. "What bruises, Daddy?"

Jesse touched the boy's back tenderly with his rough, muscle-bound hands, and the boy winced beneath his father's fingertips. "You know what bruises I'm talking about, and I'm waiting for you to give me an answer."

"Sir?"

"Boy, I ain't gon ask you but one more time."

"I don't know—I don't know where they come from, Daddy."

"You don't know? Maybe if I pull off my belt, I can help freshen your memoration." He almost never whipped the children. "You standing up there looking like two knots on Dick's dog, like you scared of me, like I'm some kind of bear for you to be scared of. Open your mouth and answer me, or I'll give you something to be scared of."

Chuck Othello opened his mouth and worked his jaws but no words formed. He put his fist into his eye and mashed a tear out, and that unstopped the dam, and now he was crying with all the dikes wide open.

The boy's tears whipped the father into a fury like a storm unleashed and uncontrollable. "What the hell you crying about? I ain't even tetched you yet." He snatched his belt from around his waist.

Mama Carrie said quietly, "Leave the boy alone. I gived him a whupping day before yestiddy."

The father was momentarily jaw-locked. Chuck was his favorite, always had been. There were many years between him and the rest of the children, except for Willie, who was playing possum in the other room. Old folks said Chuck was "the last button on Jacob's coattail." All of the rest, except Willie, as soon as they were old enough to talk back to their father and mother, were gone like chickens through the corn. Told Wakefield County "goodbye and fare-thee-well." New York, Chicago, Memphis. . . .

"You bruised this boy up like this," Jesse said unbelievingly, still staring at the welts that raised up on Chuck's bare back like whipcord. "What did he do? Rape Annie Wakefield?"

"He did the next worst thing. He raped Miss Carrie Louise."

Jesse turned toward his wife. "He did what? You crazy, woman?"

"I caught him in bed on top of her in one of the guest rooms."

"And you jus' nacherly yelled 'rape' jus' like the other white folks," he said, out of his deepest anger.

He turned to the boy again. "How did it happen, son?"

Tremblingly the boy told his father how it happened.

He turned back to Mama Carrie. "You didn't by any chance ask your own son how it happened before you skinned him alive?

[12]

I mean, you just took the white folks' word as the Holy Bible. As if they writ it."

"Don't make no difference. Even if he's telling the truth. Better for me to whip him now than for the white folks to kill him later on."

He stared at her as if he was seeing her for the first time. A familiar-looking stranger. "Woman, do you know what you're doing? You're killing him now, not later on! You're killing him now! *You,* his *own dearly beloved mother,* is killing him right this very minute! Why donchoo just take a gun and blow his brains out and be done with it?"

He was like a man reft of his senses. He seized her by the shoulders and, before he knew it, he was shaking her till she was as limp as a wet dishrag. "He ain't nothin but a little boy and you already killing off the man in him. You, his own mother, helpin the white folks put trimming on his drawers. You ain't nothin but a white man's nigger! You hear me? You ain't nothin but a white man's nigger!"

He was twice as big as she was. He could have easily broken her in two. Their boy ran toward them shouting: "Don't hit Mama Carrie, Daddy! Don't hit Mama Carrie! Please don't hit Mama Carrie!"

Jesse came back to his senses. "You ever known me to strike your mama, boy?" he said with righteous indignation.

But even as he turned her loose he told her: "Don't you ever lay hands on this boy for the benefit of white folks, you hear me? Else it's gon be me and you, and ain't nothin in the drugstore gon do you no good."

He turned back to his frightened boy. "You always wear your own britches, boy. And don't never let em put no bloomers on you. That's what they try to do to every black man ever been born of woman. Try to make him wear bloomers and suck a sugar-tit. But don't you let em get away with. Be a man, Son Chuckie. Walk like a man. Live like a man. And die like one when the time comes for it." His father's eyes had narrowed into angry slits and his eyebrows raised a half an inch like ragged window shades.

Chuck said, "Yes, sir." He had never seen his father so upset before. And he had never known him to be so angry with his mother.

His father tried to calm himself, but Chuck could still hear the bitter anger in his voice, an anger that was always there but sometimes lay dozing with one eye open, lay there beneath the surface of the calmest exterior of anybody's body in all of Wakefield County. Some folks would tell you Jesse Chaney couldn't work up enough steam to get angry with the Devil himself in person. But Chuck knew better. It seemed that ever since he could remember he had felt this thing inside his father.

"I know, son. You done seen your old daddy yassa-bossing these crackers round here, just to git along with them. But I got a limit. I got a line they bet not step across. You better believe me when I say so. That's how come they hated Paul Roberson. That's how come they ran him out the country. He was a man." His father's eyes widened now and were all aglow with pride. "Great God A'mighty! You better b'lieve he was a man! And they done outlawed a black man being a man in this country. But I want you to be a man like him. That's how come your name Othello. When you was born I looked in a magazine book, and they said Othello was Paul Roberson's middle name, cause he played it right down to the nitty gritty in that play up there in New York City."

He understood his father, deep deep in his nervous bowels. And he told his father, "Yessir."

Sleep did not come easily that night to Carrie Chaney. She could not erase the vision of their faces from her conscience, her boy's anguish, her man's anger. Faces dear to her and so much alike. Chuckie and Jesse. Jesse and Chuckie. Did they really think her a white folks' nigger? She had lived with Jesse more than thirty years, ever since she was a girl of seventeen. It was hard for her to remember when she had not known Jesse Chaney, had not loved him, had not felt his strength and recognized his weaknesses, the power of him most of the time beneath the surface like a mighty whirlpool in the river. His human weaknesses more apparent than real, his strength more real than apparent, more felt than seen. All this time and he knew so little of her. He thought she was a white man's nigger!

And her boy. She remembered a time just about a year before, when he was going on five, or maybe five already, and fearless and loving and asking far more questions than she was able to answer. And everywhere she took him, women kissed him and grown folks shook their heads and declared he was one of the Good Lord's miracles.

Old lady Brisbane said, "Lord I declare, you and Jesse ought to be ashamed of yourselfs at y'all's age. The last button on Jacob's coattail. He is one of the Lord's wonders performed right down here on earth. And he sure got a pretty head on his shoulders."

Mama Carrie was proud of all her children, especially this one, but she hoped that womenfolks wouldn't turn his head. Grown folks often talked glowingly about him in his presence, which made her mighty proud, and at the same time it embarrassed her for him. And even worried her sometimes. He would usually stand there shamefaced-looking, saying nothing, with the warmth collecting in his face. In her heart she knew that pretty or not pretty, he was black, and pretty blackness did not count in this white folks' world. He would forever have a hard row to hoe.

Sometimes she would say teasingly, "For Jesus's sake, don't say nothing like that in front of him. Lord knows he vain enough already." And his face would flush even warmer than before, even though he knew his mother to be kidding. It did not help his great embarrassment.

Other times, she would turn to him and say jokingly, "Boy, you pretty all right. Humph!—You pretty ugly, and you pretty apt to stay so, and I'm pretty apt to say so."

And his entire face would crease into a million smiles, it seemed. And he would get in his little dig. "I'm my mama and daddy's child," he would answer impishly.

It was as if it were a skit they'd made up between them and had rehearsed together many times, and now and then they put it on for other people's entertainment.

She remembered the time two years ago when she had taken him with her to see a poor white woman who lived down the road apiece away from the plantation. It had been a warm summer's day in August. She had gone to see the woman about some sewing the woman wanted her to do. Cracker woman was an openhearted woman as poor as Job's turkey, no better off than Carrie was, but poor white folks always liked to put on the dog to prove to you and to themselves that they were better off than you were. Well, that was all right with Carrie Chaney. It meant a little extra money coming in, and Lord knows it always came in handy. Cracker woman lived about a mile down the road but the day was clear and blindingly bright and it seemed that you could see a million miles to the horizon and back. It was a day for walking. And Carrie was a walking woman. She could outwalk most men half her age.

Miss Willie Belle lived on the right side of the road in an unpainted three-room wooden-frame house with a front porch that was as long as the house was wide. She was blonde and dried-out by the long hot summer's hot sunlight, so many many long hot humid summers. She had a kindly face, especially for a poor cracker woman, Mama Carrie thought. She always said, "Miss Willie Belle is a pretty good cracker." Which was the greatest compliment Mama Carrie could find in her vocabulary in description of any white woman, or man.

Miss Willie Belle's daughter was blonde and three years old and as bouncy and as shiny as a brand-new rubber ball. Baby Boo sat all over the porch in varied and various poses with her little yellow dress always up around her pink and roundish buttocks, which would have been all right if only her mother had bothered to put some drawers on the frisky child. She seemed determined to show Chuckie every little thing she possessed. She made faces at him. She poked out her tongue. She tumbled first this way and then the other.

And Chuckie had no better sense than to stare at the child and especially at the funny way her frontside was constructed, or deprived, as the case might be.

Mama Carrie tried desperately to distract her baby boy. She interrupted her conversation with Miss Willie Belle. "Look at the little dog down there in the yard, Chuckie. Why donchoo go and play with him?"

Chuck's eyes sought out the dog for a moment and found him, and it was a big mean-looking bulldog. The moment their eyes met the dog growled, and their friendship died a-borning. He looked back at Baby Boo. At least she looked better than the ugly bulldog, and much much friendlier. And she did somersaults. She tried to stand on her head. She tried to walk on her hands. But most of the time she assumed a position facing Chuckie with her bare backside exposed and her frontside too. He watched her acrobatics in open-mouthed amazement. He couldn't believe it. Somebody had chopped off the poor little biddy baby's wee-wee, he thought, and slashed her cleanly up the middle.

Mama Carrie suggested to him, "Why donchoo go around the back and look at the pretty chickens?"

[16]

"I don't want to step into no chicken mess," he answered.

Miss Willie Belle threw back her head and whooped and hollered. Her stomach shook like gelatin. "That boy of yours sure is nice nasty."

Miss Willie Belle did not seem to pay the children any further mind, but Mama Carrie was a nervous wreck by the time they were ready to leave for home.

All the way down the highway home, she tried to find a way to tell him he should not have looked at the little girl showing him her backside.

Finally she said, "It's bad for little boys to look at little girls under their dresses."

"How come, Mama Carrie?" He didn't feel bad about it in the least.

"Because it is—it's just bad—that's how come."

"I didn't mind looking at her, Mama." He laughed. "She looked so funny in tween her legs. She ain't got no wee-wee. I felt sorry for her. Somebody done——"

"Hush your sassy mouth, boy. Girls is different from boys. They don't have no wee-wees."

"What they got, Mama Carrie?"

She said, "Hush your mouth, boy." She wanted to laugh with him. He looked so serious at the moment, so innocent and serious. She wanted to take him up into her arms and tell him he had done no wrong, and let them laugh it off together. But instead, she frowned down at him and told him he had been a bad boy and he must never look under a girl's dress again.

He said, "It wasn't nothing under her dress to see, Mama Carrie. She didn't have no drawers on."

She turned her head from him and could not help from laughing deep inside of her. And somehow she knew she was saying all the wrong things to him. She should tell him that, most of all, he should not look at the girl no matter what, because she was white and because that was the way things were in this white man's world. She should have told him then and there that life was a dangerous journey for the black man as he made his way through the white man's world. She should have told him about staying in his place and talking low and bowing and scraping, and about lynching, and taught him all the rest of the Colored Catechism. The sooner he knew the way things were the better for him. But she gazed down upon him, open-faced and open-

[17]

hearted and spirited and handsome and brownish black and deep, wide, dark eyes brimming full of candor, and she could not, would not, did not, feel like putting the black man's burden on his young back with his tender years, and particularly not on this sun-washed day with such a loving softness now between them, with the fields on both sides of them alive with growth and growing, and a thousand different kinds of birds singing to each other, and honeybees and devilhorses and grasshoppers, and dicky birds sitting on the edge of the road, and rabbits darting through the bush. Her eyes filled up. She stopped and leaned down and kissed him on the cheek. He stared up at her, his face, his wide eyes, dark and full of questioning at first. Then his face creased into a smile, and her own heart leaped about with joy.

He said, "I won't look under that little old girl's dress no more, Mama Carrie. She ain't got nothing to look at." And she took him by the hand and they walked up the road together.

As she lay there wide awake beside her husband, with the moonlight dipping into the window and casting shadows up against the bed, she heard all the night noises outside—crickets and locusts and an old dog howling somewhere out there and another answering him from somewhere else, and Jesse snoring evenly beside her, and Willie and Chuckie in the next room which was their bedroom and also was the family kitchen. It all filled up inside of her and overflowed. And she began to cry and tried to stop but could not, the whole thing was too much, just awful terrible much, Jesus, too much, too much!

She cried aloud, "I'm not a white man's nigger! I'm not a white man's nigger!" She wanted her boy to be a man as much as Jesse Chaney did.

A few weeks later they moved from the servant quarters and rented a two-room shack in town.

Chapter
2

It was near the end of summer before "Mama" laid eyes on "Papa" again. He had not been to the Big House since the wrestling match up in one of the guest rooms. She missed him with a terrible passion. When Carrie Louise asked Chuckie's mother where Chuckie was, and how and why, she sensed a tension she could not understand, a hostility she would not accept. But she never got straight answers. She asked her own mother.

"Well, Carrie Louise, you know he doesn't live in the Quarters anymore." The mother vaguely remembered what the boy resembled. After all, he was just another cute little pickaninny.

"How come he doesn't come out here to visit me?"

And Anne Wakefield had the fiercest headache. It was not a most unusual condition.

"I don't know how come. Child, don't bother me with niggers." Sometimes her dark eyes were as vacant as Little Orphan Annie's.

"How come I can't go to visit him sometimes?"

Her mother sighed as if she'd been carrying a heavy burden on her back. "Well, Carrie Louise, he's getting to be a big boy now and you getting to be a great big girl, and I suspect he's made new friends and you'll have to do the same thing. After all, it's time for you to make friends among your own kind. Your own class. I mean, after all, Carrie Louise—I mean—" She thought her head would burst wide open.

The girl stared at her mother and suddenly her eyes filled up and she ran up to her own room and cried, because Papa didn't love Mama anymore. And they would never play again—together.

One day her father took her into the cotton fields in the absolute heat of a late September day and got himself a burlap bag and put another in her hand and showed her how to pick cotton. They picked for two or three hours at a stretch.

"This is honest work," he told her. "This is the source of the good life we live. This is where it all comes from. This is the fountain."

She said, yes, she understood. She wanted to understand everything he wanted her to understand.

"These people," he said, waving his hand toward the hundreds of workers (mostly black) knee-deep in white cotton, "they are also where our wealth comes from. All our comforts. The good life we live comes from these people you see here. Cotton isn't worth a hill of beans unpicked and rotting in the patches. Never look down on these people, Carrie Louise."

She looked around her and away from her at the row upon row of bodies bent deep in the cotton, black faces, black backs, sweating and glistening in the heat of early afternoon. The hot sun had no mercy on them.

She said she understood, as the perspiration poured from her.

He told her sweat was honest. Healthy. Good.

One day she went to the cotton field alone. She saw Chuckie with a group of children, black and brown and light-brown children. She ran toward him with a great big friendly smile. Her face filled up and overflowed with good feelings. She was so glad to see him she felt like crying. Chuckie was her best friend. Didn't care what her mother said. Very best friend. Only best friend. He kept working in the cotton, as if he did not see her coming. When she was almost upon him, he straightened up and turned on her with a great big smile. The other colored kids did too, as if he had rehearsed them in advance. He had waited for this moment ever since the day up in the guest room, the day his mother skinned him, her baby, alive, and held the white gal in her arms. He and his buddies stuck out their tongues at her and went into their song. The lyrics had been contributed by one of the older boys.

> *Your pappy is a pecker*
> *Your mammy from the woods*
> *They both got together*
> *And made a peckerwood.*
> *And you the peckerwood.*
> *Yes, you the peckerwood.*
>
> *Peckerwood—Yes, I say, peckerwood.*
> *Where you git that funny color?*
> *I say, it ain no good.*

[20]

I say, it ain no good.
Where you git that funny color?
Well, it ain no good.
It ain no good—it ain no good
And you ain no good—you ain no good.
And you better b'lieve it—cause you ain no good.

Carrie Louise burst into tears and turned and ran all the way to the Big House, all the way to her lonely room. The children laughed as they watched the white gal hightailing through the cotton like a scared buck rabbit. Chuck laughed far more than he was tickled. Laughed long after the fun of the thing had oozed out of him. He laughed long after he began to feel sorry for the crazy lonesome girl. He didn't want to feel sorry for her, but somehow he could not help himself. He hated the soft thing in him that made him feel sorry for her. But he had not meant to make her cry. He laughed till his stomach hurt and the tears rolled down his cheeks.

In her room now she lay on her bed and pushed her face into the pillow and cried like a motherless child, which was exactly how she felt. Motherless and friendless and loveless and misunderstood. Nobody cared. She got up from the bed and stood before her full-length mirror staring at herself. Why was she so pale and lifeless-looking, so colorless, so different from the others, like Chuckie Chaney, like most of the people on the plantation, the people her father said she should not look down upon? The people black and brown and light brown, the people, the sun-loved people, the sun-kissed people. God must surely love them to make them so black and brown and beautiful. She made faces at the girl in the mirror. So pale-faced and sickly looking. She thought, maybe Chuckie's people got that way because they picked cotton in the sunshine all day long. She thought herself colorless and ugly. She was a freak of nature. She thought, maybe if I stay out in the sunshine all day long the sun will bake me brown and black.

The years galloped by like runaway horses, and time passed as it always has a way of doing. But time did not ride its horse through Wakefield County. Time generally stood still in Carrie Louise's county, or dragged its feet when it moved at all. Time and change. The more things changed throughout most of the world, the more they remained the same in the cotton fields of Wakefield County. Yet there were changes, even here. For example, people grew older every second. Especially the young ones and particularly the old ones. Babies came into the world. Even they grew old every minute. People died and seasons changed. These were about the only noticeable changes.

Ever since Carrie Louise was seven years old she swam in the river that ran through Wakefield County. Her father taught her by just throwing her in with no previous instructions. She fought the river as if she had declared war against it, her father said, roaring with laughter. But most of the time she kept her head above water and made it back to the boat. And three minutes later she leaped in of her own accord and fought the river back to the boat again, and a few minutes later, in she jumped again, and again and again and again.

Before she stopped that first day he told her she had drunk half the water in the river. Be that as it may, she had learned forever how to swim.

Since she was ten, she sometimes came alone to swim without her father's knowledge. She was a strange child, her mother thought. Strange and moody. Most of the time she wanted people, people, people. She wanted to be surrounded by them, could not get enough of people. Gregarious should have been her middle name. Other times she wanted to be by herself and to herself. Her moods changed like the colors of a chameleon. She was happy, she was sad. She was mostly very very lonesome.

She had had a special spot, for years, where, after swimming, she would pull off her swimsuit and lie in the sun till she was baked as brown as a buttermilk biscuit. It was her hiding place, her sanctuary, a miniature arena, constructed painstakingly, with God's blessed hand, of open clearing and shrubbery and cypress trees, not fifty feet from the river's edge. None could see her save the heavens and the Good Lord up on High. She would swim and swim and swim till she had just reached this side of exhaustion. Then she would lie naked beneath the skies for hours. If her mother missed her and asked her where she had been she would tell her the first thing that came into her mind. She had been to visit this one or that one or the other. It did not take much deceiving to deceive her mother who was in a world all by herself most of the time.

Sometimes she would lie there basking and baking and browning and thinking about herself and the world and her mother and herself and the world and her father and the people on the plantation and the world, the great big magnificent world outside of the plantation. By the time she was ten years old, she had had many tastes of the wide world, but she craved to savor it in great big hunks, in its entirety.

Ever since she was very young they all went together on long train trips, ocean voyages, then by airliners. They went to New York, to California; they went to London and to Paris, to Zurich and to Copenhagen. At first her mother used to go along with her and her father just for the ride. But of late, her mother sat on the great front porch and dreamed of far-off lands and strange places. And these dream trips were sufficient. And more efficient. She could call her shots, and since she tired very easily, this way she could get off the train or the ocean liner any time she wanted to or bail out of the airplane.

Last night it had rained all night as if the sky itself were a mighty ocean with its waters overflowing and emptying onto the earth. It had stopped raining just before the day had broken red and rosy on the river's eastern shore. And now her rendezvous with solitude was a steaming jungle. Carrie Louise had come to her sanctuary shortly after the noonday dinner and had swum in the river's swollen waters—the river like a woman in the last days of her pregnancy. Now Carrie Louise lay sweetly exhausted with an open book on her belly. She stared languidly up through the tall trees, pregnant themselves now, swollen and weighted down with a wet and heavy greenness, steaming in the sunlight and still dripping from the last night's rain; she stared with her blue-green limpid eyes toward a blue and limpid sky where mountains of imagined snow moved slowly across the heavens in a never-ending procession. Sometimes she imagined the white clouds to be mountains of fluffy cotton from her father's vast plantation. She loved her jungle by the riverside. Her jungle was alive with sounds of birds and bees and crazy crickets, chirping, buzzing, giggling, and of squirrels and lizards and snakes scooting through the tall grass. The sunlight came down through the trees and choreographed a wild ecstatic dance of shadows of all sizes and dimensions. Her whole body was alive and tingling. She was at one with everything. She was one of the jungle's wild inhabitants. Suddenly her body demanded to make the shadows real to her. And she put the book aside and jumped to her feet and began to dance around and around, pirouetting, flitting one way and then the other. She was a butterfly—a bumblebee—a Juney bug. Finally whirling around and around until her head got dizzy and she fell laughing to the earth, she lay like still life for a moment, till she got her giddy self together.

She picked up the book again. As soon as she had learned to read, her father gave her all kinds of books. "I want you to know that Wakefield County is not the whole world," he told her, long before he was certain that she understood what he was trying to say. "Neither is Mississippi. There may very well be more world in any one of these books than there is in all of Mississippi." She smiled to him that she understood.

The other night he told her, "The world is in a state of flux. The days of our way of life are numbered. I want you to be ready when the time comes. It won't come in my time, I grant you. But when the change comes, I want you to be ready to change with it. I, myself, am too old and set in my ways."

Then he waxed sentimental, as he did with no one else but her. "Oh my darling, how I wish you had come along when I was a young man. I would have shown you something that would have made your eyes pop out of their sockets. It wasn't a question of getting ready for the change. I *was* the change. *I* was progress." Her father believed every word of it.

Sometimes he would talk on and on to her, and she would not understand half of what he said. He seemed to think that if he planted the seeds now and kept the soil fertile the knowledge tree was bound to grow and ripen and develop. He seemed to work upon the proposition that life was short and he would not be with his little-big girl much longer, and he wanted her to soak up everything he knew as if her young mind were a blotter. And indeed her young mind was a blotter. And books were as real to her as real life, even more real sometimes. She was like her father in many respects. With all of his talk about old age, he never slowed up for a moment. The more he talked as if death were creeping into his room, lurking around his bed, breathing down his back, the faster he ran toward life and living. Whatever happened, he would never run out of steam and sit on his porch and await Death's grim convenience. Her father was the kind of man who would be here today and gone today (not even wait until tomorrow). When the ruthless harvester came a-calling to gather Charles Wakefield to the fold, Wakefield would not linger long

[24]

and suffer. He would drop dead in a hurry as if his life depended on it.

She stretched her body full length on the cool damp earth. She smiled, remembering when she was five and six and seven years old; she used to tell him: "I wish I had lived back in those olden times. I would have been your sweetheart. I know I would."

He would pick her up in his arms and hug her and kiss her. "Yes, my darling, you would undoubtedly have been my sweetheart. There would have been no other girl for me."

"There would have been no other man for me," she unsmilingly replied. And she had meant it deeply. Very very deeply. She had meant it so deeply, she felt an awful aching in her stomach.

Sometimes in one of his more sentimental moods he would read poetry to his women, Anne and Carrie Louise, after dinner. Sometimes he would read a passage from a great novel, one of the great classics of the English language. He'd say, "Some men have written literature that transcends time and space and cultures and civilizations. Like the men who wrote the Bible, they have something to say to the ages, to generations upon generations, gone before and yet unborn. Their statements are eternal."

Anne Wakefield would contribute something like: "Before I forget it, Robert Benson called you yesterday or the day before. I don't remember what it was about."

His two favorite "classics" were, strangely enough, *Uncle Tom's Cabin* and *Gunga Din*. He read them over and over, again and again. Carrie Louise knew some passages by heart, she had heard them read so many times. Of all the characters in literature, her father favored Gunga Din the most. Every time the movie came on television he would stop everything in his frenetic life and watch every minute of it. He would call her to him and they would watch the film together.

"It was Din Din Din, Gunga Din!" She heard him saying to himself sometimes. He might be sitting with her in the back of his big black Packard limousine, with his chauffeur in the driver's seat, bumping along the countryside, and the words would come somehow from his lips unexpectedly, or he might be driving alone with her, just the two of them together, in his Jaguar sports car, or even sitting at the dinner table.

"It was Din Din Din—Gunga Din—"

The scene in the movie when Gunga blows the bugle for the

British against his own people never failed to touch this sophisticated cosmopolite, revealing a softness seldom shown to anyone except these two women in his life.

Now Carrie felt a sweet magnolia-scented drowsiness coming over her. She had swum and read and danced and daydreamed, and now she would pick her book up again and begin to read, and ultimately she would fall peacefully asleep with the book flopped open on her belly as she had done so many times before. She would sleep like a newborn babe. She had no fear of falling asleep in her sanctuary. She seemed to dare anything to happen to her. Everybody worried about her except Carrie Louise Mariah Wakefield. If life were out there to be lived she would live it and would not concern herself unduly about the cost of living or the consequences. She closed her eyes and drank in the woods with all of her senses; her ears, her nostrils, her mouth, all held the taste of the woods in them. She heard a mockingbird singing as if his life depended on it. Her nostrils sucked in the wet and heavy greenness of the forest. She drew its essence into her mouth and throat, deep down to her belly.

She opened her eyes again and sat up and stared at her body tanned by the sunlight. She was always checking on her color. She was browner than most white folks, she thought. But she would never be brown or black the beautiful way that Chuck Othello Chaney and his people were. She stood up and stared down at herself. She looked like earthenware—baked clay—set out in the sun to dry. She felt her breasts which were a newly developed wonder to her. Firm tiny mounds of sweet frustration. She stared downward at the newly sprouted darkish-blond pubic hairs. The corn silk cropping up on her arms and legs. She wished she could talk to her mother about this wonderfully terrible thing that was happening to her all over her, including what her mother called "the curse."

Carrie Louise's attitude toward her mother was one of profound ambivalence. She loved her mother because she was her mother. And she felt a great compassion for her mother that sometimes bordered dangerously on a condescending pity. Sometimes she tended to treat Anne Wakefield indulgently, as if she, Carrie Louise, were the mother and the mother were the child. Sometimes it was the simple compassion of one woman for another. There were times, on rare occasions when she witnessed scenes between her mother and father, that she would take her

[26]

mother's side, by a simple word or gesture, a show of womanly affection.

She lay down upon the earth again. She combed the curly mat of pubic hair absentmindedly with her fingertips. She turned over on her belly and buried her mouth and nose and toes into the soft, cool, dark earth. Last night her father came in from a hard day. He had asked her mother three days before to telephone her girlhood sweetheart, Jeff Winetree, and invite him to dinner for this particular night. Winetree was an architect and Wakefield wanted to discuss with him plans to build a new manor house, which would be modern and ranch-type and split-level and located at the eastern end of the plantation. While the old Big House they lived in was endowed with all the amenities and modern conveniences, it was his father's father's accomplishment, not his own. It was a monument to his grandfather, General Willie Wakefield of the 15th Mississippi Regiment of the valiant Army of the Confederacy. Charles Wakefield thought the Big House had more inherent dignity and character than any of the modern monstrosities of the nouveau riche, and was possessed of more formidable and relaxing beauty, but he was, after all, a modern man who welcomed change. He not only welcomed change, he was a changer. He himself created change. This was his preferred self-image. Harbinger of change—and changer. And he finally decided it was time for a change of residence. He would let the old house stand there as a monument to olden times and valor and ancestry and Southern chivalry and all the rest.

Her father was tired when he came in last night but in fairly good humor. He sipped his favorite Scotch and branch water. He was not a bourbon drinker like so many of his colleagues. "What time did Jeff say he would get here, dear one?"

Anne Wakefield stared at him and then at her daughter, as if she thought his question had been directed to Carrie Louise.

He sipped his drink again. "Anne, honey, what time is he coming?" With her he was patience personified, or at least, this was how he regarded himself where she was concerned.

"Who? Who you talking about, Charles James Richard?" She usually called him by all three of his Christian names whenever she was especially nervous, which was her usual condition.

"Jeff Winetree—that's who," he answered. "You did remember?

[27]

I asked you Monday morning. You volunteered Monday morning, to be more exact."

She said, "I've had a perfectly horrible headache all day long. It's been just terrible——"

"Today is Thursday," he said quietly, impatiently patient. "You were supposed to call him on Monday. I was going to call him, but you volunteered. You wanted to do it, because the two of you grew up together, though for the life of me, I don't know what difference that should have made. But you do remember promising to——?"

"All day long I've had such a terrible headache. You have no idea how I suffer, as Jehovah is my witness. Jeff and I sure used to cut a pretty figure together. I declare we did. He loved the ground I walked on. He woulda kissed my foot if I had asked him to."

"*You* suffer?" he said sarcastically. "If you drink gin and tonic all day long, how do you expect not to have a headache? You haven't got a headache, my darling sweetheart. You've got a hangover. There is a difference, you know."

Carrie Louise scolded her father. "You could show a little more understanding, Daddy. And after all, Mother has had a rough day all week long."

He growled and snapped at her. It was a rare occurrence. "And who asked you anything, my young missy? I'd be much obliged if you would speak when you are spoken to." He felt self-righteously now that he had showed Anne Wakefield all the understanding in the world. Their entire relationship had been based on him showing profound understanding and making allowances. And who was this pissy-ass girl to speak to him with such condescension? He would have to take her in hand before it was too late. He had shamelessly spoiled her. He loved her too much. All of the love, all of the affection that his wife should have received, had been lavished without stint upon this blessed child among all children. He had to reevaluate his entire approach to this sassy girl who was growing fast toward womanhood.

She said, "Yes, Daddy," tolerantly. And she left her chair and went to her mother and put her arms around her and kissed her full on the mouth.

"Poor, poor Mother dear—poor, poor Mother dear!" As if she

were caressing a picked-upon kitten just come in out of a thunderstorm.

He exploded. "Get upstairs to your room and no dinner for you tonight, young miss!"

"What did I do?" the girl said, with a poor, poor, innocent picked-upon expression in her own eyes now, as wide and deep and blue-green as the water at the ocean's edge.

"Never you mind," he said, controlling his anger with tremendous effort. "Just get the hell upstairs to your room—and I mean in a hurry."

She was a tiny girl again and her eyes filled and she thought, How can he treat me so? Doesn't he know how much I love him? But she went upstairs without a word.

And all evening he felt guilty, which made him even angrier, because he was sure that there was nothing for him to feel guilty about. He was the victim, not the culprit.

Anne Wakefield was too involved with Anne Wakefield to care one way or the other.

All evening Carrie Louise sat in her room, hungry for food, yes, even hungrier for some small sign of understanding and compassion from her mother. She was starved for motherly affection. A couple of hours later there was a knocking at her door. And she ran to open it. Her mother understood! Her mother understood! Mother to daughter! Woman to woman! Her mother had brought her something to eat, but even more, her mother had brought her love—love—love! Things would be different from now on.

When she opened the door, she saw her father standing there, tall and smiling with the hall light on his handsome face and a tray of food in his hands.

"Dinner for mi-lady—Dinner for mi-lady."

She said, "Daddy! Daddy! Daddy!"

Most of her young life she had awaited the day, the hour, the moment, when her mother would bring to her the warm food of compassion on a tray of understanding, or simply take her into her arms and say, "I love you."

Chapter 3

By the time Chuck Chaney's oldest brother, Jesse Junior, had finished high school, he had grown too big for his britches, especially around white folks, especially in Mississippi. It was during those nervous and ambivalent days before the Supreme Court decision, and the good folk of the county just were not ready for the carryings-on that Junior Chaney carried on. God bless their Christian-hearted God-fearing souls. Most white folks took a real dim view of this young black man, headstrong and handsome. And everybody agreed that he was sure enough heading in the wrong direction, the one that spelled trouble with the white man. Even colored folks agreed. Even his family, who loved him (how they loved him!), lived in constant fear for him.

It was not that Chuck's oldest brother was mean. He was as bighearted as the days were long. Friendly, always smiling, never grinning. The thing was, he didn't have any sense when it came to the art and science of getting along with white folks. He never seemed to get the hang of it, as most black children seemed to grasp instinctively from their mother's teats. He was too proud. That was the real problem. It was a sin for anyone to be too proud, and downright dangerous for colored folks. To be black and male and proud was to live with one foot in the grave and the other on a tightrope.

Whenever Junior was away from the house any length of time and was not in the cotton field, his mother lived with her heart up in her mouth. She never liked to see anybody running toward the Chaney house. She'd think it had to have something to do with Junior. He's in bad trouble. He's done hit some cracker in the mouth. As much as she loved him and as proud as she was of him (she even loved his ways, secretly), she knew he had the wrong attitude for a black boy in Wakefield County. That's all there was to it. He had the wrong attitude. Didn't know how to say Yessir and Yessum when white grown folks said Hey boy, especially if the white grown folks were little boys and girls much younger than Junior was. He'd usually mumble something under his breath. He even had the nerve to have the courage of his convictions. Which is an admirable enough trait indeed when it shows up in white people, but in black people in Mississippi, it spells *arrogance, sass, uppidy-niggerness;* put it all together it spells trouble for the black man. Even when he was a little boy, Junior would dispute anybody's word except his mother's and father's. Even with them, he would mumble his disagreement under his breath after he was a safe distance out of the reach of the backs of their hands.

One day he and Fred Douglass went into town to buy an Easter suit for Fred. Junior was nineteen and Fred Douglass was seventeen. Everybody in the county knew these fun-loving Chaney brothers. Even white folks knew them. They went into Jackson's Dry Goods Company, the biggest department store in town. First of all, the salesman wanted to sell Fred Douglass a suit without letting him try it on.

Junior said, "Naw. If he can't try it on in here we'll go over to Jacobson's. We'll take all of our trade, the whole family's, to Jacobson's from now on, and we'll tell all the other colored folks to do the same." There were only two department stores of any size in all of Wakefield City. They were Jackson's and Jacobson's, and they were always in fierce competition. And there were thrice as many Negroes as there were white folk in the county.

Mr. Dobson was a tall slim drink of pure white lightning, with ice-cold, light-brown eyes and a fancy moustache. He was a real dude of a flashy dresser, a good advertisement for Jackson's Dry Goods Company. He stared at the two nigrah boys momentarily. He batted his eyes and he looked around him; the store was almost empty at that time of day. There was not a single white customer to be seen. You could see the wheels turning in Mr. Dobson's head, and in his head you could also hear the clanking of the cash register. He didn't want any trouble with nigrahs. And there was the reality of Jacobson's just across the way. Dobson was Jackson's son-in-law.

Finally he said, friendly-like, "And, why not, boys? We always aim to please the customers at Jackson's." And he laughed at his own little joke, whatever the joke was. "I've got just the thing you'll like."

[31]

Dobson brought out a brown suit and Fred Douglass went into the try-on room and when he came out he looked in the mirror, and he looked at Junior and Junior shook his head. "Unh unh."

Dobson brought out a green suit the color of a billiard table and Fred Douglass stared at his brother and his brother shook his head. They would not even try this one on. The suit was so loud you could hear it talking. Meanwhile white customers had begun to enter the store. And Dobson had begun to sweat. But his mouth was still full of yellowish-white and smiling teeth. He brought another suit out and Fred Douglass tried it on and looked in the mirror and at his brother. Junior shook his head. "It don't fit good."

By now with white folks looking on and waiting, Mr. Dobson fought hard and valiantly to hide his great annoyance. He said something under his breath and went for another suit for Fred Douglass and when Fred came out of the dressing room wearing the suit, Mr. Dobson came to him and started to adjust the jacket this way and that, declaring that it was a lovely suit, a killer-diller, just meant for Fred Douglass, made for him and him only, and suddenly falling into a manner of speaking which was supposed to be a caricature of Harlem away up yonder in New York City. He pinched the shoulders and pulled at the back. He slapped Fred Douglass on the back.

"Boy, you sure is sharp. You gon have to git you a baseball bat to keep them brownskin red-hot mamas away from you. You is a pretty colored man."

Fred Douglass stared at himself in the mirror and then at Junior.

Mr. Dobson said, "This suit was made for you and nobody else but you. Whyntchoo just keep it on and I'll take the tags off and put your old clothes in a box?" There was a sharp edge to Mr. Dobson's voice now.

Fred Douglass looked with skepticism in the mirror at himself, and then at Junior, asking questions with his eyes.

Junior shook his head from side to side.

Dobson was obviously hot under the collar now, his cold eyes narrowing into slits. "What's the matter with this suit? I said it looks good on him."

Junior said, matter-of-factly, "Ain't nothing the matter with it. It just looks like a sack of sweet potatoes, that's all. And he can buy a sack of taters down at Piggly Wiggly's Super Market."

Dobson said, "Boy, you keep your two cents out of this. It ain't none of your business nohow." He turned to Fred Douglass. "Now, boy, you listen to me. You're my customer, and I tell you it looks good on you, and I know what I'm talking——"

Junior said, "You're my brother, and I tell you it looks like hell on you."

Dobson turned on Junior. "Nigger, didn't I tell you to shet your black mouth? I'll——"

He didn't get any further, because Junior's fist went up beside his mouth and Dobson fell heels-over-head backward over the counter and disappeared momentarily among a rack of men's suits, size 42. Clothes fell down and around him as if an earthquake shook the store. He was entangled and submerged forever it seemed in suits, size 42. Startled screams and shouting from all over now. White folk started running from all the other sections of the store.

Fred Douglass stood there mesmerized, his mouth agape, as if he were waiting for Mr. Dobson to come up for air. Junior grabbed his brother by the arm. "Come on, fool! Let's get the hell out of this damn place!"

They took off like jet propulsion toward the entrance, Fred Douglass trying desperately to disengage himself from the man's brand-new jacket as he ran. They heard frightened voices, white voices of pure and white hysteria.

"The nigger!"

"The niggers!"

"The nigger!"

By the time they reached the door Fred Douglass was out of the jacket. He dropped it on the floor as they plunged into the sun-washed street. He still wore the baggy trousers, tags and all. They ran past the momentarily startled pedestrians, ran across the court square, and ran down Johnson's Alley and through Tindall Lane. They ran all the way to Minksville. And ran clean out of sight.

The pace quickened in Wakefield City from its usual slow-drag tempo; it built slowly at first, then hurriedly, into one of hurricane proportions. The Chaney boys raced through the town and the town raced off in all directions and came together at the center—the white town, that is. Within an hour the *Wakefield*

[33]

Daily Chronicle hit the streets with the second edition for the day. The white newsboys shouted:

"EXTRA! EXTRA! BIG BURLY NEGROES RUN AMOK!"

The black newsboys were nowhere to be found.

White folk gathered quickly in the heart of town as if they were there to pray and wait for Judgment Day which was just around the bend in the road. Notwithstanding, they came most of them with arms and ammunition like the valiant minutemen of old.

Colored folks throughout the county stole quietly into invisibility. You couldn't even find a black face in the cotton patches. They stole silently into their shacks and houses and pulled down the shades on the outside world. And waited. Even the colored folks' chickens went to bed earlier that evening and sat quietly in the chicken coops and nestled in the trees.

The police came in four squad cars. They came first to the Chaneys' but of course the boys were not at home. They searched every house in Colored Town. But the boys had not even paused to catch their breath in Minksville, as it was called by some, affectionately, and by others with contempt. Late that evening as the sun sat down out over the river, some of the good church-going God-fearing white folks gathered, all decked out in their white regalia and carrying flaming torches and the Cross of Jesus. It was an awesome sight with a strange and terrible beauty. All of their faces were covered with hoods, as if they were ashamed of this strange and yet familiar ritual in which they would participate. Some came on horseback, some came in automobiles, trucks, jeeps. Others came on foot. They all came armed with the weapons of persuasion; clubs, pistols, rifles, knives. They had their little talk together. There was very little to be said. The less said the better. The act, the mission, was the thing. And they were Christian missionaries. Their cause was undoubtedly a righteous one. They would this night do a little civilizing of the savages who lived among them. So, onward Christian soldiers, marching as to war. Their destination, Minksville, or, more exactly, the home of Chaney.

"If the boy ain't home," one of the hooded gentlemen in the lead car said, "we'll take one of the others of them."

"Eye for an eye, tooth for tooth," one of the others in the lead

[34]

car sloganized. They were every last one of them ardent students of the Holy Bible.

"Burn the house down," another suggested. "You know damn well we ain't gonna find them niggers what run amuck. They still running." He chuckled, though uneasily. Nobody joined him.

The first voice said, "We ain't gon set no house on fire. That'd be burning white folks' property. We for property above everything. We ain't no bunch of Commonists."

Another said, "The thing to do is to set a nigger's ass on fire."

The hooded Christian gentlemen laughed nervously.

By the time they reached the Chaneys' it had been black dark for a long time. The streets and all the houses were blacked-out, as if war had been declared and that part of the city had been alerted for an air raid—no street lights to begin with, and no lights on in any of the houses, except there was a lamp light on in the front room of the Chaneys' for some strange and unknown reason. The valiant Christian soldiers surrounded the little house with their rifles and their pistols at the ready. Six men went up on the porch and knocked at the door. The door opened and Jesse Chaney and Charles James Richard Wakefield came out on the porch together.

Jesse Chaney said in a deep gruff voice, "Good evening, gentlemens."

The spokesman for the hooded no-faced group was speechless for a moment. He was tall and lanky, about the height of Chaney and Wakefield. It was clear he had not expected the pleasure of the company of such an august dignitary as the Duke of Wakefield County. When his jaws were finally unlocked, he said: "We-we-we come to see that justice be done. We come to get the boys that wounded Mr. Dobson."

"The boys ain't here, Mr. Jack Leonard," Jesse Chaney answered.

The spokesman took one step backward. "Don't you be identifying me, nigger." He pulled his pistol and pointed it at Jesse.

Wakefield said in a hard voice, "Put that pistol away, Jack. I also know who you are. There's not going to be any lynching here tonight. The boys are not here and furthermore you are not representatives of law and order. So call off your horses if you don't want to have trouble out of me. And I can damn sure give you a bushel of it."

Another one of the hooded men on the porch spoke up. He

[35]

was the stocky football type standing near the outer edge of the porch and seemed to be the low man on the totem pole in terms of the chain of command. "We got a job to do, Mr. Wakefield. Don't stand in our way else you'll be sorry."

"You're the one who'll be sorry, Sam Rawlins, if you don't get off these people's porch and in a hurry. I know your story." He spoke to all of them now. "The Chaneys have always been good, law-abiding, God-fearing nigrahs, and all of you know deep in your hearts they have. They have never given white folks any trouble. Now the boys made a serious mistake today. There's no doubt about it. But it's up to the law to deal with them. And the law will deal with them, that is if it catches them. But there is not going to be any lynching of these innocent people just because the boys happened to be a part of their family. We are not going to have any lynching in Wakefield County. Is that perfectly clear to everybody?"

"You talk like the county b'long to you," Sam Rawlins grumbled. "You talk like a Commonist dictator or something."

Wakefield walked across the porch to Rawlins and pulled the hood from his face. He also unmasked Jack Leonard and another of the group. "Now," he said, "I can definitely and positively identify three of you, and I got a good idea who the rest of you are. If anything happens to the Chaneys, you'll have me to settle with, I give you my personal guarantee. I'll put the Federal Government men on your tails. And I'll be the first to testify."

The unmasked ones stood their ground, which was changing into quicksand every moment and slipping from beneath their feet as sand does at the river's edge deep in bayou country. Their eyes were hard, their pale faces turning different shades of red and back to white again.

"We were just having a little old fun," Ron Flagstone whimpered. He was one of the unmasked ones.

"Don't be whining and carrying on like a old woman," Rawlins said disgustedly to his whimpering comrade. "We'll have you up on charges and kick you out the organization."

"We'll meet again, Mr. Wakefield," Jack Leonard said with dignity and the barest hint of a tremor in his voice and a whole bushel of self-righteousness.

Wakefield said, "I'm sure we will, sir. Meanwhile, make off and take your gang of vigilantes with you."

Jack Leonard and his comrades stood around and shifted and

[36]

shuffled, standing their ground and hemming and hawing, just to show each other they were not intimidated by the Great Man of the County. But they finally moved off the porch and collected their gang together and moved down the road and out of Minksville.

Standing there in the dark night on the front porch, Jesse Chaney told his friend, "I sure do thank you mighty much!" Told him soft-spokenly in a voice that smoldered on the fires of bitter anger.

"Not at all," the Great Man said magnanimously. "That's what true friends are for." Then he stared through the dark at his true colored friend. "Anything else I can do tonight?"

"No sir," Jesse answered. "I don't reckin so."

"By the way, where *are* the boys?"

Jesse Chaney stared at his great white friend and blinked his eyes. "I don't rightly know, sir."

There was a moment of loaded and uneasy silence between these lifelong tried and trusted friends. It seemed a whole lifetime of silence before they spoke again. Nonetheless, it was a silence which spoke for itself, and eloquently.

"You know you can count on me, don't you, Jesse? At least by now you ought to know who your friends are in this county."

"Yes sir, indeed I s'pect I do."

When the Great Man left, when his great car had driven out of sight, black men and boys came from all of the neighboring shacks and houses, loomed up out of the cornfields and jumped down out of the trees, came with rifles at the ready, and their rifles had been at the ready for the last two hours and a half, ever since the friendly protective black night had fallen. They came, and nervously laughed and joked seriously, and talked it over with the Chaneys. Some brought with them jugs of corn whiskey. Was there anything else for them to do tonight? Would everything be all right till morning? They chose two men to do guard duty. Each of them was to sit in trees which stood about three blocks distance from each other at the head and at the foot of the street on which the Chaney family lived. They were to fire three shots into the air if they saw the enemy approaching. The rest of them scattered to their homes to sleep nervously with one eye open.

Will Roundtree climbed up into the big oak tree at the head of the street. He took his pistol with him and a jug of the best white lightning you could find in Mississippi. And as soon as he got comfortable in his tree perch, he began to sip himself into a stupor. He fought sleep valiantly for the first three hours, but between his jug and his nervous fatigue, he did not, could not possibly, hold out much longer than that. For almost another hour he slept with one eye open, and after that—oblivion. It was the kind of night made to order for skulduggery and undercover operations. It was a totally black night without stars or moonlight. Will Roundtree fell into a deep deep sleep, the kind of sleep that comes from drinking unadulterated moonshine—one hundred and fifty percent white lightning—the kind that made you cuss the preacher and throw rocks at your great-grandmother.

About three forty-five in the morning two things happened almost simultaneously. Suddenly the moon came out and directed its powerful beams directly on Will Roundtree a-dozing in the oak tree (or so it seemed to him as he recapitulated it afterward). And just as suddenly, Will moved in his sleep and kicked the jug out of the tree and it exploded in the quiet underneath him. Just as suddenly, he awoke and scrambled down out of the tree and started firing away at the moon.

Bang! Bang! Bang! Bang! Bang! Bang! He emptied his revolver. The houses emptied themselves of sleeping men as they piled into the street in varied stages of undress.

"The enemy's attacking! The enemy's attacking!" Will Roundtree shouted. He was a veteran of World War Two, had seen action in the South Pacific. The half-asleep men ran toward him as he stood beneath the tree firing away at the undaunted moon and screaming at the top of his whiskeyed voice.

"Where's the enemy?" one man asked him.

"Where the peckerwoods?" from another.

"Where?"

"Where?"

Will Roundtree could hardly keep an upright position.

"Which way the crackers?" Jesse Chaney demanded.

Will stared at his neighbors and bobbed and wove like a punch-drunk boxer, and he was drunk but not from punching. Somehow he managed to raise himself to the dignity demanded by the grave occasion. He drew himself up and pointed to the full moon, which at the moment was yellow and mellow and basking in its own complacent radiance. "It was that feller up there in the moon," Will explained. "He played a trick on me,

[38]

the dirty hound. I thought the peckerwoods were landing by helicopter."

The men went back to their sleepless beds laughing and cussing and grumbling. And Will went home and fell into a deep deep sleep.

'Sippi legend has it that when Wakefield left the Chaneys that night he drove directly to see Rogers Jefferson Davis Johnson, U. S. Congressman, and the second most powerful man in Wakefield County. He was also owner and publisher of the *Wakefield Daily Chronicle*. It is said that Wakefield spent two or three hours drinking and arguing with the Congressman and finally convinced him that the *Chronicle* should take an editorial position unequivocally against violence and for clear heads and peaceful solutions.

Rumor also has it further that the Great Man went to see Ray Higgins, owner of the local radio station, and convinced him in the same direction. People of the county were convinced more than ever: "Wakefield is a nigger lover."

Josh Bigelow, local hardware store proprietor, said, "Hell, if I had as much money as Jimmy Dick got I'd be any damn thing I wanted to be."

That same night the boys slept (they hardly slept) way out in Johnson's Bottom. The next morning before the sun got up they began to run away and Fred Douglass didn't really stop running till he ran all the way to New York City. Jesse Junior ran all the way into the United States Army. Junior came home once in his soldier uniform, and it was the last time his family saw him. They got letters from him from a faraway place they had never heard of, that is, before the "police action" started. Korea?—Korea? At first they couldn't even pronounce it. They could hardly find it on the map. Then one day there was a telegram that would change their lives completely. LOST IN ACTION. Lost in action. And then the moments and the hours, the days and months of disbelief and unimaginable sorrow. The newspaper called their Junior a hero in the great American tradition. Even the *Wakefield Daily Chronicle* admired him and eulogized him to the heavens. Put his picture on the front page. But nothing dissolved the hard knot of bitterness in Mama Carrie's stomach, the ever-increasing anguish in the place where he had been conceived. Her Junior!

Their Junior! It was hard, Jesus! It was too much! Jesse Senior didn't smile for six whole months. They didn't even know why Junior had died, or how. They never knew what the "police action" was about in the first place. What did Junior give his life for? Maybe Junior died for nothing. This was the awful, murky, white suspicion that gnawed at Jesse Senior's entrails.

Then one day the money came from an appreciative government. But as poor as they were, more than a month passed before Jesse would have anything to do with it. It was just a piece of paper that lay on the dresser in the front room and sometimes blew off the dresser onto the floor and once found its way into the trash. But Mama Carrie put it back on the dresser again. Just in case. In a way, it represented Junior and did not belong among the trash. Jesse seemed to think he would be breaking faith with Junior to have anything to do with that piece of paper from the government. He seemed to think that to sign that piece of paper would be tantamount to signing Junior's death warrant. An act of dirty, lowdown betrayal. But Mama Carrie and Rob Rakestraw, his next-door neighbor, and others finally convinced him he was wrong.

Rob Rakestraw argued, "Ain't nothing nobody can do to bring Junior back. So the least you can do is make his death mean some little something to his family."

They were playing checkers underneath the moonlight in the backyard in the early evening. The lightning bugs were blinking and the crickets raising holy hell. They played, as usual, on a homemade board, played with bottle caps instead of checkers. Jesse looked up from the board and stared at his neighbor and shook his head. "I don't know. I-I just don't know."

"Look at it this way," Rakestraw pursued his argument. "That there check ain't from the government. It's from Junior. He earned it, didn't he? And he sending it to you from the grave. It's his last gift to his family to show you his love and his appreciation."

Jesse stared long and hard at his friend and next-door neighbor. He slapped at a mosquito which had lighted on his face. He didn't say a word. Mama Carrie, who was seated on the porch, said, "I reckin that's the only way to look at it."

Jesse Senior bought a big two-story house. With a living room and dining room and two bedrooms and a toilet inside the house! It was a house built in that part of Minksville that bordered on a poor white section. It was the prettiest house a colored person ever lived in in the county since the days of Reconstruction. With a real bathtub and everything! It had been built by a colored doctor who had come to town and left seventeen months later. The town had no colored doctor now. The Chaneys moved in in August with new furniture and everything. They were busy with a white lawyer (there were no Negro lawyers in Wakefield County) getting everything cleared away—certificates of occupancy and all kinds of insurance the likes of which Jesse had not ever heard, or suspected. They were in a hurry to get everything just so. But they didn't hurry fast enough. They moved in on a Saturday and the following Wednesday evening they all went to the regular Wednesday night prayer meeting; they went to thank the Lord for His bountiful goodness, for their new home and for their good fortune that came out of their deep sorrow. The Lord works in mysterious ways. They went also to pray again that Junior's soul was at rest in the everlasting peace of Heaven.

It was drunken Will Roundtree who brought the bad news to Jesse as he knelt in humble prayer. Jesse rose as if in shock and hurried from the church without speaking to his family. By the time he reached home, his brand-new house was one big beautiful flame that lit up the countryside for miles around. Fire engines from all over the county came and fought the fire all night long, to no avail. Jesse stood there watching the whole thing, like a curious bystander, as if it had nothing to do with him whatever. His body numb, his eyes as empty as a blind man's, his entire insides void of feeling; he wanted to laugh, he wanted to cry. As he watched the house burn down, he saw all the dreams he ever dreamed go up in flames. It was a beautiful fire to look at, and for a moment he thought he saw Junior in the burning house, standing there proud and defiant dressed up in his soldier suit.

Everything was lost. Everything except life and limb. The Lord works in mysterious ways. Some said it was the Devil's work. Some said, the work of mean white devils.

The Chaneys moved back to their little, rented, two-room shack next to the Rakestraws. They had not been moved away a week. The Lord works in mysterious ways. Blessed is the name of the Lord.

Chapter 4

The years galloped by, and Chuckie Chaney's father scrimped and saved and ate hominy grits and fatback and black-eyed peas and went without till he and Mama Carrie put enough aside to buy themselves a milk cow, so that the last child would have plenty of milk to drink. Jesse Chaney was as proud of his cow as his friend, Charlie Wakefield, was of his plantation and his Big House and his millions. It was property, it was ownership. It was status. He was at long last a capitalist. With the cow he was somebody.

They called the cow "Missy Anne" and she became Jesse Chaney's conversation piece (in place of Chuck Othello). It was as if Jesse had given birth to a newborn baby. He poked out his chest. He bragged about the poor cow every day in the week and especially on Sundays. Missy Anne did this and Missy Anne did that. Missy Anne—Missy Anne—Missy Anne—Missy Anne—

Mama Carrie told him, laughingly, "I declare before the Lord, I believe you love that cow more than you ever loved your own natural-born young 'uns."

"Never you mind," Jesse answered proudly, smiling from deep deep in his dark eyes. "Just never you mind. That's the whole trouble with colored folks. Ain't got no sense for owning property. Always beating up their gums about freedom and dignity and all that whatchamacallit. That cow is your dignity. Missy Anne is your freedom, woman. You better believe me when I say so. Freedom from an empty belly." He shook his head in smiling wonderment. "She got a sweeter disposition than a whole gang of peoples I know."

Mama Carrie said, "I hope I don't never learn to love things more'n I love peoples. That's one lesson I hope and pray black folks don't never learn from the white man."

Jesse was momentarily insulted. "There you go misreputing my words just like as usual. In all my born days, I ain't never said

[42]

things was more important than peoples. I ain't never said we should take pattern after Charlie neither. And it sure ain't no white folks' blood in my veins. Not one single drop."

She went on and on, as if she had not heard him answer her. "One thing us black folks always had is goodness and kindness in our hearts. We respects life. And, to us, peoples come before everything else. Before money, before things, before the law. Before anything and everything peoples come first. We believe in the Bible. We believe God put man over everything and ain't put nothing but the heavens over man. Put man over automobiles, airplanes, houses, cows, governments, the beasts of the field, the birds of the air—everything. White man in love with things. We like things but we love folks. We must be done brought this love we got deep in our hearts all the way from Africa. We sure God didn't find it in this place where we is now." She was out of breath from so much talk.

Jesse Chaney shook his head in full agreement. "You sure know what to say, old pretty-talking woman. You sure Lord know exactly what to say."

Their backyard bordered on the southern end of Wakefield Farms, where the corn grew tall and yellow—mellow. Jesse called his proud little backyard "Chaney Farms, Incorporated." They had, in point of fact, planted a little garden of collard greens and cabbages and string beans and sweet potatoes and green peas and strawberries and a few watermelons and sugarcane and corn and okra.

It was one of Chuckie's chores to take care of the cow, to see that she grazed properly in certain sections of the garden. Missy Anne seemed to know that Chuckie did not really have a way with women. She always gave the boy a bad time. The first time he tried to milk her he was scared to death. His buddy, Little Jake Carson, had told him you had to have a way with cows just like you had to have a way with womenfolks. Little Jake said, "Boy, you better handle her nice and gentle or strong and firm. You got to let her know you in command. I know one cow kicked a boy clean into the next damn county." Jake was one year older than Chuck and twice as chubby and fifteen times as sassy. He knew everything.

One morning Jesse gave his boy a bucket. "It's your job, Son. Go git it."

[43]

"Go git what?" Chuck looked like he'd been sent for and couldn't come.

"Go git a bucket of milk. You know how to get it, doncha, Chuck boy? You know how to milk a cow? You just oughta. That's how come I bought the sweet thing, so you could drink your guts full."

He said, "Yes sir." He didn't follow his father's reasoning, that, because his father had bought the cow to give him milk, this necessarily meant that he, Chuck Chaney, already knew how to milk the cow. But sometimes grown folks had some funny ways of reasoning. That was an established fact. So he took the bucket and went for Missy Anne. He sat there at arm's length near the damn indifferent cow, but he might have been a million miles away. He sat there for over an hour pulling on her teats, but nothing came. But sweat poured from all over his body. He could have easily collected a bucket of sweat. A thousand buckets. But Missy's teats were as empty as a well run dry. He felt like Simple Simon sitting there with his bare face hanging out, like a scared deer poised for flight at the breaking of a twig, sitting there pulling desperately on Missy's udders and Missy impolitely breaking wind and swishing her tail this way and that and Chuck expecting to be kicked into the next county any moment, and he had no business to transact in the next county, and if he did, he'd go by train or bus, or hitchhike. He went from teat to unsympathetic teat with the same overwhelming results. He threatened, he cajoled, he pleaded with the doggone cow. "Come on now, Missy Anne, you sorry heifer."

The doggone cow paid Chuck no mind at all. She just belched and farted and swished her sassy tail.

"Come on now. Just a little old biddy bit, please ma'm," he begged. "Just a half a pint at least. Just a few little biddy drops; one old lousy drop is all I ask, you no-good hussy!"

Finally, his father came to see what was keeping him so long. "What's the matter with you, son? That cow ain't nothing to be afraid of."

"He ain't got no milk in him, Daddy," Chuck answered feebly. Shamefacedly.

His father moved in toward the cow, and Chuck stepped willingly aside to gladly watch his father fail as he had failed. His father sat down on the stool. "What you reckin happened to her, boy? She gave milk yestiddy. You reckin a old possum or a coon

[44]

or something done stole in here last night and sucked her dry?"

He knew his father was poking gentle fun at him, but he could take it, because his father was his father and further because he would have the last laugh, the way he figured, since plainly the doggone cow was as dry as a summer drought. And even his father couldn't get blood out of turnip greens.

His father began to caress the cow, and Missy Anne murmured and mooed like a bashful girl with her first boyfriend. His father said teasingly, "Boy, you ain't a man till you learn how to handle teats. Where you been all this time?"

Chuck's face was flaming with embarrassment. After a few strokes on the cow's teats with no obvious results, Chuck's flushed face creased into a wide smile, and he started to tell his daddy, "It look like you could stand to learn a little biddy bit about teats your own self." He formed the words in his mouth, but he hesitated. He had never gotten quite that common with his father. Not quite that familiar. And just as he made up his mind that he was getting to be a man and his father could take a joke from him (it would not be a question of disrespect), just as he opened his mouth to tease his father, the milk began to spurt into the bucket like a jet stream.

"All in knowing how, son. All in knowing how," his father said. If Chuck had had a stick in his hand he would have hit Missy Anne on her backside, the two-timing heifer. Chuck imagined he saw the cow turn her head toward him and shrug and wink. Chuck fought hard to control his anger to keep from calling Missy Anne everything but a child of God. For he had never cussed in the presence of his father.

After breakfast Chuck went back down to see Missy Anne and cussed her with every name he could think of. "You two-faced, shit-eating daughter of a bitch's kitten. I feed you, I clean up behind you, I take care of you, and you turn around and make me look like a fool in front of my daddy. I oughta put you out to root hog or die."

Miss Anne stared at him with big sad eyes and said, "Moooo-oooo." And that was all there was to that.

The other thing, he had the damndest time learning how to stake the cow. The way he figured he just was not cut out for the country life. He would lead the cow by a rope out to the edge of the yard where the grazing was good and drive a stake into the ground and tie the rope around the stake, and he would come back ten minutes later and the cow would have pulled up stake and wandered into somebody else's yard and stuck her nose into something in which she had no business.

If you said anything against the cow, Chuck's father would simply make a joke about it or laugh it off. He spoiled the cow like she was a little old baby brat. His father said, "All these Negroes 'round here ain't hardly got a roof over their heads but they in hock to the Man for his television. Even every leaky shack out there in Johnson's Bottom got one of them aerial thingamajigs on top of 'em. But I got me a cow and that's a heap more than a Tee-Vee set."

The Chaney home was the only one in the block that didn't even have any electric lights, let alone a TV set. If it had been left to Chuck he would have preferred a TV a million times to a damned old two-faced cow.

The funny part about it, the thing that made Chuck really angry was that whenever his father staked the cow, she stayed staked. The damn cow had it in for Chuck. That's all there was to it. He began to hate the cow. Broke into a sweat every time he heard her name called. His blood percolated at the sight of her. But somehow he learned in spite of himself to milk the chick, as he sometimes called her in his rare and fonder moments.

"Come on, old funky chick," he said affectionately, "we gon get the butter from the duck today. You know you love it, dog-bite your sorry soul, so what you holding out on me for? You know I'm the best that ever did it. So come on now and get up off it."

The first time Missy put out for him, Chuck drank the first bucketful all by himself, warm, just as it came right out of the cow. He actually kissed the cow on the side of her drooling face, he was so pleased with both of their performances.

It was all of two and a half hours later in the cotton field when the first pain hit him in the stomach, and he barely made it to the outhouse. The milk went through him like a dozen doses of castor oil. And all day that day and all night long that night he beat a steady path to the outhouse and afterward to the water closet at his house. He hardly slept. Up and down, up and down, back and forth. About four o'clock in the morning he fell asleep on the toilet stool. And dozed till daybreak, when the roosters woke him up crowing all over town.

The next day he was too weak to milk the cow or even to make

[46]

it to the cotton field. He was convinced more than ever that Missy Anne had something deep in her heart against him. It was a long long time before he would drink her milk again. He thought that somehow she had probably peed in that particular bucket of milk when his back was turned.

But he grew on hominy grits and fatback grease and black-eyed peas and rice; he grew longer and taller every day. And the more he worked in the cotton patches the more he hated anything that had anything to do with cotton. He loved school but he hated the way his schooling was related to the dictates of the cotton field. Had he his way, he would have gone to school twelve months out of every year. Thirteen months, fourteen even.

"How come," he asked his father, "how come we go to school through the hot summer months and white children go in the fall?"

"'Cause fall is cotton-picking time," his father answered, matter-of-factly. "What difference do it make what time of year you go to school, long as you gits an education?"

They were seated at the supper table. It was that time of the day when all things in the whole wide world stand still and hold their breaths and the day stops dying for a moment to let the nighttime get itself together, a time when it's dark enough to need the lights turned on but not dark enough for it to make any difference. Sometimes there is just one final burst of blinding blazing sunlight, then suddenly day gives up the ghost and night falls and the lightning bugs begin their blinking and the frogs their honking and the crickets carry on like they're out of their cotton-picking minds. Chickens had long since bedded down for the night. Mama Carrie turned the wick up and lit the lamp. Chuck looked up from his peas and rice.

"You believe in magic, Daddy?"

"Naw, son. It's just magicians doing tricks."

"You believe in haints?"

"Ain' nobody ever been back to pay me no visit after they crossed over to the other side." The father laughed.

Mama Carrie sad, "They say some folks can see haints or ghosts or whatever you call it. They say them kinda folks born with a veil over their eyes."

"That's a whole heap of superstitious foolishness," Jesse said. "If my dear old mother could have come back to see me, I sure do believe she would've. Course I wouldna hanged around long enough to find out what she came back for." He laughed his great big booming laugh. And Chuck and Mama Carrie laughed with him.

Mama Carrie said, "Jesse Chaney, you oughta be shame of yourself, I do declare."

Jesse laughed. "I love my dear ones whilst they here on this green earth, but I ain't gon tell no lie. After they gone I don't want them coming back to bring me no messages from the other side."

Chuck chuckled. "Me neither, Daddy."

Mama Carrie laughed. "Both of y'all need a good old-fashioned whuppin."

Chuck stared at his plate and cleared his throat. His face broke out in perspiration. Then he said, "The Bible says the Red Sea parted and the Israelites walked across on dry land. You believe it happened, Daddy?" Chuck Othello was a Bible scholar from way back.

Jesse stared at his boy who was Jesse's natural-born spitting image. Everybody told the boy, "You Jesse Chaney up and down. Your name shoulda been Jesse Junior." So this is what his boy had been sneaking up to, to talk about the Bible. Jesse was so proud of his youngest child, sometimes he thought his chest would pop wide open. He knew the Bible better than his daddy did. "Course I believe it happened. The Bible tells you so," his daddy said.

"You do believe in magic then, don't you, Daddy. You believe Moses was a good magician."

"Hush your mouth, boy," Mama Carrie said. Good-naturedly serious now. She knew her boy was joking, but you just didn't joke with the Good Book. You just didn't.

Jesse's dark eyes laughed and twinkled. Sometimes when he looked at Chuck, he could not stop the smile from forming on his face. He chuckled softly. "That's different, son. That was God's work, not Moses. Moses just carried out his order. Moses was his worldly instrument. God can do anything. He could dry up the seven oceans if he had a mind to." He threw back his head and sang—in his big rich voice.

My Lord gonna change this wicked race.
He's gonna raise up a nation that will obey.

[48]

The boy swallowed deep into his belly. He almost could not find his voice, but he made himself speak anyhow. "I don't believe in God, Daddy." It was the first time he had said the words to anybody, including himself. It scared him to death. He knew an ice-cold fear in his mouth and throat and through his shoulders.

Mama Carrie grunted like somebody had kicked her in the stomach. "Hush your filthy mouth, boy, else I'll slap you clean 'way from this table." She was dead serious now. She stared at her boy as if she had never seen him before. She couldn't have taken his statement more to heart if he had called her, his own mother, a dirty, rotten, lowdown whore.

He said quietly, "I'm sorry, Mama Carrie. I've tried awful hard to believe in Him, but I just can't, don't care how hard I try." He felt like crying.

She drew back her hand to slap him, but Jesse grabbed her arm. "I ain't never heard of nobody ever beating religion into anybody's heart or they soul or they mind. Chuck got a better heart than a whole heap of them devils I see jumping up and down and whooping and hollering in church every Sunday. Everybody talking about Heaven ain't going there. If he don't believe, whupping ain't gon do a bitta good. How you gon ever know how come he don't believe if you gon slap him in the mouth ever time he try to talk to us about it? If he can't talk to us, who can he talk to?" He turned to the boy. "How come you talking like you talking, son? You been raised up different. We always been believers."

Mama Carrie's eyes filled up and spilled over. She looked at her boy and shook her head in pity. "Lord have mercy, Lord forgive him. Jesus! Forgive him—forgive him—forgive him! He don't know what he talking about."

Chuck asked, "Is God a white man?" He knew the boldness of his question. He did not seek to shock his parents. Sweat collected in his collar. His heart beat all the way up in his temple. In case there was a God, he hoped He wasn't listening at the moment. He hoped He was taking care of other business.

Jesse said, "God is not a white man, son. He is not a black man. He ain't got no color. And He ain't no respecter of persons, the Good Book say it plain as day."

"The Lord God Jehovah is a just God," Mama Carrie solemnly asserted.

[49]

"He's *just* all right," Chuck said quietly, bitterly. "You better believe He's *just. Just* as prejudiced as a Mississippi peckerwood when it comes to colored people."

Mama Carrie stared at him. She could not believe it was her son uttering such blasphemies. "You sure ain't never heard no talk like that in this house. And after all that Bible-reading you do. I don't know where you get it from. You sure didn't get it in this house." There was a great fear in her face, as if she thought the Lord would strike His lightning down upon their humble home. "Every time I look around, you got your head stuck in the Bible. You oughta be ashamed of yourself. God don't love ugly. He sure Lord don't love ugly!"

Chuck said, "God made me and everything else in the world since the beginning of the world. He made the heaven and the earth. Right, Daddy?"

Jesse said, "That's what the Good Book teach us, son. That's the only thing we can go by."

Chuck said, "If God made everything else, who made God?"

Jesse said, "God won't made, son. He just was. Won't nothing before Him, and everything come after Him!" There was not the great conviction in his voice that his son was used to hearing. It was a question that had plagued Jesse himself, ever since he was a boy, but he had finally accepted it on faith. Some things you had to accept on faith. Or become an unbeliever.

The boy chewed it over in his mind. Swallowed it hard into his stomach. It did not settle there. His boyish face wore a grown folks' seriousness. "I don't believe in God," he stated. "I don't believe there ever was a God."

A great sob escaped his mother's lips. She burst into tears and went quietly, quickly, into the other room.

He looked into his father's eyes, black-dark and full of trouble now. "I'm sorry, Daddy. I really am sorry. I try hard to believe, but I just can't make it. Where was God when peckerwoods were burning our house down? Where was God when Junior got killed away over yonder in Korea?" He swallowed his anguish down into the pit of his nervous stomach. "If God is good, if God is just, if He can dry up the seven seas, how come He can't unfreeze these crackers' hearts in 'Sippi?"

Jesse stared at his boy in wonderment. What could he tell him? "The Lord works in mysterious ways, His wonder to perform," the father said unconvincingly. He knew how empty his voice sounded.

Chuck said, "I don't want to hear that, Daddy. That ain't good enough no more. That ain't saying nothing to me." He got up from the table and walked outdoors into the night.

His father sat there alone at the table. None of them had finished their supper. Jesse's black unblemished skin was drawn tight as a trap drum over the large frame of his face. He frowned as he picked up a forkful of peas and rice. The food was cold and tasteless now, and no matter how he chewed, the peas and rice hung from his palate or lay unswallowed on the floor of his mouth. It was as if his gullet were stopped up like a sluggish drain. As proud as he was of Chuck, "the last button on Jacob's coattail," he worried about the boy. Lately, he did a bushel of worrying about his boy. He worried, because he knew the boy was a dreamer, and he, the father, dreamed some of the same dreams for the boy, dreams he knew the boy dreamed for himself. He had never wanted any of his children to pick cotton all of their lives. He'd always wanted something better for them, especially this last one, this one with so much fire and spirit, this one that reminded him of Junior. This one of quick tears and easy laughter, but serious deep down in his bowels. Serious. Too damn serious. This one must not lose his fire, must not let 'Sippi get him down. His eyes bleared as he thought of Junior dead and gone these many years. Jesse stared at the lamp in the center of the table and remembered their big house where they had lived for less than a week. The wick was burning low, the chimney smoking. A candlefly flew around and around the lamp like an airplane circling for a landing. It cast giant shadows against the wall and on his somber face. He knew he should get up and turn up the wick.

Jesse saw in Chuck the last chance for his own fulfillment, his own dreams. Dreams he had not dared to dream. But things were different these days for colored people. And Chuck was different. Jesse had only the vaguest notion of how his other children were doing, except for the one folks called "Crazy Willie," who worked in cotton on the Rogers Jefferson Johnson plantation and lived in Johnson Bottom and would probably live there all his days. Jesse and Mama Carrie got letters from the others. They were making their own way. They sent money orders home once in a long while and Christmas gifts. They used to come home

[51]

at Christmas and sometimes during the summer, but since the Supreme Court spoke from Washington and stirred up so much bad feeling, there was so much tension in the state that his children had stopped coming. He had an idea they were all making out. Once upon a time he had thought about Junior the way he thought of Chuck. But Junior was forever gone. He wanted this one to do better than just make out. Life must be more than making out. God must've put man here to do more than just make out. He wanted Chuck to be the proof that life was more than making out. Even a black man's life in 'Sippi.

Out in the yard Chuck stared up at the starless night. Where was God? Who was God? What was God? How? When? Why? He saw nothing but a great vast black nothingness, no stars, no moon. No God. He wanted answers that his parents could not give him. Maybe no one had his kind of answers. Maybe his questions were unanswerable. He felt a great and terrible loneliness wrapping itself around him like the heavy blackness of the night. Was Junior way up there somewhere looking down on him this night? He started to walk out toward the edge of the yard where the tall corn grew. He walked through the garden and only half-heard night things scampering around his feet. He was a very squeamish boy when it came to crawling things, like snakes and rats and lizards, but he heeded them not at all this night. He stood at the back of the garden and marveled at the lightning bugs. God made the lightning bugs. He smiled. God said, let there be light, and made the lightning bugs. Let there be noise. And made the crickets and the frogs and the old dog barking from a long ways off. And the rooster crowing in the early morn. Let there be sweat. And made black people and white cotton. Let there be hate. And made the peckerwoods. Let there be ambition. And made Charles Othello Chaney. He was ambitious and he was going to be somebody. You might as well believe it, when he said so. "I'm going to be somebody, and I don't mean picking cotton!" He started back through the garden toward the house. Let there be love. And He made sweet Miss Bessie Mae Moocho. Sweet and lovely! He smiled. God really did some making, when he got Bessie Mae together. She was honestly and truly one of God's magnificent creations. He laughed. Bessie Mae was his secret sweetheart. Chuck was so secretive about it, he had not even made Bessie Mae aware of the great love affair between him and her.

[52]

His mind made a picture of Bessie Mae of the dark dark midnight-black eyes, Bessie Mae of the dark red rosy lips and the thin dress and the roundness and the slimness, and the body smell of peanuts roasting and the sweetness of large elberta peaches, as he imagined the taste of her dark red mouth. When he thought of her, deeply of her, he was willing to concede God in all His glory and magnificence. He was willing to give the man His due.

He found his father just as he had left him, staring at the lamplight, shadows dancing on his face now creased with worrying. He said, "I'm sorry, Daddy. I didn't mean to hurt Mama Carrie's feelings."

His father said, "I know, son. I reckin I know what's in your heart."

The boy said, "We keep hearing all this talk about—you got to get an education these days. Especially if you're black, you got to get an education. But the white children go to school nine months a year and we go six. How we gon ever catch up? Six months for learning and six months for chopping and picking cotton? Go to school summer and winter—work the cotton spring and fall. How we gon ever catch up like that?"

The father merely shook his head in a show of understanding which never could be understood. Chuck said, "But God is good?"

"God is good," his father agreed. "We must believe that God is good."

Chuck said, "God is just."

"That's what the Bible say," his father answered. "Sometimes it's hard to understand."

The thing was, Chuck was on his third trip through the Bible. He knew it from cover to cover, knew it more intimately than his mother or his father. That was the surprising thing. He loved this great book. Maybe he took the book too seriously. He said, "If the Lord of Jacob is our refuge, how come He lets so many bad things happen to His chosen children?"

His father shook his head from side to side. And had no answers.

Chuck's rattle was far deadlier than his strike. He talked big, but he was still a scared boy when he went to bed that night. He was a little boy with a big mouth, a mouth that asked big questions and demanded answers. He was a God-fearing boy, who

[53]

told himself he did not believe, yet got down on his knees that night and prayed, just in case he was mistaken. Everybody made mistakes. He didn't want to take any chances of God punishing him while he slept for his blasphemy. If he woke up dead, he wanted a chance at entering those Pearly Gates. He was dying to meet Saint Peter, if such a saint existed.

The last few times Chuck staked Missy Anne in the garden, she pulled up stake and wandered onto the Wakefield plantation, and ate high off the best and tallest corn. It was as if she were determined to get Chuck into trouble. Luckily, Chuck got her back home each time before she was discovered. But one day he was not so lucky. The cow was caught in Wakefield's best corn, and one of the overseers carried her to the Wakefield cow barn. Chuck didn't know what to do about it. He was scared to tell his daddy at first. But when his father sent him for milk the next morning and he came back empty-handed, he had to tell him. His father ranted and raged far more than Chuck expected. The way he looked at it, it wasn't that much to get all het up over. A worthless, stupid, no-brained heifer.

"You are the triflinest boy God ever made!"

"But, Daddy, it ain't my fault that fool cow won't never stay put."

"He stays put for me," his father said.

"Daddy, *he* is a *she*," the boy said quietly.

"Never you mind—I know what he is. Don't be cutting the fool with me, boy. I'll slap you into the middle of next week."

"It coulda happened to anybody," Mama Carrie said. "That cow ain't never been nothing but trouble since the day we bought her."

Everything that morning made his father angrier. He usually woke up in a good humor. "I notice you don't pour his milk out," he said to Mama Carrie. He turned to Chuck again. "Can't I even trust you with a simple thing like keeping the cow in our pasture?"

"We ain't got no pasture," Chuck answered. "We ain't got nothing but a backyard."

"We ain't even got a backyard," Mama Carrie interjected. "We pay rent, but it sure don't b'long to us. We can't sell it like we can that devilish cow, which wouldn't be a bad idea. He's more trouble than he's worth."

[54]

Jesse's great voice was like angry thunder. "What the hell is that got to do with anything, woman? What the hell has rent got to do with the damn cow?"

Mama Carrie ignored the question and asked one of her own. "How come you raising all this who-shot-John over nothing? Steada just going over to Jack Tyson and telling him he got your cow and you want it? Most probably he the one that took it. He the overseer of that part of the farm. He's in charge of Mister Charlie's cows."

"I don't wanna have no dealings with Jack Tyson. You know me and him don't set horses."

Chuck sought to ease the situation with a pun. "We ain't talking about no horses, Daddy. We talking about Missy Anne and she's a cow."

Jesse Chaney just glared at him, speechless in his anger.

Mama Carrie said, "You don't want to speak to Jack Tyson, how come you don't speak to your good friend, Mister Charlie Wakefield?"

"I don't want to bother him about such a little biddy thing." He didn't like to talk with Wakefield unless he could not get around it. Since the Supreme Court spoke, he had sworn to never call him Mister Charlie again, and yet he could not bring himself to call him just plain Charles. It had become a big thing with him. The fact of the matter was, he and Wakefield avoided one another.

"Well, if it's such a little biddy thing, how come you raising so much Cain with your own flesh and blood about it?"

He glared at his wife and went off cussing to himself. More than a week passed and no cow. Every night Mama Carrie would ask him why he didn't go over and ask the man about the cow. Either man. Any man. Jesse saw Jack Tyson two and three times a day and never opened his mouth to him. He avoided Charlie Wakefield two and three times a week. It was as if he wanted to forget the cow ever existed. Tyson was the meanest cracker on the Wakefield plantation. He was especially hateful and scornful to Negroes. He would as soon call them "nigger" as he would spit outdoors. And he did an awful lot of spitting. They said he'd killed ten or fifteen Negroes in his time. Ever since the cow had been missing, Jesse had rehearsed the scene with Jack Tyson many times.

Jesse: "Mister Jack, I come for my cow."

[55]

Mr. Jack: "What cow you talking about, nigger? Get the shit outa your black mouth. Take off your hat when you come before your betters."

Then he would take off his hat and curtsy and flash a toothy grin and say: "Excuse me, Mister Jack, please suh—if you don't mind, please suh—"

But if he would not call Mister Charlie "Mister Charlie," he surely was not going to call old evil Jack Tyson "Mister Jack." Because he could never go back down that road again. Never ever could he be known again as a good old shuffling grinning darkie. But the other road was fraught with danger to life and limb, and there were only two roads. No detours and no alternate routes. There was no middle passage.

One Tuesday evening, Jesse came home tired and mean and evil, and Mama Carrie asked him about the cow again.

He shouted at his wife, a thing he seldom did to anyone, since he never found it necessary. His natural voice was thunder enough already. "I don't wanna hear nothing about that goddamn cow again, you hear me!"

They kept an argument going all through supper and into the night. Chuck wondered what it was all about. Could it be just about an old stupid knock-kneed cow? Why *didn't* his daddy just go over to stables and bring her back?

"I'll go get him tomorrow, Daddy," Chuck volunteered innocently.

"You ain't gon do nothing of the kind," Jesse growled. "I'm the man in this house, and don't you forget it. You the whole cause of this in the first damn place. You keep your big mouth outa grownfolks' business. You gettin' beside yourself here lately."

"I only thought——"

"You just shet your damn mouth 'fore I shet it for you."

Later that night Chuck was awakened by his mother and father arguing about the stupid cow.

"Why donchoo go and get him yourself," he heard his father shouting.

"I thought you were the man of the house," his mother said sarcastically.

He heard his father's hand explode against his mother's face, heard his father's raging voice. "Don't you ever forget who the man of this house is, woman." And another slap. "Don't you never ever forgit it! Don't you forgit who wear the britches! Don't you never ever forgit it! Goddamn your soul!"

Chuck ran into the other room, and saw his mother standing her ground with the tears flooding down her face and the fire poker raised above her head.

"Don't you never hit me again," she shouted to the father. "As long as you live on God's green earth, don't you never hit this black woman again, else I'm gon try my best to kill you, even if I have to steal you while you sleep."

The next day Jesse went to the grassland where Wakefield cows were pastured and unstaked Missy Anne and brought her home without saying anything to Mr. Wakefield or Jack Tyson or anybody else. And that was that.

One day Mama Carrie took Chuck aside and talked with him about it. "Your daddy is a man, Charles Othello. Don't you never let anybody tell you nothing different. He's a good man and a brave man and a proud man, and he feels his man-ness deep deep in him. But it's mighty hard to be a black man in this white man's country. I reckin it's been like that ever since they bring us here in chains. It's mighty hard, son. The odds is stacked against you. It's like robbing a bank. You ain't hardly got the chance of a gnat with cancer. But your daddy is a man. That's what make it so hard for him."

"I know my daddy is a man, Mama Carrie."

"It woulda been more easier for me to gone and got that foolish cow. Some things a black woman can get away with, a black man dassn't even try. It woulda been whole lot easier for me to get the cow, but it woulda made him feel less than a man. That's how come I kept after him to get it his own self. But every time I did it, it rubbed him the wrong way. He thought I was saying something about his courage. It was like rubbing cayenne pepper into a bad sore. He got to feeling like I was making light of his man-ness. That's how come he exploded. You understand, son, doncha?"

It was a whole heap to digest at one swallow, a great big bitter pill, but he shook his great head up and down and told her, "Yessum."

"But your daddy is man, Charles Othello Chaney. And don't you have no doubts about it."

The boy said, "Yessum."

[57]

"And he ain't never hit me before and he ain't gon never hit me again. Your daddy ain't no woman-beater. He's a man. I mean a real man."

The boy swallowed and said, "Yessum."

Chapter
5

Chuck Othello Chaney was all of thirteen years old now and tall for his age, and long and gangling like his father and top-heavy, as if he really didn't know what to do with this marvelous body he possessed, this wonderfully crazy thing the Good Lord gave him. It would be more correct to say that his body possessed him and did with him exactly as its own whims dictated. His feet went ploppidy-plop in and out of the black dust as he ambled down the sun-cooked road away from his house. He was one thing, his body was something altogether mysteriously different, and he was his body's helpless slave. Just that morning Mama Carrie told him, "Boy, you beginning to smell your pee already and you ain't hardly dry behind your ears."

He smiled to himself. He remembered the first time she'd told him that. He had been almost five years old at the time. He had put his fingers behind his ears looking for the wetness. "My ears is dry, Mama Carrie."

And Mama Carrie and Daddy and even Crazy Willie had had a big laugh at his expense. Finally it had come true though, the other part of it. He *was* beginning to smell his pee all right. Every time he went to the water closet next to the house, he took note that his pee was getting stronger and browner. The stronger the smell the greater was his pride and admiration. It meant he was growing into manhood.

He was walking down the main street of town now, Robert E. Lee Boulevard. It was one of the very few paved streets in town. Wakefield City was the county seat. A sleepyhead little cracker town of no particular significance, except that it was kind of his home town. For better or for worse, it was the only one he had. A fellow had to have some kind of a feeling about his home town. It was as if you were saddled with the meanest parents in the world, they were still your parents, even though they were stepparents, they were still your mama and your papa. You had to find some goodness in them even if you had to manufacture it. You had to find some goodness. There was a folksy sign out at the city limits (Chuck had walked out there many times and seen it) which read:

GATE CITY TO OLD TRADITIONAL DIXIE.
EVERYBODY WISHES THEY WUZ IN WAKEFIELD CITY.
A NICE TOWN TO RAISE YOUR YOUNG 'UNS IN.

Moreover, the city was in the Southern tradition. It was famous for its honeysuckle and magnolias and its great oak trees and its gracious hospitality. Welcome signs adorned the downtown area —in front of the Elks Lodge, the Knights of Pythias, the Moose Lodge, the churches, and the Stonewall Jackson Hotel, everywhere were welcome mats. They made a stranger feel at home. People sat on porches, and in summer fanned themselves with paper fans and said, "Morning," "Evening," and "Howdy," when you passed them by.

Chuck was out of the downtown area now. He stopped along the dusty highway and wiped his face with his shirttail. An old hound dog lay fast asleep on the side of the road. Great God A'mighty! It was so hot chickens were laying hard-boiled eggs. Maybe he should go back home. Go home and come another day. Two hens and a rooster walked out of the front yard of a one-story wooden-frame tattletale-gray house and cavorted up the dirt sidewalk toward Chuck, chattering and clucking to beat the band. The rooster walked a couple of paces behind the hens. Chuck wondered what they were talking about. Did chickens understand each other? Suddenly the rooster closed the gap between him and them and leapt upon one of their backs and the feathers began to fly in all directions. Chuck danced out of the way. He thought, "It's too doggone hot for such carryings-on."

He turned and stared back down the highway toward the city. The low skyline was dominated by a lofty water tank on which the name of Wakefield City could be seen from four approaches to the town and miles away. Atop the tank was a huge white cross which became proudly illumined in the nighttime. To some folk, it was the symbol of the brotherhood of man in Our Lord and Savior Jesus Christ. To others, the image conjured was entirely different. Of hooded riders of the night and strange and savage rituals.

Most of the county was low-level country, but the highway leading to the Rogers Johnson plantation went uphill for a short distance and then downhill to level country again.

From where the boy stood, the town below took on a picture-book beauty for him. It was the biggest city in the county, boasting of an ever-growing population of upward of two thousand people, the Lord giveth and the Good Lord taketh. There were four other cities in the county. But for all that, Wakefield City's beauty disappeared as you got closer to it. Chuck Chaney knew it wasn't the biggest city in the world, although he sometimes thought so, or pretended he did. Up close, it was just a typical little Southern cracker town (no more, no less) except there was a special sense of poverty here. The people and the way they lived, except for a few, seemed one jump ahead of privation. There were in Chuck's town very few colonial mansions deep into the trees away from the dusty streets with lawns that looked like campuses. The dog-eared down-in-the-mouth business district was unpretentiously defined (with rare exception) by one- and two-story raggedy-assed buildings, which surrounded the square in the middle of which the courthouse stood, taller than the rest and dominating one and all. It was, at best, a poor excuse for a city and/or county seat.

He turned and started to walk again. Something in the hushed air whispered to him: "Go back home—go back home!" He stood beneath a chinaberry tree on Swift Creek Hill in the quiet heavy 'Sippi heat of midafternoon and looked down at Johnson's Bottom, where his best buddy lived. Most people called it simply the Bottom, and Chuck reckoned it was the bottom, all right. Most of the people who lived there worked on Congressman Rogers Jefferson Davis Johnson's plantation. The shacks in the Bottom were huddled together like old folks, small and withered and ugly and helpless and shrunken, and sinking forever into the black earth that would one day receive them everlastingly. Notwithstanding the Bottom's general look of dilapidation, there were television antennae atop each lowly shack as if the shack-dwellers were listening for a message from the Good Lord up on High. Send us a sign, O Lord and Master. When will you deliver us from this unfriendly world? Send us a black Moses!

Didn't My Lord deliver Daniel?
Why not every man?

Chuck had a feeling that this day something would happen to
him. Something dangerous and different and everlasting. Whenever he came to visit Jake, he always had this funny feeling. Little
Jake Carson was his bosom buddy, his boon companion, and that
was why he was going to the Bottom. To visit Jake. He almost
convinced himself it was the one and only reason. Of course,
there was Bessie Mae Brazwell, better known as Bessie Mae
Moocho, and his mind made a picture of her, alive and warm
and disturbing, and he swallowed the peculiar taste in his mouth.
But he really had come just to see his buddy, Jake. But Bessie
Mae was something else.

A hot breeze blew from the Bottom up to the Hill and against
Chuck's face. You could smell the outhouses in the Bottom from
miles away. Some of the houses didn't even have outhouses. And
yet somehow he liked to come to the Bottom to see the Carsons,
especially Jake, and pretty Miss Bessie Mae Brazwell and all the
rest of it—Uncle Bish—

As he went downhill toward the Bottom, he began to sing one
of the songs they sang at the colored Sunday school picnic last
month in the park by the river, and he used the same outrageous
words Uncle Bish had used right after he had gotten through
eating a piece of Mama Carrie's fried chicken.

Way down yonder in my country home
I got choked on a chicken bone
Pharaoh's army got drownded
O Mary doncher weep

He laughed out loud. As young as he was, sometimes he
talked to himself, and enjoyed the conversation. As he walked
along Huckleberry Lane, he stopped laughing and shamefacedly
watched an old woman with a naked baby in her arms walk out
of her back door into her backyard and up into a green field
behind her yard. Chuck wanted to look the other way, but
something wouldn't let him. The woman didn't see him as she
looked around her; she bent over slightly, and she held the baby
as close to the ground as possible and let it do its business. Then
she spread her own legs apart and she pulled her dress outward
and sprayed the dark earth. He turned his head and started to

[61]

run down the narrow little street, hoping violently she had not wet her dress, ashamed of having spied on her, feeling a great big, shamefaced wetness gathering in his own eyes now. He was going on fourteen years old and much too big to cry so quickly. But she was too old to squat down like that, and why did she have to do her business on the ground like an animal? Why didn't she have a water closet like he had at home, or at least an outhouse? Why didn't God do something about it? Ever since he could remember, his image of God had been vivid, real, personal. God had a face, eyes, ears, nostrils. Sympathy. Anger. Passion. Love. Vengeance is mine, saith the Lord. When he prayed, he talked to God and God listened and acted. Or didn't act. And what good was prayer if God didn't listen? What good was God if He did not answer prayers? Yet, in spite of his renunciation of Him to his father and his mother that night, Chuck had not entirely given Him up. There was noplace else to seek asylum. Was there? Was there? Way down in the Land of Cotton?

He always had a funny feeling of something about to happen whenever he visited the Bottom. Life and death and laughter and hope and tears and poverty and love and hate, all of it was there just waiting to reach out and grab you, and you would never be the same again. He should go back home. He laughed at his own apprehensions and started to sing again.

> *Way down yonder where the moon shine bright*
> *Folks don't need no 'lectric light*
> *Pharaoh's army got drownded*
> *O Mary doncher weep.*

He followed a path between two shacks and came to Jake's house. It was no different from the rest of the rusty-looking one- and two-room shacks in Johnson's Bottom. Little Jake was sitting in front of his house playing checkers with his father, Bish Carson. Everybody called him Uncle Bish. Children of all sizes and ages stood around watching the game. Giggling and signifying. Little Jake was smoking a real cigarette, a roll-your-own, like a full-grown man. He looked up from the checker game.

"Well, if it ain't old Harry Belafonte hisself in person. What's happening, old baby?"

"Come on, boy," Uncle Bish said to Jake, winking at Chuck. "Keep your eye on the cotton-picking game."

"I can beat you with both eyes tied behind my back," Little

[62]

Jake told his father. Little Jake was squarely constructed, as wide as he was tall. His eyes were narrow but always full of devilment. The children jumped up and down and giggled. He was the sassiest boy in Mississippi. Nobody seemed to remember why they called him "Little" Jake. He had never been little in his life.

"Can he beat you playing, Uncle Bish?" Chuck asked.

"Who? This fathead fish beat me? You gotta be kidding. He play pretty good for somebody just learning the game. But he can't give the champ no inneresting competition. I can beat the best of them. Jake ain't nothing but a fish in a dish."

"Fool him, Devil," Little Jake said. He didn't crack a smile, as the children jumped up and down and clapped their hands and laughed and giggled. And signified.

"Ooooh—wee! I know Uncle Bish gon tend to him now!"

Uncle Bish made a couple of moves and gave Jake a jump and with one jump of his own took all of Jake's men off the board. "That's what you gits for being so sassy," Uncle Bish told him.

Uncle Bish was of medium height, a skinny, little, wrinkled-up man. From his appearance, he might have been a victim of dehydration. He stretched his legs and patted his feet and started to sing one of his funny little songs.

> *Time is tight,*
> *Money is sca'ce.*
> *Don't git better,*
> *I'm gon leave this place.*

It was more like reciting poetry than it was singing, and the children laughed. But Chuck didn't laugh. Jake scowled at his father.

Little Jake got up from his broken-down orange crate. "Let's go down the street a piece, my man, and see what's on the rail for the lizard."

"Man, I sure do wish I could git me a job. Time is really gitting tight." Uncle Bish was talking to himself as much as for the children's entertainment. "You can't even find no cigarette butts on the streets in town no more. I swan. Automation is killing the poor workingman. Hear tell Rogers Johnson gon bring in some automated cotton pickers. Hear tell Old Man Jim Sawyer say he don't need no niggers no longer. He got white gooses chopping his cotton."

The children laughed and giggled.

[63]

Jake stared contemptuously at his father. He sometimes wished that Bish were in reality his uncle rather than his father. It would be bad enough to have him as an uncle. Bish said, "John Henry sure had the right idea. Before he let that steam drill beat him down, he died with his hammer in his hand. That damn machine gon beat us all down to a natural nub." He looked up at Chuck. "You wanna play me a game, Chuck? Maybe you have better luck than this old fathead boy of mine."

Little Jake spat arrogantly through his teeth and streams of saliva splashed into the black dust. "Come on, Chuck. We got business to tend to."

"Be back directly, Uncle Bish," Chuck said. Maybe he should just play Uncle Bish one little sociable game of checkers and go home where he belonged. Maybe go swimming in the river— maybe—he had a funny feeling—maybe—

They walked down the narrow tree-bordered street, he and Little Jake. Their feet went plop-plop in and out of the black powdery dust. Naked and half-naked children played in front of the shacks and in the backyards and all through the houses.

Here and there were a few undernourished chickens. Life had slackened their pace to the tempo of a slow drag, as they went about grubbing and scrounging for their daily bread. Their eyes told Chuck the story. They were a beaten breed of hapless birds. They were not too much unlike many people in the Bottom.

Naked, brown and black and yellow babies with a brightness in their eyes and ugly potbellied stomachs. Men, old and young and in-between, sitting on the porches of the shacks that had porches and in the yards and playing checkers and cards, standing around talking to one another. You could see some folks sitting forlornly in their one room watching soap operas on television. Watching white folk cut the fool. The God-awful heat, the smell of the outhouses, the dust, the ugly rusty shacks, and the restless men, and some of the houses looked like outhouses.

An old wrinkled-up woman stuck her head out of one of the one-room houses. "Hey there, Little Jake, come here jest a minute."

Jake and Chuck stopped and stared at the woman. "Is the bug done come out?" she asked them anxiously.

"No'm, it ain't," Jake answered impatiently. "It don' never come out before six in the evening."

"Son, will you do a poor old widow woman a favor?"

"Whatcha want me to do?"

"I'm so feeble and poorly, it's a sin and a shame. And the Good Lord sure will bless you. And I sure will ask Him to be sure to bless you when I gits on humble knees tonight." The old woman spat into the yard and kicked up dust. She had used so much snuff in her day, that her lower lip stuck out all the time, snuff or no snuff.

"Whatcha want me to do?" Little Jake asked impatiently.

Her little, old, thin squeaky voice came thick and husky from her throat. "Will you go there for me to the house where the old man died yestiddy and see what the house number is?"

Jake asked her, "What you want with Old Man Ashton's number? You gon send him some flowers? He sure can't smell 'em now."

"I'd do it myself but I'm right poorly right long in here this day of Our Lord and Savior Jesus Christ. Couldn't see it good nohow cause my eyes going back on me. Don't let anybody see you copying it down. The Lord be praised on earth as He is in Heaven."

Jake repeated, "What you want with Old Man Ashton's number?"

She laughed a dry and guilty laugh. "I'm gon pray for you on my knees tonight, son. The Good Lord knows I am. Praise His name. You just bring me that number like I axed you. I'm gon play it tomorrow. You can play it too. Something tells me that's what the bug gon be. I'm gon play it in the combination."

"Did the Good Lord tell you that when you was on your knees last night?"

She laughed and cackled and then remembered to be indignant. "Git away from here you nasty stinking scamp—you sassy devil! I'm gon tell Sallie Belle on you."

Little Jake and Chuck walked off down the street.

She shouted after them. "Don't forgit to get that number, you triflin' rascal!"

They turned the corner into Drybranch Boulevard, which was a country road just like all the other dusty streets. They looked at each other and burst out laughing. They leaned against each other, and they leaned against the side of somebody's shack. They laughed and laughed. Jake said, "Ain't that a bitch? She gon pray for me when she git on her knees—She gon pray to God to hit that dead man's number—"

[65]

They laughed and laughed.

"Git the hell away from my house with all that goddamn noise!" a man's voice from inside the house shouted.

"Tell your dear old mother to get—" Jake began, but Chuck put his hand over Jake's mouth.

They fell suddenly silent and walked along kicking up black dust for a time, at home with their separate thoughts. Jake broke the silence.

"Bish sitting around on his dead ass and watching Ma go out and slave every day. Always saying that mammy-hunching song about 'Time's tight, money's sca'ce, don't git better he gon leave this place.' Why in the hell don't he git up and leave? It damn sure ain't nobody holding him."

"Where would he go? He belongs here with his family."

"Well let him git hisself a job then, goddammit. He could at least git hisself a paper route like I got. Goddamn! Do something! He git money from somewhere to sneak off here every night to buy that rotgut whiskey. His middle name oughta be White Lightning. He better not be stealing my mama's money."

"Newspaper route ain't no grown man's job," Chuck argued. "He wouldn't feel right carrying newspapers—being a newsboy. He-he-he's a man and that's a boy's job."

"Well, let him do something. He's too damn triflin' to hustle a few numbers."

Chuck didn't answer Jake. He just walked along thinking, thinking, thinking. All the children in the Bottom had loved Uncle Bish. Everybody knew he worked for Williams Furniture Company for fifteen years, till a piano fell on him and left him with a lame leg. After he came out of the hospital, they kept him on the job for six whole months out of the goodness of their pure-white hearts. But finally they had to let him go. He slowed down the whole operation. And nobody else would hire him. He'd held a few jobs since then, but not for long, because he limped so badly and couldn't get around fast enough. He was too proud for them to hire him just because they felt sorry for him. He was not that kind of a colored man. When he was healthy and working, there wasn't a steadier man in all the Bottom. On paydays he would stop downtown at the big stores in Wakefield City and buy something for all of his and Sallie Belle's children and others besides. His arms would be full when he reached

home. Chuck had been out to Jake's on many a Saturday afternoon and seen it happen.

Somebody would whisper: "Uncle Bish coming!" And all the
kids would run up the road to meet him.

Little Jake's mother told Bish a million times, "You shouldn't
be spending all your money for all this foolishness, Bish. You a
hard-working man. Both of us hard-working. You better be more
carefuller with the money. Set a little bit aside. One of these
days, it's gonna rain forty days and forty nights."

Uncle Bish would laugh and shake his head and say something
like: "Pay it no mind, Sallie Belle." In those days he stayed in
good humor most of the time. Everybody said that was sure one
man that loved his family and was good to them. Seven children.
Stepladders beginning with sassy Jake. They'd always been a
couple (he and Sallie Belle) that forever acted like brand-new
courting people. They sure did love each other in those gone-by
days. But times had changed.

He'd say, "Don't worry your pretty little head about nuthin',
Sallie Belle. Pay it no never mind. Can't take it with us. That's
one sure thing. Uncle Sam's dollars sure don't spend down yonder, or up in Heaven where you bound."

Jake and Chuck turned into the next street and three doors
down was Bessie Mae's house with all kinds of pretty flowers in
the front yard and a rose bush gleaming-full of roses climbing
arrogantly up one side of the porch and honeysuckle up the other
side. Chuck and Jake stopped in front of Bessie Mae's, and Jake
whistled his crazy whistle. Chuck knew a panicky kind of feeling.
A sycamore tree threw dancing shadows on the yard.

A soft babyish voice came from inside the shack. "What you
want, Little Jake?"

Chuck felt himself grow warmer swiftly in his face and neck
and shoulders.

"You ain't cripple, is you? Come on out and see for your own
self. Look what kind of company I brung you."

She came to the door. She was a lovely thing to look at in her
thin pink dress that looked as if it were made of cheesecloth. Her
skin was pure-black pulled-tight velvet. Her eyes were entirely
black—to Chuck Othello. Long black eyelashes. She was not
skinny, neither was she fat. She was stacked up "prettifiedly," in
the famous words of Little Jake Carson. And Chuck was inclined
to agree with him—wholeheartedly. Her bosom and hips were

[67]

those of a full-grown woman. Lord have mercy! She was bursting out all over with good outrageous health—wonderful health. Robust health! She smiled at Chuck and he felt himself growing swiftly into manhood.

"Well, well, well. If it ain't Mister Charles Othello Chaney, himself—in person. Nobody else but."

"Hello, Bessie Mae," Chuck said weakly, shyly. "How is every little thing?" There was that strange taste in his mouth again and an unremembered warmth that gathered in the middle of him.

"Just fine, Chuck. Ain't no use complaining. I'm just fine." She had the cutest roundest plumpest mouth, Chuck thought. And it did funny little tricks when she talked. He thought, Good Lord, will I ever!

Jake smiled knowingly at Bessie Mae. "You can say that a-everlasting-gin," he cracked. "You just as fine as elderberry wine. Miss Bessie Mae Moocho is moocho fine." He assumed a pose somewhere between a rock 'n' roller and a crooner with his arms outstretched. He began to sing:

Bessie Mae—
Bessie Mae Moocho

She laughed at Jake even as she smiled at Chuck. "You gentlemans come on up here and have a sitdown on the porch."

They came and they sat. She gave Chuck a roguish kind of look and her dark, dark, dark eyes sparkled darkly, blackly sparkled. Her eyes were two black shiny coals, large and wide. Her dress was too small and much too tight for her, and it hugged her thighs and ample hips in a kind of final desperation, and he could see that she didn't have on a slip and could see the outline of the elastic in her drawers, and her dress was much too short for comfort and it was awful, it was painfully disturbing.

Great day in the morning time!

Jake said, "Lord hair monkey!"

Chuck fished around in his mind for something to say to Bessie Mae, something witty and grown-up and sophisticated, something that would make her know he was a man of the world, a man who knew his way around the womenfolks. When the words came out they were: "We sure are having some real hot weather."

[68]

She looked at him and through him. Girls knew everything, doggonit! "What you need is a nice cool glass of lemonade. You gentlemens just make yourself comfortable and I'll go in and make a pitcherful." She was only a few months older than Chuck, but she acted like she was four or five years older.

"Y'all got ice?" Jake asked her.

"We *must* be got ice if I'm gon make some lemonade."

"Talk that talk," Jake sang out. "Y'all must be rich without anybody else knowing about it. Must be like hit the numbers or something." He stared at her with a real sassy open-faced look. He was the most, the everlasting most.

"I don't reckin that's none of your business," she told him, and turned and went into the house. She was time enough and overtime.

Chuck sat there growing up by the minute. He wished he could talk to Bessie Mae like Little Jake did. He would soon be fourteen, and he wished he would hurry up and become a grown man, but it didn't seem like it would ever happen. Sometimes he wished he were already his own man, but other times, when he saw what life was doing to so many of the men, and the women too, but especially the men, and particularly the women, and he thought about the mighty load that grown folks had to carry, he was willing to postpone growing up for a little while. Other times he wanted to grow up so awfully much, and be done quickly with the business of growing up, he could almost taste it. He wished he could go to sleep one night and wake up the next morning a full-grown man.

Little Jake was already grown, even though he was only a year older than Chuck. He didn't even go to school anymore. There were just too many mouths to feed and backs to put clothes on in Jake's family. Jake had gone way out in the country for a while to do a day's work on one of Rogers Johnson's plantations. Most of the Johnson workers were sharecroppers, but he always hired a few by the day. Jake would come home every Saturday night. He kept that job for about seven months—got in a big fight with the overseer about going into town one Tuesday without a pass (the croppers had to have individual passes to go into town). One word led to another, and the cracker overseer called him a nigger, and Jake tried to kill him with a hoe. Jake had had a whole heap of jobs since then, but none of them lasted, because there just were not enough jobs to go around. And Jake was too damn sassy. The newspaper route didn't bring him much money, but he didn't have to take any shit from white folks. And that was one good thing.

Jake would tell you anytime anyplace. He'd tell anybody. There was nothing white folks could do for him. He once told Chuck Othello, "Man, white folks is the most lowdownest peoples on God's green earth. They as dirty as chickens, and chickens is just about a bunch of nasty mother-fuckers. You take the rooster. That sonovabitch'll fuck his own dear mother and eat his own damn shit!"

Sometimes Chuck would sit in school and think about Jake and look around the classroom, and think about so many other children who had started to school the same year he and Jake had started. Every year a few dropped out, especially the boys, especially after the fourth and fifth grades. He didn't know where some of these children were. Working—looking for work—married—scattered—killed by TB. Some of the lucky ones had put their ages up and sneaked into the Army. One or two extra-special lucky ones were way over yonder somewhere nobody ever heard of, seeing the world and dying for their country. Like Jesse Jr. did.

Jake broke into his stream of thoughts. "She something, ain't she, boy?" He winked an eye at Chuck like a full-grown man. "If the Good Lord made anything better, that great sly cat must've kept it for His own self."

"Who? What? You better stop using the Good Lord's name in vain." Chuck laughed a weak and sickly laugh.

"Who—what—" Jake mimicked. "You know what, you sneaky rascal. Bessie Mae Moocho—that's who—that's what."

Chuck swallowed the sweet awful thickness in his mouth, and it plopped into the pit of his stomach, but the same thick taste made up in his mouth again. His face was warm and getting warmer and not only from the weather. What was keeping Bessie Mae so long with the lemonade? "She sure is something!" he had to agree.

He should be able to talk with girls as easily as Jake did. He knew the language as well, maybe better. He read more books than Jake. He read gobs of books and newspapers too and kept up with everything in the world. Little Jake didn't hardly read any books at all, or newspapers. He just seemed to know what to say when it came to womenfolks. He told Chuck one day: "Some got it, others don't got it. Some is born with it, others have to be learned it, others don't never ever learn it. I got a way with the womenfolks, cause I was born with the gift of gab. And I got sex repeal." Sometimes Chuck believed Jake spoke the gospel truth. Jake was naturally born with the gift.

"You mean sex *ap*-peal!" Chuck corrected his good glib buddy.

"Whatever it is," Jake said. "You may know how to say it better'n me, but I'm the one that got it."

Chuck repeated, "Sex appeal," because he could think of nothing else to say.

"Goddamn—Goddamn," Jake said, like he was paying reverence to the Lord on High. "Make a preacher lay his Bible down." His narrow eyes almost closed now, and his voice was low, like he was saying grace at the breakfast table. "The Good Lord made her like the stuff was going out of style and He wanted to make it perfect one more time. One more time. It may be the last time—I don't know." He shook his head at Chuck. "All you got to do is to say the right thing, 'cause she natcherly sweet on Mister Charles Othello Chaney. Lord, will I ever? No, nigger, never!"

"You oughta stop that stuff." Chuck tried to laugh. He fiercely hoped Bessie Mae didn't hear what Jake was saying. And yet somehow he hoped she heard every single word.

"I know what I'm talking about," Jake insisted. "I always know what I'm talking about. You better listen to me. 'Cause, baby, if I tell you a chicken dip snuff, you can look behind her wing and find the box. And when I tell you pretty Miss Bessie Mae Moocho is weak for you, you better believe me." He laughed at Chuck. He mimicked Bessie Mae. " 'Chuck Chaney sure is cute and intelligent too. He look just like Harry Belafonte and Sidney Porter and Ossie Davis all rolled up into one. He so nice and slim and tall for his age. His eyes so soft and wide and pretty—blah-blah-blah—And his mouth so sweet and tender-looking, but he so shamefacey.' I told her I didn't see nothing cute about that big ugly rascal, she better listen to me. But when I come around, she won't hold still for nothing in the world. Swear to my Jesus, she won't pay me no rabbit-ass mind. She ain't gitting up offa nothing for nobody, but all you got to do is to pop your finger."

Chuck started to protest again but he heard her coming through the room toward the porch and heard the clean cool clinking of ice and glass. She came out on the porch with the lemonade, and they sat there drinking it, and Chuck could feel the cool refreshment of it, as it went down his throat and seemed to spread over the length of his shoulders and all through him. It seemed to soothe the innermost parts of his body.

"How you gentlemens feel now?" She asked both of them, but her eyes were on Chuck. Always on Chuck. She was sitting in a chair and playing nervously with the lap of her dress and forever spreading it out and pulling it tightly down toward her knees, but it just wouldn't come down that far. And Chuck was growing larger and larger by the second, and he was throbbing in the middle of him.

He said, "Just fine." And he reached desperately around in the great maze of his sweet disturbance for something else to say, something smart and clever and bold and sassy, something sophisticated. It was in his mind, he could feel it there, but somehow it refused to take the trip through his mouth. Sometimes he felt, miserably, that words played tricks on him, as they lurked in nooks and corners of his mind and hid from him, like a rubber ball that had been misplaced in his house and rolled completely out of sight. He looked up at the top of the porch and around and he tried to keep his eyes away from her knees, but her knees and thighs were like lodestones to his poor lucky eyes. Her brownish-black thighs flashed at him like beacon beams and he could not keep his eyes away. He looked down at the floor which was scrubbed so clean it didn't have any color. He cleared his throat and he went through the motions of sipping lemonade, only there was none left in his glass. He sucked the ice into his mouth and let it slide back into the glass again.

Jake widened his narrow eyes and began to sing:

Come on round to my house, Baby·
Ain' nobody home but me—
Come on round to my house, Baby
I need compan—neee.
Now I ain' no iceman
Ain' no iceman's son
But I can keep you cool
Until the iceman come.
Come on round to my house, Baby
Ain' nobody home but me.

Little Jake sat there patting his feet with an innocent smile on his wide-open face, and it wasn't such an innocent smile after all. He was a signifier from way back yonder—a notorious agitator. Little Jake got up and stood in front of them and shook his fat and broad backside, while he sang:

Come on round to my house, Baby
Ain' nobody home but me—
Come on round to my house, Baby
I need compa—neee.
I ain't no butcher man
Ain't no butcher man's son,
But I can cut your meat
Till the butcher man come.
Come on round to my house, Baby
Ain' nobody home but me.

Bessie Mae tried hard to keep from smiling. "Jake Carson, you oughta be shame of yourself. I do declare."

Chuck sat there listening and throwing sly glances at Bessie Mae and feeling the afternoon heat pressing heavily down upon him and all inside of him and pushing outward against his insides. And the middle of him was throbbing throbbing more than ever. He hated that he was so shy around girls. The trees in the Bottom stood still in the heat, heavy with their bright green leaves. The bright green leaves were motionless, holding their breaths for something to happen.

Jake stopped singing and moved quickly off the porch and stood in the yard looking up at Bessie Mae and Chuck. "Well I'm gon plant y'all kitties now and dig you a little bit later on," he said. "I got me some business of my own need tending to."

Chuck stood up nervously. "Where you going, Jake?"

"That's my business," Jake answered. "I got a couple of rows to hoe, and I don't need no company tagging along with me." He looked from Chuck to Bessie Mae. Signifying. "And the way things look around here, y'all don't need no company either. See what I mean?" He stared long and hard at Bessie Mae and then he turned to Chuck and said, "Lord knows the soil around here is fine and fertile, and I know damn well you don't need nobody to teach you how to plow." He laughed a dry laugh.

"Do you really gotta go?" Bessie Mae pleaded. "Can't you stay just a little bit longer?"

[73]

Little Jake stared at her sarcastically and laughed and laughed and laughed and laughed. "What you want me hanging around for? I done already brung the great lover-man to pay you a visit. What more do you want? Y'all don't need nobody to hold the candle cause it's broad open daylight." He laughed again, this time contemptuously. "Come by the house, when you get through visiting with Miss Bessie Mae Moocho," he said to Chuck, and spat significantly into the black dust and walked off into the hot afternoon.

There was an agonizing silence as Chuck watched Little Jake ambling lazily down the dusty road. He felt somehow that Jake had led him into a trap and then run out on him; albeit a sweet and tender trap. He had not heard the birds in the trees before or the crickets, but now it seemed that the entire world around them was alive with chirping and chattering like a booby hatch. He felt a sweet kind of panic as he saw Little Jake's wide frame disappear among the shacks. He wanted to jump off the porch and run after him.

He had not been fully conscious of the smell of honeysuckle on the vine and bright red roses which came together now in one loud sweet song of fragrance and assaulted his lucky nostrils and overwhelmed his senses. He opened his mouth and sucked it all into his scratchy throat and it settled into the pit of his stomach. It was as if the roses and the honeysuckle were singing to him and Bessie Mae and to them and only them and them and them forevermore.

He looked at Bessie Mae and away again. He cleared his throat. Why did girls always make him feel so unnecessary? So sweetly uncomfortable? He cleared his itchy throat again. He blamed his sickly feeling on the flowers. He hated and he loved his sweetish sickly feeling.

"It sure is sure 'nuff hot," Bessie Mae said.

"You can say that again," he answered quickly.

She sat there spreading the lap of her skirt and pulling the hem down toward her knees, and she waited for him to say something to her.

Two honeybees left the honeysuckle climbing up the porch and chased each other around Chuck's head and then went back to the honeysuckle.

Finally she said, "I wonder when the Supreme Court gon reach way down here in Wakefield County."

[74]

Chuck said, "I don't reckon it's going to ever reach this far down. I don't reckon its arms are that long. Sometimes I think it would've been better if it never happened—the Supreme Court decision." He could outdo Jake in this kind of conversation any day in the week. But he had not known that Bessie Mae was interested in intellectual stuff and things. "The only thing it's done in Mississippi is created hard feelings between the races."

"I ain't truly never had no *soft* feelings for these crackers 'round here," Bessie Mae asserted.

"You can say that again," Chuck agreed. "But at least we were getting along together. Look at all the trouble all over the South today. It wasn't a bit like that before."

"We ain't never got along together. There was always trouble between the races. Most of the trouble was the black man's trouble. Only thing happening now is they bringing it out into the open. I'm behind Luther King one hunnert percent. I'm jest waiting for the civil rights to catch up with Wakefield County."

"I've been reading books," Chuck said. "And——"

"You must've been reading the wrong ones." She didn't like to argue with him. He knew she didn't. Yet somehow she wanted to hold him with her conversation. He knew this too. She wanted him to think like she thought. She wanted to make love to him with conversation. And he wanted to make love to her.

"I ain't no Uncle Tom," he said, defensively, "but there're two sides to every question." He looked away from Bessie Mae, staring out at the heat that seemed to be rising up like steam from the fields of green grass and the dust was rising too, black and powdery, and settling on the road and the God-awful shacks that were there before the Supreme Court decision and were there before the Great Depression that old folks talked about sometimes, and were still there and maybe they would always be there. And he should have stayed at home like he had some sense or gone swimming in the river and kept cool. But he was really hot and bothered now.

He thought about Miss Ella Mae, Bessie Mae's mother. She was another hard-working woman, always had been. Ever since Bessie Mae's father died when she was a little old baby.

Bessie Mae's mouth was round and dark red, very very dark red, like a dark red rose, and very very very moist and awfully full and terribly plump, and when she spoke, her tongue slipped

[75]

over her dark red lips and her lips were as sweet-looking as an elberta peach, and ripe and bursting.

His father talked like Bessie Mae sometimes. "Cracker this and cracker that—" but whenever the white man came around he was the politest colored man in the county. Chuck had made up his mind that he, Charles Othello Chaney, was going to be a big colored man, integration or no integration, Supreme Court or no Supreme Court. He was going to make it. He could understand Jake's and Bessie Mae's attitudes. They were not going to be big colored folks, so all that was left for them to do was to gripe and grumble and complain and wait for the Supreme Court and Martin Luther King to deliver them. He loved them just the same. But he was different. He felt sharp deep jabs of guilt for thinking he was different. But he thought it. Yes, he thought it. Hell yes! He thought it. And he *was* different.

"I was talking to Jake's daddy—Uncle Bish—just the other day," she said dreamily. "He just as skinny as the day is long in summertime. I 'member when he was such a fine-looking man. I said to him yesterday, I said, 'Uncle Bish, you sure is lost a heap of weight.' And right away I wished I hadna said it. He looked at me so funny and said to me, 'To tell you the truth, sugar-pie, I just ain't gittin' enough to eat.' I looked at Uncle Bish and didn't know whether I was gon laugh or cry. You know how he is," she explained to Chuck. "You can't never tell whether Uncle Bish cutting the fool or being serious." Her eyes began to fill.

He knew how Uncle Bish was, all right. Every time you saw him lately, there was the sweetish-sourish smell of rotgut whiskey on his breath. His eyes were like two red, tiny rocks of flint. But he also remembered how Uncle Bish used to be, when times were better for him. He looked sideways at Bessie Mae and felt a great fullness in his face and shoulders, as his mind made a picture of Jake's father as he used to be and compared it with the man he was today, and he knew that Bessie Mae had the selfsame feeling inside her. He wanted to reach out and touch her and put his arms around her, as she sat there with her dark misty eyes wearing the barest hint of a sad sweet smile, and her mouth, her damp lips spreading, her plump mouth opening slightly; he thought she might burst into weeping. Her eyes were like two large wild black grapes, like muscadines. He thought somehow if he could take her in his arms and press his mouth against hers, merging the fullness inside of him with the fullness he knew she

[76]

also felt, maybe together they could blot out the way of life in the Bottom and get rid of the shacks, and Uncle Bish would go to work again and be nice and healthy like he used to be and tell funny stories, and his own mother and father would not have to work so hard and reap so little.

He tried awfully hard, but could not keep his eyes away from her knees, so plump and round and bare, with the warm dark colors, so warm and black and brown and soft and smooth, and brownish-black and toasty brown and all the colors clashing and blending. And when he took his eyes away from her knees, there was the rest of her, her shoulders and her arms and the pushing plumpness of her bosom, that was equally disturbing. He wanted to tell her not to worry about crackers or Martin King or any of that. He was going to be a big man one of these days and take her out of all of this. Take her far away from this. Bessie Mae looked up and caught him staring at her, and she seemed to read his thoughts. "It sure is hot," she said. She seemed to always read his thoughts.

He didn't say a word. He did not trust his voice. His eyes were almost closed, his mouth in a nervous trembly pout.

"You wanna go inside and watch television?" she suggested.

He swallowed hard and said, "No, thank you."

And then there was another moment of dreadful silence, sweet and dreadful.

"Let's make some more lemonade," she suggested. "You wanna help me this time, Chuck?"

Everybody called him Chuck now instead of Chuckie. It had kind of sort of sneaked up on him. He couldn't remember when or how it happened. He thought his daddy was the first to start calling him Chuck. Anyhow, it proved he was getting to be a man. "That's a good idea," he said to Bessie Mae. "I was going to make the same suggestion my own self," he lied.

He followed her through the front room to the back room which was the kitchen. She told him to go to the icebox and take the ice pick and chop some ice.

The walls of the kitchen, like the walls of the front room, were papered with pages from Sears Roebuck and Montgomery Ward catalogues and *Ebony*, with *Ebony* pictures on the wall of Ossie Davis and Ruby Dee and Poitier and Belafonte and Sammy Davis, Jr., and Odetta and all the other black and brown celebrities. Adam Powell, Martin King, Roy Wilkins, James Farmer, and Nat King Cole and all the rest. Lorraine Hansberry, Dorothy Dandridge, and all the other colored leaders. The walls of her rooms were a gallery of a colored Hall of Fame. She favored colored VIPs. She was prejudiced that way.

Bessie Mae came over by the icebox and he could smell the heat in the kitchen and the sharp-sweet-salty-scorchy odor of her young body like peanuts being parched over hot coals, and the heat of her body and the different smell of his own hot body. He felt his heart beating violently against the ribs of his chest, he could hear his wild heart beating. His nostrils flared, his head was swimming in the pool of his angry sweet disturbance. And fine bubbles of perspiration formed over her plump mouth and on her nose. His breath came in short hot gulps now, as he made desperation conversation.

"Bessie Mae, you sure do keep a tidy house. This kitchen's so clean, I could eat off the floor."

She laughed nervously. "Well, thank you, Mister Chaney." And she opened the door to the bottom of the icebox and stooped and reached for a lemon and she brushed up against him when she straightened up and he dropped the ice pick and turned toward her and her arms around his neck and his arms around her waist and his nervous awkward mouth against her lips and her mouth beggingly open and painfully busy, and she gave in at the knees and he felt her trembling from head to foot, or maybe it was his own excited body trembling. And the lemon rolling across the floor. He held her close, so close, as if he would push through to the other side of her, as he felt his manhood growing steadily and shamelessly against her now, and she had no defenses against him or this, and he was equally defenseless. And he knew that he was going to know very soon, this day, this hour, this moment, how it felt to be a man, a full-grown manly man.

And "Chuck! Chuck! Chuck! Chuck! Have mercy, Chuck Othello!" she said to him softly. "Please have mercy on me, Chuck!" Her arms were locked around his neck forever.

Great God A'mighty! "Don't cry, Bessie Mae!" He didn't mean her any harm. But he could not have mercy on her.

Just then somebody knocked on the door and walked into the other room. "Anybody home?" The voice was cheerful—even friendly.

[78]

She fell angrily away from him and hastily smoothed the front of her dress and went into the other room.

Chuck stood in the middle of the kitchen—angry, scared, somehow relieved, ashamed of the fact that he had been about to take advantage of this poor fatherless girlchild when her mother's back was turned. At least, he told himself he was ashamed and was relieved. He *was* ashamed. Because he thought he should have been ashamed.

From the next room he heard, "Your mama at home, doll baby?" It was the voice of the peckerwood!

"Naw, my mama ain't home. You know she working this time of day. And my name ain't doll baby to you. It's Miss Bessie Mae Brazwell, if you don't mind."

Chuck listened without making a sound. He wanted to tiptoe across the kitchen and out the back door and be gone before the white man found out he was there. He wasn't looking for any trouble with white folks. He believed in minding his own business and leaving theirs alone. But his feet refused to take his body anywhere. Because, trouble or no trouble, he was not going to leave Bessie Mae in the house by herself with a peckerwood. He wasn't going to do it, didn't care how scared he was. All he would have to do was walk quietly across the floor to the back door, which wouldn't make a sound, because it was already open, and run across the backyard and be long gone. And he could tell Bessie Mae the next time he saw her that he had suddenly remembered he had some business to attend to. Some business that just would not wait. So—

"She leave the policy money with you?"

"No, sir. She say she have to catch it up next week."

"Well," the white voice said importantly, "that's what you told me last week and week before last. If you don't pay me something today, I'm just gon have to lapse y'all. And it's a sin and shame as long as y'all had this policy."

Wasn't any need of his hanging around, Chuck argued heatedly with himself. Bessie Mae could take care of herself with this insuranceman cracker. She did it every week without him. He could feel himself breaking out all over his body with a different kind of perspiration. He would see her next week sometime. He tiptoed to the back door, but something grabbed hold of his feet and kept them from going any further.

"I can't help it, Mr. Millgate. Mama didn't leave no money,

and I don't know how to make none. And I sure Lord ain't no money factory."

"If you act right," the cracker voice said, softly and trembly, "I'll show you how to make some money."

"I don't wanna make that kind of money, Mr. Millgate. I done told you that a million times. Keep away from me, man. Keep away from me, I mean that thing!"

Chuck's father always told him, "You may see your daddy bowing and scraping sometimes before them, just to keep outa trouble, just to live in their world, but if they ever mess with my womenfolks, that's the day I'm gonna meet my Maker. The thing they always did to the colored man was to keep him a boy and never let him grow up to be man. Crackers always talking about white womanhood; what they against is black manhood and they done made a million laws against it. Some on the books and some they just take for granted." He had seen his father take low before the white man many times, but when his father went before his own people, he was a man possessed of enormous pride and dignity. He was a leader in his church and in his lodges. "The thing they had against Paul Roberson more than anything else was that he was too big for the britches they wanted him to wear." He could hear his father clearly as a Sunday church bell. "He was a man and the britches they always measure for us is nigger britches meant for boys. That's how come I named you Othello—after Paul Robe-berson." The great Paul Robeson was his father's hero, the great, black, latter-day John Henry of the Negro race. He saw his father's face before him now as he stood in the doorway trembling from a shivering sweat. But Bessie Mae could take care of herself and there wasn't any need of him getting into trouble with white folks—over nothing. So *git,* Chuck Chaney, while the gitting is good. His father would never know about it. Another minute will be too late—you'll be in trouble up to your ears.

He was scarcely conscious of his own feet taking him against his will across the kitchen into the next room where Bessie Mae and the cracker were. The old floor creaked and cried like it was being badly treated. The cracker was trying to hem her up in a corner of the room. He heard Chuck's footsteps and looked around him. His thin cracker face caught on fire from ear to ear.

"Oh, so you got your boyfriend here with you?"

"So what about it if I do?"

[80]

"So you prefers this nigger boy to me, a white man?"

Chuck found his strange mannish voice from somewhere deep inside of him. He heard himself say, "Get the hell outa here!" His own words scared him half to death. He had never sassed a grown-up cracker.

"Watch out there, nigger, how you talk to a white man."

Chuck looked the cracker up and down, stared into his cat-gray-green eyes. Wild black grass sprouted out of the cracker's nostrils like jimsonweed. He was about Chuck's height and he wasn't any bigger than Chuck any other kind of way. Chuck's daddy could take this cracker and break him half in two. And you're out here in the Bottom with my kind of people, little old sawed-off peckerwood. That kind of evens things up right long in here. Chuck walked toward Millgate, feeling now the strength of his growing manhood. His heart pumping violently, afraid of his manhood. "Get the hell outa here."

The cracker's face turning redder now. He whipped a small automatic out of his pocket. "Ain't a nigger been born yet I'm scared of. I know you niggers out here in the Bottom go for bad. That's how come I always come ready for you. Y'all done let that Supreme Court up in Washington run you crazy. But I'd sooner blow you to hell as spit on the floor."

Chuck stood there watching the cracker as if he were mesmerized. There was nothing he could do but stand there. Fascinated, almost. Nothing between him and the cracker and his pistol but space and air and time and death. Nothing to hide behind. If the cracker wanted to kill him, he would just plain kill him, that was all. But he didn't want to die—Lord knows, he didn't want to die! At the same time he did not know the words that would surely save his life. He knew them but they would not come together in his mouth. He could fall down on his knees and beg this peckerwood's forgiveness. He could—he could—he could lose his life the next damn minute, but he could not knuckle down to this cracker. He did not know how to get down on his knees to white folks. His father had forgotten to teach him.

"I got a great mind to blow both of you little sassy niggers to hell and back. I'd do it too, but I ain't got the time to be explaining this, that, and the other. Trying to gang up on me and rob my money. I ought to do it anyhow." He held the pistol on them as he backed to the door and across the porch. He jumped from the porch, kicking up dust, and ran toward his automobile which was down the road apiece.

Chuck stood in the middle of the floor, more afraid now than he was when the man was there holding the gun on him. He looked down at the floor as if he expected to see his own body lying there dead to the world. Relief was mixed with a great overwhelming fear pouring through his body as the sweat drained from him. He looked up and saw Bessie Mae coming toward him, and he thought she knew how frightened he was, and had been in front of Whitey. And he felt a mighty anger building a roaring fire inside of him.

She came to him and leaned her sweet, soft, sweaty body heavily against him. And he was aware of her plump womanish softness breathing hard and up against him and he heard her swearing as if off in a distance. He smelled her young-womanish perspiration. She smelled like ground peas freshly parching. And he didn't feel like a boy any longer. He was a man. He looked down into her warm black eyes, and he felt her tremble with anger and fear. He vividly remembered the beautiful desperate want he had known with her in the kitchen near the icebox and the terribly sweet fire she had set off inside of him. It was gone gone gone. But another fire was burning. And Chuck Othello Chaney was a man. His father needn't ever worry. Even as he trembled, he told himself—his father needn't worry.

Chapter 6

"*My home is my house and my land is my land and my country is my country, even though it is not really my home, or my land, or my country. Yet it must be. And I must make it be. All by myself and single-handed, if it's got to be that way. I will be a black knight on a black horse in a black and shining armor. I will be John Henry, Robin Hood, and Joe Louis and Paul Robeson and Abraham Lincoln and Matt Dillon and Jackie Robinson and Jesse Chaney Junior all rolled into one. And I will make the land my land. Our land. John Brown was a great cat too. God blessed this land with black dirt and green grass and white fruit of the cotton and red strawberries and rivers and forests and bayous and willows and magnolias and swamps and Delta and honeysuckle and black folks and white people. Oh yes, this rich and God-blessed land will be mine one of these days. This land that the Great One up on High lavished so much beauty on. I have to have it.*

"For a man has to have a home, a land to call his own. To say: 'This is my land.' Just simply that. 'This is my land.' This is my land, this is my land—by right of everything—sweat, muscles, brains, tears, forefathers, foremothers, blood. Uncles, aunts, cousins. Willed to me by all that. And more. And nobody can give to me this land, this country, for the simple reason it is already mine. But of course it isn't really mine. And that's the catch. My claim on the land is deep deep in its black soil. Even deeper in my black soul. But as far as the rulers of the land are concerned, I cannot cash in my claim. That's what makes the whole thing sham from start to finish. One great terrible fake. And yet it isn't sham or fake. I will not let it be. I have to have it.

"If the land is already mine, then nobody can give it to me. I have to take it. I have to take it to own it, to proclaim it. I want my land to be mine, really mine, so I can have something to live for and to die for. I want to be able to shout hallelujah deep in my heart when I see the flag go by. And mean it. I want to want to pledge allegiance. I want it to be a land that I can love without holding back anything. I want it to be my land, the kind of land that I could jump up and testify about like they do about Jesus in the Hardshell Baptist Church. I'm getting to be a man every hour the Good Lord provides and a man needs a land to choke his throat off at the mention of, to wet his eyes about, a land worth living for, and dying. That is why this land is mine. And I will not let it not be mine. I have to have it."

His teacher read his entire essay, all seven pages, to the class, his teacher, with whom he had fallen in love all of the blessed way, holding nothing back. Chuck Othello was a boy who when he fell for a pretty lady, fell good and belly-busting hard, he did not stumble. Miss Ida Lee Jackson gave assignments to each member of the class to write an original essay about his home, his land, or his country. Chuck labored hard and many hours on it. He labored, with the dictionary Miss Ida Lee had lent him

[83]

within his reach. He wrote and rewrote. He erased and crossed out. Writing did not go easy with him. It was torturous, like pulling hens' teeth. He wrote some nights till his eyes hurt and the words he wrote ran together and he fell asleep writing.

And yet when she read his essay to the class, he thought he saw her slyly wipe her eyes just as she blew her nose. And when she gave his paper back to him, he saw an "A" up in the corner, and she wrote: "An excellent job of thinking and feeling!" And he felt good all over him, bursting with pride. When he took the paper home, his father read it aloud, and for months to come, it was his conversation piece. Forgotten momentarily was Missy Anne, the stupid cow. That first night, Mama Carrie came to him and kissed him and said, "It's so pretty! It's so pretty! And you do believe in Jesus after all!" She wet his face with tears and kisses.

A few days later, Miss Ida Lee told him he should send it to a colored magazine that published out of Chicago. And if he wanted her to help him, she would work with him on errors of grammar and misspelling. He was much more than agreeable, since, added to the pride and excitement of the possibility of being published, was the privilege of spending so much time with the pretty teacher. She even invited him to dinner and worked one entire evening with him.

And if he loved his teacher, the feeling was certainly mutual. He was her favorite pupil, a fact she tried unsuccessfully to conceal from the rest of the class. After his essay, she began to lend him her books to read, all kinds of books. She even gave him some books. She bombarded him with books. At Christmas, she gave him a membership in a colored book club. He was never certain that she was the giver of this great gift. He never asked her about it. But he believed it. And he loved her for it. She was the most beautiful woman in all the world, with the possible exception of Bessie Brazwell, maybe, who was not yet quite a woman but was a mighty pretty girl.

Bessie Mae's dark eyes did not miss a thing. She didn't say a word, except that one day, he of the swelled head, he, the teacher's pride and joy, asked her if he might take her books and walk her home from school. She looked up into his face and put her hands on her womanish hips and tossed her dark pretty head to one side. "Humph—I hate that about you," she said, and turned and strutted off up the road, as the swelling in his head decreased like a volleyball that had developed a slow leak which had suddenly quickened. And Chuck Othello Chaney did a slow burn, as he watched her strut up to Little Jake Carson and ask him:

"You like chicken?" She meant for Chuck to hear the conversation.

Little Jake laughed and said, "If the Good Lord made any better eating, he musta kept it for His own table."

"If you like chicken so good," she said, even more loudly than before, "why don't you just like grab a wing?" She put her right hand on her hip. And Little Jake laughed again and took her arm in his and they strutted off together. Chuck's best buddy and his sweetheart.

But for months to come he thought about this land of his. He read about the whole wide world and thought about this land of his. This land that lay so close to rivers. Land where cotton was the king, still king thenceforth and forevermore. Or so it seemed in those last years of the fifties. Oh my land is like a beautiful woman, nine to ten months out of the year from March on through much of December. Changing her gay bright garments with the style and colors of the season. My land is a lovely thing to look upon. Except, of course, in wintertime.

Luckily winter came late and left early in his land. And this last winter was one of the coldest Mississippi ever knew. It even snowed in Wakefield County, an incident that would be boasted of all the year through, as if snow were a status symbol, a thing of splendor and of great prestige. Yes, it snowed in Wakefield County. It snowed deep in Wakefield County. Biggest snow in the history of the Wakefield Weather Bureau. The children made snowmen and threw snowballs at each other. They made frozen punch. But most of that great winter there was no snow. It was just cold and barren like a desert, and without the extra trimmings and decorations of snow on the ground and icicles on the trees like the way they said it was up North. Most of the time the trees in his county stood with their arms hanging loosely downward, their thin limbs shamelessly naked. The day it snowed they made a snowman and he made up to Bessie Mae Moocho. And he walked her home from school all the way out to the Bottom almost every school day afterward, the entire winter through. It was a time when it became clear to one and all that they had a thing about each other.

One day he walked his sweetheart home—the world was cold

[85]

and ugly and naked and lonely-looking, but that night, it rained all night long and stopped right after day had broken, and That Man Up There worked hard all night in the pouring rain with his giant paintbrush dripping with light green paint and the next morning the world was all togged out in a pretty bright green garment he had almost forgotten. Then there was the next day which was prettier than the day before and the next day and the next. And he began to get that funny look about him and a queer taste in his mouth, and he smelled his pee like never before. It was sure sign of spring, the old folks said. A sign of spring and growing up. And a time for closing schools and planting cotton. It was the thing he dreaded all winter long. He hated winter, yet wanted it to last forever. Because spring meant school was over till the red hot breathless days of summer. And spring dragged its slow feet along, as usual, like a year of long hot summer Sundays. And the Man's cotton was planted. And summer finally came and school again. The happy time. Heat, flies, mosquitoes, bumblebees, Juney bugs, devilhorses, snakes, the lightning and the thunderstorms. Swimming. Sweat. And school. And girls were prettier than they had ever been since that first one was made from Adam's rib.

Even the sassy girl who lived next door to him got prettier every day the Good Lord sent. Her name was Cora Mae Rakestraw and both of her parents were cotton pickers. And she was a tall, long-legged gal who walked boyish with long strides like she was used to jumping ditches. Like she walked just for the sake of walking. She wore her hair short and close-cropped like a boy and didn't use a straightening comb. Some folks called her a tomboy and others went even further. Some of the boys at school called her a bull-diger. But Chuck had an idea that she was much much girl. But she was not as careful as was Bessie Mae as to how she sat in front of boys. And that could be disturbing. Not that Chuck had eyes for her. He only had eyes for Bessie Mae. But, after all, he wasn't blind.

Sometimes he would visit the Rakestraws, not to look at Cora Mae, but to sit with them and watch their television and keep up with what was happening in the world. Sometimes she would jump the fence that divided his yard from hers and stand behind him and watch him milk the cow and he wouldn't know she was there until he heard her giggling at him.

It always caused his face to flush and his ears to burn and his

[86]

neck to gather heat to have her stand there watching him pulling on Missy's teats. It made him feel somehow silly and indecent, like he was playing with himself in public, even though he knew there was nothing for him to feel ashamed of, which did not help matters at all. On the contrary, it made them worse.

One day he turned upon her. "Did somebody send for you?"

She stood there facing him, tall and sassy. She was as tall as he was. "Didn't nobody have to send for me. I sent for my own self." She stood there with both hands on her slender hips. Old long-legged pigeon-toed sassy-assed gal. Brown as egg-bread fresh out of the oven.

He said, "You don't get back over into your own yard I'm gonna take this stick I whip the cow with and——"

She said, "Put your hand on your hip and let your backbone slip and say you reckin."

He laughed at her weakly and picked up the stick.

She said, "Don't stand before me with your nose all snoddy, if you don't know what you doing you better ask somebody."

She was as supple as any boy in the county and could whip most of them in a fair fight. Boys didn't pick on her like they did some girls who were more tender and shamefaced. She stared Chuck down. He dropped the stick and turned toward the cow again. And she leaped and tackled him as if she was on a football field. It caught him by surprise, and he did a real belly-buster as the ground came up to meet him. It knocked the wind completely out of him and for a moment he thought he was dead. But then he got himself together and they wrestled quietly, angrily, desperately, for a few minutes as he tried to get from under her. And she whispered softly into his angry ears. "Don't mess with me, little old mannish boy, if you don't know what you doing."

He thought, Who in the hell was messing with you?

Finally he got out from under her and separated himself from her and chased her back into her own backyard, but when he thought about it later, he felt a funny kind of sensation that had nothing to do with anger. Still he told himself, and believed it, that he did not like to wrestle with girls. When he told Jake about it, Jake laughed and laughed and laughed.

"So y'all was just doing a little old innocent rassling, was you? Boy, you is the horse's ass. You just can't shit running." And laughed and laughed some more at the silly look on his bosom buddy's face.

It was the first Sunday in July, but he did not go to church with his mother and father, because he was a proud boy, and he had no shoes to wear to church. His shoes had big holes in the bottom, which were all right to wear to school. His mother put pasteboard in them. But they were not good enough for a proud courting man like him to wear to church, especially since Bessie Mae went to the selfsame church. And so did Cora Rakestraw. And Bessie Mae thought his folks were well-to-do. Didn't they live in a house in town? Didn't they own their own cow? And they had just installed electric lights. And wasn't his father Charlie Wakefield's friend? The Chaneys had the reputation of being "big colored folks." And he didn't have the heart to burst his sweetheart's bubble. Even though they hardly had a pot to cook in.

His mother felt bad about the whole thing. His father promised to buy him a brand-new pair of shoes the very next week. As they left for church they gave him a half a dollar to buy some ice and make some ice cream, which they would eat together when they got back from church. But they made it clear that the ice cream was especially for him. He walked barefoot all the way to the icehouse. The dirt burned the bottom of his feet as if he was walking on desert sand. It was one of those clear hot cloudless days in July, when you could look toward the horizon or just look outside your door or even note the way the sun dipped into your house, and you would know it was Sunday without anybody telling you. That is, if you were absentminded and lost track of summer days. It was a hot, breathless, clean-and-clear-Sunday-kind of day, with the sunlight splashing all over everything and everybody. It was a day for making homemade ice cream. Tell it like it was. And Chuck was in the ice cream mood. Tell every-thing. He stayed in the ice cream mood. It was a precious rarity in his house because ice was so doggone expensive. It was so high it was clean out of sight. In all his born days he had never gotten enough ice cream. There was this ice cream parlor down the road from the Mount Moriah Baptist Church, where the children gathered after Sunday school. Rob Jenkins Place. But an ice cream cone didn't do a thing but tease his appetite. Just enough to make him angry. He chuckled all the way to the icehouse. Singing softly to himself.

Long rangy crackers and short scrawny crackers and in-between crackers loafed around the icehouse, red-necked and pink-faced and sun-cooked, and staring into their own great emptiness. When he came for the ice they stared at him with evil white looks, and if looks could stab and kill, he would have died right then and there at the icehouse in the blazing sunlight on the warm black earth.

It had been this way ever since the Supreme Court up in Washington decided. When you walked through town and you were black, white folk looked at you with deep suspicion. There were rumors of happenings all throughout the South, black and white happenings, and even in other parts of Mississippi, but the only crops the Supreme Court had harvested in Wakefield County were mistrust and suspicion. Sometimes Chuck wished the Big Court had not spoken at all, if it wasn't going to put its money where its mouth was.

Some black folks sang:

> *This little light of mine*
> *I'm gonna make it shine—*
> *I'm gonna make it shine—*
> *Yes, I'm gonna make it shine.*

But when and where and how and what?
Jake Carson sang, jokingly, with new words to an old song.

> *I want the light*
> *From the Supreme Court*
> *To shine on me—*

As Chuck took his ice and put it on his shoulder, he heard one of the red-faced pecks say in a soft drawl—mimicking Chuck, stressing each word long and separately: *"Give me a half a dollar's worth of ice, please!"* And spat tobacco juice into the black dust. He knew the one who spat. He was about thirty-six years old, medium height and stocky, strong as two mules, brown-haired and clean-good-looking, but his eyes were as cold as the ice on Chuck's back. Chuck knew him all right. Sam Rawlins worked at one of Johnson's warehouses in Wakefield City and he was just as mean as a rattlesnake.

Chuck was broiling hot but his spirit would not be dampened.

Sam's hateful voice said, "Boy, where you steal that money from?" And then the harsh sarcastic laughter. Chuck didn't even look back. A fresh perspiration broke out all over him as he kept walking up the road from the icehouse. Those crackers could kindly go to hell and tell the people in hell Chuck Chaney sent them. At the end of this road was ice cream. And nothing was going to spoil this Sunday for Chuck Othello Chaney. Not a living ass. And Sam Rawlins was a living ass.

When he got back home he put the peckerwoods at the icehouse somewhere in the back room of his mind and went about the business of making homemade ice cream. Boiled custard ice cream. The best, the very best. He beat eggs up in the milk that was rich and fresh from Missy's teats. That was another reason they had seldom had homemade ice cream. Milk was expensive just like ice. But now with darling, sweet, affectionate Missy Anne, things were looking up. And this particular summer Sunday, Chuck forgave her everything, all the two-timing she had done him, all the trouble and the heartache she had ever caused. He loved Missy Anne this day. He added sugar and nutmeg and cooked the whole concoction to a boil, and let it cool. He poured it into the two-gallon freezer-container, put in the dasher, and put the top on. His poor mouth already watered. He put the container in the freezer-bucket and packed in salt and ice all around the sides of the container. He was glad the crazy girl next door had gone to church. And then he began to crank the old-fashioned ice cream freezer like he was cranking up a Model T Ford. He cranked and daydreamed. He would save her a little ice cream because she was his next-door neighbor. The going was easy at first, but the more he cranked the harder was the cranking, the heavier his arm became. He cranked and daydreamed.

He dreamed of the pretty teacher at the schoolhouse with whom he had fallen head over heels in love. It was not the kind of love he felt for pretty Miss Bessie Mae Moocho, he thought, but it was love and love everlasting. And it was loveless love. Maybe it was. He dreamed of going to New York City where one of his brothers lived and he could go to school nine months out of the year. Maybe even go to summer school. He would miss Miss Ida Lee Jackson, and he hated that part of it, but maybe he would suggest to her that she get a transfer up-the-country. And maybe he could persuade Bessie Mae to pick up stakes and make the journey with him. But what about her mother? He laughed. He could hardly take care of his own self, let alone Bessie Mae Moocho and her mother. He would go up there alone and go to school and graduate and get a job and send for her, if she agreed to wait that long. He was a boy who loved to daydream. He didn't build air castles, he constructed new worlds and great cities and day-dreamed great epics in which he always played the starring role. His right arm got as heavy as a piece of iron, and he changed to his left hand. He laughed. He was a switch-hitter. He was in his backyard seated on the stool he usually milked the cow from.

He sat there cranking the freezer in the quiet heat of the early afternoon. The air was hushed and motionless in the awful heat. Not a piece of breeze bestirred itself. Nothing stirred in his back-yard, not even the crazy grasshoppers, and they always liked to dance around like devils in the sunlight. Juney bugs, wasps, ants, bumblebees, lizards, butterflies, everything sat still and quiet in his yard. It was too hot to move around. Even Missy Anne had gone to sleep. He, Chuck Othello Chaney, was the only fool stir-ring in all that heat in his backyard. But he sweated for a pur-pose. Sweat poured from him all over him. It was a happy sweat with tremendous expectations in the offing. He licked his chops and sweated. He cranked and cranked and cranked, he cranked and sweated, and he daydreamed.

It seemed that the Movement, whatever the Movement was, would never make it to Wakefield County. How far in the back-woods could you be? He'd never heard anybody sing "We Shall Overcome" except over television. Names like Martin Luther King and Abernathy and Montgomery, Alabama and Daisy Bates and Little Rock and Tallahassee were like whispers in the wind and seemed a million miles away in time and space from Wakefield County, like tales of long ago, of legends and myths of faraway exotic places. He didn't care if it never reached Wakefield County, the Movement. He told himself he didn't care, because as vivid as his imagination was, he could not imagine black folks rising up in any great numbers against the white folks in this white folks' neck of the woods. Black folks outnumbered white folks in the county. When he thought of it his heart beat crazy in his chest. Out-numbered white folks two or three to one. He couldn't imagine his father really going against his great friend, Mister Charles James Richard Wakefield. The great almighty Jimmy Dick. The one and only Mister Charlie. His father's big, rich, all-powerful friend who was the Great White Father of black and white alike throughout the county. You didn't go against Charlie Wakefield. He was a good white man, even to colored people, good and white and generous and liberal, especially to colored people, but you didn't go against him. You'd better not and let him catch you at it.

You'd better accept his generosity and forget it. And you'd better never forget it.

By the time the ice cream was hard and made, his arms felt like weights were hanging from them. And he was ready for the ice cream. But he would yield not to temptation; he would wait until his folks came home from church before he began to eat. He loved his mother and father. He sometimes thought of them as aged and old-fashioned and of an ancient generation. But he loved them and respected them, and now, as he sat there in the backyard in the sweet ice-cream sunlight of his early Sunday afternoon backyard, he felt a deep shame as his mind did a rerun of the scene that terrible night with his parents about the Good Lord up on High. He felt particularly ashamed of the fact that he had made his mother cry. I'm not a bad feller, he thought. But I got a mean streak somewhere deep in me that comes out sometimes when I least expect. I got a mean streak. Ain't no doubt about it. It's the thing I got to watch.

He would just take the dasher out and eat the ice cream that clung to it, but he would not eat any more than that until his folks came home from church. His mother always gave him the dasher soon as it was ready. He took the dasher out and put it in a dish. He packed the salt and ice tight around the container and wrapped the freezer in a burlap bag. Then he took a big spoon and ate the ice cream from the dasher. It had been so long since he had had homemade ice cream. It was like a special holiday for him, like Christmastime or Easter or Thanksgiving. Thank you, Lord, for sweet Missy Anne. It had been so long. Ice was too doggone expensive for ordinary folks. And very few black folks owned their own cow. He licked the dasher dry as a chip. His father was a smart man, all right. Chuck daydreamed for a couple of minutes. To hell with television.

And Jake was absolutely right. If the Good Lord made anything better than girl-folks, he must've kept it for His own self. Girls-girls-girls-girls. Tall girls, short girls, fat girls, skinny girls, plump ones, sassy ones, shamefaced ones. Eyes, mouths, legs, bosoms. And of all the girls in all the world, there was lovely Miss Bessie Mae Moocho Brazwell. He had not seen the crazy Wakefield gal since the middle of the winter, when she passed him on the road as she sat in the back of her father's great big chauffeur-driven spank-brand-new Imperial limousine, and he pretended

[92]

not to see her. He had been walking Bessie Mae home from school. She spelled nothing but trouble anyhow.

He would just take one little old couple of spoonfuls out of the freezer and then save the rest till the folks came home. They would not even notice any missing. He dished up a heaping saucerful. After all, he made it all by his own self. He went for the ice—and all that. He milked the cow. And Mama Carrie had said it was especially for him. There was nothing to feel guilty about, he told himself. The ice cream was frozen cold and hard. He took a great big hunk in his tablespoon and swallowed it whole, and it all seemed to go to his head and lodge there and expand and to suddenly explode. He thought his entire head was frozen stiff and had changed into a block of burning ice. He slapped both sides of his head; he grabbed his throat and beat his forehead; he jumped up and down as if he had lost his marbles. He ran around in circles. His head inside was smoking-cold. When finally his head thawed, he went into the house so that he would yield not to temptation. He read the Bible for a while. It wasn't long, though, before he was back out in the yard again, staring at the ice cream freezer. Soon forgotten was his experience of a few moments back. His poor mouth watered something terrible. He had never had enough ice cream in his entire life, and after all, Mama Carrie had said it was especially for him. They wouldn't mind him eating just a little more. Just a tiny bit more. Just a tiny little biddy bit. They would hardly miss it. Each time the tiny little biddy bit amounted to a super-duper heaping saucerful. He ate ice cream till he felt filled clear up to his eye level. It seemed to be coming out of his ears. His head was clogged with ice cream. And still he shoved it in. He ate ice cream and sweated in the awful heat. He no longer dished it up in a saucer. Unknowingly, he sat on the stool now and ate with the big tablespoon directly from the freezer.

By the time his folks came home he was a human iceberg, one great big block of burning ice from head to foot. The sweat on his face now was like the steam that rises from dry ice. He heard his mother vaguely speaking to the Rakestraws. His mother and his father had walked home from church with them. "Y'all come over after while and have some ice cream with us. Or we'll send some over to you by Chuck Othello."

Cora Mae said, "I can come and get it, Miss Mama Carrie."

She always called Chuck's mother Miss Mama Carrie as if "Mama" was her real first name.

Chuck heard the conversation but he couldn't move. He was waterlogged with ice cream. His mother took one look at him and cried, "What's the matter with the baby?"

He tried to speak but all he accomplished was a chattering of his teeth. His lips felt like they were chapped forever. His eyes were bright and bulging.

She ran toward him. "Lord Jesus have mercy!"

He tried to get up but could not move at first. He was ice-cream-logged.

His father said, "He ate too much ice cream." Which statement Chuck thought to be the understatement of all times before and all times to come thereafter and forevermore even to the end of time which had no ending.

They took him into the house, which was as hot inside as it was outside. He could barely move one foot before the other. His body was shivering from head to foot. It was one of the hottest days of all that summer, a hundred and five degrees on the shady side of the street. They laid him on their bed in the front room and undressed him. His mother rubbed his feet which felt is if they were frostbitten. She tried to squeeze warm blood back into them. She rubbed and squeezed and rubbed and squeezed. They rubbed him down from head to foot with alcohol. They worked and sweated in the heat that was everywhere outside and inside the house, except in his iceberg of a body. They put him in their bed and covered him with two heavy blankets. Still his body did not cease to quake and his teeth made loud collisions with each other. His father made a fire in the fireplace and they took him from the bed wrapped in the blankets and sat him by the fire in the rocking chair. All the time he had not uttered a single sound intelligible to humans. As he began to defrost, tears began to spill from his eyes down his frozen cheeks, as if a huge chunk of ice were melting.

He tried to talk. "I'm sorry, Mama Carrie, Daddy, Mama—I—"

She said, "Hush, sugar-pie. We understand."

"Don't worry about a thing," his father said. "You're still the best that ever done it."

The more they understood the greater was his shame and guilt.

The shame was greater than the guilt. He wanted to take them

[94]

both in his arms and tell them he loved them and would love them always and forever. He loved the beauty and the goodness and the understanding in them. He was so grateful that they were not angry with him.

His mother came and kissed him lightly, warmly, on his cold mouth, and the tears really spilled down his chilly cheeks now. And as the fire from the fireplace got to him, his entire body began to leak perspiration, his face, his neck, his back, his shoulders, from his armpits, his thighs, his crotch, the water poured from him, as if he would really melt away before their eyes. And yet his body shivered.

He said, "I reckin I'm kind of a extra good ice-cream-maker. I must've made it so good, I almost ate myself to death."

His father said, "If you ain't the best in town, you a stomp-down good one."

His mother had been staring at her boy, conjuring up a tragic-comic picture of them at church safe in the arms of Jesus and their boy in the backyard shoveling the ice cream into him as if it was going out of style and he was packing it away for the entire long hot summer and all the summers that were to come. She shook her head. Her eyes filled. She felt like laughing. Laughter was so close to tears in very much of the daily drama of their lives. They were a crying and a laughing people.

Then Jesse said to his boy, "It sure is a good thing we came straight home after church, you most probably woulda——"

He got no further, because his wife erupted into gales of laughter. She could not help herself. "My baby—my baby, poor baby—he got enough ice cream *this* Sunday of our Lord and Savior to last—my baby—oh my baby—" And she went off into another round of uncontrollable laughter. And now the father started to laugh his booming thunder of a laugh. And finally Chuck was laughing. Mama Carrie came to him, still laughing, the tears flowing down her cheeks in flood tide, and she put her arms around his neck and she kissed his face all over. She covered his cold face with her warm kisses till his dear face was no longer cold. "My baby—my poor funny baby! Did you get enough ice cream, sugar-pie? My baby baby baby!" They laughed and laughed and laughed and laughed.

By the time they stopped laughing, the blankets had dropped from around him, and he was not as frozen as he had been, but he still felt like an iceberg. The room was like a furnace with the

[95]

fire blazing in the fireplace. They put the blankets back around him and put him in the bed again. In *their* bed. They would sleep in the kitchen in *his* bed that night.

When he was tucked in good and snug like winter, his father said, "Now let's us go out here and see how good a ice-cream-maker he really is. That is, if he left us any."

There was very little left to sample. Chuck had stoked away a gallon and three-quarters.

Chapter
7

Every Saturday afternoon after dinner, he would swim across the river to the other shore, touch it with his hands, and then he would push against the river bank with his feet and with one swift kick head back to his side of the river. It was not an easy thing to do, to swim the river's width and back again. It took a helluva lot of doing. In his own heart he felt about it as he imagined mountain climbers felt, when they had planned and practiced and tried and failed and finally reached the mountain top. He had read about mountain climbers in the magazines and news-papers and seen about them over other people's televisions. When he was younger he used to dream about one day climbing a mountain like great Everest. But at twelve years he grew up one day and there were no mountains in his neck of the woods. So he settled for the river. He would conquer Old Man River. Chuck planned his conquest very carefully. Scientifically.

The first day he swam until suddenly the enormity of it scared him and he lost his head and turned panic-stricken back toward shore. It was not a terribly long distance back, and he was a good swimmer even then; he would have made it easily had he not been in too big a hurry. But he started fighting the river and naturally he got out of breath before the river did. The river wasn't fazed at all. It just kept rolling along. He barely made it back to shore, and did not try again for one whole month. Then he began to really plan his conquest. He whitewashed the trunk of a willow tree that stood tall and graceful and weeping at the edge of his side of the river, so that he would have a guide post to aim at each time he turned and headed homeward. There were many weeping willows weeping down by the riverside with their great shawls of Spanish moss hanging loosely from their shoulders. He swam a little further out each time, pacing himself carefully, like a long-distance runner. He dog-paddled some of the way, he Australian-crawled. His easiest stroke, the one he used most of the time to pace himself, was an overhand stroke in which his right hand would come easily out of the water and reach out just as his head would come from under water and an easy deep breath, and his legs would kick, and his head would submerge again, and he would repeat this movement over and over with a kind of effortless, flawless, flowing motion, the whole thing smooth and fluid like pure and pretty poetry. When he grew weary, he would turn over on his back and float. The day he swam halfway across and back, his young heart shouted jubilation. Then week by week and month by month, one and one-half summers passed before the conquest was complete.

That evening after the ultimate day of conquest, he could no longer keep the secret of his battle with the river and his glorious victory. He walked all the way out to the Bottom and told Bessie Mae about it. She did not share his great enthusiasm. First of all, she did not share his great love for the river. And it *was* a love affair he was having with the river. Spiritual and sensual.

They sat out in her backyard on a wooden homemade bench, out with the washtubs and the big black washpot and kept company with the mosquitoes and the lightning bugs. And over in the bushes crickets made enough noise to wake up the dead and somewhere frogs were honking, and the whole thing was like an orchestra playing, or so Chuck Chaney imagined. He felt good. He felt strong. He felt triumphant.

Bessie Mae said, "I wish you would stay out of that devilish river."

He was brought closer to the earth by this. But he still was flying high. "How come you don't like the river, Bessie Mae?"

"I hate the river," she said violently. "I can't stand to even think about it."

"How come, Bessie Mae?" Was she jealous because he had just that very day swum all the way across the river and back? Was she angry because she could never hope to do it herself? He didn't understand womenfolks, no shape, form, or fashion. He stared through the hushed heat toward the house where the doors were open front to back. He could look straight through the house. He could see Miss Ella Mae, Bessie Mae's mother, seated in the front room sewing and fanning with her dress halfway up her thighs, unselfconsciously. Her eyes would come up from her sewing every now and then to stare blankly at the antics on the television screen of rich white folk in their swank New York apartments. The television screen choreographed a cast of dancing shadows through the house. Miss Ella Mae waved the fan about her bare knees and went back to her sewing. Chuck looked slyly at Bessie Mae, her sweet face exuding seriousness. He remembered the time they had stood so close together at the edge of Paradise Regained, as he described it in his literary and romantic mind. The same sweet thickness in his throat now and his entire body damp with aggravation.

Bessie Mae said heatedly, "When I think of how many black men that river's done swallered, how can I love the river? Sometimes I dream that one great gitting-up morning the river gon run dry and there ain't gon be nothing but black bodies lining the bottom of it. But you," she said, "you love that river better'n you do m—" She started to say he loved the river better than he loved her, but since he had never expressed his love for her in so many words, modesty made her change her horse midstream. "Better'n you love something to eat," she said teasingly. She knew he was a boy who loved to eat. She had watched him in action at the Sunday school picnics.

Chuck was off his high horse now and angry. "I don't love the river," he said. "In a way, I hate the river. I'm fighting the river, not loving it. That's how come I'm getting the best of it every time."

Sometimes she angered him the way she made a race question out of everything. What in the devil did the river have to do with black and white? Bessie Mae talked as if the river was a great white something that swallowed up black folk purely out of meanness. She talked as if the river didn't drown white folk, even when they couldn't swim. Bessie Mae was sweet, but she was prejudiced.

It was now almost a year ago when he had his first talk with Bessie Mae about the river, the day he first swam across and back. He was an expert at it now, like falling off a log. She was right though. In a way he really did love the river. And respect it. His usual routine every summer's Saturday afternoon was to eat a hearty dinner which was at twelve o'clock in the middle of the day and to laze around for about a half an hour afterward like dogs have sense enough to do after they've eaten a good meal. He lazed around to give his stomach time to get itself together. This particular day in August, one Saturday afternoon in the final days of the dog, in August, he forgot the wise ways of the dogs. He went to the river immediately after eating dinner.

He had worked all morning in the cotton, which he hated with an extraordinary passion. But out here in the river, he got away from it all. Out here he dreamed and his dreams were of a world beyond the Cotton Curtain. He dreamed of one day going away from the plantation and making a life for himself in some far-off city. He dreamed of college and knowledge and being somebody greater than a cotton picker. Although he thought of his father as a great man, he did not think of cotton picking as a great profession. In most of his dreams Bessie Mae was with him wherever he went. It was funny how when he was around her and had dreamed of her, he wanted to believe that she had lived with him the experience of his dreams. Even though he knew it was silly and childish to think in those terms, when he thought about how well he knew Bessie Mae and how many experiences they had shared together, he tended to lump actual experiences with the dream experiences. But after all, his actual experiences with her amounted to little more than seeing each other at school and church picnics and a few times out at her house in the Bottom. And walking with her home from school.

He dog-paddled for a couple of minutes, just as a change of pace, just for something else to do. He took in deep sweet gulps of river air. He thought about Jesse Junior. Sometimes he thought of Junior entirely against his own volition. He didn't want to think of sad things this Saturday afternoon of sun and water and blue skies and white sailing clouds. He wanted to just give himself up completely to his senses, which were restfully and tinglingly alive. But his contrary mind made a picture of Junior the first time he had come home from the Army in his uniform. Tall, smiling, handsome—full of confidence. You almost needed a baseball bat to beat the girls away. And he had changed—Kiss my auntie in the country! Junior had changed! Or so it seemed to Chuck, his little baby brother. It seemed to Chuck that even

Junior's voice had changed. His way of speaking. And he had been places. He'd been all the way to New York City!

The first night he was home, he and Willie and Chuck slept in the same bed together, but they hardly slept at all. They talked till four or five o'clock in the morning. Junior did most of the talking; Chuck and Willie asked the questions and listened with wide-open mouths. The places he'd been, the things he'd seen.

"When I grow up I'm gon be a soldier!" Chuck whispered.

Junior's voice lost its light tone immediately. "Boy, I hope you don't ever have to wear no monkey suit. I hope they don't have no stupid wars when you get to be a man. I hope the world has better sense by then!"

His voice assumed a lighter tone as he told them about a movie he had seen in New York City with a great black moving picture star by the name of William Marshall. Great God A'mighty! What a picture! He told them of the picture from the first scene to the end. And they never missed a single word.

It was a very hot and sticky afternoon, and the sun bounced off the surface of the river like a thousand sparkling jewels of all sizes and dimensions. Whenever he thought of the fact that he'd never see Junior again in this life he always knew a filled-up feeling all inside of him and it was just too much. He had almost reached the other side now and had not yet gotten his second wind. He turned on his back and put his hands behind his head and let the river work for him completely. One day he would teach Bessie Mae to swim and to really love the river. Then he thought, to hell with the river. He wasn't going to see this river much longer. When he grew up he was going to get further and smell a whole heap better. He was going North or at least to one of the big cities in the South like Atlanta or New Orleans. And he was going to make something out of himself, something much bigger, far more important than a cotton-picking cotton picker. He smiled to himself. And he would be a man like his father wanted him to be. A man with manhood. He would take Bessie Mae with him as his wife to honor and cherish in sickness and health, for better or for worse, or however the thing went. But it would be all for the better most of the no-cotton-picking time. He thought, Whoa there. Maybe, Mister Charles Othello Chaney, when you get to be a really big colored man, you won't want a girl like Bessie Mae for your wife. Maybe she'll be beneath your standard. After all, you'll be shitting in high cotton. And you'll be highly educated. And—

When he thought seriously about it, he sometimes had a hard time reconciling his plans for leaving home and going up North with the real deep love he had for his home and the land and the people. He had a hard time reconciling his plans for leaving with the essay he had written for Miss Ida Lee, which was published in Chicago and for which he received a check for all of twenty-five Yankee dollars. This ambivalence was a thing that came and went with him. One minute it was: "Yes, I'm leaving." The next was: "No, I think I'll hang around and see what happens."

And help like hell to make it happen. If only Junior were here with him to help him make decisions, to do things together with him. Junior had always been his hero symbol, even though sometimes here-of-late he had a hard time conjuring up a memory of what Junior looked like. Still, he hero-worshiped him.

He had reached the other shore almost without knowing it. He touched the bank and kicked backward and was homeward bound. He went through these motions, this ritual, without thinking of it. He had done it so many times, he usually negotiated the entire river now by instinct. He was taking the river for granted. "You should never take the river for granted," he scolded himself.

He thought to himself he should be ashamed of himself for thinking of Bessie Mae like that. He hadn't finished high school yet, and already he was thinking he was better than she was. He ought to be ashamed of himself. And he was ashamed. He loved Bessie Mae, even though he had never told her or even told himself until this very moment.

He thought sadly about Willie. "Crazy Willie," people called him. But he'd never called him Crazy Willie. He certainly missed him. He could talk to Willie more than he could to any of his older brothers and sisters except Junior, who was gone forever. Willie had been the baby until he came on the scene. They had shared so many experiences between them. It was really Willie who had taught Chuck the fundamentals of swimming, although Willie himself had never tried to swim across the river. Willie had taught him how to shoot and hunt. He smiled sadly. Willie had also taught him how to beat his meat. Some proper people called it masturbation.

He remembered the first time Willie had taught him what it

was all about. He and Willie and Jake Carson had been playing in a vacant shack at the other end of the plantation near the swamplands. Willie was four years older than he was. Willie asked him, "Boy, you ever fucked Minnie?"

Little Jake must have already known what Willie was talking about, because he howled with laughter, when Chuck said, "Fuck what Minnie? I don't know no girl named Minnie." Against Chuck's will, Chuck's less than noble mind made a vivid picture of Bessie Mae wearing nothing but her birthday suit. It was a terrible thing.

Willie stared at him in pretended disbelief. "Man, you mean to stand up there with your bare ass out and tell me Minnie ain't never gived you none?"

Chuck felt a heated dampness underneath his collar. "What damn Minnie you talking about?" And Little Jake fell down on the ground laughing and kicked up his heels and kept on laughing. "Boy, do you know where little babies come from?"

Willie said with a feigned seriousness, "Boy, you ain't a man till you git some from old Minnie. She got the best pussy in the whole wide world, and she'll go with you and be forever by your side in fair or stormy weather, and she won't give you the clap or crabs or nothing like that. And you don't have to worry about gittin her bigged. She might run you little crazy if you get it too often. That's about the only thing you have to worry about. Just give old Minnie a little breathing spell every now and then, else she'll run you crazier'n a old bedbug."

Jake stopped laughing long enough to put his two cents in again. This time he pointed at Willie. "That's how come you so goddamn crazy; you done fucked Minnie too goddamn much." He went off into howls of laughter again and the tears streamed from his eyes and down his cheeks.

"Minnie! Minnie! Minnie! Dear old darling Minnie the Moocher!"

Chuck said, "I wish goddammit somebody would be kind enough to tell me who in the hell is Minnie." Which statement sent Jake off into more convulsive laughter. He held his stomach. He lay flat on the earth and beat the ground.

Willie held out his right hand with the fingers spread. "These *many*, fool," he said, as he counted his fingers with the forefinger of his other hand. "One, two, three, four, five. That's how *many*. Miss Minnie Five-Fingers."

Chuck stared at both of his buddies in disbelief.

Willie said, "People always talking about, man's best friend is his dog. He might be *man's* best friend, but I'm here to tell you this afternoon, that a boy's best friend is his fist. Old Five-Finger Minnie. And you better believe me when I say so."

At that point Willie pulled his thing out of his pants and proceeded to give a demonstration with the accompaniment of poetry almost set to music.

> *I see the moon,*
> *The moon see me.*
> *Please, Mister Moon,*
> *Don't tell on me.*
> *Five, ten, fifteen, twenty,*
> *Ain' gon stop till I git a plenty*
> *Poontang's bad,*
> *Pussy is worse.*
> *Fuck my fist*
> *And play safety first*
> *Five, ten, fifteen, twenty—*

Jake was roaring now with laughter. "Look at old 'Crazy Willie,'" he said. "He can change hands without missing a stroke. He's a swinging ass!"

Chuck had gotten his second wind now and he was plowing a right pretty row on the surface of the river as he headed homeward. His entire body was a study in rhythmic movements, with every limb playing its role: head, arms, stomach, legs, like a living piece of breathing automation. He felt good all through and through from bobbing head to kicking feet. He missed Willie more than ever as the summer days romped lackadaisically by. Every day he daydreamed with the hope that any minute he would look up and Willie would come around the side of the house and into the yard and say, "Hi, boy. You been gitting any lately, or you still messing round with Minnie?" But that kind of Willie was gone forever.

It was not that Willie had gone a million miles away from home. It was just that he had suddenly grown up and moved away from the house. When Willie had been a child, he had acted like a child, but now that he had become a man he had put away childish things. And he had moved out to Johnson's

Bottom to be near a certain widow woman. And he didn't come around as often as he should. And when he did, he was so dog-gone serious. Nothing like he used to be. But folk still called him Crazy Willie.

He remembered once, a couple of years ago, they had been seated in their backyard eating watermelon. It was in the heart of melon season, and they grew great big juicy beauties in their garden at Chaney Farms, Incorporated. The first watermelon they ever grew was by pure accident. All summer long one sum-mer Chuck and Willie ate watermelons in the kitchen and threw the seeds out of the window. The next season a watermelon came up outside the window. It was nothing to write home about, a puny thing to look at. But it planted the seed of an idea in Jesse Chaney's mind. If a melon could come accidentally from throwing seeds out of the window, why not plant them on pur-pose? His question was no sooner asked than answered by him-self. He planted melon seeds in his garden and reaped a mellow harvest.

It was about seven o'clock of a Saturday afternoon, and Jesse had plucked a big fat melon from the vine and had thumped it with his index finger and had heard its ripe and juicy sound. They (Mama Carrie, Jesse, Willie, and Chuck) had just settled down for some serious melon-eating, when a long, tall, hungry-looking peckerwood came walking across the backyard toward them. He was as skinny as a stalk of sugarcane. He came across the yard and stood there watching them eating melon for a moment, saying nothing.

Chuck wondered where he came from and what he wanted and who sent him. Chuck thought uneasily, "If the Good Lord keeps the smell out of your nose, we'll sure Lord keep the taste out of your mouth." It was a saying his mother used to tease him with, when he was a little biddy boy.

The peckerwood watched them eat and his poor thin mouth watered all the way down through his Adam's apple and he swal-lowed hard and you could see his Adam's apple in a painful exe-cution. He had the largest Adam's apple Chuck had ever seen.

Finally Chuck's father broke the silence. "I don't believe I done ever had the pleasure of your kind acquaintance."

The man said, "Y'all sure do look so happy and contented. I deswear y'all do."

Willie laughed out loud.

[104]

The peckerwood's red face lost color for a moment. He said, "I got good-luck piece here for two little old dollars and itta tell you anything you want to know. Just two little old measly dollars and the whole wide world belongs to you." His mouth still watered as he watched them eat the melon.

Jessie said, "No sir, I don't believe I'm innerested."

The poor peckerwood said, "Itta tell you what the number gon be a whole week in advance."

Jesse said, "No sir, I don't b'lieve I'd be innerested. I don't play the numbers. Thank you kindly." They kept eating watermelon and the cracker's mouth kept watering.

Chuck didn't feel any meanness toward the cracker. Actually he felt sorry for him. Somehow he felt the poor man had to be in a very desperate situation to be panhandling in the colored neighborhood. Maybe it's because he isn't prejudiced, Chuck thought to himself, ironically.

The poor peckerwood said, "What's the matter? You think I'm trying to swindle you or something?"

Willie started to giggle his crazy giggle deep in his stomach, like he had a way of doing sometimes. His giggle was hardly audible. But Chuck heard it plainly.

The poor peckerwod said, "It's guaranteed to bring you good fortune. Make you a millionaire. Tell you all about who messing with your wife and who stealing your chickens. What more do you want?"

Jesse stared at the man. "Mister, did we say we wanted anything? Did we send for you?"

"Tell you all about civil rights and when you gon git it. Fact of the matter, you won't need no civil rights, you buy this goodluck piece from me. Itta tell you who gon be the next President of the Uniney States, who gon win the next world war, and all lika that. Even now tell you who gon win the World Serious and all. Anything in this life you wanna bet on, itta tell you how it's coming out. Just two little biddy dollars and your fortune is made. You don't even now have to worry 'bout being black no more."

Mama Carrie wore a great big worry in her face. Willie and Chuck were eating watermelon like it would go out of style the very next minute. The peckerwood stared at them, as if he would gladly change places with them just to get a piece of that watermelon between his teeth. He would be colored if it were required. He was so hungry-looking it was pitiful.

"Listen," he said, his mouth now watering shamelessly, slobber dripping from his lips. "I'm all for them civil rights and all lika that. That's how come I want you to have this good-luck stone."

Jesse Chaney said, "Can I ask you just one simple question?"

The man said, "You can just ask to your heart's contentment."

Jesse said, "If that stone you got is so lucky, how come you don't use it for your own self? How come you ain't rich? Or President? How come your backside so raggedy?"

The man stared from Jesse to the rest of the family. Willie burst out laughing. "He oughta be richer'n Charlie Wakefield, Daddy, with all that power in that stone."

The peckerwood saw nothing funny. His face reddened like a beet as he stared longingly at the whole half of a watermelon sitting untouched on the porch.

"Can't even buy a slice of watermelon," Willie said.

The peckerwood turned, muttering something angry under his breath, and started back across the yard.

Afterward, Willie, in describing it, said, "That cracker went back across the yard like suck-egg done been caught in a old hen's nest."

Before he got halfway across the backyard, Mama Carrie said, "Mister, you want a piece of watermelon?"

The peckerwood turned toward them again. There was this look in his skinny face of humility and gratitude. He swallowed hard into his Adam's apple. "Yessum," he said. "Indeed I sure do more than anything in this whole wide world. Watermelon is my favoritest fruit that grows out the good green earth the Lord done gived us."

She said, "Well, come on and git a piece then. Willie, cut the gentleman a piece."

The man said, "I sure do thank you ma'm, mighty much. I ain't got a thing against colored people. No-sirree-bob. I like nigrahs mighty much."

"You like watermelon," Chuck's father said sarcastically.

The river felt so good to him, so cool and soothing, like a glass of ice-cold lemonade all through his body, as the sun beat down. It was sensual, almost sexual, as if Chuck and the river made love to each other.

When you were Chuck Othello Chaney and you thought of Willie Chaney, as he used to be, you thought of things like wrestling in a hayloft and hiking way out in the woods away from everything and everybody and picking wild strawberries and blackberries and selling them to that crazy yaller-haired friendly gal who lived in the Big House. You thought of woods bright green and shimmering in the sunshine and rabbits and lizards and snakes and all kind of other things scooting through the high grass. And grasshoppers and devilhorses. You thought that Willie had to be a little crazy although you never said it aloud or admitted it to yourself and you had gotten into many fights when other boys made reference to it. He had to be a little crazy, the way he would pick up a live snake by the tail and chase you through the woods with it and finally break the snake's neck by snapping its head like he was cracking a whip. Pow! You thought of Willie and the long evenings of the wintertime and finding a warm cozy corner somewhere, anywhere, and cuddling with a book. They called him Crazy Willie, but whenever he got very quiet anywhere, you knew he had a book in his hand. He went after them like a dedicated wino after sneaky pete. He didn't care much what kind of a book it was. Is it writing? He would read it. Comic books, encyclopedias, Montgomery Ward or Sears and Roebuck catalogues. Willie Willie Willie Willie! Lots of people couldn't understand what Willie got out of reading so many stupid books, but you understood, because that was another thing you and Willie had in common. You loved books too. You were a bit more selective than was Willie. You loved them because they created new worlds for you and introduced you to other people and other places. You could take trips to far-off places without getting on a train. In a way, books, to you and Willie, were like whiskey and narcotics. You could use them to escape the cotton patch.

Sometimes when Chuck read a book, he liked to pause and try to imagine the looks of the man who wrote it. He liked to imagine that he could follow the special and peculiar workings of the author's mind. Why did he say it just like that? Why didn't he express this particular idea in another way? What did he mean by this or that? Or the other?

He didn't know what he was going to do with his life when he

[107]

grew up to be a man. But he knew one thing. He was not going to pick cotton for the rest of his days. Sometimes he thought he would be a world traveler but traveling was not an occupation that brought money in, so he would have to have a job or profession that made lots of money so he could afford to travel. He imagined that one day he would be a very rich man. And he would have a great big house full of children running and romping and having a good time with a swimming pool in the backyard and a basketball court. And he would be the most generous rich man who ever was a rich man. He would give lots of money to the poor and turn no man away from his door.

And when he grew up he would not be countrified anymore. He would be smooth and citified and Northernized like the young black man who had come among them last May. David Woodson. From the City of New York. He came asking questions, a whole gang of questions all over the place about anything and everything. About wages and hours and living situations and picking cotton and Charles Wakefield and voting and colored education and Congressman Rogers Jefferson Davis Johnson and Johnson's brother and plantation life. And so forth and so on. People were suspicious at first (even a lot of colored people were) of the slim, medium-height, soft-faced black man who asked them so many doggone questions they could hardly catch their breath, and talked with such an up-the-country accent. He almost didn't sound colored. But after Reverend Purdy introduced him at the church one Sunday and asked him to say a few remarks, suspicion died a natural death as far as most colored people were concerned.

That pretty-talking young colored man told them the South was the place where the great change would come, must come, and it was up to people like them to make the change come. He told them he, himself, was born in Mississippi, about ninety miles from Wakefield County. He told them he had been to Mother Africa, the land of their ancestors. When he first mentioned Mother Africa there were a few snickers from the congregation. The young man had to hear them, Chuck thought, and was so embarrassed he felt like going underneath his bench. But black and brown faces soon grew serious and glowed with pride when he told them they had a great history and a proud heritage which did not begin with slavery's humiliating scars. He told them he had been to Timbuktu, a city built by black men, an

[108]

ancient city in Africa which had a university centuries before Columbus stumbled upon the Americas.

"Sure-nuffs" and "Amens" and "Praise the Lords" came from all over the church, as if the young man were preaching the Gospel straight out of the Holy Book. Some tired old eyes filled up with tears of pure joy. Some old heads shook at the glory and the wonder of it all. He had opened a door that had been closed to them forever. He had brought them to the River Jordan and showed them the wondrous city that lay before them on the other side. He had somehow touched their tenderest spot.

Their hearts sang: "Oh, what a glorious city!"

After his "little talk" at the church, he came to be in great demand, like a rare commodity, to speak at this church and the other in every nook and corner of the county, at church club meetings and prayer meetings and all other kinds of get-togethers. At these meetings folks would stand up with the power and the glory shining in their faces. Young and old folks.

And demand: "Tell us about Africa and that there Tim-buck-whatchamacallit!"

Chuck went to every meeting he heard about, where it was rumored that the young man was to speak. He must have heard him speak six times—at least. And he noticed Bessie Mae at more than one of the meetings. He was jealous. He told her she was stuck on Mister Woodson. But he was somehow glad she liked the New York colored man from Mississippi who wrote books and went places and did things and talked pretty for the people. He and Chuck became fast friends in a short time. He was the Chaneys' guest for Sunday dinner at Chuck's invitation.

Reverend Purdy also came to the Chaneys for dinner that Sunday. Chuck would never forget the conversation at the dinner table. Another thing he noticed was that Mister Woodson and Miss Ida Lee were kind-of-sort-of tight and friendly too. Very very tight and friendly. Mr. Woodson was the color of chocolate ice cream (maybe just a little bit lighter). He was the most intelligent-looking man Chuck had ever met. White or colored. The girls of Wakefield County called him "cute." They said a cow had licked his forehead.

Then one day he went back up the country. Just like that, one day he up and went back up the country. But he was talked of by the folk for months and years to come. He had made a big impression.

Chuck was nearing the shore now, and he lay on his back, afloat, with the back of his head in the cup of his hands. He hoped to meet David Woodson one day soon sometime, somewhere. The thing he liked about Woodson was, with all his fame and fortune, he did not carry his backside on his shoulders. He loved people and he was as earthy as the good black soil on the farms of Mississippi.

Chuck Othello was entirely relaxed and totally lost in his daydream about this very rich and very handsome, very generous world traveler-philanthropist by the name of Charles Othello Chaney, Esquire, who somehow resembled David Woodson. Walked like him and talked like him. He was totally lost in his daydream as if he were in a deep sleep, when suddenly a pain shot through his left leg that almost made his heart stop beating. He did not panic, not at first. He turned on his stomach and tried to kick the cramp out of his leg but the pain grew sharper and sharper, as if his leg were drawing up on him. Knives were being stabbed into the calf of his leg a million times a minute. He grabbed his leg and tried to dig the cramp out with his fingers. He dug until his nails drew blood. He looked around him and nothing and no one were in sight. The thing to do was to keep his head and get to the river's bank as quickly as possible. When he started to swim, he found that he had suddenly grown very tired, and the river bank seemed miles away. And the pain in his leg was alive and crawling like a snake that was biting its way up his leg now to his thighs. His whole left leg was immobilized by a sharp, shooting, griping pain. He was fighting the water now, which was the quickest way for him to wear himself out, and he did just that in a great big hurry. And he got nowhere in a hurry. He hit several fast and desperate strokes, and thought, I'm close enough to the shore to stand up now. And he tried to stand up, his right foot reaching downward desperately for the feel of slippery earth beneath him, but his head went under water and he still had not touched bottom, and he felt the pain shoot up his leg, and the muscles of his leg contract. He struck out madly for shore now with several wild and aimless strokes of pure and simple desperation, but by now all his strength had left him and his guide mark was no longer there. The willow tree had disappeared. He had drifted downstream or upstream, he could not be certain which. And his strength was spent and he would never reach shore. He thought about his mother and his father and Willie and Jake and Bessie Mae. She had warned him that the river was his enemy.

His strength had left him, but there was nothing wrong with his lungs, a fact he demonstrated, when he let out one loud scream, as his head went under water and his feet reached desperately for a bottom that was never there:

"Help! Somebody help me!"

But nobody was in sight, and he thought he must have drunk in all the water in the river. He came up again and thrashed around in the river madly and tried to make it to the shore again, quietly fighting, desperately fighting, but fighting a very losing battle. It was the damndest stupidist thing in the world to die by drowning in the river. His river. He couldn't stay afloat any longer, because he didn't have the strength, and he was drowning. But he didn't want to die. He had too much to live for, too much to do, too much living he had not yet lived. I want to live! I want to live!

Then he saw the mirage of a white and naked body swimming toward him now with easy strokes a mile a minute. He struck out toward the yellow-haired illusion and tried to stay topside, but he was waterlogged by having so much of the river inside of him. It was coming out of his nostrils, his eyes, his ears, his mouth. And filling up all over again. She reached him just as he went under again, and she shoved him several yards toward the shore, and she said, "Stand up! See if you can stand up! It isn't deep here!"

And this time his feet did touch bottom before his head went under. But his legs were so weak that they slipped immediately out from under him and he swallowed the river again. She took hold of him and dragged him to the river bank and she laid him out on the grass and she got on top of him and she took her hands and pressed down hard upon the sides of his stomach and tried to pump the river out of him. And water did come from his mouth as if he were slobbering an entire river. She took both his arms and worked them up and down as if she were working on a pump. Then she lay atop him with her mouth against his mouth, just as she remembered her father doing once when he had rescued a drowning man a few years back. She was by now excitedly aware of who he was and of the difference of their sexes. And not saddened by the wonderful difference.

At first, he thought, before he fully regained consciousness (he

[111]

had not totally lost consciousness), that he was floating in that world of in-between. "I was drowned—and I'm dead—and dead people dream—and I am dreaming—This could not possibly be happening to me." These were his first thoughts. His second thoughts were he wasn't dead—he hadn't drowned—he wasn't dreaming. And why in the hell was somebody lying on top of him and kissing him? Still coming out of it (out of the dream or whatever it was he was still in) he thought of Bessie Mae with whom he had wet-dreamed on more than one occasion. He thought of Cora Mae, the wrestler. But he wasn't dreaming. He wasn't dreaming! Dead people didn't dream anyhow. He wasn't dead. He wasn't dreaming.

A naked girl lay busily atop him. His body felt her girlish softness from head to foot. Her mouth, her breasts, her thighs. And he came suddenly alive all over him. There was especially a growing, stiffening, throbbing, marvelous happening in the middle of him, which was attached to him, and definitely a part of him, but at the same time there was this magnificent detachment. This wonderful amazing thing of his seemed to have a mind and consciousness all its own. He, himself, was just awakening as from a deep sleep, but *It* was already leapingly alive. Her kisses were the craziest kind of suffocating kissing and almost took his breath away. If he didn't get from under her she would smother him to death. His body was vibrating now, not from cold or fear, but from a strange and surging warmth. He was a mannish boy now feeling violently his maleness, sweetly, agonizingly. Almost unknowingly, his arms found their way round her waist and held her to him, closer, ever closer. His eyes opened slowly, and slowly it came to him she was not Bessie Mae at all. His mind fought its way through the heat and smell of their young, throbbing, tingling, desperate bodies. She wasn't Bessie Mae at all, his mind said now, emphatically. She was not Cora Mae, the wrestler. But she was a very girlish girl and he was a boy knocking at the awesome door of manhood. Then his mind broke all the way through and started flashing danger signals.

She's white!

She's white!

She's white!

She's white!

When he got the message fully, he found that *It* was not de-

[112]

tached from him after all. *It* got the message too and went suddenly limp, as his hot body went cold, and his arms came from
around the girl and he moved quickly out from under her all in
one motion.

She shouted, "You're alive! You're alive!" As if she had not
known it until that very moment.

He leaped to his feet, and she got to hers. And they stood for
a moment staring at each other like boxers sparring for an opening. She was as naked as she came into the world and was getting
to be constructed like a woman with tight little, smooth little
mountains of teats and roundish hips and yellow hair atop her
head and between her legs the color of corn tassels. He was
naked except for his undershorts which hid nothing at the
moment, since *It* dangled darkly, limply, out of his shorts.

Suddenly she looked down at herself and shouted, "Oh!" And
turned from him and ran toward the woods and out of sight.

From the bushes she cried, "Go! Quick! What if somebody
caught us out here like this?"

He did not need to ponder the question. Chuck Othello split
the scene.

Chapter
8

*"About one hundred years ago, meddling Northerners broke the
peace between the whites and blacks of Dixie, and Southern men
of honor rallied to the colors and answered the clarion call of
chivalry and righteousness for His Name's sake. And after the
smoke cleared away, normalcy and the Southern tradition were
painfully reestablished, and God Almighty's will had triumphed
over calumny and malice. And now again, in our time, Southern
honor and tradition and tranquillity have been threatened.
Troublemakers are once again amongst us throughout the length
and breadth of our dear old Southland. Our honor as a proud
people once again hangs in the balance. And once again we must
unsheathe the sword, even as the knights of old, to defend and*

[113]

reaffirm those principles for which our noble ancestors to val-iantly fought.

"There are even those among us who speak with Southern accents but utter the words of foreign export. We know them too for what they are. They have the voice of Jacob, but they blabber the words of Essau. There are 'pious' black men who stand in the sanctuary of their pulpits and hide behind their inverted collars and preach love out of one side of their mouths and hate out of the other side. They preach nonviolence while they create violence. But self-styled tyrants like M. L. Coon do not speak for the humble black people of the South whom we all love and hold dear to our hearts. And thank God Almighty, Communist-inspired eggheads like Rat McGill do not speak for the white South.

"There are some goodhearted unsuspecting souls amongst us, who say: 'Go slow. Take it easy. Don't be drastic. The storm will blow itself out to sea. The crop will be all right again.' But they don't know how the seeds of Communism are planted. But, as good mother-witted farming people, we all know if the crop is bad, it's time to take drastic measures. It's time to tear it up by the roots from the soil where it is growing else the soil itself will become contaminated. We live in a time that divides the men from the boys. And we of the Daily Chronicle *sincerely believe deep in our hearts that there are still millions of stouthearted men left in old Mississippi.*

"Undaunted and unbowed, facing insuperable odds, sons of the gallant South, will *remember the glory that was once Mississippi and Alabama and Georgia and will answer the call again and take up arms (not arms of violence unless it comes to that) in her defense again. So onward, Christian soldiers, marching as to war, with the Cross of Jesus going on before. And God Almighty's will shall be done again as always and henceforth and forever-more."*

"Amen," Wakefield commented sarcastically. "Amen—and Heaven help us one and all." He had been reading the lead editorial in the *Wakefield Daily Chronicle,* as he sat at his breakfast with his wife and daughter and his hot biscuits and ham and eggs and hominy grits and his coffee piping hot and black. It was the one thing in his taste that was provincial. He loved old-fashioned Southern cuisine. He had burlesqued the reading as if he were a fundamentalistic Holy Roller in the backwoods of old

[114]

'Sippi. The *Chronicle* was owned and published by Rogers Jefferson Davis Johnson, distinguished member of the House of Representatives in the Congress of the United States from the great and sovereign State of Mississippi. Johnson was, moreover, the second richest man in the county and Charlie Wakefield's most implacable political foe. Nonetheless, they were amiable foes, for the most part, harboring no deep-seated hostilities toward one another. Outside of politics, they were friends of long standing. They were drinking "pardners."

Wakefield put the *Chronicle* aside and stared sideways at his daughter, who grew beautifully toward womanhood every single heartbreaking moment. Her hair got yellower by the day. Blue-green of eyes, impish at the mouth and dimpled at the rosy cheeks. Wakefield thought, achingly: "A child grows and grows right before your eyes and changes and changes and you are hardly aware of it from day to day, till one day, which is a day like any other day, the growth and change have changed her into someone altogether different. And she isn't your little girl anymore. She has become her own woman. Or even worse, she has become the personal property of another man, and she doesn't even carry your name anymore."

The expression on Carrie Louise's face was unusually serious this morning. Wakefield looked up toward the other end of the table where his saintly otherworldly wife was seated.

"Speaking of eggheads, Jeff Johnson is the greatest ignorance-spreader in all of Wakefield County—in all of Mississippi."

Anne Wakefield's eyes were glassy, as if they lived alone with cataracts. He had not expected a response from her. But he was a man who loved to talk. He liked the sound of words and the taste of metaphors. Sometimes his wife listened carefully enough to give him such profound responses as: "It's the truth," or "It's a sin and a shame before the Lord."

But this particular morning she was completely out of it, as was the case with her on many mornings. Her mind was a large and lonely mansion she had built painstakingly through the years, as a haven from the pathos of her life's great emptiness. Her sequestered mansion was housed with dreams and visions and magnificent ghosts of yesteryear. And men of gallantry and chivalry frequented her mansion on great white horses. Sometimes her dreams were done in technicolor. Sometimes the gallant men were black. Oh the deep dark secrets some of her dreams were! The excitement! The passion! She rarely ever wandered very far from her mansion out into that jungle that other people called civilization.

Wakefield stared again at Carrie Louise. His one and only issue. He had wanted a boy. When he passed on to his happy hunting ground or heavenly plantation, the Wakefield name would be buried with him. Sometimes he looked at his beautiful daughter and thought to himself, that, as rich and powerful as he was, he should have been able to call his shots. "God willing," he usually added, just to stay on the safe side. But most of the time he was delighted with her. Vaingloriously delighted. She was his heart. He admired the rebel in her. He'd always liked to think of himself as a special kind of rebel. He liked the way she ran headlong into life, and if she stumbled or fell, she would sometimes cry if the pain were too severe, but, cry or not, she would get up undeterred and dash headlong into life all over again. She would never be afraid of life, he thought. She would never count the cost of living. She would spend life freely. She was a spendthrift when it came to that. Sometimes she frightened him, she spent life so freely.

He slapped the paper lightly with the back of his hand. "If ever the State of Mississippi needed clear and level-headed thinking, it's at this very moment. We've got to face the situation squarely and stop this childishly blaming everything on the North and Communism. You can't agitate a vacuum. Yankees or Communists or nobody else could stir up a mess down here unless the mess already was here in the first damn place. You cannot stir up *nothing* into *something*. An absolute scientific impossibility. I've been telling them for years. The world is changing and we must change with it or be washed away by the tides of history. In the first place, their history, our ancestors, was a grandiose lie and it is an even bigger lie in the middle of the twentieth century."

The girl's serious face creased into smiles, her grayish-green eyes, her dimpled cheeks, her impish mouth. She was smiles all over herself. She loved for her father to take her seriously, to speak with her as if she were adult and equal. She asked, "Why don't you establish your own newspaper?"

He smiled at her. She thought he could do anything and everything. Sometimes he wished she would remain like this forever. A would-be world-shaker. Believing that he, her father, could really shake the world and change it. Believing that every man should try to shake it, change it. Make it different. But he knew that, just as surely as the world did change, she, herself, would surely change. That was the aching part of it. She would grow up and the stream of life would wash over her, purifying her of all her idealisms, and she would be entirely different. She would never be quite as pure-clean and uncompromising as she was this very moment, before life had washed and rinsed her heart and soul, and hung them out to dry.

He started to say to her in his own rhetorical fashion: "My darling, never let that heart of hearts of yours get frozen in the dry and deadly ice of cynicism, better known these days as sophistication. Life can be good if you make it good."

But instead, he said, "Sweetheart, you know your daddy isn't getting any younger. A newspaper—" He sighed longingly for the years gone by forever. If one could only conquer time and age. His heart cried out for his time's great waste, and he was not the kind of man who wasted time. "I got my hands on too many plows already. Too many fingers picking my pocket now with first one scheme and then another. Sometimes I don't know whether I'm coming or going." He thought of the conversation he'd had with his lawyer a couple of days before. "I told Brad Lawson just the other day, I wanted him to start a systematic campaign to take some of these leeches' hands out of Charlie Wakefield's pocket."

"None of us are getting any younger, Daddy," she said wisely, proud of her growing wisdom. "We're all growing old, every one of us. Every little biddy newborn babe." She hated to think of him growing old. She wanted time to pass, all right, but she did not want to read time's passing in her father's face, or movements.

He smiled his great age wearily, felt it suddenly all through his bones. Sixty some-odd years did not an old man make, but he knew moments of great weariness. "When you grow a little older, we will let you set yourself up in the newspaper business, if you want to, and you can crusade to your heart's content."

"Will you really, Daddy?" she asked excitedly. "Can I hold you to it?" She had eyes that seemed to be amazed at everything they saw, as if the whole wide world were one great grandiose surprise. She seemed always to be staring at skyscrapers or the seven wonders of the world.

[117]

"We can shake on it," he said. And he reached his hand toward her, but she was away from the table and back again before he could catch his breath.

"We'll put it down in writing," she said breathlessly. She wrote it all down legal and proper and he signed it with a great flourish. And she signed it as a witness to his signature. Her face was so aglow and overflowing with the moment's joy and the future's expectations, he heard his own heart cry for joy.

"Get your mother to witness it too," he said good-naturedly. In his heart it seemed such a long way off, her adulthood, and yet so terribly close at hand. He wanted desperately to believe it was a long way off. So why not indulge her in such a harmless whimsy? Or better still, why not promise her and really mean it? It would give her life perspective. Why not set her up in the newspaper business—if that was what she still wanted when the time came. Surely it was nothing for him to bother about at the moment. So long as he treated his own Negroes fair and square, he had nothing at all to worry about. He thought aloud: "It was Din, Din, Din, Gunga Din—For all 'is dirty hide, he was white, clear white inside—"

These days he often thought about Jesse Chaney. His over-active mind was a combination camera, projector, and movie screen, and on his mind's screen Gunga Din was Jesse Chaney and Jesse Chaney was Gunga Din. As the years had passed he'd seen very little of his old friend, Jesse. In a way he knew why Jesse politely stood his distance and stayed out of his way as much as possible. One of the things Wakefield deeply regretted was his calling Jesse Chaney a "nigger" that afternoon at the Big House porch when Jesse had made a fool of himself over the Supreme Court decision. He should have shown more under-standing. But he had reacted like a common ignorant pecker-wood. He remained through the years very fond of the image that was Jesse. Even though, in moments of great clarity, he realized that the image was more illusion than reality, neverthe-less he waxed sentimental when he thought of Jesse Chaney and good old Gunga Din.

"The great voice of the Nine Wise Men hangs over 'Sippi like an ominous cloud. A storm broke out all over Dixie—in Mont-gomery—in Little Rock—in Atlanta—in Tallahassee. But in old 'Sippi it just brewed and hovered, and sometimes threatened

even, and even blew into a good-sized storm every now and then, but a storm that never sustained itself, a storm that always blew quickly out to sea via the Gulf of Mexico. And the more things changed in Mississippi the more they remained everlastingly the same. If anything, things and people were worse off than they were before, because of the mounting tension between the races. Take, for example, Wakefield County.

"Wakefield County is backwoods country, as remote from the rest of the world as if it were set down in the middle of the Rocky Mountains. In a way of speaking, it is as far away as Timbuktu or Zanzibar. The Supreme Court decision of 1954 has meant very little to the people of this county. Many of them have never heard of the Court, let alone the decision. This is cotton country. The earth is black, the crop is white. The people, most of them, are black, the rulers of the land are white.

"Wakefield is one of the largest counties in the state, that is, in area. Seven hundred and fifty-nine square miles of sprawling never-ending countryside, mile upon mile of cotton plantations, the monotony broken every now and then by slim yellow corn and red strawberries and a few other crops. But this is mainly cotton country. King Cotton casts his ubiquitous shadow on the life of every person in the county. Socially, economically, politically, philosophically, and psychologically. Not a single living human can escape the great white shadow.

"While driving through the county, one can see that many of the plantations are still very much in the classical tradition, with the Mile Gate and the Big House white and awesome and the tall oak trees and the sweet magnolias and the cabins far in the rear of the Big House just as they were more than a hundred years before during the good old days of slavery. One sees black folk standing deep in the cotton and, as they straighten up to wave a hand of fellowship to a dark brother driving through, one gets the feeling that they have never strayed or ventured more than ten miles from the place where they were born and will live out their lives and go back to the earth from whence they came. The only contact with the outside world is television. For, ironically enough, though the folk are poorly paid and underfed and debt-ridden, each cabin sports a television antenna atop. The television inside the cabin belongs to the white man just as the people who live therein.

"One of the big plantation owners in the county is none other

[119]

than that estimable Congressman from the State of Mississippi, the Honorable Rogers Jefferson Davis Johnson, whose father before him ..."

It was a warm night in late August. All of the two hundred seats were occupied in the park in the grove by the side of the river. The good people of the county had smacked their happy lips on sandwiches and ice-cold lemonade. And now they waved their funeral-parlor-sponsored fans back and forth in front of their hot faces and tried to keep the children to a minimum of wiggling and giggling, as they listened to their great leader. People stood at the back of the seats and on each side and in the aisle and up near the platform. Nothing moved unless it had to in the evening heat. The leaves of the trees surrounding the grove were motionless as if they held their breaths in expectation. The army of bugs gathered around the lights up on the platform gave an eerie illusion of miniature cascades of shiny water suspended in mid-air. Lightning bugs blinked off and on as if they were returning signals to the bugs across the river.

The leader threw the periodical he had been reading from onto the floor of the platform and started dramatically to step on it, but changed his mind and picked it up again. "Excuse me, brothers and sisters, I got carried away for the moment. I reckin I take these things too seriously. I forgot that I was reading from such a august journal as the Uniney States Congressional Record."

"I wouldn've believed it if I hadna heard it with my own two ears," a woman said in clean astonishment. "The Uniney States Congressional Record."

Some of the good folks shook their heads and clucked their disapproval.

"Shame! Shame!"

"Shame and disgrace!"

"A sin and a shame before the Lord and Savior!"

A baby cried. A fat man belched and said, "Excuse me."

Good people scratched their arms and heads and hindparts and frontparts and slapped the sides of their faces as swarms of mosquitoes went on the attack with their eternal nighttime blitzkrieg. People slapped mosquitoes till their hands were bloody.

The leader held up his arms for quiet.

"I know how you feel," he told them. "I feel the same damn way, if the ladies will excuse my French."

[120]

He knew how to make them laugh and chuckle. He was their kind of man. As earthy as the sweet black dirt beneath them. He was of them, for them, by them, they thought. And he talked their kind of language. They were good, simple, openhearted country people. God-fearing peckerwoods, who didn't know what the word "malice" meant. They would give their last shirt to a poor "good-natured darky." That's the kind of folks they were.

"You tell 'em, Jeffy, boy," a real old-timer shouted.

"Give 'em hell, Jeffy!" a toothless old woman shouted. "Give 'em Hail Columbia!"

The Great One said, "The words I just read to you were from the Uniney States Congressional Record. They were inserted there by a great Yankee Congressman from the State of New York City. And where did he get it from?"

"Tell us where he got it from, Jeffy!"

"I'll tell you where he got it from, and then you'll know his reading habits."

"Tell the whole damn cockeyed world, Jeffy boy!"

"He got it from that famous Commonist-oriented periodical known as the *Democracy* magazine, but as long as I been reading it, I ain't never found anything in it *for* our democracy. Its policy is *against* this great democracy. We ought to call our little old *Wakefield Daily Chronicle,* the *Democracy.* Cause we truly for this democratic nation."

"Amen!"

"We truly for the democracy," a brother echoed from the Amen corner.

"Yi-hoo!"

"And now we come to the sixty-foe-dollar question," Congressman Rogers Johnson warned them. "Are you ready for the question?"

"Ready!" the good folks screamed in a ragged kind of unison.

"Ready!" one or two people even screamed from the little section on the right side up near the front "Especially Reserved for Colored Only."

"The sixty-foe-dollar question is—*Who wrote these bedtime stories in the* Democracy *in the first damn place!* That is the question."

"That is the question!" they repeated after him, even one or two in the proud litle section Especially Reserved for Colored Only. By now he was speaking in his most Southern, he meant,

[121]

most backwood-Southern of Southern accents. His accent was so drawled and thick he could hardly understand himself. But his audience understood him. For they were backwoods people. Good, hard-working, God-fearing, backwoods people with the smell of backwoods sweat in their bones, mixed with the sap of Mississippi pines. The salt of the salt of the salt of the earth, as he oftentimes described them. "They smell good and strong and piney-fied." Like they took their baths in turpentine. And he truly loved them, dearly loved them. He pulled off the silk pongee jacket of his two-hundred-dollar tailor-made suit. They loved to see their boy dress like they had taken good care of him. One old lady waved her handkerchief at him the entire evening through, and seemed to never tire. He rolled up his sleeves.

"Jeff boy, you sure look purty tonight!"

"You look purty and you talking good!"

There was a relatively quiet section in the audience where the quality people sat, a few doctors, lawyers, and businessmen. They loved Jeffy too. They sometimes thought he was a bit vulgar and big-mouthed, but he served their various and varied purposes, whatever they were, and he knew he served their purposes. In a way he was contemptuous of them. He could be as sophisticated as they were when the occasion demanded it. He had been more places than they had and had seen more. He thought of himself as a self-made man, as was his father (may he rest in peace) before him. And he was the second wealthiest man in Wakefield County. He let them use him because he used them in return. A good businessman didn't use his own money for his financial specula-tions, he always said, when they were not around and listening.

"Are you ready for the answer?"

"Ready for the answer!"

"The man who wrote this enlight'ning article for the *Democracy* magazine which finally showed up in no less a journal than the Congressional Record of these Uniney States of this America, was a very bright young man who came to us last year and be-took himself of our old-fashioned Wakefield County, Mississippi hospitality. Remember? I can see him now before me. He told us he was going to write a story that redounded to the good name of Mississippi. His own beloved Mississippi! A story that showed that the people of Mississippi could come together and affirm the democratic purpose for which this nation was constituted and which became the fervent hope of the civilized world in our age of the cognizance of the worth of every human being and never flinch from our atomic power and—"

Occasionally he was hung up by his own rhetorical enthusiasm. Sometimes, as now, he would begin a sentence with one point in mind but become so carried away by the sound of his intelligence that he would lose his way in the thicket of his verbiage. By the time he had extricated himself, if ever, he sometimes had forgotten what his point was in the first place. Not that it made any important difference with most of the audience. He was their man, and they were his kind of people. At least they thought they were his kind of people. It was his style that counted.

Wakefield wandered into the meeting shortly after the Congressman had begun his talk. He did not sit with the quality people as might have been expected, since he was the most bona fide quality person in all the county and possibly in the entire state. He stood with Carrie Louise on the periphery with an amused expression on his face. He once said of Jeffy Johnson: "He's the kind of man who sounds like he knows what he's talking about, until you listen to him carefully." And how many people actually listened?

"Are you ready?" Johnson shouted, with his fist balled-up and poised above his head to do battle with the Devil. He was one of the finest actors on the Mississippi stage.

"Ready!" they shouted.

"Whatchoo waiting on?" a lady shouted. And people laughed and shouted.

"All right, then. It was bad enough that it found its way in the Congressional Record. (Follow me on this in-famous journey now.) It was bad enough that the Congressional Record, which is supposed to be the most respectable record on God's green earth excepting the Good Book itself, would allow something from a dis-re-pute-table organ of Commonism like the *Democracy* magazine. (Follow me now. Keep behind but keep close to me.) But the crowning insult of all insults was that this pack of lies was written in the first instance by none other than a New York darky!" He paused. "A New York darky, born and bred in Mississippi!"

The crowd reacted. They had followed him all the way and were way ahead of him now. Booing and rebel yells and indignation and shouting to the Lord to bring down hell's fire and damnation.

[123]

The Leader held up both hands for quiet.

"Now, now—brothers and sisters, I don't mean to whip up no racial animosities. You know me better'n that."

They laughed and squealed and stamped their feet and waved their arms. Some were waving Confederate flags. He was their man. And he never did them wrong.

"No, no—" he said. "I really mean it. We ain't got nothing against our colored brethren of Wakefield County. I mean it— some of them are right here with us tonight, and I want them to know they mighty welcome. And I didn't mean no harm at all in reference to that New York darky. Darky is a term of endearment and fond affection, that is, for our own darkies. Are you with me?"

Some were with him. Some were just a few steps behind him. Some had lost their way—temporarily. Some were way out in front and waiting for him to catch up to them.

"When we call one of our colored friends in Mississippi a darky we are referring affectionately to the beautiful color of his skin, the skin the Good Lord endowed upon him to make him different from the rest of us. And that is all we referring to. But when we call a New York nigger a darky we referring to the blackness of his heart!"

"Amen!"

"Bless him, Heavenly Father!"

"Yii-hoooo!"

Rebel yells exploded in the evening heat.

They were with their Leader again almost one hundred percent.

When he got them quiet again, he said: "Deacon Robert Daniels, will you step up to the platform for a moment, please?"

A tall, brown-skinned, quiet-faced man stood up in the section Especially Reserved for Colored Only. He was well-dressed for this neck of the backwoods. He hesitated now, as if he did not know what was required of him.

"Come right up," the Leader said in a clear and friendly voice. "Step right this way, Deacon Daniels."

The Deacon still hesitated, but when the Leader beckoned him with a patient smile on his face, he finally came forward to the platform. And now they stood there side by side together on the platform. Deacon Robert "Jack" Daniels and Congressman Rogers Jefferson Davis Johnson. The Deacon was a head taller than the Leader, who was about five-feet-eight and thin and wiry

[124]

and crafty-eyed and freckled and looked the part of a homespun jackleg people's politician from the backwoods of Mississippi with a teaspoonful of book learning and a slopjarful of mother wit. But he was hardly what he seemed. The Congressman was a Harvard grad. His caricature of the Mississippi backwoodsman was consummate and purposeful. He could have made it out in Hollywood.

The two men were a sharp contrast in physical appearance. The Deacon was a handsome man, his skin was smooth and pulled tightly over the frame of his large square face. His face was intelligent. He might have been the country doctor, the college professor, or the businessman around the corner. But like the Congressman, he was not quite what he seemed.

"All right, Deacon. I want you testify in the sight of the Lord and beneath His bountiful stars and moonlight."

The moon had not come out all night that night.

The Deacon opened his mouth and contradicted his appearance. "Whachoo want me to testify about, suh?" He sounded as if he were doing a takeoff on Rochester. His voice was like scraping a piece of glass along a railroad track. Sometimes even white folk thought the Deacon had to be kidding.

"I jest want you to answer a few questions that I'm gon pose to you. I want these gentlemen of the press to hear it straight from the horse's mouth. No offense meant to you, Deacon."

Flashbulbs exploded in the night.

"Yassuh."

"I ask you, Deacon. Do you come here of your own free will and volition?"

"Yassuh."

"Where do you work?"

"I work for the Rogers Johnson Plantation, Incorporated, suh."

"It says here in the Uniney States Congressional Record that the Rogers Johnson plantation pays its workers forty to fifty cents an hour, Deacon. How much you get paid for an hour's work?"

"One dollar and fifteen cents, suh."

"It says here that Rogers Johnson plantation workers live in one- and two-room shacks. How many rooms do you live in, Deacon?"

The Deacon counted on his fingers. "We got four rooms in our house, suh. And it sure Lord ain't no shack." Pride beamed from the Deacon's childish face now.

"And do you or do you not, yourself, consider Rogers Jefferson Davis Johnson an arch exploiter of the colored people?" The Leader was a past master at the art of sarcasm and ridicule. "Do I or do I not represent the good God-fearing people of my constituency? Black and white. Did I ever keep the people of my constituency from registering and voting?"

"Hell, naw, you never kept the people from voting—not the white ones. But you damn sure ain't never given the black folks no encouragement. And I work for fifty cents an hour on your plantation too." A young angry black man had taken the floor and was waving his arms excitedly. "Don't let Jack Handkerchief-head Daniels do all the testifying. Ask me some of them sixty-four-dollar questions."

The Leader was taken completely by surprise. Reporters and photographers rushed toward the angry black man. Bulbs were flashing. People shouted for the young man to shut his damn black mouth. A group of white men crowded around the section Especially Reserved for Colored Only. One reached for the boy but he shoved him away.

The boy was screaming now. "This is a free country, ain't it! This is a free country—ain't it! This is supposed to be a free country. Go ahead and lynch me and the whole damn world will know about it. And if I'm lynched, I accuse Congressman Johnson in front of being a party to my lynching."

The Deacon was torn between two loyalties. It was his best white friend whose good name had been assaulted by the angry black boy. On the other hand, it was the crazy son of one of his best black friends whose head was about to be assaulted. He recognized the boy when he first stood up. Jesse Chaney's next-to-the-last boy. Everybody knew he was crazy as a bedbug. Hadn't been to school over three years in his entire life. But went around reading every book he could steal, beg, or borrow, books about this, that, and the other. Books had run the poor boy crazy. He was a book bug.

The boy was screaming now. "This *is* a free country, ain't it! This is a free country—ain't it? It supposed to be a free country! Is it or ain't it?"

They reached for him again as the flashbulbs went off, but a few of the people in the section Especially Reserved for Colored

Only surrounded him now and gave him protection. A tall white backwoodsman knocked a newspaperman down and tried to take his camera. People were shouting and cursing. Unobtrusively the full moon had come out, and now it beamed brightly upon the park by the river, as if it stared incredulously at the crazy human happenings.

"Git the nigger!"

"Git the darky!"

Above the bedlam "Crazy Willie's" voice could be distinctly heard. "Go ahead and lynch me and the whole damn world will know about it. You damn sure can't lynch all these newspaper people. And if I am lynched, I accuse Congressman Rogers Johnson in front of everybody in the world of being a party to my lynching. And I call on Congress to impeach!"

Crazy Willie's repeated accusation before the fact brought the Leader back to his senses. He began to pound the lectern with his gavel which he carried with him almost everywhere he went. He'd been a county judge before he became a Congressman.

"Order! Order!" he screamed. And other white men moved now to bring the other white men back to order.

When things had quieted down, comparatively, there was still a kind of buzzing in parts of the audience like bees around a rind of watermelon.

"Now—" the Leader said, "this is a free country and every man is titled to his own opinion. And Crazy Willie is entitled to his. Thank God ain't many round here that share his opinion. But nevertheless, he's titled to it. Now let's get on with the meeting."

He asked his friend, the Deacon, a few more questions, but the Deacon's heart was no longer in it. He did not like to be called a handkerchief-head, not even by poor Crazy Willie. And the audience was restless now. And the Leader was astute enough to know when he had run out the string. The meeting came to an end about ten or fifteen minutes later and without further incident.

Two nights later Crazy Willie went down River Road to call on the widow woman upon whom he had recently been lavishing his attention. And all with good intentions. He never reached the widow woman's house. And he never returned home again. He just vanished from the earth and Mississippi.

[127]

Chapter
9

They drove home in the Jaguar after the meeting. They took the long way home, Charles James Richard Wakefield and his daughter, Carrie Louise. She was sixteen years old now and had grown straight up out of her awkwardness, as slim and graceful as a stalk of sugarcane dancing in the evening breeze. She was mature far past her years. They took the long way home, followed the River Road out toward Rainbow Bend through a funnel of trees that stood tall above the highway, tall and bright green in the moonlight. The giant palmettos reached over the highway toward one another and grasped each other in a kind of ritualistic handclasp, as if they held some terrible secrets, as if down through the centuries they had been witness to some horrible happenings underneath the sun and moonlight.

Her father said almost under his breath: "It was Din, Din, Din, Gunga Din—"

And he pushed his foot further down on the gas pedal and the car leaped forward like a wild beast with this Mississippi jungle as his habitat. The speedometer needle vacillated nervously between eighty-five and ninety as if it were scared to make up its mind, as the black beast roared through the jungle night in a kind of trembling rage.

Yet the girl felt no pain or apprehension. It was absolutely the tenderest moment in the day for her, as she sat beside her father with her head upon his shoulder. She had been shaken to her very bowels by the meeting and the demagogy of the Congressman, whom she'd seen coming in and out of the Wakefield house like kinfolk ever since she could remember. She had never liked his ugly crudeness and his gross vulgarity. He was always on stage, always acting out the role of the folksy homespun peckerwood, the man of the backwoods people. He almost never dropped his guard, even though he was a Harvard graduate. And he had frightened her tonight, when she fully realized for the first time the enormity of the magical power he held over the poor and ignorant. She had read his ragsheet, the *Chronicle,* read it almost every morning of her reading life, had heard him loud-mouthing since she was a little girl, but she had never taken him seriously. How could anybody take a vulgar clown like Rogers Johnson seriously? But now she knew better. She had been especially shaken by the incident of near-violence with Crazy Willie, shaken particularly by the fact that her father never moved a muscle to go to his assistance. The problem was, with all her big talk this little girl still thought of her father as a kind of knight in shining armor, who would always and unequivocably take sides with the underdog and the poor and disinherited. And she never really understood how her father could be at home with and show such warmth of friendship to a man like Rogers Johnson, whom she imagined to be her father's diametric opposite. She thought that no two men could be more dissimilar. Her father stood for everything this man was against. She didn't understand, but there must be an explanation. She closed her eyes, closing it all out of her mind, the meeting, Congressman Johnson, Crazy Willie, everything. Let her just savor the warmth and security of her father's shoulder for the moment. She was mature enough to realize that the older she grew the rarer these moments would be.

The tires cried out as he went around a steep curve. He slowed down gradually. He had been daydreaming in the nighttime. He looked sideways at the yellow-haired girl's head upon his shoulder. He had to be more careful. He was driving with valuable cargo, to him the most valuable cargo in the world. Carrie Louise Mariah Wakefield. The countryside was alive with the sounds of nighttime people, as his baby used to call them. She was still his baby. A wild cacophony of sound, of frogs and locusts and crickets and nighttime birds of countless denominations. A million kinds of bugs and insects in the glare of the headlights gave an eerie illusion of waterfalls in miniature. Now and then a crazy bullbat would swoop down in front of the headlights and pay his respects and fly up and away again. And yet Wakefield and his daughter felt a sort of oneness with this wildness, a kind of soft serenity.

The moonlight bounced off the river like a thousand sparkling jewels. Across the river lightning bugs blinked off and on like neon signs. The man thought foolishly of the many times he had

[129]

approached the lights of New York City by ferryboat from the Jersey side.

His girl stirred beside him and he gestured toward the other side of the river. "Your granddad led a regiment in battle right over there," he told her with a great pride in his voice.

"Against the Indians?" she said sleepily. She was far from being asleep. She was just so doggone comfortable.

"Against the Yankees," he said proudly. "The Wakefields go way back in this neck of the woods. Yes-siree-bob. Nobody gave us a doggone thing. We earned our position here in this place through blood, sweat, and tears, to quote another great Anglo-Saxon. We are truly one of the first families of Mississippi." He was in an unusual mood. He did not usually carry on like this. He had the reputation of a man who eschewed wallowing in the murky waters of tradition. Change was the thing. The future was important. The past was merely prologue.

She said, "The first families of Mississippi were red men, my daddy."

"Touché," he admitted good-naturedly. "But their mistake was the failure to put it down in writing. Only men who write their history can lay any claims to making history." He paused. He chuckled ironically. "And then the fact that we had firearms and they had bow and arrows didn't help the rightness of their cause one little old bit."

From somewhere it came out of her and surprised her. She heard herself say in some kind of a singsong. "It was Din, Din, Din, Gunga—Gunga—"

He said expansively, "Any time you hear a man say, 'We won the war because God was on our side,' said man is either a fool or a demagogue. God is on the side of might, and that's all there is to it."

"Might makes right," she said, only partially realizing the enormity as well as the profound simplicity of her statement.

"You said it, Princess." He put his right arm around her shoulder and squeezed her hard. "Might and power. That makes you and me the most right people in this neck of the Mississippi woods. All along both sides of the river. Wakefield cotton, Wakefield corn, strawberries, Wakefield textile mills, lumberyards, box factories, canning. Wakefield money, power, might. And it all belongs to you."

She felt a chill go through her body which was not caused by

[130]

the specially installed air-conditioning in the Jaguar. "Money, power, might," she silently repeated deep deep inside of her, "and it all belongs to you." She shuddered and moved closer into her father's arm. She burrowed into the side of him.

"And one day you will up and marry," he said sadly, "and change your name and it will not belong to Wakefield anymore."

"I'll always be a Wakefield, Daddy." She knew she sounded foolish. As if she were saying, "There'll always be an England."

"Dynasties never last forever," he said flatly, fatalistically.

They drove all the way out to Sulphur Springs to Fat Jack's Place, which sold the best Mississippi barbecue in all the world and had the most delicious Brunswick stew. You could hear murmuring of the people at Fat Jack's Place when they drove up.

"Mr. Charlie Wakefield!"

As if he were a movie star or a great renowned celebrity.

"Who's that young cute chick he's with?"

"That's Jimmy Dick and his daughter. You better mind how you talk!"

"Jimmy Dick! Way out here at Fat Jack's. You know old Jack must be selling some damn good barbecue!"

It was the same thing everywhere he went among the just plain ordinary people. Jimmy Dick took it all in his long strides. And he walked with giant steps. No two ways about it. But Carrie Louise always experienced a profound ambivalence. She always felt somehow embarrassed in her role of the celebrated Princess of all that she surveyed, embarrassed about this power, the amassing of which she had contributed absolutely nothing to. At the same time there was an undeniable glowing that went on inside of her, a pride that came very close to sinful arrogance. It was a sin to be overly proud. Her father had always taught her it was a sin to be too proud. Pride and shame of her position, which she had done nothing to earn, merged into a sharp confusion, as she heard: "The man, himself, in person! And he got his daughter with him!" As she watched, two waiters, almost stumbling over each other, ran obsequiously out to the air-conditioned Jaguar.

They ordered barbecue "to go." And they drove back through the moonlight through the sweet-smelling jungle-clad moonlight of August, Mississippi style. When they reached home they sat in the oak-paneled den and ate barbecue as they watched the late news on television, and she drank beer and he drank Scotch and branch water. She felt so good and comfortable with her daddy this night, it was almost painful.

She looked up and around the den with its built-in sense of comfort everlasting. Wealth, affluence, comfort. She thought, Money, power, might. Everything. She missed the old Big House with its great spiral staircase, front and back, and large glittering chandeliers that hung from ceilings so high she sometimes imagined them to be stars twinkling way up in the sky like diamonds. The chandeliers had been shipped all the way from France by special order more than a hundred years ago. Sometimes she used to stand in awe of their size and beauty. She imagined that one day they would come crashing down upon somebody, maybe herself. When she was a little girl she used to use the stairway banisters for a sliding board. She would straddle them at the top as if she were riding a horse and then come sailing on her backside around the great curve and down to the first floor, which never failed to terrify and mortify her mother, on those rare occasions when her mother was herself.

"You're going to break your silly neck, and besides it's so unladylike!"

When she grew out of sliding down banisters, she graduated to running up and down the stairs. She almost never walked up or down the stairs like anybody else would do, even till the last day in the old Big House. It was almost a year now since they moved into the new one. Everything here was low-ceilinged and all on one floor, a twenty-three-room one-story ranch-type house sprawling all over the countryside, with a swimming pool and tennis court. Yet she still sneaked off and went swimming in the river sometimes.

The first big shindig in the new house was her "Sweet Sixteen" party, to which all the "young adults" of the first families of the county were invited and a few from nearby counties. Parents fought for and politicked for invitations for their children. It was the social event of the year. The Wakefield house was buzzing with activity for weeks in preparation for the great affair. Even Anne Wakefield came back to life at intervals during the preparations. In looking back, the party itself seemed hardly worth all the fuss and bother. A real live dance band, but most of the boys were pretty terrible dancers, much more awkward than the girls. The punch was ever so slightly spiked. But the breaths of some of the boys seemed very highly spiked. She learned that

[132]

some of them had brought with them small flasks of whiskey, "the real stuff," in their pockets, which was why they made so many trips back and forth to the bathroom marked "Him." Afterward empty bottles were found. The pretty dresses, the boys—some of them still pimply-faced—in tails and tux, some of them ill-fitting. The music, the dancing—from waltzing and the two-step clear across to rock 'n' roll, the Twist, the Slop, the Watusi. On the slow numbers when they danced cheek-to-cheek, some of the boys would slowly let their hands slide down the girls' backs to their backsides accidentally on purpose, and let their hands rest there tentatively.

Rogers Johnson the Third made it clear to one and all that he had eyes for Carrie Louise. He was nineteen and more mature than most of the boys. He was a Junior at Ole Miss. He was tall and danced well and was unexcitingly handsome. He looked very much like his mother, who was still a pretty woman. But when they danced and Carrie Louise looked up into his face, somehow she saw his father's countenance leering down at her. The party moved out of the house, out around the swimming pool. She stood near the pool with Rogers the Third. She looked around her at the other young adults.

"The young folk who come to your party will be the leaders of the county and the state tomorrow. Some of them will be leaders of industry, some will even go to Washington to Congress." Her father had told her this on the night before the party.

Rogers the Third would probably be a leader of industry, she thought, and maybe even go to Congress, just as his father had before him. He was the best male catch at the party, and most of the girls seemed to gravitate toward him, but he had eyes for Carrie Louise, who was, after all, the greatest catch of the county, maybe even in the state.

He took her by the hand. He said, "Let's go get some more punch."

She said, "Why not?" And why not? He was handsome and it was a party and she was having a good time. She felt lighthearted and carefree. She thought she even wished he had sneaked and offered her a drink from his flask, which she was sure he had brought with him, since he was such a sophisticated college man of the world. It was her party and these were her people, the leaders of tomorrow and all that, gallant gentlemen to the core. They got their punch, and he said, "Let's go somewhere where

[133]

it's quiet. Let's go into your father's library. I want to see what kind of books you read."

"Why not?" Why not indeed?

They opened the door to the library, and she switched on the lights. And she heard a gasp of surprise—"What!" And they looked and saw a juxtaposition of white dress and black trousers and a quick flash of disappearing bare white thighs and a quicker flash of the boy's penis as he jumped off the girl and put his sex back in his trousers. Carrie Louise's face flushed and she felt warm all over, and her hand went out as if it had a mind all its own and switched the light off again. She could hear them scrambling in the dark, as she and Rogers backed out of the room. Her mouth felt dry and her breathing was labored. Rogers led her to this very room in which she now sat with her father. He went for a drink and brought one back to her. And they drank, and as they started back out of the den, he turned off the lights. But he did not leave the den. Instead he tried to take her into his arms and she let him. Why not? And his mouth found hers and his tongue sought out her tongue, and his hand found her backside and squeezed the cheeks of her backside, bringing her thighs close up against his thighs. Her legs were trembling now, as she felt him hard against her. Then he took her hand and put it in between his legs and up against his hardening sex, and she held it momentarily as if she didn't know what it was. Then the image of the scramblers in the library flashed before her once again and she pulled away from Rogers the Third, and his face was now unmistakably the face of Rogers Junior Congressman and industrial leader. And she slapped his face, and opened the door and ran down the hall toward the back of the house.

Her father broke into her train of thought. "The whole world is one holy mess."

She had been staring at the TV, but had seen nothing till that very moment. Now as she watched, most of the late news had to do with strife and turmoil. War in Vietnam and the Congo. Demonstrations throughout Dixie, even in old Mississippi. They watched black kids sit-in at a two-bit lunch counter in Jackson. She saw them walk toward the lunchroom with a mob of white and loyal, righteously indignant Mississippians screaming at them at the top of their lungs, barking at their heels. Nice, everyday, churchgoing, God-fearing, Bible-belt white folks screaming vileness at these nine quiet-faced teen-agers, seven of them black and scared, but brave and proud. The other two were white, a boy and a girl. White and frightened and courageous. Carrie Louise felt a funny sickly feeling in the bottom of her stomach. Almost against her will she found herself identifying with the beauty of the sit-inners and feeling something very close to revulsion at the ugliness of the righteously indignant God-fearing Mississippians. The camera cut to them inside the lunchroom, seated at the counter. The TV gave a close-up of a black boy with a soft face and eyes that were dark and quiet. But she could see the trouble in them. The manager came up to them and ordered the sit-in students out, but they quietly refused. A white man came from the other end of the counter and picked up a bottle of catsup and poured it on the black boy's head. Her daddy cleared his throat long and loud and nervously. He got up and poured himself another drink.

Carrie Louise knew she would never forget the TV shot that focused tightly on the black boy and the white man. The quiet nervous resolute dignity in the black face and the sneering scowl on the white one. She felt her eyes filling up, but somehow she refused to cry.

She remembered another scene, months before, also on the late news. Little black children on their way to school amidst a mob of jeering howling white folk. Had it been somewhere in Louisiana? The glowing beauty in the children's faces. Five- and six- and seven-year-olds. The fear in their eyes. Eyes that also held a deep, dark quietness of purpose, as if they possessed a secret known to them and only them, with the exception, perhaps, of God on High. Certainly He was on their side. Compare their faces, O Lord, with those of the howlers yapping at their heels. Especially the distorted faces of the white women. She'd felt that motherhood had been despoiled. She'd felt a deep shame for these women turned suddenly into snarling beasts, into children eaters. White—Southern—Womanhood. She'd felt ashamed on all three counts. Shame for their whiteness, shame for their Southernness, deep shame for their total loss of womanhood.

She turned now to her father. "How can you be a friend of Jefferson Johnson, Daddy? I mean, how can you possibly? I mean, you were at the meeting tonight. You saw him in action—He—he—he—I mean, just how can you, Daddy?"

He looked at this lovely young woman who was his daughter and who was his life, and now she sat there in judgment of him. Children were the most intolerant people in all the world. He thought, everything is black and white to them, with no shades in between. No grays, no nothing. Everything is right or wrong, good or bad. In a way, he wished she would forever remain just as she was this moment, giving no quarter to compromise and especially to subtlety, which he fully recognized to be a euphemism for hypocrisy. He went and put his arms around her shoulders.

"The beautiful part about our relationship, honey, Rogers' and mine, is that we can disagree wholeheartedly on principle and still remain friends. By the way, that's also a lesson in true democracy. To disagree on principle, yet recognize the essential goodness and worth of the other fellow." He listened to himself and heard the lame voice of hypocrisy.

Suddenly his arm felt heavy on her shoulders. And insincere. She got up and switched the television to another station. She said, "The principle must not have been very strong or wholehearted in the first place."

All at once he felt exhausted. It had been a long day. "The things that bring me and Jeff together and hold us together go way, way back. Very, very strong."

"Stronger than any principle ever was," she countered bitterly. "You have so very much in common. Both of you're rich and white and Anglo-Saxon and Southern."

He heaved a deep sigh and blew the weariness out of him as he sank back deeply into the upholstered chair with the pillow of goose feathers, and his weariness came down on him once again. "Darling, it's been one of the nicest most delightful evenings, most relaxing I've spent in a long, long time. Let's not spoil it with an argument at the end of it."

She went and kissed him on the cheek. "It has been a lovely night, Daddy. It really truly has been lovely."

He said, thankfully and absentmindedly, "Din-Din-Din—" and then remembered. He got up from his chair and switched the TV to another channel. "I knew there was something I'd forgotten, something I especially wanted to see. It's half over already."

And they watched in silence the last twenty-five minutes of the movie, *Gunga Din*. He had seen the movie over a dozen times, but it never failed to move him, especially the scene in which

[136]

good old faithful Gunga blew the bugle for the British against his own people.

After the movie ended, he went to the library and got Kipling's *Barracks Ballads,* and read "Gunga Din" aloud to Carrie Louise.

> *With all 'is dirty 'ide*
> *'E was white, clear white, inside*
> *When 'e went to tend the wounded*
> *Under fire . . . .*

She was surprised to see her daddy's eyes fill up, as he wiped them on the sly and blew his nose. This big strong tough man of whom everybody in the county lived in awe, even and including Congressman Rogers Johnson. She couldn't understand it. Somehow she rebelled against it.

He was oblivious to her reaction. "Magnificent!" he said softly, and shook his head in admiration. "Simply magnificent! Din was a man of true nobility. Kipling knew. Yes indeed, Kipling knew. By God! How he knew! Gunga Din! What nobility of character!" He calmed down again, embarrassed temporarily by his own enthusiasm. Then—"What nobility of character! Loyalty—integrity—nobility! That's what I keep telling these ignorant peckerwoods. From Jeff Johnson down to the lowliest one of them. Treat the blacks like human beings and you got nothing at all to worry about. Kipling knew. That is the profound message Kipling left for us and it'll withstand the great erosion of the ages. Look at Din. Look at Gunga Din. No racial hostility—no rancor—man with a black skin and a white heart. Din! Din! Din! Gunga Din!"

She did not often contradict her father. This had been, as he said, a lovely night, an unusually lovely and relaxing night. She remembered driving through the noisy yet restful night and the things they talked about and the good feeling and the way she lost herself completely as she nestled against him as he drove madly through the jungle of a Mississippi moonlight. But then she also remembered the television which had given her a brand-new vision somehow, a vision she had had already, but which had been submerged in the subterranean areas of her consciousness until this night, when she saw those everlasting images on the television in her own and only Mississippi. The teenagers and the howling mob, the black boy and the white man at the counter.

[137]

He said, "There's never been another character like Gunga Din. He was the really pure in heart."

She said matter-of-factly, "He was a rat-fink, pure and simple."

He was startled. "What's a rat-fink? Who's a rat-fink? What in the devil do you mean?"

"He went against his own people. He was a fink—a traitor—an Uncle Tom."

"I—I—I don't follow you," he stammered.

She said, "What would you think of him if he were white and had blown the bugle against the British on behalf of the Hindus?"

Her daddy said, "But my baby, you missed the point entirely."

She said, "My daddy, if you don't see that he's a rat-fink, it's you who missed the point, it's you who just don't know what's happening."

He stared at her as if she were a stranger to him, his little daughter, grown beyond his recognition. Rat-fink indeed! Where in God's name did she learn such language? It was that last summer she spent with her aunt in New York City. It was—it was—it was the curse of television. He walked over to the giant-sized TV and turned it off violently.

She loved him so, she died a thousand times for him. She went to him and kissed him, her bewildered father, on the mouth and then the girl went off to bed. "I love you, Daddy." And she loved him, really loved him, more than any person in the world. She loved him, loved him, really loved him. And it was Din, Din, Din, Gunga Din!

Chapter

10

Chuck and Bessie Mae and Jake and Cora Mae and Carrie Louise-of-the-manor-house and all the boys and girls in Mississippi, all the boys and girls throughout the entire world, were growing older by the minute, the hour, the day, by the month, the year; all the boys and girls grew desperately toward the man and womanhood which some would never reach. It was a time of quiet, sometimes not-so-quiet, sometimes even violent, desperation. The highways down which they traveled toward their future lives were rutty, dark, and dimly lit. There were wars and rumors of wars just as the Bible had predicted all over the unhappy planet wherever men were civilized. In all the school books, in all the other books he had read, the history of men and women had been the history of men launching little wars, big wars, riots, battles, skirmishes. Since man could remember, it had been like this, with only a few rare moments of peace and quiet in the precious intermissions. Children's crusades, Christian crusades, hundred-year wars, civil wars, world wars, police actions, and all those glorious wars of liberation. The whole history of civilization was written in relationship to wars, or so it seemed to Charles Othello Chaney. Man was ever in the midst of war or digging himself out of the ruins of the aftermath or moving joyously toward the next one with flags waving and bands playing. It was war, postwar, or antebellum.

In this sixteenth year of his earth sojourn he did an inordinate amount of thinking and worrying about the Army and the Bomb and the wars throughout the world. His brother, Jesse Junior, was very often on his mind. He read his letters from Korea over and over again and again.

"War is a terrible thing, Mama," his brother had written in that far-off time from that faraway country. "To shoot a man down, to shoot men and kill them, men you have nothing against, to shoot them down like you were hunting possums, to murder people by the tens of thousands, war is a terrible business for a man to work at."

Chuck sat there rereading Junior's letters for the umpteenth time. It was about nine o'clock in the cool cool of the evening, and his mother and father were watching television. His father had finally broken down and bought one, but not until he had put enough aside to pay cash for it. He didn't believe in the installment plan.

Chuck looked up from one of his brother's letters. "What was he like, Mama Carrie? Who did Junior look like?"

There was a wistful glow of sadness in his mother's face. "I done told you a hundred times—you his spitting image. He was tall and lanky just like you is. He had such a soft face and the

[139]

sweetest disposition. Just like the Holy Bible say, Junior was black but he was comely."

The father looked away from the television, momentarily. "He was black *and* comely," he corrected, proudly. "Ain't no *buts* about it."

"He was black *and* comely," the mother said mischievously, "just like his black and comely daddy."

Chuck remembered his brother in vague outlines of conjured-up experiences. More accurately, he remembered what people had told him of Junior, of happenings and incidents. It was impossible to know what he actually remembered. "What was he like, Mama? I don't mean what he looked like." He confused his actual memory with the now established Junior legend.

"You remember Junior," she told him. "He was just like you in so many ways. He had a good head on his shoulder especially for books. He was nice-nasty as the days was long. He was pretty. Ain't no need of saying he wasn't. He couldn't kill a roach if it crawled underneath his shoe. And over there killing human folks." She was smiling but he saw now that her eyes were filling up. "It's been such a long long time, but it seems like only yesterday, and I still can't bring myself to b'lieve that he ain't never coming home again. Poor little Junior—couldn't kill a roach if he was 'neath his shoe. Way over yonder killing human folks. Folks he ain't had nothing against and ain't had nothing against him." She was weeping now, softly weeping.

Suddenly she laughed bittersweetly. "I declare that boy almost had me b'lieving in haints and spirits. 'Member when that old mangy dog came hanging round here? I told myself that he was Junior come back in another skin to tell me something. I used to go out in the yard and talk to that old devilish hound, but he wouldn't pay me no mind at all. I used feed him better than I did my own young'uns. Then one day the dang fool up and kicked the bucket." She laughed and laughed. She wiped her weary teary eyes.

The boy felt guilty about the whole thing now. The Devil had made him ask about his brother and open up the wound of his mother's magnificent sorrow and for the umpteenth time. Chuck tried to patch things up with: "He had to fight for his country, Mama Carrie. Junior was fighting for the free world and for democracy against the Communist threat. He was a hero, Mama Carrie."

[140]

She got up from her chair and began to walk the floor—back and forth and back and forth. Her body swayed from side to side in a kind of strange and beautiful and terrible rhythm as if she listened to a distant drummer. In spite of all of the years that had passed, the memories of Junior washed over her now like a new unlived experience. She stopped in her walking back and forth and looked up at the ceiling. It was something like a séance, as if she were listening now to other times and voices. She heard Junior clearly now, coming in from school, even heard his special footsteps, saw him sitting at the supper table. The room rang loudly with his laughter. Then she looked around her and started to walk again. She had lost him. Might as well face up to it. He was dead all these years and she must accept it. He was in Jesus's hands, and she didn't understand, could never ever understand it, but God's will had to be done. She must accept the fact that she would never see him again, except in the next world which every man inherited, one way or the other.

She sat down in the chair again. And she said quietly, "He's gone, Jesus. My poor baby's gone. Junior's gone," as if her son had just departed life, as if she had just come from his funeral. Then she began to weep and moan aloud. Her heart overflowed with her great loss and she cried and cried and cried. The boy came and put his arms around his mother. The father looked at them both, and his eyes condemned the boy, asking him why in the hell had he done this to his mother. The boy could hear his father's condemnation yet unspoken.

The more he hugged his mother the more the storm of her great sorrow broke over the dam of her resistance. He said, "I'm sorry, Mama. I'm sure 'nuff sorry I brought Junior up." It was true. He had resurrected Junior. "Please, don't cry no more, Mama Carrie!" If he uttered another word, his own floodgates would break loose and run amok.

Jesse Chaney said, his deep voice gone husky: "Ain't no needa you carrying on like that, Carrie. Ain't no need atall." He came and put his strong arms around both of them.

She stopped crying and sucked the tears back up her nostrils and swallowed the terrible sorrow down through her bosom and deep into her belly. She looked up at Jesse and then at Chuck Othello. She said quietly, "Before I see another one of my babies killed in another one of these white folks' wars, I'd take a gun and blow your brains out my own self. I swear to my sweet Jesus!"

"Don't talk like that, Mama Carrie!" He had never heard such bitterness pouring from his mother. It scared him half to death.

The father said, "Be shame of yourself, Carrie baby. You just a little upset right long in here. Just a little bit upset right long in here. You'll be all right directly." He was massaging her shoulders now with his tough and tender strength. "You'll be all right directly. You'll be all right directly." Like the refrain of some forgotten hymn.

Yes, he was reaching toward his manhood now, and he had seen many things on television. For the last few years, and sometimes even after his father put the antenna atop their own house, he had sat next door, out of habit (as he explained it to himself), sat in the sweet cool of the evening and held hands with Cora Mae on the sly and watched the world burning and borning, tearing down and building up, exploding and uniting. He'd seen men whirling through space like crazy.

The first time they held hands so slyly and so shyly had been the evening they watched a fellow black 'Sippian walk through a jeering mob at Jackson to attend Ole Miss, that nostalgic giant-of-the-gridiron and keeper-of-the-Holy-Grail-of-White-Benevolence. They usually sat (Cora Mae and Chuck Othello) in the dark part of the room, that part which the dim lamp near the TV barely reached. They watched their fellow 'Sippians give a glorious demonstration of traditional Southern hospitality. As cheers of angry welcome from the white-faced mob grew louder and louder, Cora Mae's hand went out to him and their fingers staged a silent wrestling match. He sensed her entire body quaking with deep feelings, and he knew her eyes were filling up. It had not been the first time he had witnessed the "tomboy" of Wakefield County change suddenly into an out-and-out cry baby.

Early one morning quite some time before this time, one September morning, he had been milking Missy, when the tomboy vaulted the fence and ran toward him like the law was chasing her, and grabbed hold of him. He thought she wanted to wrestle like she usually did. And he was not in the wrestling mood. She had wakened him from one of his daydreams. He had been staring down the dim highways of his life's future. In his mind's ear he heard that old song over and over.

Look down
Look down
That lonesome road
Before you travel down.

His road was long and lonesome with an awesome white fog that always hung down upon it like a great smoke screen that was always and forever there, and if you were black you could easily lose your way, which was why the fog was there, in the first place.

There were questions that continually demanded answers. Where are you going, Charles Othello Chaney? And how? When? What? Why?

She said, "Come! Come! I want you to see it! I want you to see it! I want you to see it on television! They're fighting for us! They're fighting for us!!"

Chuck looked up into the tomboy's face and saw the first tears he had ever seen her shed, and they were flowing down her cheeks like rainfall. He ran with her and they both leaped over the fence. And they stood side by side in the front room of the Rakestraws and they both cried that morning, two big overgrown cry babies cried for joy as they watched the soldiers, black and white, in Army trucks with guns mounted, in jeeps with rifles at the ready, serious-faced soldier boys rolling endlessly into Little Rock to protect the right of eight black children to a first-class education. They cried and wept for joy upon this great occasion.

Her mother and father were already at work knee-deep in Mr. Wakefield's cotton. Cora Mae didn't know that Chuck was crying also. She was so ashamed of her own self, great big girl like her, crying like a newborn baby, she could have gone straight through the floor. She turned to Chuck and laid her head upon his chest.

"I'm not crying," she said. "I'm not crying. I'm really laughing. I'm so happy!" She sucked the tears back up her nostrils. "Them soldier boys just look so pretty to me this morning."

"Yes!" he said. He didn't trust himself to speak further. He himself was so filled up.

She was talking through her tears. Little overgrown black girl-child. "Look at 'em! Look at 'em, they still coming. Look at their faces! Black and white ones! In them pretty soldier suits! I ain't never felt good in my heart about the Uniney States Army till this very morning. But I'm with them all the way this morning, 'cause they come to pertect them poor little black children. They

[143]

pertecting me this morning! And I love the whole Uniney States this morning like I ain't never did before!" Her voice choked off.

When she found her voice again, she said softly, "Don't that spangled banner look pretty! Look at it waving from that truck! Look at it flapping in the morning breeze!"

Her voice choked off again, and she started to say, "I'm not crying—" but she looked up into his face and saw that tears were spilling from his eyes, and she knew he understood.

Chuck understood, because he felt the same way she felt at that moment, because he had felt the same denial. He had always had that same feeling toward his flag that a loveless stepchild has toward his stepparent, overflowing with love but getting no love in return. At his school they celebrated all the patriotic holidays. They celebrated the Fourth of July (Independence Day), and did not have to go to school, which did not make him happy, because he loved school and hated holidays. They celebrated Washington's Birthday and all the others, excepting old Abe Lincoln, understandably. Chuck tried terribly hard, but no matter how beautiful the Washington Day program was, no matter how pretty the story about the cherry tree, he had trouble with the image of honest George as his father of all fathers. He tried hard, sometimes he almost cried he tried so hard, to feel what he imagined the other kids felt, or at least, the white kids in their white schools. But he just somehow could never make it. He thought that maybe the Devil had something to do with it. He thought that maybe he had too much of the Devil or the evil spirit in him. But he doubted it. When he thought of flag and government and patriotism, he wanted a chill to run up and down his spine, but he usually conjured up his brother Jesse Junior's face as he imagined him somewhere far off in Korea, in the cold frozen reaches of Korea. Red snow and a purple heart. And he felt as he imagined Cinderella must have felt. Only there were no fairy godmothers for black children. There were no black fairies, no black fairy tales. Even when they stood in school and swore allegiance, he felt the same ambivalence. He was loyal to his country, he wanted desperately to feel loyal, but what he wanted to feel, but could not, was that his country was loyal to him. And loveless love grows sour, makes the heart cold and the stomach sick.

That historic "Little Rock" morning was the first time they kissed each other. The big tomboy cry baby stood there boohooing joyously in his arms, and he didn't know what to do about it. He just tried to keep himself from crying. He thought that men should never cry.

"I'm not crying," she repeated over and over. "I'm not crying. I'm just so glad and I'm so happy."

He said, "Who said you were crying?"

Which seemed to turn the silly girl's faucet on more than ever, as she rained tears onto his shirt. He didn't know what to do about it. He said, in his toughest and his tenderest voice, "Now come on. Stop that!" And he said, "There now!" Softly and tenderly. And he wiped her eyes with his hand. He had no handkerchief. And finally he kissed her lightly on the cheek, innocently. And she came alive and started to smother him with kisses. He held on to her more tightly than before, aware of his manhood now, and he tried to kiss her back, kiss for kiss, but she kissed him too hurriedly, too fiercely, too desperately, all over his mouth and the rest of his face. The poor child slobbered shamelessly as if she had starved for kissing all her life and a feast had been placed before her. He wanted to savor the taste of her kisses, but all he tasted was mucus from her running nose. He hung on in a kind of desperation. But he had been only twelve years old, and had not known what to do about it.

It had been in Chuck's sixteenth year that Uncle Bish got religion. He had tried just about everything else. It was at a Wednesday evening prayer meeting at the Mount Moriah Baptist Church. Reverend Clarence Purdy was the pastor. People called him "Purty Purdy" or "Pretty Purdy," depending upon how many days they stayed in school before the cotton patch snatched them out of school forever. Reverend Purdy preached on Sunday, worked weekdays in the cotton fields, when he felt like it, ran a combination barber shop and shoe shop, owned a few acres himself, where he grew a little cotton and corn and snap beans and a few strawberries. And yet his people did not look upon him as a jackleg preacher.

It was a funny thing how he seemed to change his way of living, after that young Mississippi writer from New York City came to town. It was as if Reverend Purdy had a hidden fountain in him filling up, up, up, and nearly brimming over, and David Woodson had turned the spigot on. Some folks said: "Reverend Purdy been born again!"

Almost every sermon he preached thereafter had something worked into it about freedom or justice or civil rights. And he preached straight out of the Bible. Reverend Purdy was an old-fashioned country-style preacher.

Sisters and brothers came from far and wide and deep deep in the sticks to hear him. His sound effects were tremendously dynamic and entirely dramatic. He walked up and down and neighed sometimes like an excited stallion. He wheezed as if he had asthma, as if he were breathing his last breath. He could outsing anybody in his choir. And sometimes he mixed his singing with his sermon. It didn't make any difference. He was preaching the word, singing or talking or shouting. One day, when he was much younger, he preached so hard and the sisters and brothers shouted so loud, a pair of buggy horses broke away from a post they were tied to outside the church, and took off madly down the highway. He had the reputation of being the preachingest Negro in Wakefield County, and there were some preaching Negroes in the county. Anybody would tell you. When he mixed up Luther King with Moses it was a sight to behold and a thing to listen to. His church was always packed. Even a few white folks came, and sat in the back—over to the side. Chuck had seen Carrie Louise over there a time or two.

The day Bish Carson got religion and joined the church was Independence Day.

He told his family all week long that Wednesday prayer meeting would be on Independence Day and he was going to get his independence. He was going to free himself from sin. "Maybe it'll change my luck."

Little Jake, who was just about a grown man now, said, "Shee-itt!" underneath his breath.

Miss Sallie Belle said, "Man, if you went to church you'd probably knock at the door. It's been so long since you seen the inside a church, it would snow in Mississippi on the fourth day of July."

He shook his drunken head and said, "Ne'er mind, baby darling. You'll see me there come Wednesday night."

Nobody believed him, but come Wednesday, Independence Day, and there he sat at the Wednesday night prayer meeting. Usually Reverend Purdy didn't do much preaching at prayer meetings. It was mostly singing and praying. But this time he did it differently. This was Independence Day. He preached a solid hour and took his text, not from the Good Book, but from old Frederick Douglass. After he gave the hymn in common meter:

> *Amazing grace*
> *How sweet the sound*

After the humming of the last verse died away, he stood up in the pulpit, walked dramatically toward the rostrum, and opened up a big black book and said:

"I take my text this evening from the book of *Negro Orators and Their Orations* from the words of Frederick Douglass. Page one hundred and seventy-five."

He paused. David Woodson had sent him the book, *Negro Orators and Their Orations*, collected by Carter G. Woodson. And Purdy already had read it three times from cover to cover.

Most good folk in the congregation wore shocked and puzzled faces. Some of them cupped their ears with their hands and strained to hear their pastor better. Some waved their paper fans before their faces. It must have been a question of mishearing. His texts had always come right out of the Holy Book. There sure wasn't any book of the Bible by the name of Frederick Douglass.

"What does your Fourth of July mean to me, a slave?" Reverend Purdy asked rhetorically.

"Ask the question, Purdy!" Brother Jimson shouted. "Ask the Man the question!" Anywhere Reverend Purdy got his text was all right with Brother Jimson.

"What does your Fourth of July mean to me, a black American?" Reverend Purdy rephrased the question ever so slightly.

"G'wan, Purdy! G'wan Purdy!" one elderly sister raised her hand and waved her handkerchief back and forth at him.

"Why did you invite me here to speak to you on this occasion?"

"Why!" Brother Jimson shouted. "Tell us why, Reverend Purdy! Tell us why!" Everybody said of Brother Jimson that he always started shouting before the preacher got warmed up good. He always ran way out ahead of everything and everybody, even ahead of Reverend Purdy. And that took a bit of sprinting. And that could also be disconcerting.

"Thus spaketh the great Fred Douglass," Reverend Purdy continued.

Brother Jimson said, "Lord knows that's what Fred Douglass spaketh." Brother Jimson had picked cotton all his born days, ever since he could remember.

[147]

Purdy was a square-shouldered coal-black man of middle age and medium height. His head was entirely without hair except around the edges. His was a large and round and handsome head, which shone as if he used shoe polish on it—regularly. He was a man who looked good in his clothes. A gold tooth glistened from his mouth. He exuded power. He might have been a fullback had he made his way to college. By the very grace of God he had made it through the seventh grade in the Louisiana swampland. By the grace of God and his own determination, he had made it out of the swamplands all the way to Wakefield County, Mississippi. He was a self-educated man with all the strength implied and all the limitations. Some said Clarence Purdy picked cotton and preached his way all the way from the Louisiana bayous to Vicksburg, then to Wakefield County, stump-preaching in every little country byway and picking cotton in every patch, doing both jobs to keep body and soul together.

When Purdy first started preaching in Wakefield County, Bish used to say about the preacher: "Talking about he was working in the cornfield and he looked up in the sky and saw God's handwriting—G-P-C. Telling him to *Go Preach Christ*. And he threw down his plow and picked up the Bible. *Go Preach Christ,* some stew beef! God was telling him to Go Pick Cotton!"

"And then Brother Douglass preached his sermon."

"Tell us, Purdy, tell us! Don't hold nothing back!"

"It was on the fifth day of July in 1852, way up yonder in Rochester, New York." He shook his head from side to side and drew a deep breath. "That's a long long ways from here, almost all the way to Canada. Some of y'all ain't even been to Jackson or Yazoo City. Scared Old Massa won't like it and won't give you some more crumbs from off his table. But Douglass went, and ahh Lord, he was born a slave. But he went and spoke to them white people way up yonder and he told them 'bout themselves."

Purdy paused and laughed sarcastically. "Yes, he was born a slave, but aah Lord, he whipped his great big white whipping boss and escaped to freedom, and fought till his dying day for the freedom of his people. He told those Rochester peckerwoods where to get off, and you here living in this mordren age and talking all your big talk and this and that and scared to join the NAACP. Well, you a lie and the truth ain't in you."

The congregation laughed now a kind of bitter masochistic laughter. Some patted their feet, some said Amen.

The Reverend Purdy carried on like this for almost an hour. He would read directly from Douglass's speech and then give his own interpretation and then preach at his congregation.

"Fred Douglass died a free man—yes he did—and you ain't free yet—naw you ain't—'cause your soul ain't free and your heart ain't free and your mind ain't free."

"Preach freedom, Reverend Purdy!" another lady shouted from near where Chuck was sitting. She was elderly and wrinkled and her hair was completely white, what there was left of it. "Preach it! Preach it!" Then she mumbled to herself, "Lord have mercy I never thought I'd live to see 'em preach freedom from the pulpit!" She laughed to herself. She shouted aloud, "Thank you, Jesus! Preach freedom, Purdy! Preach it!" She began to pat her feet in a kind of chaotic rhythm. And she wiped her eyes now with a handkerchief. "I'm so happy! I'm so happy, Jesus!"

"The white folks done enslaved you and messed your head up so bad you run around here talking 'bout 'I like them high-yaller women with blow hair.' Talking *down* everything that's black, talking *up* everything that's white."

"G'wan, Purdy! G'wan, Purdy!"

"Talking 'bout 'good hair' and 'bad hair.' If your mind was free and wasn't so messed up, you'd know that God A'mighty made all kinds of hair for human folkses. He didn't make no good hair."

"No he didn't!" Brother Jimson shouted.

"He didn't make no bad hair!"

"God ain't never made no bad hair!" Jimson shouted.

"All the hair God A'mighty make is good. The only thing you got to worry about is when you git like me and ain't got no kinda hair at all."

The congregation broke up with laughter, as Purdy rubbed his handsome shiny dome.

"Douglass told them crackers up in Rochester that the Fourth of July was the celebration of a great big fat lie, as far as black mens and womens was concerned."

Then as if someone had disputed Reverend Purdy's word, or some unseen unheard spirit had denied the fact, Purdy said, "Yes he did. And he was talking to good crackers, friendly crackers, supposed to be friendly. But he didn't care. Friend or foe, it didn't make him no never mind. He believed the truth would

[149]

set you free—everybody free. White, black, red, yaller. The truth ain't got no color."

He paused. "But you scared of the truth. You been lying so long, you been living so many lies, backbiting and backsliding, and bearing false witness and coveting and stealing, and fornicating, you wouldn't know the truth if it walked up to you and said Good Morning. You here every time the church door open and jumping up and down and shouting and carrying on. But the Good Lord want to know—is you your brother's keeper? Douglass was his brother's keeper. Tubman was her brother's keeper. Great God A'mighty, old Nat Turner was his brother's keeper. Y'all better git your house in order 'cause the train might be here this very night, and everybody talking 'bout Heaven ain't going there."

Pretty Purdy was walking back and forth across the pulpit and sweating now, beautifully sweating. He wiped his beaming forehead with a large white handkerchief. "Douglass and Tubman and Turner was they brother's keeper. Yes they was. When they theyselfs got free, they didn't stop fighting like you woulda done. They dedicated they lives to the freedom of they black brothers and sisters!"

"Tell it like it *i–s is*, Preacher!"

"Yes they did, and the Bible say, If you say you love the Lord who you ain't never seen and you don't love your brother who you see every day, you are a liar, and the truth ain't in you!" He paused and wiped his face again.

"Running around here talking about it's a free country and talking about you a citizen, and yet you scared to go down to the courthouse and register to vote. Well, you a lie and the truth ain't in you.

"Talking about you tryna make a better life for your childrens and yet you scared to do a little old thing like register to vote. You a lie and the truth ain't in you!"

"Preach it, Purdy!"

"Preach it, darling!"

"Tell the truth and spite the Devil!"

Purdy said, "God don't love liars. Naw He don't!"

"Naw He don't! He sure Lord don't."

Purdy said, "Lying is ugly."

"Yes it's ugly!" the old lady shouted.

"And God don't love ugly," Purdy told them, almost quietly.

[150]

"Naw He don't!"

"Lord knows He don't!"

"And when you don't vote," Purdy said, "you cheating your childrens and your children's childrens. And cheating is ugly and God A'mighty sure don't love ugly."

"Yes! Yes!"

"Amen! Amen! Amen!"

He started to sing, softly at first.

> *The little black train is coming*
> *You better git all your business right*

The choir picked it up and finally the congregation. He had a big voice, big and grand and melodious. And he loved to sing.

> *You better git your house in order*
> *'Cause the train might be here tonight.*

They sang four verses and some of the brothers and sisters were openly crying and shouting now, weeping for the hope and shame and joy he had inspired in them. The old lady near Chuck felt so good, she started to fling her arms up and down.

"Are you ready for the little black train?" Reverend Purdy asked.

"Yes!" they shouted. "Yes, I'm ready!"

"Yes, we ready!"

"Are you ready for the freedom train? That's the train I'm talking about this evening."

"Yes, I'm ready for that freedom train," the old lady shouted. "I'm ready for that freedom train! I'm ready for that freedom train!" She was flinging her arms up and down wildly now, and Chuck was scared that she would hurt herself. At the same time he felt his own eyes filling up. The man on the other side of her said, "Help me try to hold her, son."

And Chuck took one arm and the man took the other, but she had gotten strength from some secret source, because she almost flung Chuck down beneath the benches. He was strong as two oxen, but it was all he could do to keep hold of just one little old arm of this withered-up old lady, while the man on the other side had a devil of a time with the other arm, as she flung both arms up and down, up and down, with a certain definite rhythm now.

And "Yes! Purdy, Yes! Preach freedom, sweetheart! Preach it, darling! Let the train be here tonight! I'm ready for it! Ready! Ready! Ready! Ready!"

Reverend Purdy sat down in the big chair behind the lectern and wiped his face again with his large white handkerchief. Brother Sam Jenkins, the ice-cream-parlor man, led the congregation in a lengthy prayer for freedom. When he was finished, Reverend Purdy rose again and started singing. Everybody joined in the song which was an invitation to the sinners, to the sheep who had strayed from the fold. The doors of the church were thrown open. They sang:

> *Whosoever will,*
> *Let him come.*
> *Let him come.*
> *Whosoever will,*
> *Let him come.*

About ten sinners, most of them children, came slowly, shyly, down the aisles to join the church and be saved and their sinful souls converted. And finally Uncle Bish Carson came, and people wept all over the church. He came quietly down the aisle, his red eyes flooding with tears, crying unashamedly. He had sworn that he would this night come sober to the Lord, and he had laid off the bottle all day long, but at the last moment he had taken just one little old nip, just to get his nerve up to make this great historic trip to Jesus, and one nip had led to another, as it always did with Uncle Bish. And now he almost flowed up to the mourners' bench. But he held his head up high and he flowed with dignity. He sat on the bench with the other sinners who were being saved, and then they all knelt at the altar. And when the ritual was over, he tried to get up as the others did, but he was so drunk he couldn't make it.

His face flushed with great embarrassment, and his breath almost knocked the preacher down, as he helped him to his feet.

Bish mumbled his apologies. "I reckin I got the spirit in me just a little bit too much tonight. I must be overcome with that good old spirit."

The good shepherd, Purdy, softly smiled and agreed with his lost sheep who had at long last found his way, although it was still a shaky and a rocky one. Shepherd Purdy said ironically, "You sure got the spirit in you tonight, Brother Carson. Lord in Heaven knows you got the spirit."

[152]

For two whole months afterward Uncle Bish didn't take a drop to drink. Every day he went out in search of work, with little or no success, but he went limping every day. He was a changed man. Anybody would tell he was, including himself. He had religion. He had been born again. He was converted. Even his luck changed—finally. He got a little job as a night watchman in a warehouse in Wakefield City. He held his head high and began to put on weight and started to favor somebody. His limp was barely noticeable. They didn't give him a pistol in his watchman job for some reason or other. They just gave him a big stick with which to guard the premises. He walked around the yard with his flashlight dipping into corners, and he felt damn good about it. But most of the night he sat in his little cubbyhole at the warehouse and read the Bible and studied for the ministry. He wanted to be ordained. He didn't care if he never became the pastor of a church. He just wanted to be ordained and preach just one time in the Good Lord's temple. He wanted to be a witness for Jesus who had saved his sorry soul from hell's fire and damnation. Purdy gave him much encouragement. Sometimes he would come by the warehouse and help Bish with his Bible lessons.

His ordination was set for the middle of September, not long after Big Meeting time. Every late afternoon, a couple of hours before he went to work, he would come by the Chaneys to get Chuck to help him with his sermon.

Chuck tried to beg off at first. "But, Uncle Bish, I don't know nothing about preaching no sermon. And anyhow, it supposed to be in your own words from your own mouth."

"That's all right about that," Uncle Bish argued. "It can be from my mouth and from my heart but from your brain. You know I don't know enough to preach that first sermon. I'm subject to get up there and start cussing and carrying on. You want me to keep my feets on the straight and narrow, doncha?"

"Of course I do, Uncle Bish. You know I do."

"Look at my eyes. You want them to stay like that now, doncha? Or may you don't care no more about your Uncle Bish."

You're not really my uncle, Chuck thought. But he looked into the man's eyes. And it was true. Bish's eyes were as clear and as innocent as the eyes of a newborn babe. Yet Chuck had a feeling he was being had and he resented it, but—

Bish said, "You your brother's keeper, ain'tcha?"

Chuck said, "All right, Uncle Bish. I'll do what I can—"

[153]

Each late afternoon they worked on the speech together, which actually meant that Chuck did all the work and Bish did all the talking, mostly off the subject. But he wanted to take his text from the Book of Job. He wanted to talk about Job's trials and tribulations. "Put some big words in there for me, Chuck Othello. I know you got 'em in that head of yourns and I want 'em in my sermon."

"How come you want big words, Uncle Bish?"

" 'Cause I'm a big nigger, that's how come." He laughed slyly at Chuck. He knew Chuck did not like to hear the word. Yet he used the word deliberately, teasingly. "You just put some big words in my sermon for this ignant nigger to say so they'll think I'm smart."

Chuck said, "Uncle Bish! If you going to keep saying nigger this and nigger that all the time, you can just forget about my helping you write the sermon."

Bish looked at Chuck in all solemnity. "If you write me a good jim-dandy sermon, with some great big words and everything, I promise you, I swear to the Good Lord up on High, I'll never say nigger again the longest day I'm on this earth."

Chuck had a feeling, ever increasing, that he was being had, but Uncle Bish was an irresistible force.

One Wednesday evening, Mama Carrie and Jesse went to the Willing Workers Club meeting at the church. It met early before the regular seven-thirty prayer meeting. They left the house right after supper and left Bish and Chuck working on Bish's ordination sermon. When Bish left for the warehouse, Chuck came out and sat on his back porch, and when he looked around him, he saw the long-legged short-skirted tomboy sitting, careless, on her porch. She was staring straight at him, and their eyes met and he felt his face grow warm, and he tried his darndest to outstare her, but he finally looked away.

"I hope you know me the next time you see me, Mister Chaney." She was the freshest sassiest girl in Wakefield County. Chuck Chaney bristled. She really knew how to get next to him.

He said, "Beg pardon?" Nervously.

She said, "Don't be begging my pardner. What you looking at me so hard, you little mannish puppy? What you tryna do? Tree me? You don't look like no hound dog, and I sure God ain't no robin redbreast."

[154]

He said, "I was not staring at you. I wasn't paying you no mind at all."

The sun was bedding down out over the river and splashing the horizon with all kinds of crazy pinkish-bluish-reddish colors.

She said, "How come you so stuck-up and hankty? How come you ain't neighborly like Reverend Purdy says we're s'posed to be?"

Chuck said heatedly, "I don't know what the devil you talking about." She knew how to rub him the wrong way and with hardly any effort at all.

She said, "Why don't you come on over here sometime and sit a spell? That's what I'm talking about. The sunset just as pretty from my back porch as it is from yourns. It sure ain' nobody over here gon bite you. I ain' that hongry and you sure God don't look that delicious."

He sat in silence for a moment, mumbling angrily to himself. She could really bug him, when she set her mind to it. He got up and came slowly across the yard and jumped the fence and came up on her porch and sat within arm's length of the sassy girl and stared eastward across the rolling fields of corn and cotton toward a great conflagration which the sun was building on the surface of the river. The sun always seemed to be setting the river on fire or sinking forever into its gentle waters as if sucked in by some mighty hidden whirlpool.

She broke into his thoughts with: "If you just come over here to sit and think thoughts to yourself, I sure hate that about you. You coulda stayed at home. You must be think you cute or something." She stopped and waited. But when he would not be baited by her, she followed up with: "Ain' nothing cute but babies and monkeys, and you too big to be a baby."

His streak of meanness got the best of him. He said, "How come you wear your hair so short? You ain't no boy." He had stabbed her with a deadly weapon, and he knew it. And immediately he felt terrible for having done it.

She said, "You better b'lieve I ain' no boy. If you think I am, just try me—one time. I'm more woman than you'll ever be a man."

He said cussedly, "How come you don't wear it long and straighten it like most girls do?" His face had broken out into a cool damp sweat.

" 'Cause if the Good Lord hadda wanted me to have white

folks' hair He woulda given it to me. That's the trouble with colored folks. All of them tryna be white." Her voice choked off, and now he heard a tremor in her voice. "I thought you was different, but you just like the rest of them. Yesterday I was walking downtown near the courthouse, and I saw some little biddy children going somewhere and big ones too, and all of them started laughing at me. I mean colored children." He would not look at her but he knew somehow her large wide eyes were filled with tears. "They said, 'Look at that ugly African tomboy.' And all of 'em laughed at me." She was sobbing now. "It didn't make me feel bad," she lied, "but I felt so sorry for all those poor ignorant colored people. Little biddy children. But I expected different from you. I don't know how come, but I——"

He said, "Cora Mae—" He felt awful, something terrible. He said, "Cora Mae, I—" All inside of him was like he had swallowed razor blades—and double-edged ones at that.

She said, "Get offa my porch and go home, you color-struck bastard. You just like the rest of them." She ran into the house through the kitchen to the front room. Her folks were at prayer meeting. He followed her. He felt mean and hateful, as if he had betrayed his mother and his father and the entire colored race.

She turned on him. "Get outa my house. What you following me 'round for? You don't like girls with kinky hair. You like girls with 'good' hair. Good hair—good hair—good hair! You like yaller gals!"

He said stupidly, in anguish, "My hair is kinky too. Ain't no such thing as bad hair. All hair's good hair." He ran his hand over his head of short-cropped hair. His face, his shoulders, warm with enormous guilt, great big hard knots in his belly now.

Tears streamed down her burnished-brown face. "You think I'm just an ugly tomboy too!"

"I think you're pretty, Cora Mae. I think you're really beautiful!" Her tearstained eyes were wide and warm and soulful. He had not known she had such warm eyes till now. They were brown-on-brown and so sensitive and so full of hurt now. Her face was the color of dark-brown half-burned toast.

"Naw you don't, Chuck. Naw you don't! You a lie and the truth ain't in you!"

As tall as she was, she looked so much like a little girl now, a lonely scared little baby girl, who was lost and looking for her parents. There was a terrible beauty about her look of loss and helplessness, which lit a fire of great compassion in him. He reached out and took her into his arms. She tried to wrest herself from him at first.

"Naw you don't! Naw you don't! I don't need you to feel sorry for me. Damn your hinkty soul!" But despite her great strength, he held her steadfast in his arms, and finally she leaned her head against his chest and cried and cried and cried, until his shirt became wet with her tears.

He massaged her shoulders, he ran his fingers through her hair. She said, "You don't like me! You don't like me!"

"Yes I do!" he said softly. "Yes I do—I do! I do!" He was warm all over now and not from the evening's heat. His body knew a heat that was altogether different, and he felt his vaunted manhood growing steadily against her. It embarrassed him at first, because he knew she must have felt it too. His proud assertive manhood. But she had long since ceased to struggle in his arms. They kissed, and, at first, she was in sole charge, as she had been a time before, when he was young. As before she smothered him with her hungry kisses all over his face. She was never actually in charge. She ran way out ahead of herself even. But ultimately he caught her mouth with his mouth and held it and stilled hers for a moment, and made her know he was behind the wheel. He was the driver.

She dissolved then and there in his clumsy tender arms, and her knees buckled and she went down to the floor, and he went with her. And they made a pure and desperate kind of love with each other right there on the floor beside the fireplace, as the moonlight spilled upon them through the window. And a big cat watched them from a corner. Cora Mae and Chuck made love together.

Awkward love.

Painful love.

Tender love.

Chuck wrote Uncle Bish's entire speech in longhand. Afternoon by afternoon they worked. Finally the great night was upon them. Bish got an old buddy of his to pinch-hit for him at the warehouse. When Bish came by the house that night to pick up his speech, he was as sharp as a pitchfork, duded down from

[157]

head to feet, and he walked so straight and upright, Chuck's daddy got suspicious. He was so sharp and steady he was hardly limping. He could have walked a chalk line all the way to Jackson City.

Chuck's father eyed him with suspicion. "You all right, ain'cha, Bish? You ain't got the spirit, is you?"

Bish drew himself up with enormous dignity. "Not the kind you talking about." But you could hardly understand him. The wad of gum in his mouth was so large, it was a wonder it didn't choke him to death.

Chuck himself got angry with his father for insinuating that Uncle Bish had fallen off the wagon on this night of all nights. He felt himself to be a part of this big night, not unlike the opening night of a play, and he was the author and Uncle Bish was the star performer. His daddy should have had more feeling for Bish than to kid around with him on such a night as this, as if a man could not be born again. Chuck was dead certain Uncle Bish had not fallen off the wagon, but Chuck was curious about the big wad of gum in Uncle Bish's mouth. And when Chuck gave him the sermon, and Uncle Bish put his arms around his shoulders and thanked him, Chuck did get a whiff of something sweet and sharp on Uncle Bish's breath and it was not exactly chewing gum. But, well, it must have been. He was letting his father's prejudices affect his own high opinion of this reformed pious person who was the man of the hour. Daddy was jealous of Uncle Bish. Yet and still, there was this faint and sweet aroma.

The church was almost jam-packed. Chuck had had no idea that their "debut" would be such a smashing success. Wow! Great God from Tallahassee! He sat on the front seat. And he was as nervous as he imagined Reverend Bish (he meant Uncle Bish) was. He really meant Reverend Carson. It was hard to think of him as anybody but Uncle Bish. He'd been Uncle Bish so long. And Reverend Bish didn't look nervous at all, as he sat there calmly in the pulpit smiling piously, as if he would take wing any moment and fly away to Heaven. He was sharp as a machete. He was so sharp it was a wonder he didn't cut himself. It was a wonder he wasn't bleeding like a hog in killing-time. Uncle Bish was a Bish and a half, a cow and a calf. He had on a brown suit that was pressed pretty and creased to kill. He crossed his legs like important people have a way of doing and pulled up his trousers nonchalantly, and as far up his legs as you could see you saw nothing but Miss Sallie Belle's best pair of nylon stockings. It was then that Chuck saw that the Reverend was wearing sneakers. Nylon stockings and brand-new sneakers!

The ordination ceremony went off smoothly. And then there was another song and a prayer, and then Bish was introduced to give his ordination sermon. Chuck went bug-eyed as he watched Uncle Bish take the big wad of gum out of his mouth and stick it under the rostrum chair. But then the very recent Reverend Carson walked up to the pulpit and gave out his text and then he started preaching pretty for the people. It was a good sermon, even if Chuck did say so his own self. Chuck followed the Reverend from sentence to sentence and paragraph to painful, eloquent paragraph. He heard the sisters and brothers Amening their agreement. Sometimes Chuck caught himself softly repeating the sermon along with Reverend Carson. He knew it all by heart. The brand-new preacher compared Job's trials and tribulations to the trials and tribulations of those black and noble sons of Ham who dwelt right here now on this earth in the land of Mississippi. But Job had faith and we must have faith. And Job had confidence and Ham's children must have confidence. And Job had patience. "God is testing us black peoples." He went on and on and on, tying things up one with the other. And he had the church slightly rocking. Rock, church, rock! And Bish began to rock and sway. His mistake was when he came around to the side of the lectern and started to lean upon it and began to wave his arms as he had seen Reverend Purdy do so many times.

First of all, he lost his place on the paper Chuck had written for him, and he never did find it and so he was strictly on his own thenceforth and forevermore. The more he didn't know what he was talking about, the more he began to wave his arms and rant and rave about absolutely nothing. His wife, Sallie Belle, knew what had happened and laughter started to bubble out of her in spasms and she could not help herself from laughing. He was sweating now and carrying on, and finally he located one of the really big words he had insisted Chuck include, and he tried to pronounce it once, he tried to pronounce it twice, and he tried to pronounce it thrice. On the fourth go-round, he wound up like he was Satchel Paige and he flung the big word mispronounced out at the startled congregation, threw the great word with such momentum that he fell out of the pulpit. Miss

Sallie Belle fell out on the floor in laughter uncontrollable. Chuck and Little Jake sprang from their seats and ran toward the altar over which Uncle Bish was draped as if unconscious. People gasped and shouted. Others sprang to the boys' assistance.

But suddenly the Reverend straightened up and brushed them away and brushed himself off and climbed over the altar railing and put his head up in the air and strutted with a great and limping dignity up the aisle and out of the church. And never did come back again. Some said Bish walked straighter than he ever did even before the accident.

Some said, when they spoke of the memorable night and of the Reverend Carson's fall from grace: "That Bish was a preaching fool!"

A few weeks later, Bish explained his downfall to his mentor.

"Chuck Othello, you know doggone well God ain't call me to preach no Gospel. That's how come He knocked me outa the pulpit. God knowed I ain't had no business preaching. But I always wanted to be a preacher every since I was knee-high to a hoppergrass. Cause womenfolks do love preachers, and I sure do love womenfolks. The Good Lord knows I do. When I was a boy, I used to want to be one of them kinda country preachers that made the womenfolks beat the benches, come up to the altar and fall out and kick up they heels. Great God A'mighty! Most preachers say the Good Lord called them, but ain't nobody called me but the pure-dee Devil." He laughed and laughed. But he could not hide his deep disappointment from his mentor, Chuck Othello.

He never forgave Sallie Belle for laughing at him, even though she got down on her knees and begged forgiveness. And sometimes he said he would have made it in spite of the Devil, if Chuck hadn't put such big words in his sermon. "Chuck Othello, you ought to be ashamed of yourself, tricking your Uncle Bish like that. God don't love ugly."

It just wasn't Uncle Bish's night that night. It was the one night in the year that the bossman came around to the warehouse and found Bish's pinch-hitting buddy fast asleep.

And on the following night, Uncle Bish reenlisted in the army of the unemployed. Notwithstanding, it was not a voluntary reenlistment.

[160]

Chapter
11

It seemed, of late, that every time the doors of the Mount Moriah Baptist Church opened, Carrie Louise Mariah Wakefield was seated in the back, over on the side. Some folk wondered if she'd bought herself a private pew. She would sit there sometimes as if she were possessed, shaking her head and patting her feet and swaying from side to side like she had Soul and true black folk's religion. To some black folks it was a most peculiar sight. At the end of the services, some of them would walk over to her and shake her hand and try their best to make her welcome.

Others scowled. "Why in the devil don't she go to her own church?"

Little Jake said, " 'Cause they ain't no Soul in them white churches. She looking for something."

Old lady Boswell said, "Humph! Aah Lord! She looking for something, all right. And if she don't mind she sure gon find it soon enough."

Bessie Mae's reaction was: "What would happen if one of our menfolks put their black feet inside of Wakefield First Baptist?"

Every time one of the good members of Mount Moriah would come up to Carrie Louise and give her his or her right hand, she always had to fight hard to keep her eyes from filling. When she went to her own church and sat there and heard them sing their stiff and sterile songs and talk their talk, she tried very very hard, but she never could feel anything. She just felt a great big emptiness inside. An intellectual and emotional emptiness. She gave generously to the collection plates at Reverend Purdy's Mount Moriah.

Old lady Boswell said, "She tryna buy her way into the Kingdom."

But most of the members didn't mind her frequent visits. They either ignored her or they welcomed her. And even Bessie Mae Moocho did not organize any opposition to her. Nobody threw

Carrie Louise down the steps like they did black folks who tried to worship in white churches. Bessie Mae just grumbled. She had always felt deep inside of her that the old rich yaller-haired white gal had eyes for Chuck Othello Chaney. She didn't even remember when she first began to suspect it. But then, when it came to Chuck Chaney, she suspected everyone who wore a dress and was under forty-five or fifty. She admitted to herself she was a jealous woman when it came to Chuck Othello.

Somebody wrote Charlie Wakefield that his daughter had joined the "Nigger Baptist Church." He laughed it off, ignored it. But then he got a few more letters and a couple of phone calls. He talked with her after supper one night in his study in the new house.

She drank Scotch and soda now, so he poured both of them a drink.

She sat back in one of his leather chairs. It was comfortable but cold. Like Daddy is sometimes, she thought. And yet she dearly loved her daddy. Sometimes, here of late, she called him "Charlie," with all its Negro connotations. Sometimes when she was angry and felt soulful, he was "Mister Charlie" to her. And he knew the Negro "Charlie" connotations, and it always made him angry for her to put him in this category.

She said, "All right, Mister Charlie, like what's happening?" She'd spent two summers in New York. She was *hip*. Or at least she thought she was. And she was in one of her anti-Daddy moods.

He pretended to ignore her flippancy. "Baby, where're you going to school next fall?"

"I already told you, Mister Charlie. I'm going to Wexler College way up north in New York City, just a stone's throw from Soul City. I mean Harlem, U.S.A. I'll be there, at Wexler, I mean, while the great school celebrates its diamond anniversary. And wouldn't that be loverly?"

"How about Radcliffe? I'd prefer—I mean I've had five or six of them investigated. I'd prefer Radcliffe or Vassar. I mean——"

She said, "Oh, so you have your own private bureau of investigation. Well, my dear father, I will go to Wexler College, or I will not go to college. Period. Exclamation point, for emphasis." She poured herself another drink. He thought, not quite eighteen, and she pours herself another drink in front of her father and

[162]

without a by-your-leave or an if-you-please. Times sure had changed—in Wakefield Manor, even.

She had grown into such a beautiful young woman. He hated these fights he had with her lately. "All right, my dear, we will discuss it some other time. There's no big hurry."

She said, "I disagree. We might as well discuss it now. It's later than you think, Charlie my boy. Like you always said, the world is changing, time is passing. And they're rioting in Africa."

He changed the subject. "How is your Wednesday Night Bridge Club, sweetheart?"

She said, "D-U-L-L spells dull, and that's the word they invented for the Wednesday Night Bridge Club." She sounded slightly tipsy.

He changed the subject again, apparently. "What's this I hear about you joining the Mount Moriah Baptist Church?" He laughed to let her know that he knew it was one enormous joke, too ludicrous to take seriously.

She said, "So you also have your bureau of investigation spying on me here in Wakefield. Well, let me tell you something. There's nothing happening in our dear old tradition-ridden lily-white Wakefield First Baptist. And the only reason I wouldn't join Mount Moriah is they probably wouldn't have me. I mean why would they take a pale-faced fink like me unless they just felt sorry for me. I mean Afro-Americans are a forgiving non-vindictive people, but there is a limit."

He went to her and put his arms around her. He said, "Darling, I don't understand. I mean you're speaking a different almost foreign language to me tonight. I mean what in the devil's happened between us?"

She had never seen her father like this before, almost stammering. He had always been self-confidence personified. He'd never needed to be arrogant. He'd always been too self-confident to be arrogant, to brag or boast. She felt like she had lost something with him, something she would never find again. And it was all her fault. Her stomach felt as if she not eaten for days and days. She moved away from him, shaking her head now.

"Daddy," she said, "Daddy! Everything I am you made me. Everything I know you taught me."

"I don't know you!" he shouted. "I don't know you! You're my own beloved little girl, and I don't know you anymore." He was almost whispering to himself now. "What's happened to us? We—we—we—"

She said, "We've grown up. That's what's happened to us."

He said, "I don't understand."

She said, "Daddy, when I was in New York last summer, I heard a man speak, a beautiful black man named David Woodson, and he said the Bible Belt lived, slept, and ate Christianity more than any other place in the whole wide world, they read the Bible morning, noon and night, and yet he said the same Bible Belt was the most racist-minded, the cruelest, the most ignorant, the most inhuman and God-awful place in the whole United States. And he was talking about the people—not the place. You understand, my daddy? And that included Wakefield County, that included Mississippi. The Bible Belt—the Bible Belt—the pious, gospel-preaching, Holy-Rolling, everloving Bible Belt—"

He seemed to only hear "beautiful black man." He kept mumbling to himself, "beautiful black man—beautiful black man" like a broken record.

"Mister David Woodson said the only place in the Black Belt where Jesus could be found was in the black churches in the black hearts of black people. That's what he said, Daddy, and my own white heart cried out and I knew he spoke the truth. He was my black Jesus. And he, himself, was born in Oculmugee, Mississippi."

She poured herself another drink. "He was my beautiful black Jesus, and he taught me love again as I remembered love to be somewhere way back yonder when I was young and gay and believed in love."

Her father said, "You say this to me? You loved a nigger?" He seized her by the shoulders. "You loved a nigger?" He was shaking her unknowingly.

She moved away from him again. "You got it all wrong, Daddy. We didn't sleep together. He doesn't know me. I didn't even get to shake his hand. But he stirred my soul. He stirred my soul, not my clitoris."

He slapped her face. It was as if his hand acted of its own volition.

"Oh no, it wasn't like that at all, although I was given to understand while in New York that quite a bit of hanky-panky goes on down in the cotton patch, where Old Master always exercises his God-given prerogatives. I mean high yallers do not drop like the gentle rain from Heaven. But you never explained these kind of things to me."

He stared at the nervous, sure-of-herself, beautiful, yellow-haired, blue-eyed, long-legged, bosomy stranger. He should have taken her in hand long ago. But she had always been able to out-talk him, and it was all his fault, whatever she had come to—whatever. Anne Wakefield always told him, "She's going to make you cry one of these days. That very girl's going to break your heart. You just wait and see."

"Oh, I'll get New York out of me soon enough. Just give me two or three weeks with the young ladies of the Wednesday Night Bridge Club, and you wouldn't be able to distinguish your li'l ol' angel-pie from any one or the other of those sweet little deli-cate souls." She mimicked the most delicious of Southern accents. People in New York immediately recognized her Southern accent, but some folk in Wakefield County thought she talked with an up-the-country brogue. Putting on Northern airs.

He said, "I must have had too much to drink. I just don't seem to understand." Life was becoming much too much. It ran right out from under you. It was getting too damn complicated. And he was getting old. He didn't want to get old while his girl was still so young. And beautiful.

"You always taught me that the world was changing and we had to change or be swept aside by history. Well it's already here, my daddy, in our time. And I want to live it. I want to live it, and I want you to live it too."

He said, "We'll talk about it some other time, sugar. I'm tired —I—your daddy's very very tired. I——"

She said, "I'm going to Wexler, Daddy. And there is no more Gunga Din. Gunga Din is dead, Daddy! There is no more Gunga Din, and I doubt if there ever was one, except in your imagina-tion, Rudyard Kipling notwithstanding."

"I'm very sorry, sweetheart," he said, "but your dad is very very tired this evening. So very tired. I just don't know, I need a rest. Possibly I need a vacation."

He sank down in a leather chair, and he looked old far far beyond his actual age. He had always been a young man to her. It was a shock for her to see him look so old, and even old-fashioned now, which was the worst aspect of it all. His eyes were old. Suddenly his face was wrinkled. She was filled with great compassion for him. She went to her daddy and put her arms around him. "I love you very much, Daddy! I love you very very much! I love no one in the world but you!"

He mumbled something incoherently.

That fall she went to Wexler College on the outskirts of Soul City. It was all right, because Wakefield's sister lived in Manhattan and would surely keep an eye on her favorite niece. True, his sister was one of those way-out artists. True, she had almost lost her Southern accent. In a way, Carrie Louise felt closer to her aunt than she did to her own mother. Her aunt was fabulous, flamboyant, called to Carrie Louise's mind the image of Rosalind Russell's "Auntie Mame."

Charlie Wakefield knew his sister was "way-out." But she would see to it that Carrie Louise didn't travel too far down the road to Nigger Heaven. His sister had not been that long out of dear old Mississippi.

Chuck was just eighteen now and getting mighty close to graduation time. In another month he would really be a high school graduate. Such as it was at Booker High. He would graduate—then what? One thing was clear. There was no money for college. Another thing was clear to Chuck that might not have been quite as clear to his mother and his father. Come September he was not going to stand knee-deep in Old Man Wakefield's cotton. That was for damn sure.

About a week before graduation in the hot dog-days of August, Mr. Wakefield sent for him. He went wondering what the Old Man wanted with him. If he wanted to talk to him about working on the plantation, he might as well forget it. He had not gone to school through twelve long hot summers to become an educated cotton picker. That was one sure thing. No kind of sweet talk from Mr. Wakefield could make him change his mind. It had been made up long ago. There were no words in Wakefield's vocabulary to convince Chuck he should live out the rest of his life picking cotton. He was not going to begin—in the first place. As soon as school closed he was going to leave Wakefield County even if he had to walk every step of the way to wherever he was going.

Now he stood before the big man like a soldier standing at attention. Wakefield was seated behind his desk with a cigar in his mouth. He stood up and shook the boy's hand warmly. Like

[166]

man to man, like equals. And he sat down again with a broad smile on his face. It was almost a grin.

"You're sure your papa's young 'un," he said.

"You sent for me, sir?" Chuck said, with a nervous kind of dignity.

"Boy, I remember the very day you were born. Yes indeed I do! A few days right after I came back from the war in Europe." The man laughed warmly at the memory of it.

The boy stood tall and straight and silent. Serious-faced. What was the big deal?

"Take the load off your feet," the man said. "Sit down. Relax."

Chuck sat down and waited. He did not relax.

"You graduate this month, don't you, boy?"

"I graduate this month, yes sir," Chuck answered. Now it was coming.

"What're your plans?"

"I have no particular plans, sir." Except that I plan not to work on your plantation. It was getting warm in Wakefield's air-conditioned office.

"Your daddy and me have been friends since we were knee-high to a mosquito," Wakefield said warmly. "You're like one of the family to me. Like a nephew."

White folk were the everlasting most, Chuck thought. All of this beating around the bush just to get him to the cotton patch. He decided to play it close to the vest. He just sat there saying nothing.

"I've had plans for you since the day you were born," Wakefield said.

I'll bet you have plans for me all right.

"I've had my eye on you all along."

I'll bet you have. I just bet you had your eyes on me.

He seemed not to notice the boy's lack of response. Maybe he simply thought it best to ignore it. "Yes indeed, and I know how well you did in school." He paused as if he had run out of steam. Momentarily. "And I got plans for you."

He stared at Chuck till Chuck felt the heat collect in his collar. "Well, what do you say?"

"Say about what, sir?" He had an idea that the man was playing cat-and-mouse with him, and he had a good idea who was supposed to play the role of mouse. And he didn't feel like being Mickey Mouse today. Or any day.

Wakefield picked up some papers from his desk and dropped them onto the desk again. "I've made all the arrangements for your college education. I made them for you the day you were born."

Chuck was speechless now, and not by design. He did not really know how he felt about the great and sudden revelation. Images went on a rampage in his mind, colliding with one another. Images of Chuck Othello Chaney leaving Wakefield County for a college campus; images that conjured up old dreams he had not dared to dream and yet had dreamed somehow deep in the place where dreams had a way of spawning themselves, notwithstanding the realities.

Wakefield saw himself as a warm and generous-hearted human being, and he relished his role of Great White Father more than any other of his roles. He was a man who played many and varied roles. But he knew that if there was one Christian truth that would withstand time's great bent for obsolescence, it was the one that said it was more blessed to give than to receive, and especially if you gave to the poor downtrodden colored people. He looked at the speechless boy and he imagined the profound emotions of humility and gratitude the poor boy must be experiencing at the moment, experiencing so deeply there were no words to express them. Relax, my boy, relax!

"Well, what do you say, boy?" Wakefield asked him, smiling understandingly.

Chuck felt like crying out for joy; at the same time he knew that dignity dictated that he keep his feelings under wraps. There was this other feeling of ambivalence, an uneasiness lurking somewhere in the far reaches of his consciousness and flashing danger signals. What're you getting out of it, Mr. Wakefield?

"I don't know what to say, sir."

"Well, please don't say, 'thank you, sir.' Because it is not necessary. The world is changing, son, and Wakefield County has to change along with the rest, and it'll be up to young folk like you to see that things change in the right direction when the time comes. All I ask is that you do your best at the University and come back and serve your people. When the trouble begins there'll be rabble-rousers a dime a dozen, and your people are gonna need young, clear, educated heads like yours to guide them. That's all I ask. Go prepare for leadership. That'll be reward enough for me."

[168]

Something deep in Chuck told him to look the gorgeous gift horse in the mouth and down his throat and even up his hinder parts. But he consciously stifled all misgivings and accepted Mr. Charles James Richard Wakefield at face value. The man was generous and sincere and farsighted. Racial prejudice could be double-edged, Chuck Chaney told himself. And he wasn't going to let it blind him to the goodness in some white men. Wakefield was a good white man. There were good and bad in both the races.

He got to his feet. He wanted to leave the Great Man's presence now. He would get the details later. He wanted to be gone, to get out into the open so that he could give vent to his feelings. He wanted to tell his mother and his father. To go all the way out to the Bottom and tell Little Jake and Bessie Mae Moocho. Tell Cora Mae and Miss Ida Lee. Shout it from the hilltop and from the river banks. He wanted to laugh and cry and jump up and down and act like he was eighteen, because he was only eighteen. But he played it cool.

Wakefield got to his feet and put his hand out toward the boy and seized the boy's limp hand in a warm handshake. "You'd better get yourself together—get your things ready. This is August the twenty-third and the University opens the second week in September. I'll work out the details with your daddy."

All the boy could say was, "Thank you, sir."

Three weeks later he went to Douglass University in a city in a neighboring Southern state.

PART TWO

PART TWO

Chapter

1

Everything about the University campus frightened him at first. Life was lived at such a swifter pace, it seemed to him that every living soul ran everywhere he went. His first impression was that everybody, students and teachers, dashed madly about from class to class, from place to place, across the campus, to the dining hall, to the Students Union, to the gymnasium, to the dormitories. Everything was one mad dash headlong into—Where in the hell was everybody going and in such a great big hurry? Suddenly Chuck felt old-fashioned and awkward and slow, with two left feet, big and ugly, and stumbling about and getting into everybody's way. It was a feeling he had never experienced before.

His second impression, equally disquieting, was that everybody talked a different language from his, with quick and very proper accents. They used words with such great ease, words he'd never known before except in library books, words he had never ever heard spoken by real live human beings. White Southern accents, it seemed, emanating from black mouths. Northern accents, Western accents. Foreign accents from African and Asian students.

And the way the students dressed was not to be believed! Some of the boys were very very proper and expensive dressers, with skinny neckties (he couldn't get over those skinny neckties) and skimpy continental and Ivy League suits. He had secretly laughed at them at first, until he realized that they were in the latest style. Others went to the other extreme with sweat shirts and dirty sneakers and long hair and long and unkempt whiskers. And there he was, caught in between the two extremes. Suddenly, in his own eyes, he stood out like a bump on a log, his clothes ill-fitting and countrified. He had always prided himself on being from the city. Wasn't Wakefield City the largest city in the county? Yes. Wasn't it the county seat? Yes! Didn't real honest-to-goodness country people come to his city every Saturday to city-shop and see the sights? Hell yes! Didn't Wakefield have great tall buildings? Skyscrapers?

Well—after he boarded the bus on the seventh day of his first week at the University and took a trip downtown and walked around the downtown section of the city, he thought that at last he knew what a really big city was like. And he had to admit that he was just a country boy. That first day downtown, he got an eyeful of the city. He also got a sore neck gawking up at the tall skyscraping buildings, fifteen and twenty stories high, reaching up into the clouds. He bumped into other pedestrians.

"You better look where you going, boy."

"You can git em out the country!"

He walked in and out of the big department stores. With moving stairways! Escalators! It was too much! It was just too much! It was enough to take your breath away. And automobiles! All sizes and denominations! He saw more cars that day in downtown Johnsonville than there were in the whole of Wakefield County and Dawson County combined. He never knew so many cars existed.

The crowning insult of all was when his roommate nicknamed him "Lil Abner." Affectionately, of course. His roommate was from New York City. The whole thing boiled down to one word. The people at the University were sophisticated. And he, Charles Othello Chaney, was unsophisticated. After the third week, he was ready to go back home. And forget it. "Lil Abner!"

And the teachers were different. Man! The teachers were entirely different! Different and impersonal. They couldn't care less, or so it seemed to Chuck Othello. It was confusing to him. While the teachers were distant and aloof and impersonal, at the same time some of them were very informal and chummy with some of the students, especially after classes.

And the girls paid him no mind at all. As bashful as he always was, at home he had always been one great big continuous hit with the girls. He couldn't help it. But here, on the University campus, they didn't even notice him. And when they did look at him, they laughed at him inside of themselves, or so the self-styled country bumpkin imagined. The girls were different and more stylish than he'd ever known that girls could be. They were bolder and sassier than girls should ever be, according to his rustic standards. Bold and fast with strong opinions of their own.

[174]

And like the boys, they dressed from one extreme to the other. Some dressed in the latest style, but others dressed in sweat shirts and dungarees and sneakers, when they were outside the class-rooms. But sneakers or high-heeled shoes, they were the prettiest girls he had ever imagined. And they didn't pay him any rabbit-assed mind.

It was a Saturday in the middle of October of his first semester. He had been at the University for almost a month. His room-mate, Ronnie Gilbert, had tried to get him to go to the football game which was being played on campus, but he had not felt like going. He had not felt like doing anything but moping around and feeling lonesome and sorry for himself and homesick and wallowing sublimely in his homesickness. He lay on his bed and stared at the ceiling and thought about home and about his mother and his father and the old cow, Missy Anne. He thought of the girl next door and thought of the girl out in the Bottom. His mind even made a picture of the crazy girl who lived in the Big House but who had gone to college up-the-country in New York City. They all liked him. There was no doubt about it. They liked him very much, even if the girls on the campus paid him no rabbit-assed mind. He longed to be away from this place, this campus, this glittering city, and back to his home town, back to Wakefield County, where life was real, and people were honest-to-goodness, whatever they were that's what they were. But the big city where the University was, was as phony as a nine-dollar bill in Confederate money during Reconstruction. And he was weary of it. He longed for the country roads, the sweet aroma of the flowers in bloom. The strong sweet smell of pine and cedar. He longed for the noises of the backwoods country, the rooster crowing in the early morn. The racket that the crickets kept up in the evening, the honking of the frogs, the chirping of the birds, the pure clean air, the wide openness of everything. He lay on his back on his bed and wallowed in the sickish sweetness of his great profound nostalgia. He was going home. Everything about these last four weeks was phony. The college was phony, the teachers were phony, the campus was phony, the fellows phony, and most of all, the girls were phony.

His mind made a vivid image of the house he had grown up in, and it was all prettied up now in technicolor stereovision. His father and mother and the girl next door. How beautiful his home was. He saw his home town now in a different light, all aglow in its unpretentious beauty. He missed Bessie Mae and Little Jake. He missed everything and everybody. He thought, you never miss the water till the well runs dry. Even the shacks in Johnson's Bottom were not ugly now. They were picturesque. And down by the riverside, his river, with the weeping willows kneeling at the water's edge, with the Spanish moss like shawls thrown around the willows' shoulders. And where could you see sunsets like the ones in Wakefield County? A great big bursting brilliant disk of fire and brimstone sitting down upon the river, slowly sinking like a ship at sea.

He felt his nostalgia deep deep in the depths of his belly, felt it deep down in his bowels, tasted his dearly beloved homesickness in his mouth and throat and through his nostrils. He got up and got his rags together, which was how he thought of his clothing. He had once pictured them as "glad rags." But now he knew that they were very very sad. He was going home. The big two-faced city was not for Charles Othello.

By the time Ronnie came back from the game, Chuck was packed and ready. "What the fuck you think you're doing?" Ronnie asked him. Ronnie was of medium height and broad-shouldered. He looked just like a college fullback. He had a big round handsome head, a heavy head of deliberately unkempt hair. At the moment, his large face was framed by a terrible black beard. He went through all kinds of changes, somewhat like the weather and the seasons of the year. Some kids on campus called him "Castro." Chuck was a head taller than his roomie, but Ronnie was ten pounds heavier.

"I don't think I'm doing anything," Chuck answered heatedly. "I know exactly what I'm doing."

"Let's start all over again then, baby. Now, exactly like what in the fuck do you know you're doing?"

"I'm putting this phony place behind me. That's what I know I'm doing."

"Shee-itt!" Ronnie sneered. "So Lil Abner is going back to pick Ole Massa's cotton for him. You one of his good hard-working niggers. You're going back so he can sincerely work your crazy ass off! Ain't that a bitch!"

Almost effortlessly, Ronnie had punctured the balloon of Chuck's divine nostalgia, which did not make Chuck feel any better toward the glib New Yorker. "You wouldn't understand," he said to Ronnie, with an unfelt condescension.

"I understand all right, Lil Abner. You're homesick, aren't you, baby? You got that old nostalgic feeling, hunh?"

"Yes, that's it. I'm really homesick."

Ronnie said, "Like you miss Whitey's old mule farting sweetly in your stupid face." He took a whiskey bottle from his topcoat pocket. "I know what you need, old baby!" He put his arm around Chuck's shoulder. "Baby needs the boppie. Daddy's going to give the baby the boppie." Ronnie's whiskeyed breath almost knocked Chuck over. Chuck pulled away.

"I don't have time for none of this shit! I'm going home!"

Ronnie sat down heavily on the side of his bed. "I know what the trouble is with you. You need the boppie and some poontang. Ain't nothing wrong with you that a little pussy wouldn't straighten out. Am I right or wrong?"

"You can do me one great big favor," Chuck said, "and mind your own damn business."

"I thought you Mississippi spooks were into something. I thought you cats had testicles. Shee-itt! You sitting up here look-ing like two knots on a dog's dick talking about you homesick for Missy-goddamn-sippi! You had one little taste of homesickness and you ready to split the scene. Ready to run back home to Mama. Shee-itt! Home wasn't all that great, and you know it. Wakefield County, Mississippi! I doubt if it's even on the map. Ain't that a goddamn shame! I guess you just can't wait to get back and pick that cotton, or maybe you one of Ole Massa's house niggers, hunh?"

Chuck sat down on the side of his bed. Ronnie was absolutely right. He didn't have a damn thing to go back to. Go back to picking cotton? "Shee-itt!" he heard himself say slowly. And he thought his eyes had begun to fill, out of sheer frustration of it all. Maybe he *was* one of Ole Massa's house niggers! And he started to laugh and he couldn't stop laughing. Maybe that's why Ole Massa sent him off to college. Shee-itt! Ain't this a goddamn shame! Going home to what? He stopped laughing and he thought to himself: What you going back home for? Going home to Missy Anne? And he could see the soulful face of the cow before him. Missy Anne! Missy Anne! And he began to laugh again, and he laughed and laughed and laughed.

Ronnie handed him the bottle and he took one long swallow and the whiskey seemed to set his insides on fire and came back through his throat and nostrils and almost strangled him to death. Ronnie pounded him on the back and gave him a glass of water.

"Goddamn, baby!" he told Lil Abner. "You're a real greedy boy. I sure hope you aren't that greedy about the pretty little pussy cats around this place. You sure won't last long if you are. You're either all or nothing at all, aren't you, baby?"

It was not that he didn't do well in his studies. He would always do well scholastically in almost any situation. It was just that he had to work much harder to keep his head above water. Back at Booker High, book learning came much easier for him. He made his A's with very little effort. But here in this place, he realized how sadly his education had been neglected. Sometimes a teacher would discuss things with the expressed understanding that: "You had all of this in high school. I just want to see how much you have retained." And then he would go into a lengthy dissertation, and all of the students excepting one or two, always including Chuck, would seem to have a frame of reference and know what the teacher was talking about, whereas he would be lost in the fog of his disgraceful ignorance. He began to develop an inferiority complex. And he was much too proud to ask stupid questions of the teachers, questions the answers to which everybody else seemed to know.

The first two months he was hopelessly and helplessly behind in most of his classes. He went through periods of great depression, a kind of thing he'd never experienced before, a deep sense of personal inadequacy. Chuck went from one mood to another. He was especially astounded at his roommate, Ronnie, who involved himself in civil rights, did his share of partying and dating, loved his bull sessions, and yet found time to study and seemed to know most of the answers in the classroom. Ron tried in vain to interest Chuck in extracurricular activities. Chuck did nothing those first two months but go from class to the library to his room to study.

Ronnie said, "Damn! I ain't never seen anybody like you before. You're no fun at all, you know that? Always got your head buried in some goddamn book. Everything isn't books, baby. Part of education is living, you know. All work and no play make Jack stupid as a mother-fucker."

Chuck said, "Do me a favor, Ronnie. Shut your damn mouth, or get lost."

Sometimes he would just sit there staring into his books, as if he didn't hear his roomie at all. Some nights he studied far into the early morning, and some days he would fall asleep in class. He had to make up for lost time, those springs and autumns he'd spent chopping and picking Mr. Wakefield's cotton.

One of the teachers spoke to him after one of his classes. Walked with him to the Students Union. "Do you have trouble with insomnia, Mister Chaney?"

"Sir?"

"You have trouble falling asleep at night?"

"No, sir. Once I go to bed I don't have much trouble going to sleep."

The teacher's name was Philip Jacobson. He was a youngish man, dark brown of color, and baby-faced; he was often mistaken for one of the older students. He taught Freshman English. "But you've fallen asleep in class a couple of times. Do you stay up late nights?"

"Yes, sir."

Dr. Jacobson had a reputation with the students as being one of the Negro teachers who was concerned. Some cared, others didn't. "But how do you expect to make it, Mister Chaney, I mean, if you don't apply yourself?"

"I do apply myself, Doctor Jacobson. That's just it. I stay up late studying every night."

Dr. Jacobson said, "I see. Well, you know, there is such a thing as overdoing it. There is such a thing as the law of diminishing returns."

Chuck said, "I don't know what law that is, sir, but I do know one thing. I got a lot of catching up to do. They gave me a country school education. I went to school six months out of the year. Look at all those months I've got to catch up with."

Dr. Jacobson's face warmed up with compassion for this boy. He thought to himself, it was boys like Chuck that made you think that teaching was worth the energy expended. All kinds of energy—intellectual, emotional. You certainly didn't teach because of the mighty paycheck. Was it G. B. Shaw who said, "Them that can't, teach?" Maybe that was it. Maybe you taught, because there was nothing else for you to do. In any event, it was worth it when you ran across a student like Charles Othello Chaney, who was serious, who wanted to do better than he was doing, a student who gave a damn and had not come to the

University just for the ride. Phil Jacobson himself had come from a little country town in Georgia. He knew about the colored educational system built around the superior priorities of cotton chopping and cotton picking. He had come directly from the plantation to Morehouse College in Atlanta, Georgia, thirteen years ago. A lot of water had flowed under the bridge since that day in late September. But he still remembered. He could empathize with this soft-faced boy who walked beside him, because he still remembered.

They stopped outside the Students Union. He told Chuck that in staying up half the night studying he was defeating his own purpose. First, he would work himself sick or into a nervous breakdown, and what good would that do? Second, after you put in a certain number of hours of studying, you've had it. After that, it becomes a waste of energy. You don't retain anything further. You just work yourself into a nervous state for nothing. "And what's the good of it if you fall asleep in class?"

The boy said, in a tone of quiet desperation, "But how'll I ever catch up? It's impossible to study in the dorms in the daytime. Too much noise. Too much going on."

Phil Jacobson invited him to his apartment the next evening for dinner, and they worked out an arrangement, whereby Chuck could use the apartment as a place to study, whenever Dr. Jacobson was not using it, which was often enough, since he spent a great deal of time in his office, when he wasn't in the classroom. Chuck shut everything out of his life those next two or three months and dedicated himself to the desperate business of playing the game of "catch-up." Dr. Jacobson gave him a few hints about good studying habits, a few pointers about what to read and study in order to catch up, not only in English but in all of his other subjects. It was difficult at first, with all the activity going on around him at the University. Football games, then basketball, debates, dramatics, civil rights activities, and girls. Girls, girls, girls, girls! All sizes and denominations. But he drew a strength for concentration from somewhere. God knows he knew not where his strength came from, and he put everything else out of his mind, almost, and dug in for a season and a seizure of book-learning. Dr. Jacobson did most of his own studying and class preparation in his office in Abraham Lincoln Hall, the academic building. Chuck saw very little of his roommate during

[180]

this period, and usually that was either late at night or early in the morning and on weekends.

On Wednesdays, Chuck had no classes at all in the afternoon. That first Wednesday he hurried over to the apartment after gobbling up his lunch. He unlocked the door, and went into the living room. As he switched on the lights, a half-naked woman leaped up from the living room couch where she had been napping with her legs spread-eagled.

She let out a loud shriek as she leaped three or four feet from the couch, and poor Chuck must have leaped five or six feet straight up. He started to back out of the door, but then he looked at the number outside the door, and it was "Philip Jacobson—Apt. 35." He was in the right place. He had been coming there since last Thursday.

The woman stood before the boy in her slip and bra. "Who the hell are you?" she asked. "If you don't git outa here right away, I'm gon call the police."

She was a plain-faced, sensual-mouthed woman, medium-brown of skin, with a bra brimming over with healthy breasts, and with panties (which he could see through the flimsy slip) full of roundish thighs and plump hindparts. The Professor had characteristically forgotten to tell either of them about the other.

They stood there staring at each other. He felt a warmth collecting in his face. Finally his voice came back to him. "I'm a student at Douglass," he said.

She stared him down and said, "So what? That don't mean you got no license to come busting in on a lady——"

He said, "But I study here every day. Doctor Jacobson gave me the key. He—" He showed her the key. He stopped. Why should he be on the defensive? But before he could ask her what in the devil was she doing in Dr. Jacobson's apartment, she put him on the defensive again. She told him, "I hope you recognize me when you see me again. You looking at me hard enough."

His face grew warm again. "Who are you?" he finally asked her. "What are you doing here?"

She said, "I'm the cleaning lady. I come every Wednesday, and I was just taking me a little old fifteen-minute break. I been working since early this morning. Sometimes I comes in the morning. Sometimes I comes in the afternoon. It depends——"

He said, "I'm sorry I——"

She said, "Come on in and shet the door. Keep the neighbors out your business."

He shut the door and still stood near it.

She said, "You sure is fresh the way you look at a lady. Turn your back, so I can make myself presentable." He turned his back and she went into another room.

Chuck went into the little room next to the bathroom which was Jacobson's study. And he buried himself among his books with his long legs propped up on the Professor's desk, and he read and read and read, but digested very little. He heard every movement the lady made inside the small apartment. She used the vacuum cleaner. She went to the bathroom. He thought he heard her peeing, and he heard the toilet gurgle. He got up and closed the door to the study, but it did no good at all. He could not shut out her presence. She was a very very physical woman. And he thought to himself, "She sure is noisy and heavy-footed."

Just about the time he had convinced himself that he was concentrating, she knocked at the door. He jumped. His heart-beat quickened. His face grew warm. He was not as annoyed as he pretended to himself to be. "What do you want?"

She opened the door and strutted in with a tray. "I don't want nothing. I just thought you could take a little cup of coffee or something." She bounced into the room, her buttocks quivering like Jell-O, newly made, and she put the tray on the desk before him. Hot coffee and two slices of buttered toast.

He mumbled, "Thank you, m'am," and he could not keep his eyes from watching her plumpness, as she bounced out of the room again. It was outrageous she was so doggone healthy-looking. He tried very hard. All afternoon he went through the motions, but he got very little done. He was so painfully aware of her presence. He was stupidly aware of her presence, he told himself. And she was old enough to be his mother. She wasn't that old, and Chuck Othello knew she was a long way from being motherly. Ronnie was right, he thought to himself. All work and no play made Jack pretty stupid. Very stupid. A man needs to relax sometimes. Man needed woman. He laughed quietly to himself. Ronnie told it like it was. Man needed poontang. The door was closed and she was in the kitchen which was the farthest room away from him, but she must have heard him laugh, because she came now toward the study.

[182]

"Did you say something to me, Mister—" She opened the door and stood there. "I don't even know what your name is."

"My name is Charles Othello Chaney."

She smiled. "That's a whole heap of name you got. It's right pretty too. My name is Naomi Hester, and I'm mighty please to make your acquaintance."

He said, "The pleasure is all mine, Miss Naomi."

She said, "Well, I'm through with my work, and I'm gon be saying goodbye, hear? I be seeing you next Wednesday, if I live and nothing don't happen."

He said, "I'll be seeing you, Miss Naomi," and watched her as she bounced over to the closet and got her coat and went into the Professor's bedroom and closed the door. He saw her again as she came out fully dressed and said goodbye to him again, and he heard her bouncing toward the front door and the door closing behind her. He got up and went to the bathroom and stared at himself in the bathroom mirror. Sometimes he thought he looked just like he remembered Junior used to look, especially the time when Junior had come home in his soldier suit. He thought proudly, "We could go for natural twins." Other times he thought he was Willie's spitting image. But Willie and Junior did not resemble each other that much. Nobody would've mistaken Willie and Junior for twins. Of course they were every one of them Chaneys, unmistakably Jesse's children. His mark was on every last one of them. Today, Chuck thought, I look just like Junior. I'm his natural-born spitting image. And the ladies don't find me hard to look at. You'd better believe me when I say so. He twisted the faucet and cupped his hands together and dashed handful after handful of cold water on his face. A man needed a woman. Poontang. Ronnie was absolutely right. Poontang—pussy—poontang! But he would do without for a few more weeks, maybe months, till he had accomplished the goal he had set for himself in his Operation Catch-up.

His mind made a picture of Miss Naomi, full-bosomed and jiggling and bouncing all over everywhere and leaving a trail of feminine smells all over the place. He couldn't understand how she managed to smell so good as hard as she worked and as much as she bounced around. As he thought of Miss Naomi in her apron, slip, and bra, he felt a great warmth move all over him and settle in his loins. Man needed woman. Yeah!

[183]

Chapter

2

Unlike Charles Othello, Carrie Louise's first year at Wexler College was not dedicated to the pursuit of book-learning but, rather, to the pursuit of life and living. The way she figured she had a lot of catching up to do in this department. And there was a lot of life to be lived in this giant of a city.

The city was sound. Backfires, horns honking, screams of joy and fear and agony. The sound of music, jazz, opera, symphonic, calypso, Afro-Cuban, Puerto-Rican, Rock 'n' roll.

The city was motion, breakneck speed. Everybody running for the subway, buses, taxis. In the air and underground.

The city was violence. Murder, rape, mayhem, insurrection, riots, snatching pocketbooks, mugging.

The city was people. Millions of them, shoving, pushing, fighting, struggling, working, drinking, balling, dancing, laughing, crying, living, dying.

The city was man-constructed monstrosities—Chrysler Building, Empire State, Rockefeller Center, Hotel Americana; the city was everything she'd heard the city was and more. It was a city of love; it was a city of hate.

The city scared her half to death, and yet she loved this frantic madhouse of a city with a burning passion. She had been here many times before, but she'd never had the city to herself before. She'd never thought of it as her very own.

Those first few months she walked all over Manhattan. Uptown, Downtown, East Side, West Side. She'd never seen so many foreigners. She gawked deliberately and unashamedly. The Fulton Fish Market, the Brooklyn Bridge, the Woolworth Building, Wall Street, Broadway. It was her fourth or fifth sojourn in New York, but she had never really seen it before. Like this. Never like this. On her ever-loving own. At the outset she was completely uncritical of the city. Even Forty-Second Street, which she recognized as Queerville and Whore City and Decadence Incorporated (designations she had learned from sophisticates at Wexler), and just around the corner to ugly, gaudy, unbelievable Times Square, she loved it all. Lived in awe of it, yet divinely loved it. One Saturday in broad-open daylight, she walked along Times Square from Fiftieth Street down past the Astor Hotel, down past the Paramount Theatre, and turned right into Forty-Second Street and walked underneath that long line of theater marquees stretching like a gleaming, blossoming apple orchard all the way to the Eighth Avenue subway, and she was propositioned five times by a motley variety of punks, pimps, and Lesbians. She was thrilled to death by it all, even though she was so scared she almost put a puddle in her panties.

It wasn't just that the city was so large. It was the tremendous anonymity she immediately achieved. She was just one little old solitary "me," out of a city teeming in the tens of millions. Nobody was particularly impressed by her name, or her father's name, for that matter. Nobody cared where she came from or where she was going. In Wakefield County, when they drove through town, she could always hear the comments from the lesser natives, white and black: "There goes the Man!" "There goes Jimmy Dick!" Even if she herself happened to be driving, it was still: "There goes the Man!" And the Man was Wakefield. The Man was anybody to whom the great name was attached. It didn't matter the sex or age or gender. Her Uncle Jeffrey used to say, before he died, "In the beginning was the Word and the Word was Wakefield and the Word was with Wakefield." There were other words and other men like Rogers Johnson and his brother and Mayor Brady, but there was really only one Man, one Word, and the Man and the Word were one and the same, Wakefield—Wakefield. Suddenly, in New York, the name was dispossessed of its magic and its power. Even black folk here were unimpressed. It was indeed a very peculiar thing, how you could get on a jet and just one hour and twenty minutes later, a name so powerful at its source came to mean precisely nothing in particular, except that it was a name.

She told her roommate, "Down home, I was a big frog in a little biddy pool. Up here, I'm a little teenie weenie frog in a great big pool. And I love it!"

Her roommate said, "I'll just bet you love it up here, honeychild." Sarcastically.

Up here even black folk were entirely unimpressed. "Ironies

of ironies," her roommate told her that first day. "You got your-self a black roommate." Her roommate was some kind of a big frog in a big pool. Her roommate was Cheryl Kingsley, nick-named Sherry. Her father was a prominent lawyer and a New York State Senator. "I am a child of the big black poverty-stricken bourgeoisie," she had a way of saying, overdramatically, in a kind of ritual of self-deprecation.

Sherry was an excellent student, effortlessly so. She seemed to spend no time at it at all. A few people called her father a modern-day Uncle Thomas, and she seemed eternally dedicated to making up for it. She knew her father was a dedicated and courageous man and was not an Uncle Tom, but he was her magnificent hero image and she demanded a standard and a mili-tancy which was impossible for him to attain, in his position. She was his greatest admirer and his severest critic. She was, as the French say, *engagé* up to her ears. She was totally involved. She'd been to Mississippi the summer before and worked on voter registration. When she was twelve or thirteen years old she joined the picket line in front of Woolworth's on Fifth Avenue in the city. She had been arrested five or six times by New York's Finest at some demonstration or other. In Times Square, it was against Vietnam; in front of the United Nations against apart-heid in South Africa. Out in Brooklyn, she lay down in front of a truck during the demonstration against a hospital for not hir-ing Negroes. She went to the Statue of Liberty with Belafonte and Poitier and David Woodson. Already she knew such people as John Lewis, Jim Foreman, Martin Luther King, Julian Bond, and David Woodson. Two summers before, it seemed to her father, the Senator, that he spent most of his time that summer down at the Tombs getting her out of jail. Even Sherry's mother got swept up in the civil rights excitement that glorious summer and, embarrassment of embarrassments, his excellency had to spring Mrs. Jeffry A. Kingsley, Jr. one bright summer day. In her more exacting and sarcastic moods, Sherry addressed her father as "Your Excellency."

At first, Carrie Louise resented them, of all things, assigning her a Negro roommate, although she would not admit it even to herself. For after all, she was a special kind of Southerner who possessed not one single trace of prejudice against the Negro. She was a Wakefield and the very name itself meant enlightenment. Nevertheless, she went to the office and asked for another room.

[186]

Dean Benedict asked her what was wrong with her room. Was it that she did not like the view? She could see the Drive and the river from her windows, and she could see New Jersey on the other side. Was it that she didn't like her roommate? Miss Kingsley was from one of the very best families of Brooklyn. Could it be the color question? Carrie Louise would not, could not, admit that her request had anything to do with color. She was too intelligent, too sophisticated, too emancipated to be prejudiced. Wasn't she?

One night Carrie Louise lay in bed staring back through her life's short span. Her eighteen years seemed so long in the living of them, it seemed that she had been alive ever since way way back as far back as she could remember which seemed to her much much longer than eighteen little old measly years. She was glad to be in New York even though this night she felt a kind of sweet nostalgia that put a sugary aching in her stomach and a taste of wine of blackest sweetest berries in her mouth. It was one of those nights in which an elusive sleep seemed just beyond her body's lovely drowsiness. Her body glowed and smoldered with good feelings. She could feel her body glimmering.

Sherry had come in from some kind of meeting about fifteen minutes before and had undressed quietly and had taken care of her nightly ablutions and had gone silently to bed. Carrie Louise had remained as quiet as the mice on the night before Christmas. When Sherry came in, Carrie Louise had been at the very outskirts of sleep at the city limits of the Land of Nod. But now she was fully awake. She listened sharply at the night noises so different from the noises of jungle nights in Mississippi. Horns honked here in the place of the bullfrogs of her beloved Mississippi jungle. Instead of the late night sounds she was used to of some old dog howling somewhere near or far, on her father's far-flung plantation (a sound that was a sure sign of death), she now heard a distant sound of fire engine sirens blasting through the stillness of the night. She believed there was not one single moment in the twenty-four hours of each of the three hundred and sixty-five days of the year when fire engines were not en route to a fire somewhere in this terrible and wonderful city. This city was always burning.

She turned on her side and stared through the darkness at her roommate in the bed on the other side of the room. She whispered softly, "Sherry!" She received not one single bit of the

[187]

slightest hint that Sherry heard her. "Sherry! Please!" Where she had heard nothing from Sherry's bed at first, now she heard a deliberate and a labored breathing. Sherry turned over in her bed from one side to the other. It was the movement of annoyance. She was definitely trying to say something to Carrie Louise, but the Wakefield girl was so hung up in what she wanted to say to Sherry, how could she be expected to get the message? Sherry's message.

She said, "Sherry! Are you asleep?"

Finally Cheryl gave out with a deep sigh of disgust. "Of course I'm asleep, you Mississippi peckerwood. What did you think I was doing? Standing on the corner of a Hundred and Twenty-Fifth Street and Lenox Avenue giving out membership cards to the Mississippi Ku Klux Klan?"

Carrie Louise jumped up and sat up in bed. "I knew you weren't asleep." She was as excited as a little girl. "I just knew you were playing possum!"

Another sigh of disgust came from Sherry's bed.

"I just want to talk a little biddy bit," Carrie Louise said.

"Try talking very very softly in your sleep," Sherry answered, and turned over on her other side with her back toward the girl from Mississippi.

"I'm just so happy being in New York City I declare I don't know what in the world to do."

"I have a suggestion," Sherry answered. "Go to sleep and tell me about it some other time. Like mañana, which never comes."

Carrie Louise spoke as if she had not heard her roommate. "I was just telling Barbara Weeks, you know she's from Cleveland, Ohio, that swarthy redhead in our history class. I told her just tonight at supper. 'Real white top-level Southerners get along with colored folks much better than Northerners.' We know them better than these hypocrites up here in the North. We live with them. Why they're just like one of the family. We love them like they're our own blood relatives."

"A whole heap of them are your relatives, honeychile. Especially on your pappy's side."

It was a very peculiar thing, even to Carrie Louise, herself, the transformation she was undergoing, not unlike a metamorphosis. Back in Wakefield, she sounded like a Northerner to the natives, not only in her accent but in her attitudes and in the content of her speech. But here in New York City, she sounded Southern even to herself. And she was always on the defensive. Defending a way of life she had thought she'd outgrown. Something seemed to push her onward almost against her will. "Northern white folks don't love colored folks, else how come you have Harlem up here, that ghastly ghetto. It's because folks up North don't love colored, don't want them to live among them. That's how come. Why back home colored folks live in the same house with us."

Sherry sat up drowsily. "Colored servants," she suggested.

"That's right, colored servants," the Mississippi girl admitted.

"They all live happily in the servant quarters," Sherry suggested, with as much sarcasm in her voice as she could muster upon this sleepyish occasion.

But her sarcasm was lost on Carrie Louise. "Yes, in the servant quarters. I really did love the servant quarters. I used to romp and play down there so much, my mother used to say, 'You go down there so often you going to turn into one of them!'"

When Carrie Louise thought about her childhood and the servant quarters, her mind always made an idyllic picture of the Chaneys, and in that picture there was always Aunt Carrie, good and honest and warmhearted. When the Chaneys had moved away from the servant quarters into town, she had cried her heart out, she had missed Aunt Carrie so. Then there was Uncle Jesse, so tall, so black, so humble and sincere. When she thought of him now, she could not help thinking of that noble savage, Gunga Din, her father's favorite fictional character. It was very funny the way she seemed to adopt her father's view when she was away from him. The longer she stayed in Yankee-land, the more she felt like a true Southerner and the more she believed, or pretended to believe, in the Southern way of life.

She thought of the servant quarters and she also remembered the summer afternoon she intruded upon the man-and-woman wrestling match, better known as playing "Mama and Papa." Even now her face grew warm as she remembered it, and especially the time she played it out with Chuck Othello, so many many years ago, it seemed, upstairs in a guest room in the old Big House. How could she have been so stupid? Or was it mere stupidity? Was there an even deeper motivation? And then he moved away and they never played together again.

"When I was a girl," she said, "I grew up with the cutest little old colored boy. We would romp and tear something terrible all over the place. Nobody could do a thing with us. They were the best years of my life, I declare they were. He didn't have any rancor in him at all, no hostility against white folks, or nothing like that. His——"

Sherry said sleepily, "Let me help you out. His name is Tom, and when he grows up to be a man, you're certainly going to call him Uncle." She turned over on her side again, with her back to the poor little rich girl.

"His name is not Tom," she said heatedly. "His name's Charles Othello Chaney." Her entire body glowed as she remembered the time she gave Chuck mouth-to-mouth rescuscitation, both of them in their birthday suits, and both of them much too big by then for such carryings-on. It was a sin even to remember it. Lord have mercy! She could die right now just thinking of it— and after all this time. But it wasn't a sin. It could not be a sin, because it was entirely innocent.

She said proudly, "He was almost like a brother to me. My father even arranged for his college education. He's at the University right now, just because my father sent him." She would have continued, but this time there was no mistaking what had happened. The soft even snoring from the other bed told her Sherry had gone to sleep on her, and for real this time.

One day Sherry came in the room with some books under her arms. "Look, Carrie Lou, you are the most know-nothing chick it has ever been my misfortune to encounter anytime, anywhere. Maybe even anyhow. Let's see if we can't boot you a little bit since you want to talk about the question, eternally. I mean, you run off at the mouth, but you don't ever say a damn thing."

Carrie Lou said, "I don't know what you mean—I—" Sherry had taken her down a peg by shortening her from Carrie Louise to Carrie Lou. She had objected at first but had been overruled. So she was Carrie Lou all over the campus.

Sherry said, "I mean, if you're going to insist on talking about some of your best friends, culyud that is, you might as well know a little bit of something about which you're talking. Here, dig into these, and then look me up for some intelligent conversation, I mean, for a change." She threw the books, one by one, at Carrie Lou, who was lying on her bed. "Frederick Douglass, Aptheker, Du Bois, John Hope Franklin." The first book struck her on the face, glancingly, and landed on the floor. Carrie Lou leaped to her feet angrily. "Now wait a minute!"

Sherry did not even look up, nor did she break her rhythm. The second book landed on the bed. Carrie Lou sat back on the bed and caught the third one, then the fourth. "Baldwin, Jones, Lomax." She stopped, empty-handed. "That'll be enough for your pretty little messed-up head for a start. You aren't ready for David Woodson yet. And don't you mention the race question to me again until you make your way through these books."

"But I know David Woodson!" Carrie Lou exclaimed, ecstatically. "I heard him speak—I heard him speak! And I admire him greatly. I——"

"You heard him speak, but have you read him? That's the question. Have you read him? Since we have been roommates, I have seen you read all those phony Southerners like Faulkner and Robert Penn Warren and all that bunch of faggots that make up the old New Critics and the new Old Critics. But this is the moment of truth with you and me. Pee or get off the pot. Read *me,* or forget it! I have no time to waste listening to your stupid inanities. What I mean is, I think you're a first-class fourteen-carat phony, which is oaky-doak with me. Just don't do me any favors like talking to me about the race question. I mean, I'd rather we didn't discuss at all. I could really do wonderfully without it. But if it'll kill you if you don't, then learn something about it before you open your mouth again. I'm sick and tired of you making a fool of yourself!"

Sherry was sitting now, on the side of her bed. The thing had been building up between them since September, and here it was past the middle of November, and twenty-nine shopping days before Christmas. The thing had been boiling up inside the girl from Crown Heights in the Borough of Brooklyn in the County of the Kings. The more desperate Carrie Lou became in terms of proving her friendship to Sherry, the more hostile Sherry Kingsley became, or so it seemed to the girl from Mississippi who had always had her way with everybody she had known. She sat there now among the books Sherry had thrown at her. She felt put upon, and at the same time she had a contradictory feeling of tremendous guilt. Why should she always be put on the defensive? She could not assume the guilt of the whole white South. She had lynched no Negroes. She had never meant anything but good toward them. Even a couple of the other colored girls in their group at Wexler had told Sherry in Carrie Lou's presence that she was wrong in her attitude toward white people. Lumping them all together. It was discrimination in reverse. Carrie Lou had thought many times of going to the office again and getting herself moved to another room. Since that first time, she had been to the office twice and had turned around at the last minute, and decided to stick it out. She would make this arrogant colored girl love her. Or else.

Sherry said, "The one thing I always admired about the white Southerner, you knew where he stood. At least they weren't hypocritical like the Yankee bastards. I mean you knew what to expect from the Senator from Alabama. But here you come, a dyed-in-cotton peckerwood from the backwoods of Mississippi, and already you're the great friend of the colored man. Why, honeychile, you're pure white Anglo-Saxon Southern womanhood. You're the emblem of the Ku Klux Klan. You're their *cause célèbre*. Your lily-white body is the rationalization for every lynching, every indignity, a black man ever suffered in the last one hundred years. Like you're just about a bitch, you know that?"

Carrie Lou felt as if she had been stripped stark naked and lashed until her entire body bled. The whole thing was too much for her. It built up up up from her bowels through her stomach through her chest through her throat into her cheeks and now it was spilling from her eyes. She overflowed. She could not hold back the flood, and the tears spilled down her cheeks. She said. "I don't under—I mean—I just don't understand—" She moved like she was sleepwalking from her bed and sank beside the other girl on the other side of the room. She blew her nose and wiped her eyes and mumbled, "Why are you like this? Why? What have I done to you?" Her voice choked off. She leaned her head on the other girl's chest. She wanted Sherry to take her into her arms and show her some compassion. She sobbed uncontrollably, as she waited for the other's love, her womanly compassion, to triumph over hate, the love which she knew nestled in the breast of every black human being. And she needed it, demanded it.

She almost fell to the floor when suddenly Sherry pulled angrily away from her, and stood above her. "I ain't your black mammy, baby. I know I don't look like Aunt Jemima. Don't get your people mixed, doll baby. I know you people pretend that we all

[192]

look alike. You might have been suckled by a black woman, but this one isn't going to give you any titty!" Sherry put on her coat and walked out of the door and slammed it shut behind her.

Carrie Lou sat there stunned for a moment. Then she cried some more and then wiped her eyes and went to the phone and called her father down in Mississippi. She told him she was coming home the next day.

He said, "What's the matter, baby? You want me to come for you?"

She said, "No, Daddy, that won't be necessary. I'll catch an early morning plane. I'll send you a telegram in the morning and let you know what time to meet me."

But she slept on it, and the next morning she felt better about it, and she sent him a telegram that she had changed her mind. She was going to spend the weekend with her aunt down in the Village.

The next few weeks every chance she got she dove into the books Sherry had given her to read. Her head exploded with information and points of view she had never dreamed existed. The more she read the more she wanted to kick herself for some of the conversations she had gratuitously imposed upon her room-mate. And she had known better—or hadn't she? She remembered talks she had had with her father, and how different she had felt with her advanced viewpoint, how different she had felt she was from the rest of the peckerwoods in Wakefield County! She had thought of herself as a radical, or at the very least, a liberal. But as soon as she had gotten to New York and with her colored roommate, somehow she had felt dedicated to the entire South-ern position. She had felt a loyalty which she did not really deeply feel. Or did she? Sherry had brought to the surface all of her hidden Southernness, hidden even from herself. It had given her a strange kind of fascination to hear herself talk like Rogers Johnson's daughter instead of Charlie Wakefield's. And she did not understand what had motivated her. Or, at least, she pre-tended not to understand.

One day, a few weeks later, she said to her roommate, "How can I ever thank you for lending me those marvelous books?"

Her roommate said, "Don't mention, honeychile. I'm always doing missionary work." She never called her anything but honey-chile or Carrie Lou.

Carrie Lou said, "I really mean it, I appreciate everything you've done for me. I know how I must have been a real pain in the neck."

"In the hindparts, honeychile, in the very very hinder parts." Sherry laughed a short laugh, and this time not derisively, Carrie Louise hoped.

"In the very very very hindparts," Carrie Lou agreed. "Can we be friends?" honeychile asked timidly. She held out her hand toward Sherry.

Sherry pretended not to notice. She walked toward the door and looked back at Carrie Lou. "No sweat, honeychile. You're not that hard to take. Just don't work so hard at it. I mean, with the yackety-yack. I mean, like relax sometimes." She left Carrie Louise standing in the middle of the floor.

One evening in the middle of winter, Sherry broke down and took Carrie Lou to a party with her. "A culyud party," Sherry told her in advance. They had been out together a few times before. They had spent the night at Carrie Lou's way-out aunt's house in the Village. Slept in the same bed together. But when Carrie Lou tried innocently to cuddle, Sherry turned definitely and deliberately away from her. But Sherry was attracted to Carrie Lou's Aunt Daphne and she liked her, as much as she could like any white woman from the Solid South. Carrie Lou could tell that Sherry liked her aunt. She was one of those Southerners who had almost made the change to a Greenwich Village native. She had practically lost her Southern accent and her Southern attitudes—against her will almost. Sherry looked upon her as a slightly younger version of Tallulah Bankhead, in looks and manner as well as in her speech and her sophistication.

Sherry and Carrie Lou went out to dinner together a few times with some of the other girls. And each time Carrie Lou made a point of picking up the check. She was also picking up New York slang as rapidly as possible. She'd pick up the check, and when others asked her what their share was she would say, "Everything's cool. I'll take care of it this time."

The fourth time she pulled this, Sherry checked her. "Oh no," she countered. "Everything isn't cool at all. That's very uncool. We've all got daddies, honeychile. We were all getting to our grits before you got here."

The party was in Brooklyn in the Crown Heights section on President Street. They caught the Seventh Avenue—Flatbush

Avenue subway. About nine o'clock back in the Barracks, as they called Jefferson Hall, their dormitory building, Sherry had almost finished dressing for the party, when she noticed that Carrie Louise was still lounging around in a sweat shirt and in dungarees.

Sherry had shrugged her way into her own dress, and she turned to Carrie Lou. "Well, honeychile, are you going or are you going to get left? If you're going, you'd better get the lead out."

"Of course I'm going, Lady Kingsley." Some of the girls called Sherry "Lady Kingsley" because of the way she carried herself. She told them it was because of the way she denied their image of humility which was the hallmark of the "noble savage." "I'm already ready. I'm waiting for you."

Lady Kingsley faced her. "You're ready for what? Where in the hell you think you're going? To some Mississippi peckerwood hoedown? Or maybe you think you're going slumming with the funky nigrahs? If you're going with Lady Kingsley, you'd better get up off your sorry pale-faced rusty-dusty, and get your best rags on. You'd better get yourself together, baby. You look like dammit I'll bite you."

Honeychile got up off her pale-faced rusty-dusty in a hurry and got herself together in her best glad rags. She told herself one had to have her kind of broad sense of humor to enjoy such a colossal joke on herself. She told herself that she was big and secure enough to indulge this black girl in her childish tantrums. She told herself the black girl really liked her but put up this great bluff in order to hide her deepest feelings. She likes me but she has to have a white scapegoat, because she's pretending, at this stage, to hate all white folk. And I don't mind being her scapegoat, after all her people have suffered at the hands of my people. She's getting even with the whole white race by taking everything out on me. Carrie Lou felt good, felt like a martyr. A beautiful magnanimous white martyr. If folks at home could see her now, they would not believe their eyes or ears. *Me, I,* Carrie Louise Mariah Wakefield, the Princess of the Wakefield Manor, the one and only Queen of Wakefield County, taking low before an arrogant sassy bourgeois black gal. It was ludicrous, and you had to have a sense of humor. But deeper than the sense of humor was the sense of awe that Carrie Lou felt for this daughter of a slave ancestry.

She moved swiftly now. "It won't take me long to change," she said, apologetically. Why would Sherry invite me to her party, if she didn't really like me?"

"You're going to have to go through a whole lot of changes, honeychile, if you're going to join the human race."

Carrie Lou would never get over the New York subway, thundering along underneath the city, sometimes at unimaginable speed, people pushing off and on, everybody and everything in one great big hassle of a hurry, going, going. It didn't seem to matter where you were going, so long as you were in motion going somewhere. She sat there next to Sherry watching the faces across the aisle, watching people pushing on and off, noting the smoky smell of the subway when it roared into the Wall Street Station, as if Brooklyn Bridge were burning down, the pungent smell of perfume mixed with body sweat. She thought she loved to ride the New York subway, the wonderful New York subway, the filthy New York subway. As it rumbled underneath the river, a jet stream of air seemed to come from somewhere and whirlwind after whirlwind of dirt and old pieces of dirty newspaper blew around the subway floor. The dirt got into her eyes, and a dusty dirty page from the *Tribune* wrapped around her leg. She kicked it away, and she thought how ironic it was, for them to get all togged out in their glad rags, and then have to ride the filthy New York subway. She thought they would look like refugees from a minstrel show by the time they reached their destination. Something (she had no idea what it was) prevented her from voicing her thoughts to Lady Kingsley.

When they walked into the block on President Street, she was stunned by the aura of affluence. The wide lawns, the large two- and three-storied mansions, brick and limestone. She blurted out before she thought it over, "Sherry Kingsley, I thought we were coming to a colored party."

Sherry came back with, "I just wonder what made your little old mind jump to that conclusion."

She never knew how to take Sherry Kingsley; that was one of the problems of their relationship.

In the middle of the block Sherry led the way down the walk toward a three-story mansion that loomed upward into the night. It was a red-brick house, and Carrie Louise noticed the ivy growing up the sides of the house from the bottom to the top. Except for the third floor which seemed to disappear up into the darkness, the house was bursting with brilliance. Lights were on in every room. And she heard the sound of voices and of music coming from the house. Sherry absentmindedly took a key out of her pocket, changed her mind, and rang the doorbell. When the door opened a handsome black man of medium height and middle age welcomed them into the house. He was one of the most distinguished-looking men Carrie Lou had ever seen. He was brownish black. His face had a hard, firm quality about it and yet there was a definite softness. It was his eyes that were full of softness, the softness of self-confidence, which this black man exuded. He smiled as he took Sherry into his arms.

"My baby! You did come, after all." And then he unfolded her from him, yet held on to her hand, as he looked at Carrie Lou.

"This is Carrie Louise Mariah Wakefield, Father. My roommate from below the border."

He extended a hand toward Carrie Lou. "Yes, of course!" he said in a soft melodic voice. "Sherry has told us so much about you."

Carrie could just imagine what Sherry had told them about her, if indeed she had mentioned her at all. His large hand enveloped hers in a warm handshake. She thought, he is a charmer. She thought, this man has dignity to burn. How in the devil could he be an Uncle Tom, a Gunga Din?

A tall black man came forward and took their wraps, and Senator Kingsley led them to a table in the high-ceilinged, cathedral-type, oak-paneled dining room. "You might as well get a little refreshment, Miss Wakefield, before Sherry takes you on a round of introductions."

A black bartender, dressed immaculately in white, stood behind the table. They both got Scotch and soda and then they began the round of introductions from the dining room through the wide foyer to the living room, one room flowing into the other, giving a sense of depth and spaciousness. There must have been fifty people in elegant attire, except for one or two sloppy-looking bearded ones who seemed to be escapees from the avant-garde. A long heavy chandelier hung from the middle of the ceiling in the dining room; a delicate-looking chandelier hung lightly and glittered brightly in the living room. She met Dr. Jackson and Mrs. Blakeley and Judge Goldberg, a tall handsome black man, and they left the dining room when a tall-for-a-woman aristocratic lady came toward her. She was copper-colored and fortyish and of slim and queenly carriage; she was all grace and graciousness. She took Sherry into her arms and when she released her, she took both of Carrie Lou's hands into her hands warmly.

"We are so delighted to have you visit with us, my dear. Anyone whom Sherry loves, we take to our hearts ipso facto, as Adam would say." She turned to Sherry. "Did Miss Wakefield meet your father, dear?"

"Yes, Mother. The very moment we arrived."

This was really Lady Kingsley, Carrie Lou thought, almost against her will comparing Sherry's mother with her own. Mrs. Kingsley signaled for one of the white-jacketed men who was floating around the rooms with a tray and she took their glasses and set them on the man's tray and gave them fresh drinks, and she signaled for another man to bring them hors d'oeuvres, and —"Enjoy yourself, my dears," and she was gone toward other guests.

There were a few white people sprinkled over the party here and there, apparently, for the sake of composition. Tokenism. In any event, it gave Carrie Lou a kind of feeling of security that she was not the only one. She did not fully understand her own reactions to the party, to this spectacle of black affluence. It was not that she had thought that all Negroes lived like Negroes lived in the shotgun shacks in the backwoods of plantation Mississippi. She knew that some Negroes lived middle-class lives in the South as well as in the North. She'd seen copies of *Ebony*. It certainly wasn't that she was unused to this spectacle of affluence. The tradition of wealth and affluence went far back in her family more than a hundred and fifty years. The old Wakefield house and the new house made the Kingsley home look modest by comparison. And there was more evidence of conspicuous consumption in one corner of the Rogers Johnson Big House than there was all over the Kingsley mansion. It wasn't the evidence of affluence at all that shocked her. It was just that somewhere deep inside of her, she had expected, desperately wanted, almost against her will she had wanted, needed even, to find black affluence dissipated on bad taste and gaudiness, and here she found herself in the midst of quiet splendor, an aura of relaxed elegance. She had so much to learn. As Sherry always told her, she had a lot of changes to go through.

She looked around her and unknowingly, like a little child, she put her arms around Sherry. Perhaps the Scotch had gone to her head. "Thank you, darling! Thank you! Thank you!"

Misunderstanding, Sherry pulled away from her. "Thank me for what?" She didn't like for white folks to paw at her.

"If you had really hated me, you would have let me come to your party in my dungarees and made a damn fool out of me. Or worse, let me make a damn fool of my own self."

Sherry stared at Carrie Lou and suddenly both of them burst into laughter as their minds shared a picture of Carrie Lou at this party in her sweat shirt and her dungarees. Sherry mimicked, "Donchoo know I loves you, honeychile?"

As far as Carrie Lou could see, they were the youngest at the party. Most of the folks were between thirty and fifty. As they made their way toward the living room, Carrie Lou saw a group seated on one side of the room in a kind of circle. A couple of people sat on the floor in the middle of the circle. As she neared the circle she felt her heart pump faster. Almost of their own accord, her legs stopped walking and her hand went toward her forehead. It couldn't be! Her eyes were playing tricks on her. She turned to Sherry for confirmation. Sherry gave her that blasé expression of hers, which sometimes infuriated Carrie Lou. But this time she looked back toward the circle and into the smiling face seated on the floor in its center. Dressed in slacks and sport jacket and perfectly at home, it seemed. Was it really Harry Belafonte! She thought she'd sink right through the floor. She turned again to Sherry. "It's Harry Belafonte!"

Sherry said, nonchalantly, "You were expecting maybe Barry Goldwater?" But she didn't fool Carrie Lou this time. She could hear the deep pride in Sherry's voice. It was then that Harry saw them. He got up and left the circle and came toward them, and Carrie Lou thought she would faint away right on the spot. He came and took Sherry into his arms and kissed her on the mouth. "My own true love," he said. "My one and only love."

Sherry was in heaven. Carrie Lou sensed it, even though Sherry carried the whole thing off with sangfroid and savoir faire and all that jazz. She said, "Harry, darling. There's never been anyone but you."

Finally, she ungathered herself from the tall, slim, agonizingly handsome brown-skinned man. "Harry, this is my roommate,

[199]

Carrie Louise Mariah Wakefield all the way from Wakefield County, Mississippi."

She was so thrilled she hardly heard him say, in his husky voice, "How are you? Delighted to meet you." That is what she quoted him as saying when she told other folk about a million times afterward at the college and back home in Wakefield County. She didn't remember what she answered in return. She remembered thinking as Sherry introduced her, Why does she have to always drag my name out like that? And why does she have to tell everybody's body I'm from Mississippi? She'd never thought she'd ever feel this way about her native state. She just knew at this moment that she wanted to get away from the proximity of this man as quickly as possible before she made a fool of herself. She didn't know what to say to him. She was too mature to grin and giggle. She felt like shrieking like a teen-ager at a Beatle Jamboree, but she had more dignity than that. He kept one arm around Sherry who stood by his side, even as he talked with her, the girl from Mississippi. How were things in Mississippi? How was the civil rights movement down there? He would very much like to pay the place a visit. Don't ask her how she answered him. She thought she remembered saying something stupid and insincere like, "We'd be mighty delighted for you to pay us a visit, Mister Belafonte."

Centuries later they went downstairs to the basement where the joint was truly jumping. Stereophonic high fidelity playing rock 'n' roll and modern jazz and calypso and high life. Here was the younger set seriously engaged in their gyrations and libations. It was a finished basement that went the entire length of the house, pine-paneled, built-in bar, built-in fluorescent lighting. The basement was swinging. It was saying something. The ages down here ranged from about eighteen to twenty-eight. Sherry introduced her roommate to a few of the folks. "She's trying her damndest to acquire a little soul before she goes back to Bad Cracker, Mississippi."

"You got to pay your dues, before you can sing the blues," one of the young men cracked. Sherry left Carrie Lou to her own devices, as she danced calypso with a student from Nigeria. Carrie Lou panicked, as Sherry left her standing with the tall young man who had cracked to her about dues payment.

He turned to her. "You want to dance, Miss Carrie Lou?" he mimicked.

It was kind of a moment of truth for Carrie Lou. She had never danced with a black boy before. Indeed she had never been this close to dancing with a black boy. None had had the temerity to ask. None had had the opportunity. She said, "I don't think I know how to do that dance." It was really weird how she tried to disguise her Southern accent these days, and how it always seemed to her to come out more pronounced than ever.

He said, "You sure ain't going to learn how to get your hog maw and chitterlings just standing on the sidelines with your finger in your ear. Soul does not drop like the dew from heaven, Miss Cotton Blossom."

He ushered her out onto the floor and took her into his arms and before she could resist, she was dancing, she was trying to keep in step. He was a good dancer and as good a teacher. She could not do all the fancy steps he executed as he danced away from her and back again with his slim grace and his swivel hips. He kept her off balance most of the time, and she was almost glad each time he danced back to her and took her in his arms again. She was in his arms now, his black arms, as she imagined them, and the roof had not yet fallen in. She thought to herself, deliberately, I'm dancing with a big black burly nigger and the roof has not fallen, the earthquake hasn't happened yet. If they could only see me now way back there in Wakefield County. I'm dancing with a nigger! I'm in a big black nigger's arms! I'm dancing with a nigger!

The music had stopped and he led her toward a corner of the room where a bull session was underway. What had she expected? That he would try to drag her into another room and have her? They were supposed to be hot-natured, weren't they? That's what the Negro Revolt was all about, wasn't it? Miscegenation? She knew it wasn't true. Notwithstanding, thoughts leaped around in her mind like grasshoppers in the Mississippi sunlight. Were black men really such great champions in bed? She wondered. The girl from Mississippi wondered. Against her will, against her intelligence, she wondered.

One of the fellows in the bull session was making like a Muslim, as Carrie Lou and her dancing partner approached the group. "If a white man is not a blue-eyed devil, what is he?" He was a short, skinny young man, who looked as if a good strong wind would put him into orbit.

[201]

"He's a brown-eyed devil, if he has brown eyes," another boy said.

Still another said, "How about the white womenfolks, man? Like are they blue-eyed devils too?"

Short-and-skinny said, "You haven't ever heard the old man talk about white women, have you? I mean the Right Honorable Elijah Muhammad. Hell naw, and you aren't going to ever hear me low-rating Mister Charlie's wenches, especially his lily-white ones."

Somebody whistled, "Whee-eee!"

Carrie Lou heard the quiet laughter, some of it not so quiet.

Her dancing partner waving his hand in front of him as they walked up to the group. "As-Salaam-Aleikum. All praises due to Allah."

Somebody answered, "Wa-Aleikum-Salaam."

Carrie Lou saw Sherry opposite them in the inner circle of the group, where she would be if she were anywhere in the vicinity. She would always be in the inner circle.

One young man gestured toward Carrie Louise's dancing partner, whose name was Elwood Robinson. "There he is, old Elwood Triple-X himself. Now we can call the mosque to order."

Sherry said, "They wouldn't let Elwood get anywhere near the mosque. He refuses to give up his soul food, pig knuckles, chitterlings, and poke chops."

Elwood had to laugh himself, as did the others, except for Carrie Lou.

Sherry said, "Besides, when have you ever heard tell of a Muslim standing that close to a white lady?"

The soul folk cracked up with laughter. The short and skinny one said, "Behind that, Elwood, you ought to pack up your tent and slink away."

Carrie Lou's face turned red, lost color, turned red again. These people didn't want integration. Every time anybody put out a friendly hand toward them, they tried their best to bite it off. Didn't they know this was not the way to win friends and influence people?

The short and skinny young man said, "Like you know Elwood never went for that Black Nationalist bit. My man is an integrationist. Nonviolence is his stick."

Elwood said, "You are so right, baby. I would not want to live in a world that was of black people, for black people, and by

[202]

black people. There would be too much black in the picture. I like contrast."

He looked around at the rest of them. They had been putting him on, but it was obvious now that he was getting serious. "I mean, like we're all Americans, right? And look at all the progress we've made. I mean we even have a Negro Cabinet member. The things you chaps have to learn is a little objectivity. There are two sides to every story."

Sherry said, "You're damn right there're two sides. The wrong side and the right side."

Another fellow said, "Elwood is right. We segregate ourselves. This is a new day. We have to learn to stop thinking Negro and think American."

Sherry said, "If you cats are so patriotic, why is it you're always trying to figure out some new gimmick to keep you in college longer? How come you don't volunteer for Vietnam?"

Elwood said, "I have two years to go to get my Masters or else I sure would enlist tomorrow morning. I'd rather fight them over there than to wait till they come over here and attack us."

Short-and-skinny said, "Can't you just imagine the great big old bad Viet Cong coming way over here across that ocean in great big old rowboats and attacking the poor defenseless little old United States? My heart of hearts bleeds for the dear old peace-loving U.S.A. Our hearts are always in the right place. Yet and still, nobody ever trusts us. It just isn't fair!"

Short-and-skinny knew what to say to make them laugh. And they laughed heartily. Sarcastically.

A tall, massive, dark-brown young man said, burlesquing, "Yeah, picking on us just because we're bigger than them. It isn't easy to be cast in the role of a big bully, especially when you're tenderhearted underneath. But by God, we can't give up the ship now, no matter what anybody says. We'll enforce peace and democracy upon those yellow hordes even if we have to destroy every stinking last one of them."

They had another good laugh, except for two or three of them. And Carrie Lou. She felt she had to say something. She felt that it had to be a two-way highway. If she was willing to walk toward them, they had to move a few steps down the road to meet her, even if not all the way, they had to make some kind of motion toward her. If she were willing to listen to their side of it, then she had a right to be heard, they had a responsibility to hear her side. She took a quick look at Sherry, then she took a deep breath, and to herself she said, Here goes. And she said, "Admittedly there have been misunderstandings among the races in our country."

She heard the laughter, quiet and derisive, like they say some horses laugh. She felt a warmth collecting on her neck and face. "I mean, we all realize that the change has to come. Even the poorest white man in Mississippi knows it in his heart, I mean, that the change must come. It's just that you have to give him time for his heart to send the message to his mind. Then the white man will be ready to accept the colored man as his equal."

"That's right!" Elwood said, but without the old enthusiasm.

The tall massive one said, "Lady, the so-called Negro is not sitting around on his black ass waiting for the white folk to accept him. Those days are gone forever. The question is, whether we want to accept you people or not. You can't accept me, baby. Excuse me, please. I mean—Miss Anne."

Elwood said, "The lady simply meant racial tolerance. That's what we're all working for, isn't it?"

"Who in the hell wants her to tolerate me? It isn't up to her to tolerate. Like David Woodson says, 'The big job facing the white man is to get himself in some kind of shape for the rest of the world, which is colored, to accept *him*.' I mean, like, the onus is on Whitey to prove himself worthy of acceptance. And, me myself, I doubt if the cat will make it."

Sherry said to Elwood, with as much scorn as she could muster, "What the hell do they teach you up at Dartmouth? Good Lord, they integrated you right out of the colored race."

Elwood said, "I mean like what did I do, baby? What did I say wrong? I'm one hundred percent for the rights of the little people, the underdog, the colored man."

The tall massive quiet-faced soft-voiced young man could be a mean man once his hackles were up. He said sneeringly to Elwood, "Baby, you are beneath contempt. Just because you want to get into Miss Whitey's drawers, you don't have to kiss her hindparts in the bargain."

A couple of people drew deep breaths. The short and skinny fellow laughed. Carrie Lou's face was afire with humiliation. She buckled as if he had kicked her in the solar plexus. She turned and stumbled over Elwood's foot, but she caught herself in time. And she straightened up and then walked quickly across the floor

[204]

of the basement, her eyes filled now, bumping blindly into people dancing; she blundered toward the stairs. Before she reached them she broke into a run.

Sherry turned to the tall massive one. "You do play a little rough sometimes, Lorenzo. I mean like really. After all she *is* my house guest and my roommate." She stood around for a moment, then walked across the room and up the stairs.

By the time Sherry got upstairs, Carrie Lou had gotten her wrap and gone.

Chapter
3

Gradually he caught up with his work as the seasons raced toward Christmas. Gradually the boy relaxed into his new and nervous manhood. Now and then he would go out on the town with Ronnie, what there was of the town to go out on. Ronnie said it was strictly from Hicksville. Chuck still went every chance he got to Dr. Jacobson's to study. He could concentrate at Jacobson's better than he could anywhere on the campus. In the dorms it was either rock 'n' roll or modern jazz or Ellington or Ray Charles or Max Roach or blackjack games or poker or the bull sessions that seemed to go on interminably. The dorms seemed to him to be one great cacophony of sound. He could concentrate at Jacobson's every day, that is, except for Wednesdays. He would wake up every Wednesday morning conscious of what day it was, conscious all the way down in the very middle of him. He felt his manhood painfully. He went around till noon very much aware of himself and trying hard to keep his manhood from sticking out all over. At noon he would make a beeline to Jacobson's apartment which was about three blocks from the campus. By the time he got there he would really be wrought up, and as he put the key in the door he would wish desperately that she was already there and in the state of undress like the first time. At the same time he would wish that she had not come at all. She wore a dress now whenever he was around.

It did no good; he stayed upset. His manhood was self-conscious.

If she came after he arrived, he would sit at the desk, immobilized, with a hardness and a throbbing in the middle of him, he'd be leapingly nervous like a cat on a red-hot stove. Every time she came later than he, she would always come into the room where he was and look him over, up and down and sideways, and give him a "How you, Mister Charles Othello." And a few moments later she would come bouncing in again with coffee and toast or cookies or something. And she would always look him up and down, as if she knew exactly what was troubling him.

One afternoon she teased him. "What's the matter, honeybunch?"

He said, "Nothing's the matter."

She said, "You so serious and everything like something troubling you or something." She looked him up and down and his sex throbbed like a heartbeat. "Don't you let them little fresh college girls worry Mama's baby. You keep your mind on all that book-learning. You hear?"

He said angrily, "Don't worry about it!" He did not like her to tease him. He told himself he did not like her to tease him.

One Wednesday he came, and she was already there, but he didn't see her till he came into the study and saw her seated at the desk with a book in her lap and her legs up on the desk as he sometimes had a way of doing, except that he always wore trousers. He could not help seeing over halfway up her skirt, her naked, plump, and roundish thighs flashing brownish black and blackish brown.

At first she just looked up at him and said, "How you, Mister Charles Othello?"

He swallowed hard and said, "I'm fine, I thank you. How are you?"

She said, "Just fine." And then, "Oh, excuse me." And she took her legs down off the desk and pulled her dress down to her knees. She stared down at the book in her lap and then up at him again. She said, "Psychology. You know, I used to want to go to school and get a college education and really be somebody and maybe be a nurse or a teacher or maybe write a book or do something like that important, doncha know? But both my mama and papa up and died and I had to take care of three children under me, and I raised them all right out the white folks' kitchens, till the last one got to be eighteen, and then one day they didn't see me no more, cause I just up and left Birmingham, and I ain't been back since. But I really woulda made something outa myself. I really mean it. I just know I woulda."

What could he say but—"What do you mean? You certainly did make something out of yourself."

"What?" she demanded. "A general cleaning woman." She laughed derisively. "A woman that do days work from house to house, in and out folks' houses every day excepting Sunday? What is that? That ain't nothing."

He smelled a strange smell coming from her that he did not relate to as her usual smell at all. It was strange and yet somehow familiar. And then it came to him she had been drinking, and she had not been drinking coffee. Her dress slid slowly up above her knees. He said in a strange and gruff voice. "You're just as good as anybody else." And meant it.

"I ain't nothing!" she said. "But I know one thing, I sure ain't nothing common. I'm honest. I don't ask nobody's body for nothing."

He said, "I think you're a fine person. I mean I really do."

She said, "Thank you, Mister Charles Othello. Thank you very much, but I ain't got no education. I'm ignorant."

He said, "You *are not* ignorant. And furthermore, education isn't everything. There're a whole lot of educated fools in this world."

She said, "Thank you." She wiped her eyes. He hoped desperately she wouldn't cry. She said, "Well let me get up from here like I got some sense and git to my work and let you git to yourns. Cause you a gentleman with important work to do."

He said, "I really hate to disturb you."

She was back before he could get to "the" in his history book, back with coffee on a tray, two cups, one for him and one for her. And she sat across from him sipping hers and eyeing him. "Whew! I sure can use this coffee this afternoon! I got the awfulest old headache." He said that he was sorry. Her dress was too short for his comfort, and he could not keep his eyes away. He wondered if she had been drinking Dr. Jacobson's whiskey. When he finished his coffee, she took it from him and took herself to the kitchen, and he sighed and picked up his book again. But by now he was throbbing with excitement.

About fifteen minutes later, he almost bolted out of his chair, as the record player in the living room suddenly gave out full blast with a great one by Ray Charles, the one and only.

> *I got a woman—way over town*
> *Good to me . . .*

She came into the study again and she pulled him from the chair. "Aren't you going to ask the lady for a dance?" And now she was heavy in his arms as they danced around the study and he felt his manhood grow steadily against her. Shamelessly, he felt his manhood hardening against her thigh. His face broke out into a sweat and he felt some hot air in his collar now. She leaned her head against his cheek and it was terrible the way he felt so good, and she was old enough to be his mother, he told himself, knowing she could not possibly be more than ten years older than he was.

She looked up in his face. "How come you so serious?"

"Who said I was serious?" He thought to himself, everything is out in the open between us now, because she's got to know that I'm hard against her. I mean a woman old as she is, she has to know this isn't a hammer in my pocket.

The song was ended and she stepped away from him and looked him up and down. "Thank you, kind Mister," she said impishly and did a curtsy. "And now I must git back to my work and you must git back to yours." But he didn't do much concentrating that particular Wednesday.

He heard from home at least once a week. Mama wrote him, or Bessie Mae or Cora Mae. He even got a couple of letters from his namesake and his benefactor, Mister Charles Wakefield himself, in person. Some good news, some bad news. A storm was gathering all over Mississippi and lightning striking close to home. The real big thing was voter registration.

Mama Carrie's letters were usually filled up with who died, who got born, and who got married. Birth, marriage, death, but she always closed with some kind of wisdom for the times. "Lord have mercy, we finding out, every day the Lord sends, just how much the white folks really hate us." And she always ended with "Write us and let us know how you getting along, and pray regular. God help us."

Bessie Mae was the news commentator on the happenings. Cracker plantation owners in nearby counties were running Negro croppers off the land for registering to vote. Churches were dynamited. Four Negroes in Barksdale County found murdered in bed, on the roadside, in the woods, and in a public park. Nobody had been arrested. But the people keep on registering. And Little Jake walking around talking about organizing a Wakefield County branch of the Deacons for Defense and Justice. "The *Chronical* say it ain't nothing but Commonism pure and simple. And it shall not come to Wakefield County. And I reckon that make me a Commonist, cause I'm with the whole thing all the way. If the little black train come this way, I'm sure Lord gon git on board. Uncle Bish is going down slow. He's drinking hisself to a early grave. He done left home or Miss Sallie Belle done put him out. He living with a no-good woman over in Tybeeville in East Wakefield over by the paper mill. Some folk say he working for the police, say he a spotter, but I don't believe Uncle Bish would stoop to that." She wished Chuck Othello was there with them. They needed young blood, especially with an education, to lead the struggle. "Cause it's coming just as sure as guns is made of iron."

Cora Mae's letter went along the same line. "We digging in to fight the crackers. Get an education and hurry home."

Ironically, Charles Wakefield's letter expressed some of the same concern for him to get an education. "We'll need calm, intelligent, young militant leadership to cool down the hotheads and the know-nothings of both races. And that's why I'm counting on you to fill the bill on the colored side."

Letters from home often left him in a strange kind of mood, difficult to put his finger on the way the letters left him feeling. Was it guilt? Sometimes he felt guilty no matter how emphatically he denied it. Felt that he had run away just as the fight was to begin. Sometimes he felt that his being at the University was one great big tremendous irrelevance. Ronnie was always talking about dropping out of school and going to 'Sippi or 'Bam and joining the Movement. But it never left the talking stage.

Othello went to see Dr. Jacobson one night and talked it over with him. He was learning good words now. "I feel totally irrelevant now," Chuck said. He was building his vocabulary, becoming articulate, he thought. "Here I am stuffing my head with Shakespeare and Keats, Yeats and Plato, and Western Civilization, and history in my time is about to be made right down there in the county I was born in."

Jacobson had given him a can of beer when he came in. He

[209]

sipped it nervously. Jacobson was the kind of listener who listened so attentively you could almost hear him listening. He was all attention and concern. He looked you in the eyes and mouth and seemed to try to anticipate the words before they issued forth. He was sipping Scotch and soda. He said, "What you're asking me is to advise you to quit school and join the Movement, but I simply cannot do that in good conscience. Either that, or you want me to convince you that it is proper to remain in school, and I cannot tell you that either. It is a decision you will have to make. But I will say this. The longer you stay in school the more valuable you will be to the Movement in the long run, once you leave. And I guarantee you it will be a long run. As David Woodson says, there is no revolution yet, but the revolt, the rebellion, has begun and it will eventually develop into a full-grown revolution."

The boy looked down at his shoes; he looked up and around the living room. He looked back at Dr. Jacobson. "But where does that leave me?"

"It leaves you at the University soaking up an education instead of dropping out to join the Movement and probably ending up in Vietnam shooting other colored people. They're drafting drop-outs like crazy, you know, especially colored ones."

Chuck stared down at his shoes again. He thought painfully of Junior.

"When and if you finish college, what're you going to do? Go back and live in Mississippi?"

He downed the rest of the ice-cold beer. He turned the question over in his mind. Did he really have this fierce dedication to the Movement and the Southland? Or did hearing from home merely bring to the surface the deep guilt in him, a guilt that told him he had no intention of casting his lot with Bessie Mae and Uncle Bish and Cora Mae and Little Jake and Daddy and Mama Carrie and living out his life in 'Sippi. Somehow he was angered by Dr. Jacobson's question. Somehow he felt righteously indignant. He almost stammered. "Why—what do you mean?"

"I mean, are you going to stay with the South or will you head north? It would certainly be understandable if you did."

He said, too forcefully, "Of course I'm going to stay in the South! What do you think? It's my home!" He lowered his voice. "I'm going back to Wakefield County. What do you think, I'm a fink or something?" Then he stopped and shook his head. "The truth is—I don't know what I'm going to do."

But like Ronnie, he stayed in school.

Ronnie told him a few days later. "Like I would really split this scene, old broad, and do duty in 'Bam or 'Sippi, but I'm not ready for no extensive ocean voyage, if you know what I mean. That Viet Cong over there is kicking asses and taking names. And I love Sister Gilbert too much to make her into one of those unhappy Gold Star Mothers."

Christmastime came and Chuck went home; he was astonished at the way the town had changed. Everything everywhere else in the world was expanding, and here in his own home town and county, things seemed to be shriveling up, withering away, things and people. It was just like Ronnie had said when he kidded him. Wakefield City was a one-horse whistle-stop. No more, no less. Ronnie had said, "Baby, the train doesn't stop in your home town. They got a sawdust pile on the edge of town and they just slow up and you jump off into it." At another time he'd said, "Wakefield's so small you can stand in the middle of town and piss all the way to the city limits."

Folks in Wakefield County looked at it differently. It was their Chuck Othello who had changed, not they. Not that they blamed him for changing. You were supposed to change, or what was the use of going to college? Just so he had not changed in his heart. He went to church that first Sunday with his parents and they were bursting wide open with pride. He was the first Chaney to ever study at a college, and that was really something. It was a grand achievement. Reverend Purdy welcomed him back to the church as if he were a cross between the prodigal son and a very important person. Asked him to stand so that everybody could see him, as if he were a celebrity from up-the-country. When the services ended he stood near the door shaking hands with the brothers and sisters, old and young, who came up to him. Some of the older sisters hugged him to them, some of them kissed him.

"Done gone up to that college place and got pretty as a Georgia peach."

"Don't even sound like you used to."

"Boy, don't you put on no college airs with me," Miss Ella Mae said to him devilishly as she put her arms around him and kissed him loudly on his cheek. Her daughter, Bessie Mae, stood just behind her, her sweet face blank and noncommittal.

When Miss Ella Mae released him, Bessie Mae walked up to him and held her hand out limply to him. "You ain't been up to that University so long, that you forgot the way out the Bottom, have you?"

He said lamely, "Are you kidding?"

She said, "Well, you sure didn't answer nobody's letters. That's one thing and that ain't two."

He went to see her one evening, and sat in the front room watching television along with Miss Ella Mae, who, after a miserable half an hour passed, got up and excused herself. "I'm glad you came to see us, Mister College Man. I'm sorry I got to leave you right long in now," she said with a twinkle in her eyes. "But I promised Sister Carson I was gon drop in on her tonight. Sallie Belle gits along right poorly sometime here lately."

Miss Ella Mae did not get very far down the road before Chuck gathered Bessie Mae into his arms and his body hard up against the softness of her anxious body, his mouth against her soft red lips, her mouth open greedily, and their tongues staging a kind of war of quiet desperation, his chest against the softness of her busy bosom, stomach to quivering stomach, hard thighs against soft thighs, his sex was hard as a brick now and big against the region where her sex lived leapingly, and even still they tried to get closer. They sighed, they hugged, they kissed. They came up for air. "Chuck Othello, how come you didn't answer my letters?" . . . "I was so busy, Bessie Mae—I was so busy catching up —you have no idea—" . . . In a clinch again they tried to get closer than before, which of course was not possible. She tasted so sweet; smelled so good like he remembered! Felt so good, Great God A'mighty! If this wasn't love it would have to do till the real thing came along. She said, "Sugar-pie, I can't stand it!"

They swapped spit crazily. They could feel and taste and smell the want they shared for one another. "You got another girl beating my time up there at the University?" He said, "I swear to the Good Lord up on High, there is no other girl, there is no one but you!" And kiss and tongue and swap spit and press hard up against my love and my hand slides down to the plumpness of her precious ass and pull her up against me even closer, till I feel a glorious wetness and my love drips slowly from me.

He tried to slide her dress up as they stood there in a darkened corner of the room, but she pulled away and backed away, "No, Chuck Othello! Please, doll baby! Mama might come home any minute! Please! I beg you! Naw! Naw!"

He murmured, "All right, I'm sorry." But when she went into his arms again, his hands seemed to have a mind of their own as they sought to raise her dress again, and she stood with him for a moment and all up against him and mouth to mouth her body trembling for the moment of sweetness unbearable, but when he tried to pull her pants down she pulled away again. And she started to cry. The whole thing was an exercise in sweet frustration. She went into the kitchen and got a cold glass of water and drank it down. She came back into the front room with a glass of water for her love. He drank it down.

When he had finished, she held his hand, but stayed out of his embrace. "Chuck Othello," she said, "baby doll. I feel the same way you do, but there's a time and place for everything. Maybe if you send for me, I'll come and spend a weekend with you up there at the University."

He tried to imagine Bessie Mae Moocho at the University. The picture somehow eluded his imagination. Maybe he could rent a room somewhere in town for her, just for a weekend. He said weakly, "That's a good idea, Bessie Mae."

She said, "You just send for me, and I'll come a-running."

Then she said, "You seen Little Jake since you been home?"

He said, "I just got home two or three days ago."

She said, "Let's go see if we can catch up with him. I think I know where he hanging out."

They walked down the pitch-dark street of the dusty road, and he remembered walking down this road so many times, in that far-off time of just three or four months ago, when he'd thought that Wakefield was the center of gravity of the whole magnificent universe. She said, "I expect he over to the Harlem Hideaway. That's the new place we got out here for colored." She laughed masochistically. "It's the only place out here for colored. And it ain't new, leastwise the building ain't. It used to be a grocery store. Old Man Ridley's, but we boycotted that mean old pecker-wood and run him outa business. He was selling meat you could smell five blocks away. He put fist and meat and maggots and all upon them devilish scales of his and charged you for the whole damn mess."

They heard Harlem Hideaway blocks away, and it was jump-

[213]

ing. You could hear the jukebox blasting with rock 'n' roll à la Little Richard. You could hear talking, could hear laughter.

Chuck thought, I got plenty of nothing and like nothing baby is sure nuff plenty for me. He thought, My people are the happiest people in all this world. He said aloud, "We sure are some happy people."

"What we?" she asked him. "You mean you and Miss Mama Carrie and Mister Jess? Y'all all that happy?"

He said, "You know, I mean, we colored people."

She said, "Speak for yourself and your University people. Cause I sure am one Negro who ain't all that everlasting happy."

He said lamely, "Always laughing and dancing and singing. You know now, Bessie Mae, colored folk ain't got a care in the world." He was half-teasing and half-serious. "Always whooping and hollering even in church. Shouting all over the place."

She said heatedly, "They sure don' teach much mother wit up at the University, I can state you that. If you don't know why black folks shout so much in church, you ain't got as much sense as you had when you left the county. You can believe me when I say so. Black folks get so happy in church cause that's the only place they can be happy. This old white world is hard; that's how come they seek a little peace every now and then with Jesus."

He knew she spoke now deep from inside of her, and he wondered at her ability to dig so deeply, and wondered at his own superficiality, which he admitted silently to himself. She was a full-grown woman and he was still a college boy. She had had to come to grips with life and he had put it off for a time.

The man charged fifty cents apiece at the door of Harlem Hideaway and the big sport from the University gave him a dollar bill and he entered with his lady from the Bottom. He looked around the crowded room for Little Jake, but he could hardly see four feet in front of him for the smoke screen sent up by tobacco smokers. At first, it was like walking into a darkened movie house; it took him some time before he could make out faces through the man-made fog. On one side of the floor were a few tables where men and women sat and drank their troubles and laughed and talked. On the other side was where the action was, all kinds of action, most of all, all kinds of dancing. The Twist, the Frug, Watusi, the Bird, the Dirty Dog, this and that, it seemed a hundred variations. There was a pungent smell of inexpensive perfume and body perspiration and rotgut whiskey.

[214]

The floor had been concrete once upon an ancient time, but now it was mostly dirt, here and there covering a few patches of cement. It was, moreover, dirt sprinkled with sawdust, which made a crazy combination.

"There he is," Bessie Mae said.

They made their way through the fog and dancing people toward Little Jake as he sat at one of the front tables with two other young men, drinking beer directly from the bottle. A good warm feeling coursed through Chuck, as he neared his childhood buddy. "Hey there! Little Jake himself, in person, beating up his gums as usual!"

Jake was talking a mile a minute and waving the beer bottle as if it were a baton. He looked up, and his wide face cracked into a great big smile. "Kiss my Auntie in the country!" he exclaimed. He got to his feet and he seized Chuck at the shoulders and he took Chuck's hand and started to pump it like he expected to get water. "Goddamn old rose! Look who's here! Look who's here!" He introduced Chuck to his friends at the table, Noah Abernathy and Willie Banks. "Set down—set down!" He pulled two chairs from another table. He stared hard at Bessie Mae and looked back at Chuck. "And I see you in good company just like usual." He ordered beer for them. "Well! Well! Well! Kiss my Auntie in the country."

Bessie Mae said laughingly, "Watch your language in the company of a lady." It felt good for her to see these two together, and with her; to feel that Chuck was still a part of them, to feel that their lives were interwoven with his forever. She had never felt she could hold Chuck to them, really hold him. Ever since she could remember, he had always come out to the Bottom and shared two or three hours of their lives and then back he would go to Minksville, where the living was easy, by comparison. Only by comparison. And when he went off to college she thought surely he had left their lives forever, their small, cruel, penny-ante, uneducated lives. She had loved these two boys, now reaching manhood, ever since she could remember. Loved Jake as a brother, loved Othello as a lover of all lovers. Her heart had placed him on a pedestal.

When Othello left for the University, she, in a kind of last-ditch desperation, created within herself an unquenchable thirst for knowledge, a starvation for the written word. Since college was out of the question, she decided she would educate herself by reading everything she could lay her hands on. She had a job working in the white folks' house for thirty dollars a week and she spent much too much of her salary for books. She borrowed books, stole books. All kinds of books. She wanted to increase her vocabulary, to build up a store of knowledge inside of her. She went to see Miss Ida Lee. Miss Ida Lee lent her books about the Negro. All kinds of wonderful books. She filled her head so full of books she sometimes thought it would burst wide open. She had to do something to at least keep within shouting distance of the University man. She told herself, she had to.

Little Jake explained to Chuck that Noah and Willie were from a nearby county where they worked day and night on getting the Negro to register to vote. "We going to be doing the same thing right here in Wakefield County." Chuck stared at his buddy. Little Jake had changed. It was hard for Chuck to put his finger on the precise nature of the change. In the first place, of course, he had become a man. Boyhood was gone forever. But there were other changes. Ever since Jake had dropped out of school a few years back, he had ambled along from job to job with a kind of studied aimlessness. Most grown folk said he was just a "don't care" rascal. Little Jake used to say about himself, "I don't give a good goddamn if the sun don't shine tomorrow morning and if it don't never shine no more." But now there was something new about him and his face was all alit like someone who had been born again and whose soul had been converted to a new kind of religion.

"We gon stand this county on its ass, excuse me, Bessie Mae, I mean its hindparts, old buddy, and you just ought to be here."

"He ought to be up there at the University just like he is, getting some sense and education in his head."

Jake stared at Bessie Mae Moocho. He had always been in love with her ever since he could remember. "I knew you was going to take up for his side. You always did and I reckon you always will."

The jukebox was detonating eardrums now with an old blues fragment by Lightning Hopkins. Real honest-to-goodnes, down-in-the-bottom, gutbucket blues. Slow drag blues.

I'm jes settin' here with my arms fold-ded

The dancers of all ages and descriptions went *scrunch—scrunch-scrunch,* as they scraped across the dirt and cement and

[216]

sawdust, the couples holding each other tightly and close together, thigh to thigh, belly to belly, cheek to cheek, as if this were the last dance before the Day of Judgment. It was like an act of pure and simple, sweet and lonely desperation.

Scrunch-scrunch, scrunch-scrunch.

Chuck felt a kind of guilty feeling as he looked from Jake to Bessie Mae and back again. "Don't you worry about a thing, Little Jake," he said. "I'll be back in the good old summertime."

Jake said, "I ain't worried, buddy. I got enough to worry with these bad-ass peckerwoods."

Noah Abernathy said, "We gon need mens with a good education. Ain't no doubt about it."

The sassy look on Jake's wide face had changed to one of seriousness. He loved Chuck Othello like a brother, and like a brother he was jealous of him, sometimes. "You really coming back ain'tchoo, buddy boy? We really truly need you bad!"

Chuck thought his eyes might be filling up. He didn't want these people to depend on him. He was embarrassed by the love and trust and huskiness he heard in Jake's voice, saw in Jake's narrow eyes. He got up and shook Willie's and Noah's hands and lastly Little Jake's. "I've got to be going now. I'll see you again before I go back to school." The two friends looked into each other's eyes. Warmly. Chuck Othello's voice was husky now. "For God's sakes, take care of yourself, Little Jake. And give my love to Miss Sallie Belle and Uncle Bish. But for Christ sakes look out for these peckerwoods."

Bessie Mae got up to leave with him. She said goodnight to Jake and his buddies and they made their way through the man-made fog of tobacco smoke and dust and dirt and sawdust being kicked up by the dancers who were doing frantic gyrations now to the tune of a wailing cat named Leon Bibb singing "Dink's Blues" like it was supposed to be sung. The guitar was naturally talking that talk.

If I had wings like Noah's dove—

They walked around the Bottom in the dark that night; his senses drank in all of the sounds and smells and tastes and sights of that night in the Bottom with Bessie Mae at his side, his hand staging a quiet wrestling match with hers. They stood in the dark grass beneath a chinaberry tree and he held her in his arms and

[217]

promised to come back to her and Jake and Wakefield County in the summertime.

And he meant to keep his promise.

One night in the early fall of that year, late September, Jake's father had gone down on Douglass Avenue which was the street where the colored businesses were situated. One short block of colored business right off Rob Lee Boulevard. He went from Douglass Avenue into Douglass Alley and got real juiced at a juice joint that sold the kind of "white lightning" that made you cuss your preacher and play the dozens with your mama. He was roaring drunk. Actually he had drunk the kind of whiskey that would not let you walk. It made you run. He was running drunk. He lost his sense of direction, and there he was running through a very very lower-middle-class white section of Wakefield City, when he saw an automobile coming toward him down the street. He must have thought he was in the Bottom, because he stopped and stood in the middle of the road, trying to flag the car down.

There were five white men in the car and they were cruising, trying to see what was happening in that part of town that time of night, figuring if anybody was on the street of the opposite sex, she would not be coming from prayer meeting.

"I shore could use me a nice piece of tail, the Good Lord up in Heaven knows I could," Matthew Billings said. He sighed. "Something about fifteen years old, a pure divine white virgin. I'd like to bust that cherry and feel the blood all over my old joy stick, I deswear fore God I would."

Otis Millgate, who was driving, said, "Man sir, I could use me some good juicy black stuff tonight. Ain't nothing in the whole wide world like a nigger cherry. Fourteen years old and red hot as cayenne pepper. You can smell it a mile away. Great God A'mighty! Put ten long extra years on to your life."

Lionel Sandford chuckled from the back seat. "Both of y'all oughta be shame of yourself. It's all in your mind anyhow. Y'all better leave that young pussy alone, if you know what's good for you. Itta kill you just as dead as you got to die."

Sam Rawlins said, "We oughta go out into the Bottom and find us a nigger and cut his nuts out and hang em on a telegraph post and put up a sign saying, 'This Poor Black Ignant Bastard Insisted on his Civil Rights'!"

Millgate said, "If you go out to the Bottom tonight, you damn sure won't go with me and in this car. Them some bad-ass niggers in the Bottom. I oughta know, cause it's part of my goddamn policy debit." He was an insurance agent.

Sandford said, "Ain't had no trouble outa our niggers here lately about that civil rights mess, so we better let well enough alone."

Rawlins said, "The thing to do is make a example outa one of em and make sure ahead of time that they don't get no more funny notions in they head."

Sandford argued, "I say, as long as the nigger don't step outa line, let him be. He got a right to live as much as anybody else."

Rawlins laughed. "Boy, if I didn't known you all my life, I'd swear fore God you wasn't nothing but a straight-out nigger-lover."

"And if I didn't known you all my life, I'd take you outa this car and give you a swift kick in your asshole."

The entire car erupted with drunken good-natured laughter.

Just as the laughter died away, Rawlins said, "Whoa!—what is this the Good Lord done set before us? I knowed to my pure white heart he was listening to my prayer."

Millgate brought the car to a halt, and there stood Uncle Bish in the direct beam of the headlights not more than seven feet away.

"Hey!" Uncle Bish shouted. "Nigger, take that goddamn light out of my face!" He staggered closer toward the car. "Take that goddamn light outa my eyes, mother-fucker!"

"Watch your tongue, you black sonuvabitch!" From the car.

"Who you calling a black sonuvabitch, mother-fucker? And take that goddamn light outa my eyes!"

The white men got out of the car, Sandford weakly protesting, and they dragged Uncle Bish to the car and threw him into the back seat, and beat him all about his head and pistol-whipped him; then they drove him out of town in a northerly direction and drove off the road into a thicket of bush and pine and cypress trees, and they dragged him out of the car and threw him into the clearing, and trained the headlights on him.

Bish looked up at them as they stood around him, three of them with pistols drawn. He knew his time had come and his race was run. He began to plead with them. "Please white folks, I ain't done nothing to nobody! I ain't done nothing to nobody!"

"Shet your black mouth, nigger!" Rawlins said, as he went upside Bish's head with his heavy shoe. Bish was bleeding from several bruises on his head and face now.

"Please don't lynch me, white folks! I swear fore God I ain't done nothing! Please don't lynch this poor black nigger!"

Rawlins said, "I hear tell all you black boys got great big black ones, boy. Pull it out and let me see it."

Millgate had warmed up to the game by now. "Yeah," he shouted. "Pull that black thing out, boy. I want to see is it true what they say about Dickie." He started to sing: "Is it true what they say about big black Dickie?" And they all had a good laugh, excepting Sandford.

Sandford said, "Come on, let's leave him out here. We done taught him a good lesson."

Bish said, "I don't know what you gennermens talking about."

Rawlins said, "We talking about that little biddy old thing you got in tween your legs. We want to see how big it is."

Bish still cringed before them. "I ain't did nothing, white folks. What is I done for y'all to do this to me?"

"Nigger, if you don't pull that black thing outa your britches, I'm gon personally kick the shit outa you."

Bish stood up and faced the white pranksters. "Well, goddammit, all right, you pale-faced mother-fuckers. Kill me! I don't give a good goddamn!"

Rawlins walked up to Bish and put the nose of his pistol up against Bish's forehead and cocked it. "Pull it out, Sambo, before I count to three, or I'll blow your black ass into hell."

Sandford said, "You better pull it out, boy. He'll kill you sure as Heaven's happy."

Sweat rained in torrents from all over Bish's body. He pulled his thing out of his trousers.

"Goddamn!" Matthew Billings shouted. "He got something hung on him like a co-cola bottle! That black bastard got a mule dick!"

"Shit!" Millgate said contemptuously. "It ain't big as my little biddy pinkie on my left hand." He spat on Bish's baggy trousers.

Rawlins said, "Give us an exhibition, boy. Let's see you play with it."

Bish said, "I don't play that, sir. Nawsir, I don't play with it like that, sir. They say that'll run you crazy."

Millgate pointed his pistol at Bish. "Play with it, you civil

[220]

rights bastard! Or all us will blow your head off at the same damn time."

Bish looked around at them. All of them had their pistols pointed at his head, except for Sandford who was unarmed.

Rawlins pulled a long switchblade out of his pocket and clicked it open. "All right, Mister Civil Rights, you don't give us a little ole exhibition, I'll cut it off all the way up to your ass-hole!" He came up close to Bish, and Bish felt the sharp edge of the cold steel on his penis.

Millgate said, "That's how come so many niggers go crazy, they play with themselfs too much, and that's how come they dicks git so big. They hand-maiden."

All the white men laughed and cackled. An owl hooted from nearby. A rabbit scooted through the brush. The wind blew through the cypress trees.

"Fuck your fist, you black civil rights bastard!"

"No sir! I ain't never had nothing to do with no silver rights. I declare fore God I ain't!"

Rawlins laughed and said, pleasantly, "I'm gon count to three, and if you ain't fucking your fist by the time I say three, we gon blow your nappy head off."

"ONE!"

"And I'm gon slice it half in two."

Frogs were croaking to beat the band.

Bish could feel the increased pressure of the sharp edge of the switchblade on his penis. He thought the cold steel had cut him to the bone.

"TWO!"

And Bish began to fuck his fist.

"That's more lack it!" Rawlins said.

Millgate said, "You ain't punishing that nigger none. That nigger's having himself the time of his life. Ain't nothing being punished but his fist. He's like a rabbit in the briar patch."

And the white men whooped and hollered.

Sweat poured from all over Uncle Bish, as he pumped on his penis for the amusement of the playful white men.

"Beat it harder, boy!" Matthew Billings shouted. "You ain't even got it stiff yet. Great God A'mighty! Daisy Belle should be here to see this sight. She ain't gon b'lieve it when I tell her!"

Rawlins agreed. "Yeah, we ought've brung the girls along."

"Beat it faster, boy! Git a hard on! You ain't no sissy, is you?"

"Whoever heard of a nigger who couldn't git a hard on?"

"There's some nigger sissies too. I done heard tell of em."

It was true. No matter how fast Bish pumped, his penis would not get hard. But sweat rained from him and tears cascaded from his eyes.

Millgate said, "We oughta have a naked white woman out here. I'll bet it 'ud git hard quick enough, I betcha."

Mosquitoes, candleflies, praying mantis, and a million other insects held their orgy around the headlights.

Millgate dropped his trousers and his drawers and tucked his penis out of sight between his legs and shuffled toward Uncle Bish, wiggling and twisting, imitating a flamboyant faggot. "Just make tend I'm a woman, black boy, and a pure white woman at that. That oughta make your nature rise."

Sandford looked on in disgust. "For Christ sakes, Millgate!" The other white men howled and hollered.

"That's the best-looking pussy you ever seen, ain't it, nigger?" He waltzed around Uncle Bish and did a little dance.

"For Christ sakes, Millgate!"

Millgate came up very close to Uncle Bish and rubbed his pubic hairs against Uncle Bish's manhood. "That oughta git it up quick enough, I reckon."

Rawlins said, "To hell with that shit!" And pushed Millgate aside. He put his pistol up against Bish's head again. "Nigger, I want you to tell me who it is around here stirring up this here civil rights mess."

"I declare fore God, I don't know a thing about it, Mister Rawlins."

"Don't you call my name, nigger. You don't know me."

"Yes sir, I know you all right, Mister Rawlins. Known you nearly 'bout every since I known my own self."

"You call my name again and I'm gonna blow your black brains out." He shoved his pistol up against Bish's forehead. "You gon tell me the name of the civil rights niggers or ain'tcha?"

Bish shook his head, as sweat poured from him. He was leaking perspiration. "I deswear fore the living God, I ain't know nothing 'bout no silver rights. No-sir-ree-bob!"

"Git down on your knees, nigger!" Millgate said to the others, "I'll show you how to handle the bastard."

Bish got down on his knees. Millgate stood naked to his waist. "Open your mouth, black boy."

Bish opened his mouth. Millgate stood above him and close to him. "Nigger you gon tell us who that head nigger is in this civil rights mess? That foreign nigger from out the county?"

"I don't know no foreign nigger. I deswear fore God."

Millgate shoved his penis into Bish's mouth. "You bet not bite down on it, else I'll send your black ass straight to hell!"

Bish fell backward and puked his guts.

Sandford said, "Goddammit, Millgate, I b'lieve you one of them funny fellers."

Millgate turned toward Sandford, waving his gun. "I don't take that shit from nobody."

Sandford said, "I didn't mind what you did to the nigger, but you sure did make like one of them funny fellers. I mean a man doing it with another man."

"He ain't no man, he's a nigger. That's the point I was making."

"The only point you made was, you kind of a funny feller your own damn self."

Millgate lunged toward Sandford, gun in hand. "I don't take that shit off nobody's body."

Rawlins stepped between them. "All right, boys. That's enough of that now."

Millgate was almost at arm's length from Sandford. He pointed his gun at Sandford, almost touching his forehead. A great bull-bat swooped down toward the headlights and away again. Millgate said, "I don't take that kinda shit from nobody!"

Sandford reached out quickly and grabbed Millgate's gun hand. And they began to wrestle. By the time Sam Rawlins parted them and they looked around for Bish Carson, he had taken off into the bush.

Chapter
4

He was glad to get back to the University. He hadn't realized
how much it had grown on him, till he went home that first
Christmas. It was not that he did not enjoy his Christmas back
in Wakefield County. He told himself, it was just that he was
impatient to get through his years at the University and get out
into life and living. It took a few days to get back into the
routine at school, especially to get back into the discipline of
studying. Dr. Jacobson offered his place for studying again, and
Chuck accepted.

That first Wednesday, he spent five hours of nervous expectation and absorbed very little of what his eyes beheld on the pages
of his books. She did not come at all that first Wednesday. And
for an entire week he wondered about her. What had happened
to her? Maybe she had quit her job? He started many times to
ask Dr. Jacobson about her, but he yielded not to the temptation. On the second Wednesday, he was truly in a nervous state
by the time he got to Jacobson's. It took him minutes to fit the
key into the lock, and when he entered he was disappointed
again; as he went from room to room he felt his growing disappointment, until he came into the kitchen where he found her
fixing coffee. She uttered a happy noise of surprise and dropped
the coffee container and came to him and threw her arms around
his neck and kissed him joyously full on the mouth. She pushed
her mouth against his mouth momentarily, and then she pushed
him away from her, and looked him up and down, with her
happy glowing insinuating eyes, as she had a way of doing, making him feel wonderfully uncomfortable. Her eyes almost always
seemed to be amused at him.

"I'm so glad to see you, baby sweet," she said. "I really missed
you awful much. I thought you wasn't coming back." Then she
turned from him and made two cups of coffee and gave him one,
and he stood there like two bumps on Dick's dog, staring at her.

She laughed at him. "All right now. Gwan get your school work. And I sure Lord got my work to do."

He went to the study, and she did not bother him again till she was ready to leave. Then she came to his door and said, "Goodbye, now. See you next Wednesday, if I live and nothing don't happen. I was sick as a dog last Wednesday, and you didn't even send me a little old git-well card."

He said seriously, "How was I to know? And I don't even have your address."

She said, "I forgive you this time. My address is four-five-seven Ludlow Lane. All right now, I'mon see you, hear?" And she turned to go and got to the front door and came back to his door again. She said, "What you doing Friday night?"

He said, "Nothing."

She said, "How come you don't come over to my house and git a home-cooked meal for a change? I don't like to brag, but I can really mess up some somethin' to eat."

He said, "I'll come if I'm invited."

"You invited, Mister Charles Othello. Four-five-seven Ludlow Lane. Seven o'clock'll be just about right. I don't live but 'bout four blocks from the campus."

Friday night came, and as he walked through the cold night, he was sharply conscious of the neighborhood surrounding Douglass University. He had noticed long before the sharp contrast between the University and the neighborhood. Douglass sat smack down in the middle of the city's largest slum, and had practically no visible relationship to the slum, except that most of the people on the Douglass campus were of similar pigmentation to the people of the neighborhood. As he walked now with his coat collar up around his neck, his eyes took in the two- and three- and four-room houses, dying of old age and lack of attention. The black ghetto in this glamorous city was not too much different from his Minksville in Wakefield County. He saw a woman come out of her back door and watched her walk shivering down a path that led to an outhouse about twenty yards away. She opened the door and disappeared inside. He couldn't help imagining how cold her bare backside would be when she went about her business. Then he noticed that all the houses on the street had their little lean-tos in the back. They looked as if a good strong wind would put them into orbit, folks inside of them and all. Somehow a memory came to him from somewhere

[225]

out of the past. And he was a boy again, walking down the hill to the Bottom to see Jake and Bessie Mae and Uncle Bish, and an old lady carried a baby in her arms and walked out into the backyard and squatted to do her business. He felt an angry warmth now gathering in his collar, even as he had felt an angry wetness in his eyes on that summer day so long ago. Douglass University sat among the groaning misery of this sprawling ghetto like an oasis in the middle of a barren desert. Douglass sat there in its tower of indifference in an aura of total contempt toward the people of the ghetto. And Chuck Othello was a part of Douglass.

Naomi Hester lived in a two-room wooden-frame house. The aroma of home-cooking assaulted Othello's nostrils as he came up on the porch. Fried chicken! He knocked. It seemed like centuries before he heard her coming to the door. And when she opened it, he stood there momentarily, staring at her. She was dressed to kill, with her hair combed in an upsweep like Josephine Baker. She wore a blue print dress (it looked brand-new) and her large earrings did something for her eyes. He had not noticed that they were so large and dark and wide before. She wore a gingham apron over her dress.

She smiled. "Come on in and close your mouth. The something to eat ain't quite ready for you yet."

He laughed weakly. "Am I too early, Miss Naomi? You so dressed up, you must be expecting company."

"You the only company." She laughed. "Come on in and leave all that weather outside and take the weight off your feet."

He walked in and closed the door. And she led him to a couch in her front room which functioned as a living room and bedroom combination. The back room was the kitchen where the action was. He could hear and smell the action.

She left him and brought back a glass of beer, and left him again. They had supper a little later. Fried chicken, creamed potatoes, snap beans and roasting ears, and a home-made coconut custard pie and hot coffee. They ate supper at the kitchen table. He told her if she wasn't the greatest cook in town she was a stomp-down good one. And he meant it. She knew she could throw some grub together. And enjoyed it. When they finished she led him to the front room couch, after he had protested lamely that he would do the dishes, at least help to do them, at least dry them. A few minutes later she came toward him taking off her apron, wearing the widest smile he had ever seen any human smile.

She sat near him for a moment trying to get a conversation going, but what did she know about how people talked at a university or even what they talked about. Then she got up and turned on her radio to a program of dance music, and she turned toward him and held out her hands and they were in each other's arms dancing to the crazy music. They Frugged at first and then Watusied. Then a slow one came over the radio, and they slow-dragged. She was not heavy this time as before, even though she leaned hard up against him from breast down to her thighs. And he knew she was a woman. And she knew he was a man.

She looked up into his face. "You the most seriousest boy I ever did see in all my born days."

He said stupidly, "I'm not serious."

She said, teasingly, "Oh—so you're just playing around with me, hunh?"

He was warm all over. "No m'am, Miss Naomi. You know I'm not playing around."

She laughed at him. "You the sweetest little old shameface thing I ever did see."

When the music stopped, he did not let go of her, and he clumsily sought her mouth with his mouth, and they kissed, and this time her tongue went in search of its opposite number. And found it. And she whispered softly, "My baby! My little biddy serious pretty baby!"

And they sat back on the couch. And he stared across the room and tried to think of something to say to her. He wanted her so badly he could barely keep his knees and thighs from quaking. What did you do with a woman her age? Just take her into your arms and be about the business? He didn't know. He wasn't sure. He didn't want to get out of line. But since she invited him there to be alone with her, she must've been ready for the challenge. She would think he was queer or something, if he didn't make his bid. He was a man, she was a woman, and he had to make his bid. He turned toward her. "Miss Naomi—"

"Yes sir, Mister Charles Othello?"

"I—er—mean—I don't want you to call me Mister."

"And I don't wantchoo to call me Miss. Whatchoo want me to call you? Little Brother?"

[227]

He said gruffly. "I'm not little, and I'm certainly not your brother."

She said, "Let's dance. You're getting too serious again."

And they were in each other's arms again, and this time she put both of her arms around his neck, and his face was a mask of seriousness now, even more so than before. She asked him, "What's the trouble?"

He said, "If you don't know by now, it sure won't do no good to tell you."

When they sat down this time, he took her into his clumsy arms, and he put his warm hand on her thigh, and then he put his hand up her dress, as he held her mouth fastened desperately to his mouth and tongue to tongue. But she pulled away from him. "Oooh-ooh-wee! You are a sassy boy! Miss Naomi going to give you the worst old spanking." And she got up from the couch and left him. "You just wait there till I git back." And she went through the kitchen to the back porch where he guessed the toilet was. He did not want to believe she had an outhouse. When she came back from the porch she wore a bathrobe with a nightgown underneath. And she told him to get ready, if he was going to spend the night.

He went through the kitchen like a man sleepwalking. He went out on the back porch where the toilet with running water was, the kind with the chain and bowl above. Out there in the cold, he wondered why he had gone out there. He had no bathrobe or pajamas. So he urinated.

When he came back inside, she told him, "You can undress in the kitchen."

He felt ridiculous as he stood in a corner of the kitchen undressing. By the time he had finished, she had made the sofa down into a bed, and was tucked in already. As he came toward her she began to laugh softly at him.

He got hot behind the ears. "What the hell you laughing about?"

She said, "How come you got your drawers on? Everything showing anyhow. You just sticking out all over." She laughed at him.

He stared down at himself and saw that she was absolutely right. He was sticking out all over. He came and got into the bed. And he turned toward her and took her in his arms and found that she was in her birthday suit. He wondered what had

[228]

happened to her bathrobe and her nightgown. But he did not wonder long. She was luxuriously equipped from head down to her foot. He rolled over on top of her and tried to get his member in without ado.

But she said, "Baby! We got all night long. Tomorrow is Saddy. Don't be such a greedy boy. Mama isn't ready yet." He tried to relax, as he felt her hands all over him. And she took one of his hands and guided it to the cave of love surrounded by the precious grass of life. And she said, "Play with me!" And she took his head and guided his mouth to one of her breasts. And he wasn't sure what she wanted at first, until she whispered, "Mama's baby suck the titty!"

And as he put his finger inside of her sex, he sucked from one breast to the other. And the woman squirmed and twisted beneath him. "Oh bay-bee! Oh bay-bee! My sweet sweet baby!" Her eyes closed, her face aglow with love and love's anticipation. She had her hands all over him. She held his sex in one of her hands. She squeezed it and she squeezed it. He had never felt this way before, never ever. His manhood was so hard he thought it would break off in her hand.

Finally she cried softly, "Now! Now! Put it in now!" And he tried desperately and clumsily and without success to probe her love cave, and finally she took matters into her own hands, and put him into her, and they made love.

And "Bay-bee! Bay-bee! Bay-bee! Oh! Oh! Oh, my baby!" Even the sofa bed itself cried out in a kind of vicarious association with the rapture of the love being made. Miss Naomi and Mister Charles Othello rode the winds of love together, they rode the love winds in each other's arms, together they rode the winds of love until they reached the glorious city at the very same millionth of a second. And they overflowed together, as they both shook like St. Vitus and the bed moved out from under them, surely the bed moved out from under them and the room shook like an earthquake. And love spilled over everything and everybody.

He awoke a few hours later. He did not know where he was at first. He awoke, and had been having a sweet dream, the very sweetest dream he ever had, and he thought he was still asleep, even though he was wide awake. He felt a kissing of his ears, a gnawing and a tonguing really, and he felt a warm hand in between his legs. The room, the bed were filled with love, and

[229]

his nostrils drank in the sharp and salty odor of the love already made. He closed his eyes and opened them again and turned over on his side and stared into the face of the woman whose face was all alit with love. She was a good-looking woman to begin with, but the rapture of the love they'd made had transformed her into the loveliest of women, physically, spiritually. She was beauty and beauty was Naomi Hester. She was the glorious black angel of love and beauty. He felt his throbbing sex grow in her hand, and he rolled over on Miss Naomi, glorious Naomi, sweet and lovely lady, wondrous woman. And they made joyous love again.

Chapter 5

It was a rough, white, hard and ruthless winter, in New York town, the kind of winter that kept your nostrils blowing and your eyes forever full of tears. It was a cold, cruel, white winter, especially for Carrie Louise's roommate. It was a winter when Death grimly stalked the land. Carrie Louise could not get over the fact that her roommate, not quite nineteen years old, would go out each morning to the newsstand on Broadway near the subway and buy *The New York Times,* and come back to the dormitory and turn first of all to the obituary page. After she scanned the bad news, she would usually let a sigh of relief ooze out of her. "Hooray and hallelujah, everybody who's anybody made it through the night." Then to the other pages.

This ritual began sometime in autumn of the time when Death would stalk the winter months. The trouble with Sherry Kingsley, she really knew almost everybody who was "black-and-anybody" in the Arts and in the Movement. First, there was Sam Cooke, whom she had met just once out at Town House Restaurant on Eastern Parkway in her native Brooklyn. She owned every record he ever made. And she was shaken at the news of his "crazy senseless death. Honeychile, it makes no damn sense at all!" And there was Nat Cole at the ripe old age of forty-five! She

sat around and played his records one after another, and her eyes
filled, and she sat around and swore to herself, "Goddamn!
Goddamn!"

She had very little to say to Honeychile that winter. She just
studied and played her records and swore softly to herself, as
Death grimly stalked the earth. Sometimes she gave Carrie Louise
such devastating looks, the girl from 'Sippi felt like crying out:
"Please! Please! You know damn well I'm not to blame for
deaths! You can't blame white folks for everything bad that happens on this earth. Even so, you can't blame me for being
white!"

She thought she heard Sherry mumble to herself one day,
"Death is a goddamn white man!"

When Lorraine Hansberry's new play, *The Sign in Sidney
Brustein's Window,* opened, Sherry and Carrie Lou went to opening night. Sherry laughed and wept throughout the entire play.
Afterward Sherry took Carrie Lou with her across the street to
Mama Leone's Restaurant to an opening-night party for *Brustein's Window.* Sherry went up to Lorraine, who was seated at
the head of one of the long tables; she was emaciated and racked
with pain—lonely-looking in the midst of a crowd of friends and
admirers. Sherry smiled her widest and most beautiful smile in
her whole repertoire of smiles. She did not have many smiles to
choose from. She was not a dedicated smiler. She threw her arms
around Lorraine.

"Oh darling! Darling Lorraine, it was so lovely! So beautiful!
It was poetry! It was Shakespeare—it was Shaw! It was Hansberry!"

Lorraine said, "Lord have mercy! You really liked it, Sherry?"

Sherry shook her head. "Liked it? I didn't like it—I loved it!
And I love you!" And she kissed Lorraine and turned away,
almost colliding with her roommate standing behind her, red-
faced with compassion. She mumbled, "This is my roommate,
Carrie Louise Wakefield." And Carrie Lou took the great young
woman's hand and said, "I'm mighty pleased to meet you. I think
the play was just wonderful!"

And bleary-eyed, Sherry led Carrie Lou over to a table in a
corner of the room where a crowd of people, black and white and
brown, were seated, including some of the members of the *Brustein's Window* cast and also including David Woodson. And of
course, Sherry knew Woodson. Woodson got up from the table
and took Sherry into his arms.

[231]

And "Sherry baby! How's the college girl?"

She introduced Carrie Lou to Woodson and the girl from 'Sippi felt her heart beat faster and a weakness in her knees. He made room for them and they sat there talking about the play and about everything else under the sun, with Carrie Lou staring directly into Woodson's mouth; he did not appear to notice, and Sherry, who rarely drank except on special occasions, began to drink herself into forgetfulness. Carrie Lou got drunk off the atmosphere and the conversation, which she thought to be the most brilliant she had ever heard.

Then one cold white morning a few weeks later, Carrie Lou went instead of Sherry over to Broadway and got the paper, and when she returned she scanned the front page and she said aloud almost unknowingly, "Oh no!"

Sherry said, half-jokingly, "Oh yes, honeychile. You don't expect to rule forever, do you? How many registered in 'Sippi this time? Fannie Hammer is my patron saint. Believe me when I say so."

Carrie Lou said, "Lorraine Hansberry!"

Sherry turned toward her, dropped the hairbrush from her hand. "Oh no! I don't want to hear it! Please! Do not read it to me! Do not read it to me!" She sank into a chair and sat as quietly as death itself. Carrie Lou knew Sherry was trying her best to cry, to wail and moan and let the ocean flood wash away the sorrow in her soul with tears. But Sherry just sat there, numb and dumb. Finally the tears began to spill quietly down her cheeks. She didn't bother to wipe her eyes or blow her nose. She looked like a little girl lost and scared and lonely. She uttered not a single sound, not a sob; she just sat there, let the tears spill down her cheeks.

Carrie Lou went with her to the funeral up in Harlem at the Church of the Masters. A cold white spell lay all over New York that Saturday. It had snowed all day and night the day before and all that Saturday morning. The church was packed with somber faces. Carrie Lou saw many famous and familiar faces among the honorary pallbearers. Sammy Davis, David Woodson. A soft-spoken minister, Reverend Callender, gave a quiet funeral oration. The great Paul Robeson spoke and Shelley Winters spoke and Ruby Dee, and Nina Simone played the organ. How she played the organ! People were wiping their eyes all over the church, some of them crying openly.

[232]

Outside the church, afterward, the snow still came down. Photographers made a nuisance of themselves taking pictures of celebrities who were in attendance. Sherry introduced Carrie Louise to Paul Robeson, Eslanda Robeson, Ossie Davis, Irving Burgie, and a tall rangy handsome red-bearded man by the name of Malcolm X. She called him Brother Malcolm.

The next day, which was Sunday, Sherry did not get dressed. She sat around all day and moped and sank deeper and deeper in a kind of morbid torpor of despair and helplessness. Late that afternoon she looked up and stared at Carrie Lou and said deliberately and slowly, "Death is a goddamn white man! Death is a goddamn white man!"

It was a silly thing to do, but Carrie Lou felt that she must somehow come to the defense of white manhood. "Come on, Sherry, I mean, be reasonable. You can't blame death on white folks, you just can't blame the white man for all the evil on this earth."

It was the bitterest look she had ever seen on Sherry's face. "Well now, honeychile, just like who has been responsible for centuries for the mass murders of mankind? I mean who killed six million Jews? I mean who killed sixty million blacks? I mean who dropped the bombs on Hiroshima and Nagasaki? Who is it spending billions for mass murder and trips to the moon while millions of humans starve all over the earth and others die of cancer?"

Carrie Lou's face reddened like a ripe pomegranate and then turned white as biscuit dough. "But you can't lump—I mean, collective guilt—I mean—"

Sherry's staring at her now was like spitting in her face. She could almost feel the spittle. "I'll tell you what I mean. I mean you white folk have the stench of death all over you."

Then a few weeks later the world stood still. It was a Sunday afternoon, and Sherry had gone to a meeting up at the northern tip of Harlem. She went almost every Sunday afternoon. Carrie Lou had asked her once or twice if she might go along with her. And Sherry's answer had been unequivocal. "I really think you'd better not." Unemotionally. Just—"I really think you'd better not. I mean, I've tried to expose you to as much blackness as your white soul could absorb, but this would be a little too rich for your blood. I mean, this one is for black folks only."

About three-fifteen that February afternoon, the girl from

[233]

Wakefield lay on her bed with a book in her lap, listening to music over the radio, and staring at the words in the book, seeing nothing. The girl was miles and miles away from where she was, in the sweet and crazy land of her daydreams. Then it happened.

We interrupt this program to bring you an important announcement. Black Nationalist leader Malcolm X has just been shot down while he spoke to a group of faithfuls at the Audubon Ballroom in upper Manhattan. It isn't clear yet how serious the wounds are. Stay close to this station for further developments.

She dropped the book and jumped from the bed. She had shaken his hand just two or three weeks ago at Lorraine Hansberry's funeral. She felt a great overwhelming helplessness. And she quaked all over as she remembered that Sherry was at the meeting at the Audubon. She went every Sunday. And Sherry loved Malcolm. Loved him selfishly and selflessly and completely, holding nothing back. Well, maybe, the girl from 'Sippi thought, maybe it isn't serious. Surely it isn't serious. It couldn't possibly be fatal. Malcolm exuded such a sense of indestructibility. She'd felt it when she'd met him at the funeral. Then the music was interrupted and the flash came that would change the world.

MALCOLM X IS DEAD! MALCOLM X IS DEAD!

Her eyes filled up. It could not be, and yet deep inside of her, she knew it was. It was! And always would henceforth and forever be. He was dead.

SHOT DOWN BY BLACK ASSASSINS,
ALLEGEDLY MUSLIMS . . .

She was ashamed of the relief she felt that they were black men, the assassins. They were nonwhite. She was glad they were nonwhite. The news kept coming every other minute.

THIRTY-TWO BULLETS ENTERED HIS BODY.

She stared at the radio in a hypnotic state of disbelief. Surely it was a dream, a nightmare, and she would wake up after awhile and later Sherry would come in and tell her about the meeting and how handsome Malcolm was and how manly and how he was the hope of black America, which was the hope of all America, all humankind. But she knew she was not dreaming. The finality of the statement.

[234]

MALCOLM X IS DEAD.

It was as if the radio itself had murdered him. Once announced dead, he was dead forevermore. Eternally dead everlastingly. There was no appeal from death pronounced by radio.

When Sherry came in a few hours later, she was calm, as if nothing had happened at all of a catastrophic nature, as if the sky had not fallen in on her. She said, "Hi, honeychile," and she got into her pajamas. And she got a book and she clicked on her desk lamp, as if she were going to dig for the night into some intensive concentration. She read for almost an hour. Then she looked up briefly and said to no one in particular, "Book-larnin', that's the only salvation for the nigrah." Bitterly. And she looked down at her book again.

There was another spell of silence in their room, a brief spell that seemed like hours to Carrie Lou. Then she said softly, tenderly, "But, Sherry, I mean, didn't you go to the meeting today? I mean, don't you know—" Her words hung in mid-air and no more words would issue forth from her.

Sherry looked up from her book and turned toward her roommate, her large eyes widening more than ever, like a little frightened girl lost in the Mississippi jungles. She stared at Carrie Lou. "Why don't you keep your damn mouth shut?" And the dam broke loose and the so-called tough one disassembled.

All that had been building up that day, those months, those years, everything in flood tide now. She stood up from her chair. "He's dead! He's dead! The last man on earth is dead! The last man in this land is gone! Everything is dead and dying! Malcolm's gone! Malcolm's gone!"

Carrie Lou stood up, as Sherry walked toward her, and Carrie Lou put her arms around her, as Sherry came up to her, but Sherry shoved her violently clear across the room and went and fell upon her bed and cried as if it were the last day on this earth. "He was the very last angry man!" she sobbed. "He was the last man in this land of queers!" She sat up and looked up into the girl from 'Sippi's frightened face. "Don't you understand? He was the last black hope. He was the last hope that black folk could achieve manhood." She fell on the bed again and cried and laughed and blurted out words interchangeably. "They killed black manhood! Killed black manhood!" Crying, laughing, sobbing. "He was the last man!" She mumbled, "Where is Robeson? Where is Robeson?" She sobbed, she blurted, "What's to become of black folk? What's to become of black folk?" Every time this tough sophisticated New York lady screamed now, Carrie Lou's belly did a flip-flop. She felt an overwhelming compassion and she went and sat beside the girl and lifted her to a sitting position and put her arms around her, and Sherry could resist her arms no longer. She turned and wept unashamedly in Carrie Lou's arms, as Carrie Lou massaged her shoulders and ran her hand through her short-cropped hair. Girls, hearing the screaming, gathered in the doorway of Carrie Lou's and Sherry's room.

One of them asked, "What's the matter with Sherry, Carrie Lou?"

Sherry stared up at them. "Get out of my room, you murdering bitches! You bloodthirsty bastards!"

Carrie Lou was frightened. She felt her own eyes filling up. "But, darling, the radio said Negroes killed him."

"Yes," Sherry said, almost quietly, "The miserable black contemptible bastards, they did their masters' bidding." The hysteria was almost absent from her voice now, replaced by a tone even more frightening in its quiet understatement. "The poor ignorant sons-of-bitches killed their black Messiah, the only one who could have saved us from our miserable existence. The only one who could have saved America."

Off and on, she cried for more than three weeks, and despite her growing hostility to whiteness (she even loathed the winter snow), she and Carrie Lou drew closer together, even against Sherry's own volition. Sherry was like a person nearing seventy year of age or thereabouts, who had lived a life of waste and felt dear time slipping from her grasp and felt Death's cold white breath panting wildly on her neck. She talked continuously about death and dying. Between Lorraine and Malcolm, another dear friend had died. Lively, vivacious, beautiful Beverly Robinson. Sherry got into a habit of talking to herself. "I know I'm going to die at a very early age. I'll never see twenty-seven. Something or somebody will strike me down. I know it; I feel it in the very marrow of my bones."

Then one day she came into their room and sat down on her bed and started to cry again. "Malcolm! Malcolm! Brother Malcolm!" She uttered the name reverently, tenderly, helplessly.

"Will to us some of your anger, dear Brother Malcolm. And your great strength."

Carrie Lou came and sat beside her and put her arm around her shoulders. She was smiling through her tears now. Sherry was. "He was so beautiful, you know. So manful. An anachronism in this age of fashionable objectivity and cynicism and faggotism. A knight in shining armor. He was a charmer. All the image of him created by the American press and TV was entirely false, deliberately false. He didn't hate white folks, he loved black folks. And that was what was revolutionary about him. He loved black folks. And that's where he was so far ahead of most of the so-called militant colored leaders and writers and artists who expend so much energy hurling dirty words at white folks, whipping sick white folks on their asses with wet towels. Either that, or talking to white folks endlessly about the degradation of the black man. But Malcolm loved black people, he believed their salvation was in their own hands. Therefore he talked directly to them. That's why they ordered his assassination. He's gone now. And black folks are defenseless. Brother Malcolm was our lover. Our one true only love."

She started to weep again now, silently. She said, "I'm sorry you didn't meet him, honeychile. He was so beautiful."

Carrie Lou said, "But I met him. You introduced us."

Sherry repeated, "I'm really sorry you didn't get a chance to meet him."

And Sherry broke down into weeping again, quiet weeping. And the girl from 'Sippi found herself weeping softly now, as they wept unashamedly in each other's arms.

Because a man had died.

Chapter 6

More and more and little by little, Chuck Othello adjusted to the University and made the University adjust to him. More and more he relaxed into the pace of things. He had at long last caught up with the pace, and sometimes he even ran far out ahead. Not very very far, of course. Ronnie and Jacobson had been a big help, and especially Miss Naomi. He went to dinner at her house almost every Friday night. And almost every Friday night she taught him about love, and lovemaking. And it was good.

They talked easily with each other now, about everything. Politics, war, peace, civil rights, the Movement. She thought he was going to be a great race leader. "And stand in Malcolm's shoes!" is what she told him. He looked forward to those Friday nights.

Ronnie told him, "One of these Friday nights I'm going to tail you, Lil Abner. I don't know—but you must be doing something right. You're going through so many changes."

One Friday evening after dinner, he sat on the couch at Miss Naomi's and she sat on the floor beneath him with her head leaning on his thighs. She said, "I like basketball, Othello. I wished you'd take me to the next game."

His face flushed hot with shame, as his mind made a picture of him escorting a woman to the game who was old enough to be his mother. "I hate basketball," he lied. He really hated the hypocrite in him. He knew by now there wasn't that much difference in their ages. Not more than ten years, maybe less, and she looked even younger than she actually was. And he looked older than he actually was.

She was quiet for a moment, for a hateful moment. Then she said, "I thought you said you loved basketball. I thought you said you used to play it good back home."

"You must've thought it," he said. "I hate it more than any game I know."

She said, quietly, "Well—there's nothing to jump so salty about. I just asked you."

"Who's jumping salty?" he almost shouted.

"You is," she said, never raising her voice one octave.

"Forget it!" he said.

"All right, baby sweet." And she got up and went through the kitchen to the toilet on the back porch and got ready for him, and he was ready for her when she returned, and had taken down the sofa bed. And she gave him love. And tried tenderly to teach him how to give love in return.

One Saturday night Chuck and Ronnie went to a party off

the campus at the home of a wealthy white liberal—an interracial party, which was becoming the fashion in certain circles, even though the circles were very limited in circumference due to the good, old, tried and trusted mores of the gallant South. Notwithstanding, with a very precious few, it was the "In" thing to do. There was Scotch and bourbon a-plenty at this particular party and Chuck was shocked to see some of the teachers, especially the white ones, gulping it down along with the students. This was real democracy. Authentic liberalism. True racial tolerance. And a whole lot of other good and wholesome things in the American tradition, this was. But somehow he was not as sophisticated as he had thought he was, especially when he saw the teachers pawing the students, especially the colored ones. So there was drinking, there was smoking, there was dancing. And of course there was discussion of the question. Always and forever there was discussion of the question.

Ron came up to him and drew him aside. He had been downing the white folks' Scotch like it was going out of style. He said, "Baby! Drink em up and make Mary. Mary is the blonde bitch standing over by the bar."

Chuck stared at his buddy, his face growing hot, and he looked around to see if anybody else had heard him.

Ron said, "You don't fool me, baby, with that innocent look. You ain't no angel. You're a bitch with your shit. I have checked you out, old baby. I have checked Lil Abner out." He was loud-talking now, and Chuck was getting uneasy. "And Lil Abner ain't Lil Abner *enty* more.

"That group over there sitting on the floor is talking about the Movement. They expect every black boy here to be a Negro leader. They expect pearls of wisdom to drop from every living black mouth. Have you heard that Godfrey Cambridge record? He wasn't lying, baby. I'm going to establish a 'party nigger' agency, right smack down here in this chickenshit Southern town." He was supposed to be whispering, but he was loud-talking and broadcasting, and Lil Abner was getting nervous. "Ron Gilbert's Nigger Agency—Hire your party niggers by the night. Good, glib quiescent niggers."

Chuck stared at him angrily now. "Like let's change the subject, hunh? Or else I'm splitting."

Chuck watched Ron move toward the bar and lead the

[239]

blonde girl to the area where folks were dancing. He also watched some of the others watching Ron, especially white men watching closely, as Ron danced with the blonde one cheek to cheek and belly to belly, and talking a nice brand-new hole in the lady's blonde head. And each man to his own imagination as to what Ron was discussing. Chuck was annoyed by Ron and yet admired him. He knew Ron was doing this deliberately to antagonize the good well-meaning Southern liberal white folk and to set their smiling teeth on edge. Chuck moved toward the group of talkers seated in a circle on the deep red plush carpet.

A pleasant-faced complacent-looking young Negro man was sucking on a pipe and saying quietly, "Oh, *yah,* Malcolm had no following at all. He spoke for nobody. He represented nothing. Television made a big man out of him. Like Carl Rowan said, he was a bum, a pimp, a hustler."

A thin-faced white man said, "Precisely. He represented nothing but hatred and violence. He was a racist, pure and simple. That's why his own folk shot him down. He lived by the sword and died by the sword. Poetic justice. Pure and simple." He had a Southern drawl that was long, deep, thick, and wide. And somehow what he said rubbed Chuck the wrong way, the words, likewise the music.

Another Negro whom Chuck had seen many times at the University felt he had to say, though timidly, "But don't you think, Billy, that he served a useful purpose? I mean, didn't the alternative of him standing in the wings have a positive impact on the national power structure as well as the civil rights establishment?"

Othello was still standing and he heard himself say, with stifled excitement in his voice, "Malcolm was one of the best things that ever happened to the Movement. He was the spur. He taught Negroes to love themselves. As for Whitey, Malcolm didn't teach Negroes to love *or* hate Whitey. He taught them they were their own salvation and that loving or hating Whitey had nothing to do with anything." Othello surprised himself making such a "long" extensive speech. He had not said so much since he had come to the University. They all looked up into his face, and he almost panicked at his own audacity. He looked away and saw his roommate coming toward them. He said, "Tell them about it, Ronnie. You know the score about Brother Malcolm." Ron had talked him deaf, dumb, and blind about "Brother Malcolm." According to Ron, he had known "Big Red" personally. He had talked about him to Chuck so much, Chuck felt that he had himself known Brother Malcolm, personally.

He had had the fiercest kind of arguments with his roommate on the question of Malcolm X. He had argued that Malcolm was a fraud. Malcolm was trying to lead black folks down a dead-end street. He was a demagogue. Malcolm was prejudiced. He preached nothing but hate and violence. It was as if Othello (subconsciously or otherwise) offered up all the established clichés that formed the popular American image of Malcolm, so that Ron could break them down, one by one. It was as if he deliberately picked Ron's brain, so that he, Othello, might be de-brainwashed in return. In their room they sometimes argued almost to the point of violence and far into the night. And finally Othello had himself become an avid Malcolmite, who could argue Malcolm's cause as eloquently as his roommate.

"Baby! I don't waste my breath on Whitey," Ron said disdainfully. "Shee-itt! I don't come to these parties for Whitey to pick my brain. I come to drink his whiskey and ball the jack. And I don't feel no qualms about it either. Whitey owes black folk so much, we're going to always be playing catch-up. Shit!" Ron stared down at Bill, the pipe-sucker. "I leave it to old William "Gunga Din" Davis to put these people on. You'll tell Whitey what he loves to hear, won't you Gunga Din?"

There was a bit of embarrassed laughter from the colored brothers and sisters in the circle, except, of course, the old philosopher, young Mister William "Gunga Din" Davis. He sucked on his pipe and countered with, "That's right, Ron, old boy. You did join up with the Muslims, didn't you? Hence the beard."

Everybody was listening now. All had gathered from other parts of the room, white and black and brown, girls and boys, men and women. The blonde was standing next to Ronnie. Ron said, "Don't try to put me on, old Gunga, you miserable clown, or I'll put you down right in front of all your kindly masters. Like yeah, I started to join the Muslims. Why not? As a religion, it's just as legitimate a hustle as any of the others. I went to several meetings at the mosque in Harlem. Malcolm was the greatest black man in this decade.

[241]

"The man at the mosque said, 'You want to join up? You'll have to give up smoking.'

"I said, 'That's cool. It'll be a little hard, but I've been known to go through changes.'

"He said, 'You'll also have to give up whiskey.'

"I said, 'Well, you know, like I do love my Scotch and soda, and a little sneaky pete every now and then, but I can rise to the occasion and fight through to a genuine adjustment. I mean, like no sweat, Brother Triple-X. Everything's cool.'

"The man said, 'You'll have to give up soul food. Hog maw, chitterlings, pork chops, fatback, pig feet, knuckles, and all that stuff.'

"He had me vacillating for a couple of minutes. I was thinking to myself, a soul brother without his soul food, that's like a Kentucky colonel without his Jack Daniels and branch water. But I pulled myself together. I said, 'That's okay. Anything for the cause. As long as I can still make it to my hominy grits and black-eyed peas and hush-puppies. Everything's cool. Turn to Allah—Pray to the East!'

"Then old Triple-X lowered the boom on me. He said, 'You'll have to give up white women!'

"Like man, when the words sank in, I just executed me a fast about-face, and walked out of that mosque, and like I ain't never looked back until this very day."

There was a moment of terrible silence, and then some damn-fool black mouth snickered and all the colored brothers and sisters cracked up with laughter, all, that is, except Gunga.

Ronnie kept a straight face. "Well, what the hell—admittedly, it's a back-breaking job, and I'm a Black Nationalist and all that, but after all, who's going to pleasure white women if black men cop out? White men're too damn busy mothering one another."

The party broke up soon thereafter. It was time.

It was sleepy time down South.

They had eaten and made love and he felt comfortable and sleepy as he wallowed in the aroma of the love already made. The sharp sweet salty odor of tidewater flooded all his senses. He really had it good. A good-looking woman, experienced in the art of making food and making love. A generous tender-hearted woman, who gave her all, asking nothing in return.

[242]

But love, which was everything to her. Almost. All the students gave out with the universal gripe against the mess that passed for food in the campus cafeteria. But he, Charles Othello Chaney, country bumpkin, Lil Abner, if you please, had a refuge to which he could escape each Friday, and maybe even other days. But he would not run things into the ground. He would not take advantage of her goodness. You lowdown bastard, he thought complacently to himself, you are already taking advantage of the lady's goodness. And he felt neat little stabs of guilt about it, but most of all he felt damn comfortable. He turned toward her and moved his body up against her naked body, and he kissed her. He thought, boy, you're really smelling your piss.

She moaned and squirmed and groaned. "Baby! Baby! Baby!"

Then she said, "Will you do something for Mama, doll baby?"

He felt so cocky he could hardly bear it. She had taught him confidence around the womenfolks. She'd taught him how to turn a woman on. "Anything, sugar-pie. Like you just name it and, baby, you got it!" He liked the sound of his almost-brand-new bedroom voice. Low and deep and husky. He had listened to it changing, month by month. He was going through so many changes these days, sometimes he hardly recognized himself. Christ! She was so good to him, how could he deny her anything?

She said, "I wanna go to the Spring Dance at Douglass. Will you take me?"

Right away he broke into a sweat. Suddenly his precious bed had rocks in it. Somehow she felt his great uneasiness. He knew she felt it. She said, "What's the matter, baby sweet?"

He said, "Nothing's the matter. What made you think there was?"

She said, "Will you take me to the party?"

He said, "You know I don't know how to dance."

"I can learn you," she said.

He caught himself in time. He'd started to correct her, to tell her she should have said, "I can teach you."

She said, "It's more than a week away, and you can come here every night, and you can have dinner with me, and we can practice."

"I don't like to go to dances!" he told her heatedly. He felt

[243]

a great and guilty anger. He knew his good thing was in danger now. His playhouse was about to topple. He knew that behind it all was the same motivation which was behind her basketball enthusiasm. She wanted to bring their relationship out into the open. She was honest, and she wanted to make them honest with each other. She was proud, and she wanted the whole wide world to know it. And he was a lowdown goddamn two-faced snob. He was contemptible was what.

She turned her back to him, and he heard her weeping, softly weeping. And a tide of great guilt flowed all through him. But he summoned up inside of him a feeling of righteous indignation. They always cry, he told himself, like a man who'd had a whole world of experience. Goddamn their time! They take advantage of you with their tears. They thought if they fed you once or twice or gave you a little poontang, they thought they owned you heart and soul and mind. He had learned all of this lore about women at the barber shop in Wakefield City and from the dormitory philosophers, both profound, tremendous sources of such knowledge. But his rationalization did not hold water—not even for Chuck Othello. He still felt guilty. Deep in his bowels he felt stabs of shame and guilt. He tried to take her into his arms. He tried to be tough and tender too. "What the hell are you crying about?"

She pulled away from him and got out of bed and put on her gown and bathrobe. She said, "I ain't crying. It's just time for you to go back to your college people. And you can go straight to hell for all I care." The tears streamed down her face in cascades, as she stared her lover down.

"What's the matter?" He was sitting up in bed now, uncovered to the waist. Phony bastard. He knew what the matter was.

"Ain't nothin the matter. It's just done got late up in the evening, and my eyes just done got opened, and I'm wide awake and sleepy. So you best git back to your college world."

He should ask her to turn her back, and he should get out of the bed and get into his clothes and be long gone. He knew he should, but knew he wouldn't. He had to rationalize himself to her, to him. "I don't understand. I-I-I mean, the least you could do is tell me what's the matter. I mean, surely we owe that much to each other."

"If you don't know, sugar-pie," she said bitterly, "ain't nothin

[244]

Mama can say to explain it to you. And as for us owing each other something, you ought to be the last one to bring that up." She picked up his trousers from a chair and handed them to him. "I'm sorry for the last thing I just said about who owes who what. I'm very sorry." She walked into the kitchen and closed the door behind her.

He got dressed slowly, turning it all over in his mind. The fact of the matter was, he loved to come to her behind closed doors and have a party with her at the table and in bed, but he wanted that to be the end of it. He wanted to believe in the magic loaf, to eat his cake and still have it and never have to pay the baker. His relationship with her had been fake on his part from the go-go. He was the taker, she the giver. But hell, he was younger than she was and was a college boy and had more class, so she was getting her side of the bargain. He was dressed now and he opened the door and entered the kitchen where she sat at the table drinking coffee, looking older than her years. She said, "Why don't you get the hell back to your University? I'm sick of looking at you." She spat the words at him, even as she rose from her chair and poured him a cup of coffee.

She sat opposite him now and she stared at him, her large, wide, dark eyes narrow slits of bitterness. "You're a phony little pissy-ass stuck-up sonofabitch," she said, almost without rancor, tears cascading down her cheeks again. "You know that, don't-choo?"

He said, "Naomi—that is—Naomi—" His voice came from deep in his scratchy throat.

"Miss Hester to you, if you don't mind."

"I mean I didn't know you were that serious about going to the dance. I mean, I'll take you if you want to go."

She said, "I'm good enough for a free meal and a good screw, but I ain't good enough to meet your University friends. They're too far above me. I'm too old, I reckon, and I'm too ignorant. I ain't been to the University. I don't know the big proper words to use. I ain't been through the high school less 'lone the University."

He said, "I told you I'd take you to the dance. Can't you hear me?"

"Ain't this a goddamn shame? All that big talk about the Negro this and the Negro that! Well, I'm the damn Negro, I'm the black folks, I'm the Afro-American, or howsomever you call

[245]

it. I'm the black folks, not those goddamn phony prissy-assed proper-talkers at the University!"

"How many times do I have to say it? I'll take you to the party!"

"Don't do me no favors, little boy. I don't wanna go to your old party. It would most probably bore me half to death. I'm above those little chickens at the University. I mean, I figure I'm a better woman than any woman in Johnsonville. I don't beg nothin from nobody. To hell with your Spring party. I just asked you to see what you would say. And you flunked out, Chuck Othello Chaney. You failed the test. I don't know what they teach you at the University, but they sure don't teach you manhood."

He was whipped. She had stripped him naked. "You just don't understand. I mean——"

"Oh I understand all right enough, I reckin. You a big race-pride man, but I reckin I just ain't quite the right color for you University Negroes. I ain't no high-yaller, my lips too thick, I——"

He said, "Right color! Good Lord have mercy no! You know me better than that."

"You a big race man, but you just like the white man, you just out for little old sport on the dark side after the sun go down. I got your number, sugar-pie."

"You got me so wrong," he pleaded. "I care about you very much. I'll take you anywhere you want to go. I'll do anything you want to do."

She smiled a slow soft smile. And she said quietly, "You will? You'll do anything I ask you?"

"Of course I will! I'll take you to a basketball game and the Spring Dance. Football—baseball—I'll do anything. I'm very proud of you. You're the greatest."

"I sure is glad to hear that," she said slowly and deliberately, "cause I'm bigged, and I want you to marry me. You know, I'm in a family way."

He had stood up to go to her, but now he sank back down in his chair. "You're what?"

"I'm bigged, and it's your baby."

He broke out all over in a cold sweat. "How do you know?"

"You ask me how I know? Do you think I'm a whore or something? I know because ain't nobody but you been screwing me. How do I know? You lowdown bastard!"

"I didn't mean that. I meant, how do you know you're pregnant?"

"How do other womens know they pregnant? Because I missed my period and because the doctor told me so."

He lowered his face into his folded arms. "Great God Almighty!" He felt as if he were drowning in the river that ran through the place where he had lived out most of his life, his young life, all of his planning going down to the bottom of the river with him. He had thought that because he knew how to swim so well, there could be no danger for him ever in the river, and he had gotten careless, and just as the shore came into sight, he was being swallowed up by the river, all of his plans going down to the bottom with him. He stared at her, relishing a great anger that was growing in him. With one sentence she had killed all the dreams he ever dreamed. He said, "But you, I mean, I thought you were protecting yourself. You're old enough—experienced—I mean you know better than to get caught like this—"

She smiled bitterly at him. "Man and woman appoints, the Good Lord disappoints." She laughed.

His stomach was a fiery furnace. "But-but-but what're you going to do about it?"

She laughed at him. "Ain't you got it kinda ass-backwards? I know they teach you how to make a sentence better'n that at the University. Don'tchoo mean—What*choo* going to do about it? I mean *you*, Mister Charles Othello Chaney." She laughed some more at the silly, stupid expression he imagined he was wearing on his face. He hated her for laughing at him.

"You ain't gonna let me down, are you, doll baby?"

"What do you mean?" He knew damn well what she meant.

"You gon do the right thing by poor Naomi, ain'tchoo? You gon act like a man supposed to act?"

"I don't have any money," he said. "They say abortions are expensive. I'll see if I can't scrape some up, a little cash and go half and half with you—maybe."

She was crying again now. "I ain't gon git rid of my baby. I ain't gon git rid of my baby, you mean heartless bastard! I thought you loved me. I thought you'd be a man about it.

I thought you'd take me in your arms and tell me everything was all right and you would marry me."

He felt sorry for her and angry with her at the selfsame time. "But I'm too young to get married. My whole life—my future."

She said, "What about my life? What about my future?"

He said desperately, "But maybe we can do something—maybe it's not too late. I mean—maybe the doctor is mistaken——"

She said in a flat and toneless voice, "Forget it. I made it all up. What kind of a fool you think I am, to let you big me? I just wanted to see what you would say. I thought you was different, but you jes like all the rest of them college boys, they don't ever grow up to become mens. I was jest testing you again, and you flunked out again."

He got up and walked toward her. But she looked up into his face and said, "Goodnight, Mister Charles Othello Chaney."

And he knew she meant goodnight, and so he said goodnight in return.

He never saw her on Wednesdays again at Jacobson's. She would come very early and leave before he arrived. And he missed her more than he would ever have imagined he could miss her. He missed her moving heavily around Jacobson's apartment, missed her interruptions and even found himself expecting them. He missed the Friday nights, which he now saw in retrospect as things of treasured beauty, rather than just food and poontang, as he had somehow unconsciously regarded their relationship. But most of all, the thing that really hung him up was the discovery of his own hypocrisy and snobbishness, his opportunism. He would never forgive himself, the way he had exploited her. How could he become so bourgeois in such a short time, so bourgeois that he could be ashamed to be seen with such a wonderful woman at a crummy college basketball game? At a phony chickenshit Spring Dance? Was it that he thought Naomi not good enough to socialize with the "sophisticated" college girls? What had made him kick her in the face like that? Had he come to the University for them to turn him into a first-class middle-class phony-baloney? He walked around the campus with the image of her face before him. He daydreamed of her in the classrooms.

One day Dr. Jacobson told him, "Miss Hester told me to give you her best regards."

And a great shame swept over him and he turned his face away from his teacher, and his face filled up and tears spilled from his eyes, and he walked hurriedly away in the opposite direction.

Meanwhile the days passed into weeks, passed into months, and spring came and green grass and midterms and girls prettier than they ever were and trees now heavy with a newborn greenness and brand-new fragrances of flowers blooming, flowers, some of which were nameless to Chuck, but no less beautiful. He knew the look and smell of honeysuckle and magnolias and morning glories and dandelions and red rose bushes and daisies and brown-eyed susans. Spring was also blue skies and thundershowers. Spring was everywhere all around him moving rapidly toward summer, but Chuck could not shed the winter coldness which had seized his heart and soul and mind. Naomi had warmed his body and heart and soul in the wintertime, and when her great warmth was withdrawn, a cold spell set in upon him, a spell that springtime could not thaw.

One day in late spring, Ron met him in front of the dormitory.

"Man, why didn't you tell me you had such a fine thing for a cousin right down here in Johnsonville?"

"What kind of cousin? I don't know what you're talking about."

"Miss Naomi Hester, baby! She's fine as wine. Cousin Naomi, baby! She came by here about an hour ago looking for Cousin Charles Othello. Man, where've you been hiding the lady? Baby, she shook me to my natural chittlings!"

Chuck said, "Thanks." And turned and walked back across the campus where shadows danced darkly to the crazy music of the crickets. Darkness was falling all over the world, all over Johnsonville. It was night by the time he arrived at Miss Naomi's. There was one street lamp on her street at the intersection, and she lived in the darkness of the middle of the block. He felt a kind of shamefaced nostalgia as he saw the little house standing in the softened shadows of a towering sycamore tree. His heart began to thump and pound as he walked across the yard and up on the porch, and he hesitated before he knocked on the door. He had his nerve ever coming to her house again after the way he had acted the last time he had seen her. Maybe he should turn around and walk down off the porch and away from the house and never show his face around this place again. He did not deserve her love or friendship, even if she were ready to forgive and to forget.

[249]

He knocked softly, timidly, at first, then, what the hell, he rapped loudly with his knuckles. Then he had a sinking feeling that he should disappear before she got to the door, but he made himself stay. If she came by to see him, then he was going to find out what she wanted.

The door opened and there she was, more beautiful now than he had ever seen her before or ever imagined. She said, "Come in, Mister Chaney."

He came in and she led him to the sofa and she sat in a chair opposite him. "Well-well-well," she said. "Look what the cat dragged in."

He said, "How've you been, Naomi?"

She said, "Just fine, I thank you."

"You came by the campus?"

"Don't worry. I told them you was my cousin."

"I'm not worried. I thought maybe you wanted something."

She laughed. "I told them I was your ignorant cousin, the one didn't have no education."

He said, "Stop it! Will you stop it?"

She said, "You had supper?"

He said, "No, but I didn't come for supper. I—"

But she got up and set the table and they had supper, and she talked all during supper like a tape recorder that could not be shut off. She talked about the ways of white folks, she talked about civil rights, about this and that, would not let him get a word in edgeways. And when they finished eating supper, she rose from the table and he got up and came toward her and tried clumsily to take her into his arms, but she told him quietly, "No sir, I thank you. It can't never be like that again." And she led him to the door and said goodnight to him.

Summer came early, came in noisily and violently with the flashing of lightning and the crashing of thunder; it seemed the whole sky had declared war against the entire earth, and didn't it rain!

It rained ten days and eleven nights.

It rained clean through until the day school closed.

It poured the day Chuck caught the bus for Wakefield County.

[250]

PART THREE

PART THREE

Chapter
1

It was hot as hell in Wakefield County all that summer.

There were wars and rumors of wars between the colored and the white all over peaceful Mississippi. Some folks said the trouble started when the Supreme Court struck its first blow for "Commonism" way back there in 1954. Some folks went much further back, way back to the days of the gallant and courageous men, sensitive souls, like Rob Lee and Stonewall Jackson and good old Jeff Davis, God rest his peaceful soul in Heaven as it was on earth. And ungenteel uncultured bastards like Grant and Sherman. Some folks blamed the North and the "Commonist-inspired EN-DOUBLE-A-SEE-PEE." The whole damn thing was a plot, according to Congressman Johnson, against the Southern genteel way of life.

Between letters from Bessie Mae and Mama Carrie and Cora Mae, Othello had been kept fully posted about the happenings, about the growing confrontation between the colored and the white. He could hardly believe it could be happening in his county in his 'Sippi. He could hardly believe black men could muster so much courage. He even received a letter now and then from his magnificent Great White Father. In the letters from Bessie Mae he watched her style change from letter to letter. He watched her vocabulary expand and grow more flowery from week to week. She wrote at least once a week. She even used the word "perspective."

As far as the county itself was concerned, white folks said (and a few colored naturally said Amen) that the trouble started when the two Negroes from the next county came meddling over to Wakefield last December just before Christmas. Noah Abernathy and Willie Banks. They talked first to Reverend Purdy, then to old man Deacon Rayfield Jimson. The Deacon had passed his eightieth season a few years back. They talked to Miss Ida Lee, the schoolteacher. They came out to Johnson's Bottom and talked with Bessie Mae and Little Jake. They talked with red-eyed Uncle Bish. They talked with a quiet-faced sharecropper by the name of Luke Gibson.

Bish told them, "Not me. I ain't gon git in that nigger mess. Y'all ain't nothing but agitators."

Somebody said they saw raggedy-assed Uncle Bish one day over in Tybeeville (better known as Black Tybee), standing in Miss Easter Lillie's front yard, and Uncle Bish waved at him friendly-like, but the man said he didn't wave back because Uncle Bish was so raggedy, the man mistook him for a scarecrow put out there to scare the birds out of Miss Easter Lillie's garden. Miss Easter Lillie was Uncle Bish's ladyfriend. A tall, buxom, high-yaller woman.

Willie and Noah also talked with Jesse and Carrie Chaney. They looked worriedly at the two strange men at first. But finally they said they would think it over. They didn't want any trouble from the white folks. Mama Carrie wrote Othello up at the University all about it. He talked it over with Ron. He felt so far removed from Wakefield during those last months at the University. He could almost be "objective" about the whole thing.

"Meaning of course," Ron told him heatedly, "you can almost look at it from the white man's point of view. The white man's P.O.V. is the most subjective objectivity the world has ever known. It's a load of horseshit. *Period!* Excla-goddamn-mation point!"

They had been having dinner down at Chicken Charlie's, a place where students went when they were slightly financial in order to get a brief reprieve from the menu at the Greasy Spoon, which was the name used by the students when they spoke of the University cafeteria, a name they used derisively with fond affection. Ron and Othello had been eating fried fish at Chicken Charlie's, when Othello showed Ron his mother's letter.

"You're going to tell Mama and Papa to join the struggle, aren't you, old baby?" Ron demanded. "I mean, what're you, a Gunga Din or something?"

He answered absentmindedly, as if he were thinking out loud and to no one in particular, "I don't know. It might just get them into a whole lot of unnecessary trouble. They've had a hard life already. And after all the jumping up and down it wouldn't accomplish a damn thing. It's so difficult to know how to advise them." Wakefield County seemed so far away in time and space. He sometimes found it hard to believe that he had lived there all his life until just a few lousy months ago.

Ron had guzzled down three bottles of beer. "You're putting me on, you fink! You must be putting me on! You'd better be putting me on!"

Othello stared at his explosive roommate. He said quietly, "Maybe so—maybe not."

Ron shouted softly, "Why in the hell you think they're sacrificing like they are to send you through school? So you can get some sense up in your big ugly head to stand up to those peckerwoods. It's up to people like you to go back and give leadership to the Movement."

He smiled at Ron. He shook his head slowly from side to side.

Ron said, "Goddamn liberal-ass white kids flocking down there in multitudes to fuck up the Movement and you can't even get young-ass Negroes who were born and bred down there to take a stand. We are a fucked-up race, you hear me?"

Ron put all white folk in the same category, Othello thought. Everything was black or white to him. But what if Othello told him his parents hadn't sacrificed to send him to college, a fact Ron took for granted? What if he told Ron he was being subsidized by one of the last of the Great White Fathers? Great White Fatherism was one of Ron's favorite topics. "It's not just all black and white," he told Ron, philosophically. "It's more complicated than that. Black and white relations in the South are very complicated. You Northerners just don't understand the subtleties." Even to himself, he sounded phony. He sounded to himself like one of those liberal white "philosophers" who were always sounding off at the interracial parties. Ron and Othello went to quite a few of them during those winter months of their freshman year.

Ronnie ranted and raved and guzzled his beer and called his roommate all kinds of Gunga Dins and Uncle Toms and sell-out artists, called him everything but a dedicated follower of M. L. King. All the while Othello sat opposite his roommate, quiet-faced and soft-spoken, never raising his voice, which made Ron even angrier than he would have been. But in the final analysis, Ron convinced him. He wrote his father and Mama Carrie that the franchise was the black man's birthright, his only hope, and Negroes in the county like Negroes throughout the nation must stand together and fight for it. And go down fighting, if it came to that.

"But please be careful. Don't jump way out in front and take unnecessary chances."

Back in Wakefield County somebody took the voter registration story to the Man, and the courageous *Wakefield Daily Chronicle* blasted it in big black bold headlines across the top of its front page.

NORTHERN BLACK REVOLUTIONISTS INFILTRATE COUNTY!

The lead story went on to say that the *Chronicle* knew the names of the Northern infiltrators, and would be able to lay its hands on them any moment when the time came. But the *Chronicle* was fair-minded and was giving them fair warning to get out of Wakefield County. If the black Northern infiltrators did not take heed and take to their raggedy heels, the *Chronicle* would take steps to expose them to the citizenry. It would have no other alternative. "Down through our glorious history Wakefield County has had a proud record of harmonious relations between the races. And we shall not sit idly by and see those relations jeopardized!" On the editorial page it said, "Our good kindhearted colored folks are not listening to these Northern infiltrators. They know they're welcome to the vote. All they got to do is register, and nobody is keeping them from the courthouse. Whosoever will, let him come. Amen."

"Amen!" Little Jake repeated softly, as he and Bessie Mae and the two Northern infiltrators and Jesse Chaney and Josh Hemlock, and Reverend Purdy and Miss Ida Lee and Deacon Jimson and three others, and Miss Ella Mae, nodding and napping, sat around Bessie Mae's long wooden kitchen table, with the lone light bulb hanging over the table from the ceiling. "Amen," he said one more time, as he put the newspaper aside. "Whosomever will let him come. We coming all right, Mister Congressman Peckerwood and our head ain't gon be bending low. You better believe me. And we thank you for the invitation." Bessie Mae's mother, Miss Ella Mae, had suffered a stroke in January. She had not fully recovered.

On the table before them they had a road map of the counties in that neck of the 'Sippi jungle. "We're Northern infiltrators,"

Willie Banks said smilingly. He was black of face, quiet-voiced, but he was capable of exploding when the occasion demanded detonation. He pointed with the index finger on his left hand to the town where both Abernathy and he had come from, the place where they had lived out most of their lives. "Northern infiltrators. This place we come from is north all right. North of West Hell, but it sure is south of Wakefield County."

The men and women at the table looked around at each other, chuckling nervously. They knew that at least one of them had carried tales back to the Big House. Someone had finked on them. Was that someone seated at this very table with them? Sharing their confidences? If the *Chronicle* had done nothing else it had thrown mistrust into their midst. They would from here on in look upon each other with suspicion.

Abernathy said, with cheerful bitterness, "Well, the one good thing about it, the *Chronicle* say they welcome colored folks to the courthouse for registration. So it's up to us to make em put they money where they mouth is."

Even though they were a long ways from the eyes and ears of white folks, way out yonder in the Bottom, Johnson's Bottom, they spoke in whispers as if they thought somebody was eavesdropping from the next room.

Lester Primrose said, "Now wait a minute. Let's don't run out here half-cocked and cut the fool. You know these white folks ain't studying about being serious when they say they welcome us to register and vote. Common sense'll tell you better'n that."

Deacon Jimson said, "It don't make no never-mind. I'm gon reddish anyhow. That's how come we meeting and planning together, ain't it? So we can stick together, if white folks don't like it when we reddish."

"That's right," Little Jake agreed. "If Whitey git mad, he can scratch his ass, I mean, scratch his mad place and git glad. Excuse me Reverend Purdy and Miss Ella Mae and Miss Ida Lee, and you too, Bessie Mae Moocho. Now looka here, Brother Abernathy and Brother Banks is come way over here and gived us they valuable time and thoughts and put they life in danger for us. And now it's time for us to act. It's time for *us* to put our money where our mouth is." He winked an eye at Abernathy. "Now the man say he welcome us to register. Well, how many can we git to the courthouse to put him to a test next Wednesday? This is Friday. That give us five days to go tell it on the mountain. All of us good church members," he said gratuitously, unsmilingly, even though everybody at the table knew that the last time Little Jake had been inside the church was the night his daddy fell out of the pulpit. "We all go to church so we know what pledging mean. Each and every one of us gon make a pledge right now, as to how many soul peoples we gon git to come to the courthouse on next Wednesday."

Lester Primrose said, "How we gon pledge for other people. You know how scared niggers is of——"

"*Negroes*, Brother Primrose," Reverend Purdy corrected him with his Baptist-textured voice. "It's just as easy to say Negro as it is to say nigger. Before we can stand up to the white man, we must teach ourselves to respect ourselves. Great God Almighty, we got to git that nigger feeling out our system. We got to purge it like we taken castor oil."

"Forgive me, Reverend Purdy. May the Good Lord up on High forgive my wicked soul. I meant to say, we know how scared colored folks is of Mister Charlie."

"Forgiveness b'long to Him, Brother Primrose, not to no mortal human being like me."

Noah Abernathy suggested, "In a way, Brother Primrose may be right. Perhaps it would make more sense for us to start the pledges with our own selves. How many of us are ready to make history on next Wednesday? If we pledge ourselves first, then we'll make sure to get other folks to come with us, cause fear sure does love a heapa company, not that there's anything to be scared of, but everybody know there sure is safety in numbers."

Redheaded Josh Hemlock graduated high school three years ahead of Chuck Othello. He worked hard and shot crap and saved his money and hit the numbers and by the time he was twenty-one (he was twenty-three now), he had opened a little grocery store right smack down in the downtown district. He thought of himself as a "big important nigger." And he had just begun to run his race. He was "high-yaller," and his head was crowned with a head of what he and some other Negroes termed "good hair," meaning it was of the kind that white folk wore atop their skulls.

He shook his head now from side to side.

"The colored man is backward, and he going to always be backward. He got no power. No economic, no political power.

Power runs the world, and spooks ain't got no power at all. And ain't got no get-up about 'em to get no power."

Deacon Jimson's eyes were almost filled up now, as was his husky voice. "I sure would like to cast my vote just one little old biddy time before they lay my weary soul to rest. Just one little time," he chanted almost to himself. "Just one little time. Just one little time."

"I don't blame the white man," Josh Hemlock said, "for keeping the darky in his place."

Reverend Purdy said, "Can we stick together just one time, brothers and sisters? Just one time on our weary journey through this life?"

Abernathy looked from face to face. "How many gon meet me out in front of the courthouse at nine o'clock next Wednesday morning?"

Little Jake's hand went up before Noah's last words were out of his mouth. Then Bessie Mae's hand went up. Then Reverend Purdy's. Then Miss Ida Lee who had been quiet throughout the entire meeting. And then no more hands went up, but folks looked uneasily at one another. You could hear a strong breeze blowing across the backyard. The light bulb hanging from the ceiling swung a slow pattern of shadows back and forth across the table.

"Well," Little Jake said, "four beats a blank." He looked angrily from face to troubled face. He cursed them and he cussed them with his angry eyes. "Four do beat nothing at all." He was trying to convince himself as much as to bolster up the others' spirits, which at the moment were dragging the natural ground, from Little Jake's way of thinking.

Then his heart thumped wildly in his chest, as he saw Chuck Othello's father stick his hand up toward the ceiling. Jesse Chaney never learned to whisper. His voice was much too big and powerful. "Me and Mama Carrie—we'll be there—if we live and nothing don't happen."

Hemlock jumped up from his chair. "Shh! Shh!" He walked over to the back door and opened it and stared outside into the empty chilly darkness. A dog was howling somewhere, howling like he'd lost his mind somewhere out there in the darkness of the Bottom. He stood in the open doorway for a moment.

Little Jake said, "Close the door, man. You letting all the hot air outa the lady's place."

He closed the door and came back and sat down at the table. "I thought I heard something moving around out there in the back. Can't be too careful with these peckerwoods."

Little Jake said, "You ain't got to worry about no white peckerwoods messing around out here in the Bottom. It's the black peckerwoods you got to keep your eyes on."

Abernathy said, "Any more volunteers for registration?"

Deacon Jimson's hand went up. He held up both hands. Another, then another, and finally Sister Ella Mae woke up after Bessie Mae kicked her shins underneath the table, and put her weary hand aloft. Abernathy sat at one end of the table. He smiled a big, wide, solemn smile. He put out his big-boned hands toward the center of the table, and Jake put his work-callused hands toward him and they clasped each other's hands as if they swore an oath together. Then Noah Banks' hands went out and seized theirs. Then Deacon Jimson's withered hands went out to join them. And another and another and another black hand slowly joined, Bessie Mae and Ida Lee and all the rest. Black and brown hands. Finally even timid Lester Primrose got to his feet and joined his hands with his black brethren. All were standing now with their hands joined with each other, except Joshua Hemlock. Finally he stood up and joined them.

Abernathy said in a gruff voice, "We are making history, brothers and sisters. Let us always stand together, as we stand right here tonight."

Reverend Purdy said, "Say Amen."

And the brothers and the sisters said Amen.

Their faces glowed, their lives had changed.

Othello read about his county in *Democracy* magazine. David Woodson had returned to Wakefield County and talked to the people and witnessed the struggle and had gone away to tell the people's story to the nation and the world. Woodson had become a writer whom the whole world listened to.

The courthouse clock was striking all over town that next Wednesday morning, and seventeen brothers and sisters stood in front of the courthouse in the chill of early morning. Jesse and Carrie Chaney, Little Jake and Miss Sallie Belle and Bessie Mae and Deacon Jimson and Lester Primrose and Reverend Purdy and the Rakestraws and Miss Ida Lee and others. Josh Hemlock was in bed with the flu. Banks and Abernathy thought it best that they not show themselves around the courthouse that morn-

[260]

ing, unless they were needed, in which case they would come a-running. But otherwise it was agreed that the two foreigners from the next county, Northern infiltrators as they undoubtedly were, might very well grate on the white folks' tender nerves, which were bound to be in bad enough shape under the best of circumstances. The brothers and sisters stood there among themselves staring up the long white walk to the courthouse, making up their minds to take that last mile and go inside and register. It was the longest fifty yards in all the world, a hundred years long, even longer, and who among them could predict the consequences, could foretell the next half hour?

Lester Primrose expressed the fear they all felt deep inside of them. "One thing my daddy always did tell me. You wanna stay outa trouble, son? Keep away from the white man's courthouse."

They looked at him and laughed nervously. And seriously. He suggested, "How come we don't put it off till next Wednesday? Haste can make a whole heapa waste."

Some of their faces showed shamefaced relief. He had said it. They hadn't. But they would not fight him over it, since it was a good idea. It was common sense and mother wit. A few of them turned to leave and the others probably would have followed. They would never know precisely.

Because the Deacon stood his ground. "I'll be eighty-four years old next month. Next week ain't promised to me." And he began to walk with Mrs. Jimson up the long white walk toward the white and awesome building. Reverend Purdy made his move next, then Little Jake, and then they all decided to do the thing which they'd made the trip to town to do. White folk stared at them as if they had never seen that many colored people going toward the courthouse. White folk were the most nervous people in the whole wide world. Up the steps and inside the building, now, and down the corridor, they walked like soldiers in a strange land on a lonely beachhead with land mines all around them which might go off any minute.

And then the great letdown. They got no resistance from Ned Haverstraw, the registrar. Nobody bothered them at all. Ned Haverstraw smiled his great big ugly smile. "Well I swan!" He was tolerantly amused. "And folks say y'all nigrahs don't never read the paper."

They say, when all the "nigrahs" had made out registration blanks, all seventeen of them, Ned closed up shop and made a beeline over to the mayor's office. "You wouldn't believe it, Mack, goddammit. Seventeen uv em, just as big as life. I'm telling you it was a sight to behold."

Mayor Mack Brady had a real good laugh. "Just goes to show you, eveybody got a sense of humor in Wakefield County. Niggers just as well as white folks."

Mack Brady passed the joke on to Jim Dante, who also had a good laugh. "Niggers are the cutest chillun in all the world. Sometime you have to indulge them a little. So long as things don't git outa hand."

When Charlie Wakefield heard the news, he was tickled to death. "I think it's just wonderful. It just goes to show you."

"I don't know whatchoo so tickled about," Congressman Johnson told him. "It's all right long as they don't git no funny ideas that's alien to our way of life."

"Don't worry so much, Jeff. This is a healthy development. A good way to help get them to believe in the American way, the Southern way. And ain't no harm done. Seventeen voting sure isn't going to change anything overnight. This diversion must be heaven-sent."

There were a few worried and conservative souls, but all in all, the quality white folks took it in good stride and had a good laugh at the expense of their "nigrahs."

But Reverend Purdy and Jake and Miss Ida Lee and Noah and Willie went all over the county spreading the gospel of registration, mostly under the cover of darkness.

Reverend Purdy said, "Registrate! Registrate! Registrate!"

They even invaded the plantations.

Registrate! Registrate! Registrate!

Bessie Mae, and even Deacon Jimson, when he wasn't too poorly, preached the gospel of registration. Here lately, Deacon Jimson tired very easily.

One day he was sitting on his front porch with two of his buddies in the cool of the evening in early spring, chewing his tobacco, and two young men came up the road and paused for a moment in front of his house which sat right in the bend of the highway. One of them asked him, "Grampa, will you settle a argument for us? Who won the Silver War? The North or the South?"

Rafe Jimson didn't have to study a second about it. "White folks won it," he told them without blinking, as if surely they must have known the answer to such an obvious question. His tobacco-chewing cronies sitting on his porch with him laughed and chuckled their agreement. And spat tobacco into the yard, stream after stream.

The young men roared with laughter. "Grampa, you something else!" And they walked off up the road. They had asked him the same question (must've been a hundred times) and always got the same response. "White folks won the Civil War."

"That's how come you ain't free yet," he shouted after them. "Cause you didn't win it. Git your hindparts down to that courthouse next Wednesday morning and registrate!"

Miss Ida Lee called a meeting of the teachers, all seven of them, who taught with her at the Booker High School. Most of the teachers were openly hostile. All were frightened and suspicious.

Bill Judson said, "You're out of your mind fooling around with an ignoramus like Purdy." Judson was an unconfirmed bachelor and had been in love with Ida Lee Jackson ever since he could remember.

Another teacher, Professor Wilson, said, "I own a pretty little bungalow and I buy a brand-new car every three or four years. And I got a family to think of. I own a telephone and bathroom with running water. What more do I need?"

Ida Lee Jackson answered Wilson, but she was staring hard at Judson. "You need dignity and manhood."

Wilson told her, laughing bitterly, "I can't afford them. My notes are too high."

They all laughed masochistically.

Bill Judson said, "You're not fooling anybody but your own self, Ida Lee. All of us live out here on Strivers' Row, that little biddy one block of nice little bungalows, and if we go against the Man one day, he can call all of his notes due on the following morning."

Perspiration on her full shapely mouth now. She was not used to arguing and persuading folk to action. "How can you consider yourselves teachers? How can you teach citizenship to our children when you're afraid to be citizens yourselves?"

Stella Roberts had taught school almost since anybody else in the room could remember. She taught Ida Lee in fourth grade. She burst into tears. She dabbed her eyes with her handkerchief. "I just can't see it! I just can't see it, don't care how hard I try!

[263]

I can't see this integration. I just can't see myself teaching white children. I wouldn't know how to go about it!"

Ida Lee said, "Miss Stella, we're talking about voter registration, not integration."

"Deep in my heart, Ida Lee, I know you're right, but I reckin you just can't teach an old dog new tricks."

Bill Judson said, "All right, Ida Lee, I'm with you. I'll be down there next Wednesday morning." There was no conviction in his voice.

White quality folks laughed about it over their bourbon and branch water all that weekend. But on the next Wednesday morning, they were shaken to their hominy grits by the sight of more than a hundred Negroes standing in the registration line. At the end of the afternoon, Ned Haverstraw, chief registrar, stared at the books and scratched his backside. One hundred and twenty-three nigrahs had applied for registration! He called the mayor, and the word got around like brush fire, and the smart white folk detected a trend and called a meeting.

Attending the unofficial meeting were, of course, Mayor Brady and Ned Haverstraw. And Jule Babcock (better known as Badcock), the county prosecutor, Jack Wimbush, farmer and merchant of medium means, Rab Johnson, farmer and head of the county's White Citizen's Council and brother of the Congressman, Judge Marshall, a fair-minded peckerwood, Tricky-Dick Bilgewater, president of Wakefield City Savings and Trust and friend of the colored race, Congressman Johnson himself, and Sylvester Caswell, plantation owner and Grand Kleagle of the Wakefield County Ku Klux Klan. And a host of other highly respected and respectable and respectful quality people. Charlie Wakefield was the last to walk into the meeting.

"They have their black spies amongst us. We got our black spies too amongst them," Bessie Mae wrote to Chuck Othello. "That's how come we know what happened at that first meeting in the mayor's conference room. You remember Rob Digby? He's the porter down at the courthouse. Thirty-three years of faithful service. He walked in and out of that meeting all night long. Emptying spittoons and ashtrays, and fetching this and bringing that. They saw him and they didn't see him."

The meeting started off quietly enough, but it was thrown into an uproar, when the registrar reminded the gentlemen that there were roughly fourteen thousand blacks in the county and six thousand whites!

Rab Johnson calls on all the white folks of the county to stand together against this nefarious plot to integrate the Southland, for which he blamed the two Northern infiltrators. Wimbush's soft-spoken voice is drowned out by the others, as he tries to point out quietly and irrelevantly that the infiltrators come from Saxton County which is actually south of Wakefield. Judge Marshall and a couple of other trembly voices speak for moderation. "In all things, moderation." "Temperance is the watchword." But Congressman Johnson leaps to his feet and almost breaks the meeting up when he shouts at them about the possibility of "a black shaff!" (meaning sheriff), "a black mare!" (meaning mayor), "a black Congressman!" He almost loses his voice, but somehow he tapped some source of reserved strength, as the Congressman from 'Sippi shouted hoarsely: "What's happening to our fair county while some of its most prominent citizens are walking around nonchalantly like every week is be-kind-to-niggers week? It ain't nothing to laugh about, Jimmy Dick. You got more to lose than anybody else. So git your hind-parts off your shoulders."

Charles Wakefield said quietly, "It's the biggest joke in the last one hundred years. A half a hundred colored people apply to register to vote which they always had a right to do under the Constitution and the whole county acts like Judgment Day has come."

Jack Wimbush said sarcastically, "That's exactly what we scared of, that Judgment Day might come one day right smack down here in Wakefield, and the judges might be nigrahs."

Somebody took him literally. "Great God A'mighty! Scare you to death just studying about it. Black nigger judges!"

The Congressman said, "Let's take a vote. How many think like my radical friend, Jimmy Dick Wakefield, raise your right hand." Four raised their hands: Wimbush, Bilgewater, Judge Marshall, and Sid Burnstein. Jimmy Dick Wakefield did not bother.

"Now," the Congressman shouted, "how many think about it like I do. How many think the situation serious?" All the rest of them raised their hands and shouted, "Aye!"

"All right then," Johnson said triumphantly. "Here is what we got to do."

And it was at that point that Digby, the porter, achieved his visibility. They ordered him to get out and stay out. And Jimmy Dick left shortly afterward.

Here of late Mama Carrie's letters always repeated the same refrain. "We never dreamed that white folks had such hatred deep down in their hearts for us."

Jeremiah Hagan, white plantation owner of acre upon acre of cotton and corn, wanders way out in the cotton field to talk with Josephus Hagan, colored, who is busy cultivating cotton.

After inquiring about the family, the wife, how's Josephus' big boy doing in school, etc., Jeremiah broaches the question of registration.

Josephus straightens up and stares at the friendly-faced boss-man long and hard, Hagan to Hagan. "Well, sir, I sure been studying about it, but I ain't made my mind up 'bout it—least-ways not yet awhile."

Years and years before either of them came into the world there had been this relationship between white Hagans and black Hagans. Sometimes Josephus wondered what his real name was. He heard Malcolm X best a white man on television about two years ago, and it set him to thinking. Then he saw Malcolm on the evening news on television speaking on a street corner in Harlem to a crowd of Negroes. "Your name ain't Smith! Your name ain't Jones! That's your slavemaster's name. Your name is Nkrumah! Your name's Lumumba!" It sure did set Josephus to thinking.

His white, paunchy, red-faced counterpart says, "Well, Jose-phus, like I always told you, you and your flock got a home on this plantation for the balance your days, and your young 'uns' days. We go way back. Your family just as much a part of this plantation as mine is. And you a man just like I am, and I ain't got nothing to do with it, but if I was you, boy, I'd stay away from Wakefield City right long in here."

Josephus says nothing for a moment. Then his sole comment is: "You would?"

Jeremiah stares at him trying to look inside of this soft-faced black man, whom he has known all of his life, and he suddenly has an eerie frightening feeling that he's never really known him. It was really kinda spooky! He tries to look through to the real man. He's been too soft with his nigrahs was the trouble. He's been a sentimental fool. "It's a damn shame, Josephus. The nigrah got just as much right to vote as anybody else, but it ain't gonna be nothing but a whole mess of trouble, just as sure as my name is Jeremiah Justine Hagan. Too many radicals and hot-heads. Just as sure as me and you been friends just as long as we can memorize it, it ain't nothing but heading for trouble."

Josephus looks away across the field over the acres upon acres of cotton and corn all the way to the horizon and then looks back at Jeremiah. Joe's eyes seem to gaze at nothing in particular. When he finally speaks, his extended comment is: "It ain't?"

Rab Johnson, the Congressman's brother, leaves the Big House and jumps in a jeep and drives over to a group of sharecropper shacks which are located in the foreground of a background of miles and miles of corn and cotton. He talks with Luke Gibson, tall, black, sad-eyed man, outside his two-room shack, which houses his wife, his mother-in-law, and seven children. Some of the children are running around under their feet, skinny, pot-bellied, and half-naked, and a baby is crying inside the shack.

"Me and you good friends, ain't we, Luke?"

"Yes, sir. I 'xpect we is."

"Mama! Mama!" one of the boys yells. "Lil Bud got a dead rat in his mouth!"

"Leave me alone! Leave me alone! He b'long to me! I seen him first!"

Luke walks over to the two boys and takes a big dead field rat out of one of the boy's mouth and slings it as far out into the field as he can heave it. Rab Johnson's face is losing color. But he gets himself together. "Don't you listen to them Northern infil-trators. They ain't nothing but troublemakers."

Luke says, "Yes, sir. But something tells me I'm going over there and registrate. I b'lieve I'll make myself a citizen. I b'lieve itta be the best thing for me all the way round."

"Stay away from Wakefield City, boy. You hear me?"

"Yes, sir, I hears you all right, but I spect me and the madam both gon over yonder and registrate. I b'lieve itta be the best thing for us, specially my chillun."

Mister Johnson loses his poise. "You do, boy, and I'll run you offa this farm, you hear me? Run you and your family clean out the county!"

[267]

"Yessir, but no matter, I b'lieve we still gon registrate, sir. I ain't gon tell no lie about it."

Sylvester Caswell, another respectable citizen whom Rob Digby had seen at the meeting in the mayor's conference room, is standing on the back of a truck. He is medium height and stocky. He wears a big wide hat as if he might have been from Texas. His black croppers and renters and day-workers, their wives and half-naked snotty-nosed children looking blank-faced up at the panic-stricken white man, as he belabors them about that "politic thing" over in Wakefield City and warns them against Purdy and old Rafe Jimson. "This is a free country!" he shouts at them, "and y'all don't never have to go into Wakefield City if y'all don't want to. But I ain't worried bout y'all nohow. Cause y'all don't never want to. And y'all don' never go into that sinful place without permission nohow." He works himself up into a rage and fury. "I'm giving each and every one of y'all a fair and friendly warning. I'm here to pertect you against that damn sanctimonious Purdy preacher. If he come smelling 'round here, y'all just let me know, and I'll show you how fast a weasel can run! This is a free country! Y'all don't have to vote! Don't y'all let nobody tell you no different!"

One of the older black men applauds politely, anxiously even, but the rest of them stare up blank-faced and noncommittal at their great white protector. One man, name of Rufus John, mumbled, "Damn I reckin! It must be something to it, he so worked up about it. I best git my sorry hindparts into town and look into it. I hear tell of it the other day, registrating, but I ain't thought nuthin uv it till this minute. Thank you, Mister Bossman."

On a truck in town in front of Hemlock Groceries stand Reverend Purdy and Little Jake Carson and Miss Ida Lee and Bessie Mae, talking to a group of black farmers and renters and croppers and workers. Purdy is also telling them, "It's a free country! And if y'all let Cap'n Charlie scare y'all out of your God-given rights as first-class citizens, shame on every last one of you. And God won't bless you! And you'll always be poor and powerless and your chillun hongry and ignorant. God A'mighty wants us to stand up and be counted. Jesus Christ Hisself said, 'I came not to bring peace, but a sword.'" They answer him,

[268]

"Amen." "The white man is scared of us voting, not because he thinks we want his kind, his womankind, but because he want our sweat and muscle for two dollars a day. He want us to work from kin to caint. But if we registrate and vote, we can run that kind of white man out of power!" Most of them applaud him with "Amens" and "Tell the Truth" as Abernathy and Banks and a few others pass out mimeographed leaflets. But a few of the brethren shake their heads. They just don't know. "White folks mean enough as it is, just dry 'long so. It don't do to git them all het up."

Hemlock tells Reverend Purdy afterward, "I'm with you all the way, on registration and all like that, but find somewhere else to have your meetings besides in front of my grocery store. I don't want to have a whole gang of trouble with every white man in the county. I done worked too long to build my business up."

By summer more than a thousand Negroes had registered.

By summer the drive was on to drive two thousand "niggers" out of the county by primary time in August. Dispossess them, drive them from the plantations where they were born and had worked all their lives. Knew no other place to live or work. Starve them out. Harass them. Still the registration increased. On the streets in the city, white folk looked at Negroes differently. Black visibility increased a thousand percent. Hate stalked the downtown streets like invisible evil spirits. Zombies of hate and tension. Registration ever rising.

"All right, I warned you. You got till Saturday to vacate the premises. You and your family."

"But where I'm going? I ain't never been nowhere else."

"That ain't my problem."

By the time Othello got home from school the war was on. Sometimes the highways looked like one of those rerun movies on television about World War Two with those ragged refugees on the highway going anywhere and nowhere. All their lives they had worked for Mr. Caswell and Old Man Johnson and Cap'n Watson. It was the only world they knew. Entire families, with no place to go, slept out in the open, on the side of the road. Nothing to do, nothing to eat. Nowhere to go.

Luke Gibson was a crazy "nigrah." He told Mr. Johnson, the Congressman's brother, he was going to stay right where he was. "You want me out, you gon have to put me out. I got seven children and wife and a mother, and all but the baby done give you time. We done already earned our way to live in this little old run-down shack forevermore, even if we never hit another lick at snake the longest day we live."

A week later the sheriff and his deputy came and moved his things out to the side of the road. A few hours later, Luke and Reverend Purdy and Little Jake put them back into the shack. This happened at least once a week.

The shaff (sheriff) came one day with eviction papers. Luke told him he had other papers which entitled him to stay in the shack, papers that entitled him to stay on the plantation as long as he wished as long as he had not broken his part of the agreement, which he hadn't. Rab Johnson's first wife, just to spite him for chasing after "nigger women," had signed a work contract with Luke which did not expire within Luke's lifetime. Lizzie Johnson could get away with this because she controlled the purse strings, and she was a spiteful woman—a man-eater, a castrator was the name some men had for her. Lizzie Johnson had long since passed away, but the contract remained intact, and very legal, as Luke found out by making a trip all the way to the colored lawyer in Jackson, when the trouble first began.

The sheriff said, "Show me them so-called legal papers."

Luke said, "I'll produce them when the time come. You just git a warrant and bring me to court. Me and my lawyer'll be ready. And the Federal Gov'ment gon be ready too."

The sheriff scratched his hindparts. He said, "Federal Gov'-ment?" He didn't want any G-men smelling around. The sheriff ran illegal whiskey stills.

Othello never did meet Willie Banks again, one of those famous Northern infiltrators, from Saxton County, Mississippi. The second week Othello was home, an old peckerwood found Willie's body a few feet off the road on a lonesome highway in a very short and shallow grave.

Oh yes, it was hot as hell in Wakefield County all that long hot summer.

But Chuck Othello Chaney escaped the heat, that is, for the most part, since he spent many hours in the rarefied and air-conditioned atmosphere of the brand-new Wakefield mansion and in an air-conditioned Cadillac.

Chapter
2

The Man must have had spies around the place. The next morning after Othello's return home for the summer, Charlie Wakefield sent for him.

It was Saturday, and at first he went to Wakefield's office in the city, but they told him Jimmy Dick was working in his office at his new house that particular morning, as he sometimes did on Saturdays. So the young man from the University walked out to the new house.

Manicured hedges, ten to twelve feet high, fenced off the new house from the highway. Beyond the hedges, for two hundred yards, giant oak trees stood in staggered formation, exactly one hundred in number. They were formidable and awe-inspiring like soldiers on guard duty. Beyond the great trees was the manor house, a low-slung rambling ranch-type mansion sprawling awesomely and arrogantly all over the bright-green countryside. Othello stood now facing the front of the mansion. God only knew how many rooms there were, or even how many wings, since they seemed to go off in fifty-odd directions. He stood for a moment making up his mind. The thing was this. All his life till last September, he had always gone around the back, and even this time, he started automatically in the backward direction, but pulled himself up short. He thought of Ron, he thought of the interminable discussions he had had with Ron about black manhood, about Malcolm, about Martin Luther King and John Lewis and Whitney Young and Wilkins and all the rest, James Farmer, James Foreman, but especially John Lewis and Malcolm, because Malcolm was Ron's patron saint. And John Lewis was the shining prince. He thought of Naomi Hester. Beautiful, glorious, wonderful Naomi Hester. After all, he *was* a man. He looked around him, as if he thought Lewis or Naomi or Ron were watching him. He was different, wasn't he? He was different from the boy who'd left Wakefield County in the autumn time. Why go to the University if you didn't change? He was different because he had been away somewhere, he himself had seen new places, talked to different kinds of people. He had been to college and it had spoiled him for the back-door entrance. It was his Great White Father's fault for sending him to college.

He wiped his face with a white handkerchief and started for the front entrance and pushed his finger on the thing that made the chimes go off inside the house. He swallowed hard and dug in like Willie Mays at home plate.

He waited in a nervous sweat and thought the door would never open, hoped the door would never open. Maybe no one was at home. Hopefully. Come again some other day. But he learned that doors do open finally. The butler was a small black man, a family retainer from way back.

"Boy, ain'tchoo Jess and Carrie's young 'un?"

"I'd like to see, I mean, I have an appointment with Mister Wakefield."

Old man Ross Baker said, "Boy, I know your mama and papa taught you better manners than that. You go around the back now, and I'll tell Mister Charlie you looking for him."

"I am not going around the back." He felt sweat pouring from all over his body now. He had taken a good bath in the big tin tub before leaving home, but it was all washed away in sweat now. "I am not here looking for a handout. Mister Wakefield wishes to see me. If you'll——"

"College sure do turn some people into a educated fool!" Ross Baker offered his opinion. Gratuitously.

They stood there staring one another down, young black face versus old black face. Baker would guard the sweet white sanctuary with his very life, and Chuck would guard his young black manhood. A good-natured, tolerantly amused voice broke into the hateful standoff. "All right, Uncle Ross, show the gentleman in. I'm expecting him."

"But he—I mean——"

"Show Mister Chaney in, Uncle Ross. Is your hearing good?" Even though Othello felt relieved, he didn't like the amusement

[272]

he heard in Wakefield's voice. Mister Charlie was having himself a ball at the expense of his two favorite "niggers."

He walked past the grumbling butler and followed Wakefield down a long corridor and turned left down another corridor and finally reached the Great Man's office, which was an inch deep in carpeting. Chuck thought his feet would disappear from sight. The Great Man went behind his desk and sank back into a swivel chair, sighing deeply. "Sit down," he said. "Sit down—sit down and make yourself at home."

Othello sat down and his whole body almost sank out of sight, this time for real among the goose-feathered couch. It was as if somebody had pulled a chair out from under him. The Great Man knew what had happened and was smiling, actually laughing at him beneath his composed face. Which did not help Othello's frame of mind or disposition.

"Don't let Uncle Toms like Ross get you upset. They'll never change," the Great Man chuckled. "But they don't really mean any harm."

Othello's voice almost trembled with his anger. "Sir, I believe you sent for me."

Mister Charlie said, "I certainly did. I certainly did." Then he looked up at the ceiling for a moment, then back at Othello. "Oh yes. What are your plans for the summer, son?"

I am not your son. "I don't have any definite plans. I'm going to get some kind of job." But not in your cotton field, old buddy. Wakefield's hair was as white as balls of cotton now and ebbing at the hairline. He looked ten years older than Othello remembered him looking when he'd left for the University. He was still an impressive-looking bastard, but time was suddenly and swiftly etching the story of his life in deep lines upon his face. He was aging in a hurry, although he carried himself like a man fifteen or twenty years his junior. He got up and walked around the desk and rested his backside on its edge. "What are you majoring in at the University?"

"I haven't decided yet—I——"

"Business Administration. That's the main problem—your race don't know anything about administration. It's not you all's fault. You never had the opportunity for experience."

Othello stared at Wakefield. Before he'd gone to the University, he had never thought of Wakefield as talking with a Southern accent, but now he sounded as if he were coming on strong with a caricature of a Mississippi peckerwood. It was fantastic how the man had changed, Othello thought. Or maybe the change was in Othello's hearing. In his perspective and perception.

"Business Administration would be just the thing. And this summer you can work for me and I'll teach you something about business from actual experience." The Great Man had developed a twitch at his left cheekbone. "Do you have a driver's license?"

"No, sir."

"We'll take care of that on Monday. You take the weekend off, get yourself together. And report to me here on Monday morning bright and early. You'll be working some of the time right here in this wing of the house. So you don't need to come through the front door and give Uncle Ross an ulcer at his age. He's got enough complaints already. There's a——" He stopped. He stared at Othello who was staring at him blank-faced now. "It has nothing to do with your color. I'm above those kind of considerations. It's just more convenient. I had this wing built to function as an office away from the office. I use this entrance sometimes my own self, when I come from town and I want to come straight to my work. You understand?"

Othello said he understood.

All through the long hot summer, he kept cool. And saw very little of Jake and Bessie Mae and Cora Mae, who were in the heat of things. He reported at the side entrance to the mansion every weekday morning at eight o'clock, and Wakefield was usually there and explained to him some aspect of his forty-million-dollar empire. Some mornings, Wakefield would take him on a tour of the Wakefield complex which stretched out all over the county and for miles and miles. Wakefield Textile was in Yazoo City, Wakefield's Department Store in Jackson. "Keep your eyes open, boy." It wasn't long before Othello figured what his job really was to be that summer. He was a glorified chauffeur. After all the Wakefield "horse-manure-à-la-Business Administration" was cleared away, he was a chauffeur pure and simple. "Learn everything about the Wakefield operation, boy. The day is coming when colored men going to be managers of things. And I want you to be ready. The Negro race needs experienced, intelligent, educated leadership, instead of all this violence and hotheadedness."

[274]

It was all right with Othello, the chauffeur's job. And it was a whole lot better than other jobs, or no job at all. And at least once a week, he drove the Great Man somewhere outside the county. And he liked to drive and he liked going places, seeing other faces. He saw very little of Carrie Louise that summer, just fleeting glimpses, here and there, because he always used the side entrance, and she was almost never in that wing of the house. Which was fine with Chuck Othello. The only other place he saw her was in church. She still went to worship at Mount Moriah Baptist Church at least twice a month.

He arrived for work one Monday morning in the middle of July, and Carrie Louise was seated behind her father's desk.

She said, "Good morning, Othello. How was college?"

He said, "Where is Mister Wakefield?"

She looked him up and down. She was as fresh-faced as she'd ever been. When she smiled her entire face smiled with her; her eyes, cheeks, teeth, lips. "I asked you a question first," she said, "Didn't they teach you any manners up at your college?"

He did not like to be laughed at, especially by a rich, empty-headed white bitch like this one. His face grew warm now, and he tasted his great anger on his lips and in his mouth and throat. "College was just fine. Is your father coming to the office today?" Wakefield was ever punctual.

"My father is a little bit under the weather this morning."

"Anything serious?" If she wanted to play the game of smiling stares, he certainly was not going to let her stare him down. He was not going to let her castrate him. So he stared back at her and through her, blank-facedly, as if she were invisible, or better still, nonexistent. She got the message.

"Nothing serious," she said. "He'll be at his post tomorrow. Generally speaking, he's as healthy as a horse. I expect it was a case of one Scotch and branch water too many." She laughed. "Sit down, Othello Chaney."

"Did he send me a message or something? Is there anything special this morning?"

Her whole face smiled at him. "I'm afraid your colleague was in no shape to send messages this morning. Will you please sit down for a moment? You certainly are a fidgety boy."

He sat, wondering now and curious too, as to what this white girl thought there was for the two of them to talk about in 'Sippi. He sat and waited.

[275]

She said, "You sure have grown. I remember you almost as long as I remember my own self."

He thought to himself, "What is this? Reminiscence Week?" He stared across the desk at the yellow-haired white girl. He wasn't exactly smiling at the moment, but during his sojourn at the University he had developed an expression which made it seem as if a smile were always lurking just out of sight beneath the surface of his face.

She said, "Do you remember how we used to romp and tear together over in the other house?"

He said, "I remember." What in the hell did she want from him?

She said, "We were such good friends in those days. Then one day we grew up and I don't know you anymore."

He said, "*C'est la vie.*" What else is new?

But he remembered all right. He remembered the romping and the tearing, but there were other memories he remembered. He had been about five years old when he learned the difference between black and white, and he had learned his lesson painfully. His mother had whipped it into him. And this girl across the desk had been the instigator with her Mama-and-Papa business. The two of them naked and belly to belly in the guest room in the Big House. He never would forget the incident. After his mother whipped him, later in the day, he'd seen the white girl weeping in his mother's arms. It was a long time afterward that he was able to understand the terror which must have struck his mother's heart. A black boy and Miss Rich White Bitch belly-to-belly in Big House, Mississippi. But the white girl in his mother's arms was something else again.

Carrie Lou's face turned red like a beet, as she remembered now the time when she lay on this black boy naked as she came into the world and mouth to mouth out in the woods that day when he had nearly drowned. She felt a strange heat move all over her body, and she could no longer look him in the face. She had never related the incident to a living soul. How could she? Even now as he sat there, she was so embarrassed, she thought she would go right through the floor. Or was it really embarrassment? But it had been completely innocent. Hadn't it?

She told him, speaking quickly now, about her college roommate who was a Negro. He said, "Oh." Cool as dry ice. The girl's

[276]

name was Sherry Kingsley and her father was a famous lawyer in New York and a state senator, and wealthy, and she and Sherry had become good friends. Othello's comment was "That's good," a bored expression on his face. Sherry Kingsley was into everything, she knew everybody. "David Woodson, John Lewis, Martin King, all the leaders. Foreman, Farmer, Malcolm X." The girl was almost out of breath. "I met some of them my own self." Othello thought, Big deal. But he was entirely unimpressed. It was strange, he thought, to hear this 'Sippi white girl namedropping colored VIP's as if she herself were basking in the sunlight of their celebrity.

She looked him in the face again now. "Were you active in the Movement at the college?"

He had almost relaxed, but with this question, all his danger signals started flashing again. "What movement?"

"The Movement," she said, almost impatiently. "The civil rights movement—the black revolution."

He stared, wordless, at the girl. What the hell did she know about the Movement? "I'm afraid I spent most of my time with my head in the books."

She said, "And what about the Movement around here? Is anything happening?"

He said, "Happening?" So that was what she was all about. She wanted information about the Movement here in Wakefield County. She just wanted to do a little old espionage for the cause of white supremacy. Just a little old harmless espionage by getting this stupid colored boy to spill his chitterlings. She probably had made up that wild story about having a Negro roommate, Sherry Whatchamacallit.

She said, "You know what I mean. Is anybody into anything?"

He was glad he could say truthfully he knew nothing about anything, he had been too busy. At the same time he was somehow ashamed that he had kept himself aloof, aloft. He said, "You know as much about it as I do."

She said impatiently, "Oh I know all about the voter registration drive, and I think it's simply marvelous, but I want to know the inside of everything. I want to be a part of it. I know they've put hundreds of good colored folks off the land for exercising their constitutional rights. I know they've set up tents for some of them to live in on a couple of acres of land owned by the

Mount Moriah Baptist Church. And I think it's a sin and a shame, and I think it's just marvelous how the colored stick together, and live in tents."

She knew more than he did already.

She said, "You've been over to Tent City, haven't you?"

Othello had not been over to Tent City. He had heard his parents mention it, in passing. He had read what David Woodson had said about it in *Democracy* magazine. He thought, Well, my little spy, you will not get anything from this interview, for the simple reason that the man is ignorant of what is going on. He don't know nothing and don't say nothing, he just keep rolling along.

He stood up and told her, "I can't help you at all. And I have to be running along. Tell your father I'll see him tomorrow morning."

He went over to Tent City that afternoon, where about forty-five families were living in Army surplus supply tents. Some had been there since the middle of winter. Othello asked one elderly lady how they made it, especially in the wintertime. She said, "Indeed, darling, in some ways it's better than them shacks they moved us out of. It was like living outdoors in them doggone things whenever the weather got bad. It rained inside them devilish shacks and leaked outdoors."

Tent City was four rows of olive-drab pyramidal tents. The men had built an outhouse at the edge of one end of the row of tents and a common kitchen at the other end. Children ran around all over the place and especially underfoot.

David Woodson had interviewed every family in Tent City for his article in *Democracy* magazine.

"My name is George Booker. I'm fifty-five years old. I've cropped shares for Mister Billy Watson since I was eleven years old. I've always lived on the Watson plantation. And likewise my wife, Sojourner. I and her has five children. Cropping shares is the only work I ever known. What is we going to do?"

"My name is Matthew Jackson. I'm seventy-five years old. Mister Johnson told me, me and my family had a place to stay as long the Johnson plantation existed. I done worked for Mister Johnson all my life. He always told me I and mine was like one of the family. And that ain't too much of a big lie, cause some of mine sure do favor some of his mighty much. I has five chil-

dren and eight grand. Six of the grand lives with me and Queen
Esther who is my first and only wife."

Othello stopped at the end of the second row of tents. An
old withered black woman sat in front of the tent in an ancient
cane-back chair. She was mumbling something to herself. Her
face seemed to wear a thousand wrinkles. He seemed to be drawn
to her as if by an invisible magnet. What was she mumbling to
herself about? Was she trying to say something to him? He stood
above her now and saw her old lips barely moving.

He said, "Yes, m'am, what is it you're saying?"

It was her eyes that held him, fascinated him, mesmerized him.
Large and wide and luminous were her youngish eyes, filled with
the pain and anguish of the ancient ages. "I don't understand
you, Mama."

Her eyes appeared to him to be all-knowing and all-seeing. He
thought she said, "Ain't this a damn shame? Come almost a hundred years down this long and lonesome road to go on to Glory
in a doggone tent. Worked in the Master's vineyud all my life.
Always sowing, never reaping, and come to the end of the row to
die in a damn tent!" She laughed and shook her head from side
to side. "Jesus darling, you sure got a funny sense of humor. I'm
tellin' you the natural truth." She laughed some more. Bitter
laughter. "Niggers sowing—white man reaping. He got the whole
world in his hand. Splain it to me, Jesus. Don let your servant
stop believin! It's too late, Master! Too late! Too late!" She was
laughing and crying simultaneously. Laughing, crying, mumbling.
"You is mysterious, Jesus darling. You is really somethin!"

He felt his own eyes filling up, and he moved away from her,
stumbling over a tent stave. He somehow managed not to fall.
He'd wanted to plead with her, tell her not to stop believing. A
hundred years of walking down that long and lonesome road to
sit and die outside a tent at the journey's end. As he walked away
from the camp ground he ran into Carrie Louise, who was just
driving up in a Jaguar. She bounced out of the car with her arms
full of packages.

"Give me a hand," she told him.

He took some of the packages. "These are for the campers!"
she told him, almost gaily. "Thought you told me you'd never
been to Tent City."

"This is my first trip," he said weakly, angrily, as he followed
Lady Bountiful, which was how he thought of her now, as she

[279]

strode up the row of tents toward the outdoor kitchen. "This is Luke Gibson," Lady Bountiful told Othello, as they gave the tall black man the packages. He seemed to be in charge of the kitchen force.

She didn't need to introduce him to Luke Gibson. He had known the sad-faced man all of his life. She was bubbling over with enthusiasm. "Luke doesn't live here. He's a volunteer worker like you ought to be. He still lives on Rab Johnson's plantation. He refused to move. Isn't he heroic? Everybody loves him. Every time I bring something, I tell him to take some of it home to his own family, wife, mother-in-law, and seven children. And he always says, 'Yessum,' but he never takes a thing. He is as true a Christian as any white man in all of Mississippi."

Chuck Othello slipped away as she went from tent to tent asking the campers how they were doing this beautiful summer afternoon. She wanted them to love her, even as they all loved old stubborn old Luke Gibson.

And they really did love old Luke Gibson, and the stand he was taking against one of the "baddest" Mister Charlies the state had ever known. Everybody talked about it everywhere Othello went among his kind of people. He heard his own mother, Mama Carrie, pray for old Luke every night. Luke and his wife and his mother-in-law and his poor little innocent children. Especially his children. Everybody admired Luke for his stand against the Man, even as they feared for him, because the Man he'd picked to stand against had a fearsome reputation when it came to colored people. Almost overnight, soft-spoken, churchgoing, God-fearing Luke Gibson had become a folk legend and a hero. Before now, folk had thought of him as the gentlest kind of a man. Wouldn't harm a gnat if it were sipping in his buttermilk. And suddenly—strength. John Henry. "Should've been named John Henry steada Luke Clarence Booker Gibson."

One night Othello ran into Uncle Bish. He was stoned, drunk as a cooter, and was finding it almost impossible to navigate. He emerged from Douglass Alley and stumbled along Walnut Street, half-walking, half-running. "Hey there, Chuck Othello." He looked like an accident going somewhere to happen. He had put on weight around the middle and lost weight in his face and shoulders, and was just as Othello's father had described him:

". . . as raggedy as jaybird in whistling time." Othello never found out when "whistling time" was. But he had heard the expression all his life. And it seemed to fit Uncle Bish at the moment.

Uncle Bish walked now rocking and reeling with his shoulders thrust forward as if he were bucking a tornado, but there was no wind stirring in the air at all. He was so high a good strong wind would have put him into orbit. He walked a little ahead of Othello about half of a step. "Let's go git us a little old taste, Othello. Don't worry 'bout nothing. I got the money. I'm a working man. I'm the establishment soup-pen-tendant. That's what my bossman said I am. I got a good job. Don't pay no tention to these niggers round here." Othello's father had told him about Uncle Bish's job as porter at the *Wakefield Daily Chronicle,* which was edited and published by Congressman Rogers Jefferson Davis Johnson.

"No thank you, Uncle Bish. I got to—"

Uncle Bish stopped and turned toward Othello and his feet got tangled with each other and he went down in a heap. "Somebody tripped me," he mumbled. Othello went to pick him up. "I don't need no help," he said, using his body to keep Othello from picking him up. "I can git up by my own self!"

Othello released him and he tried to get up through his own efforts and fell flat on his face. He rolled over and looked up at Othello. "Goddamn!" he said, laughing masochistically. "I'm like Dusty Fletcher—I ain't never seen no whiskey that wouldn't let you go *no*-where!" He stared up at Othello through bloodshot eyes. His red eyes looked like lighted lanterns. "Whatchoo standing up there looking like two dogs on a knot's dick? Ain'tchoo gon help the old man git to his feets?"

Othello helped Bish to his feet and Bish draped his arm around Othello's shoulders and they made it up the dimly lit street. "Come on, Othello, let's go git us a little taste. I got plenty money. Don't worry bout a thing. Open the door, Richard. The man's out here. Wheee-eee! I would holla but the town too small!"

"You don't need no more whiskey, Uncle Bish. I'm going to take you home."

"Whoa—there," Uncle Bish sang out, and imitated a donkey, as he became suddenly immobile and balled up into a knot and used all his strength to keep himself immobile, in very much the manner of a stubborn jackass, which is what Othello was just ready to call his childhood hero. A damn jackass!

"Come on, Uncle Bish, doggone your time!"

"I liked to heard you then, boy! You watch your langwich! I'll rap your platter till your head git flatter. I'll wash your mouth out with lye soap, you don't mind." They were underway again. "You doin the right thing, Othello. Tell em your name is West and stay away from all that nigger mess. A nigger ain't shit no way you take him. I oughta know, cause I been a nigger all my days. I tol' Mister Congusman Johnson, I'm a xpert on niggers. Been one all my natural life—been one all my life."

Othello closed his eyes momentarily as they stumbled up the streets. A single tear spilled down his face, as his mind conjured a memory of Uncle Bish when he was his childhood hero. He was almost every black child's hero. He'd had the biggest heart in Wakefield County. Generous to embarrassment. And the children loved him. And he loved the children. "The black man's future," he would say, "is our childrence." Speaking proper, putting on airs. "They our treasure, more valuable than gold. Can't take it with you nohow. Some of these white folks think they gon pay their way through them Pearly Gates. Gon bribe Saint Peter." He used to be hard on Mister Charlie Peckerwood. He didn't even sound like Uncle Bish anymore.

"This ain't the way to Bennie's," he said, pulling himself up short again, rearing and bucking.

They were going through Crackerville now, where the really poor white peckerwoods lived. They got underway again. "Even a poor white trash is better'n a nigger. A nigger ain't shit! I sure am glad you one nigger boy got sense enough not to git mixed up in that nigger mess with silver rights and all that shit. Silver rights! Silver rights! Voter reddistrayshon! Ain' nothing to it. How it's gon be anythin to it when it's niggers running it? Stands to reason."

They were at the edge of Crackerville now where it ran smack into Black Tybee. Ragged-assed white kids were playing ring games beneath a lamp post.

> *Little Sally Walker*
> *Sitting in a saucer*
> *Cryin and a-weepin'*
> *For all she has done—*

When they saw Bish coming, the game broke up and they ran toward Bish and Chuck Othello with their hands held out. "Uncle Bish! Uncle Bish!"

Before Othello knew what was happening, Bish was emptying his pockets of coins and throwing them to the children, who scrambled for them on the ground in front of them. A dark-brown-skinned little girl ran from across the road toward the crowd with her hands out. "Git back, black bitch!" Bish shouted at her. "Don't you put your black hands on my money!" He reached in his pockets and started to hand out dollar bills to the happy peckerwood children. "Here, pretty children! Here! Here! Git back, black bitch!" He kicked at her. "Git back, black bitch!" The little black girl's eyes filled and tears spilled down her cheeks; she turned and ran back into the darkness from whence she had come.

"Uncle Bish!" Othello cried out. "What's the matter with you? Are you losing your mind, or something?" Othello snatched some bills from Bish's hand and shooed the white children away. "All right! All right! That's enough of that! Give Uncle Bish his money back." The children scampered.

And they got underway again going up a dusty road of a street that was entirely blacked-out. No street lights anywhere at all. They were truly in Black Tybee. "What in the devil you want to give your money away like that, Uncle Bish?"

"Don' worry bout nothin! Donchoo worry bout a thing."

"If you're going to give a little money away, why to white children? Why'd you chase the colored girl?"

"Cause she was black. That's how come."

"What's that got to do with it? That's how come she should get a preference, if anything."

"Cause she black and her foots stink and she don't love Jesus and God don't love ugly and a nigger ain't shit!"

They were in front of his house and started into the yard, and Othello felt a wetness fall upon his sock. He held out his free hand palm upward to see if it were raining. It wasn't raining. And then it reached his nostrils, and he knew that Uncle Bish was pissing his pants. Then Bish broke wind protractedly, like rifle fire, and another kind of stench assaulted Othello's nostrils, turned his stomach over. "Uncle Bish!" He knew somehow that Uncle Bish had shitted in his pants. They had reached the steps by now, and Bish stood still as death, but his pants did not keep quiet, as he lost control of all his functions. Crying, breaking wind, urinating, defecating. He sank down upon the steps and wept like a lonely child without a loved one in the entire world.

Miss Easter Lillie, a stout, tall, high-yaller woman came to the door. "Lord Savior, do pray!" she murmured. And she and Othello struggled with him to get him into the house. Uncle Bish mumbling all the while, "A nigger ain't shit, Chuck Othello. A nigger ain't shit! You stick with Charlie Wakefield like you got some sense. Stay way from that fool boy of mine in the Bottom. Stick with Charlie Wakefield. A nigger ain't shit! I oughta know. I'm a xpert on niggers. Been one all my life!"

And all the way home that night Othello's eyes were never dry. He wept for Uncle Bish, for the man he remembered Bish once was and for the thing he had become. He woke up off and on all night long, and each time it was thoughts and dreams of Uncle Bish that waked him. How had it happened? How in God's name had it happened?

The next night he went to see Little Jake and Bessie Mae Moocho and talked to them about the Movement. They were up to their ears, committed and active. They moved him with their dedication, but he could not be involved, he really could not. He was just too doggone busy. He held hands one night and swapped spit with Cora Mae Rakestraw, and she talked on and on about the Movement. It was unbelievable. Maybe it's a fad, he tried to rationalize it. For hundreds of years, black folk had laughed or wept only on command, only with permission from their kindly masters. "If Cap'n Charlie shouted 'Shit!' you squatted and strained lustily," in the words of Othello's roommate, Ron. No back lip. Just hang your head when Cap'n speaks to you. Don't fret your head about such things as citizenship and ownership. Only men can vote and have possession. There are no such things as black men. The only men are white men. So you must govern yourselves accordingly. But suddenly black men appeared as if from nowhere, appeared in all their blackness. Black men stood straight, and white men scratched their heads in consternation. Some even panicked.

His mother and father, humble, God-fearing people had begun to talk about Charlie like a dog. Reverend Purdy and Luke Gibson were on every black lip in the county. To the city fathers they were wanted men, public enemies. One and Two, in the order named. One evening after work, Othello stopped by the church to see his pastor, who invited him to dinner at the parsonage. He drove an ancient Packard and was probably the world's very worst driver, as he sped along at ten and fifteen miles an hour. Othello felt naked and exposed as they drove nonchalantly through the downtown area. He could feel the stabs of hatred from the angry looks of white folk, as he drove around with Public Enemy Number One. It seemed to Othello that his pastor had to make a million stops before heading home. It was nerve-racking. One of the last stops was at a bakery shop, and he had to park the car on an incline. Purdy got out of the car unconcernedly and took a brick out from under his seat and put it behind a back wheel to keep the car from rolling back downhill, and he ambled into the bakery. Othello thought his pastor would never return, as cracker after cracker drove alongside and stared at the car, and threw angry white looks at Othello, or so he imagined. Reverend Purdy stopped by his combination barber shop and shoe shop. He stopped at this place and that. It was a long time after dark by the time he headed home for real. He lived out in a brand-new settlement for Negroes, where the teachers and the preachers and the mail carriers and Pullman porters lived; people E. Franklin Frazier called "black bourgeoisie," but whom ordinary folk called "nigger rich."

There was no moon out that night as they sailed down the main highway at thirty miles an hour. Then they turned off the main highway and onto a dirt road which led to the new development. They had gone about two hundred yards, when a blast of siren broke the silence of the peaceful countryside. Out of nowhere a squad car flew past them for about fifty yards and threw a roadblock across the narrow road; two cops emerged from the car and came running toward the old Packard which had chugged down to a halt.

One of the policemen threw the beams of his flashlight onto the windshield, temporarily blinding them. The cops came up to the car, one on Reverend Purdy's side, the other on Othello's. They dipped the beams of their flashlights into their faces again, and then into the back of the car.

Reverend Purdy asked politely, "What's your problem, Officers?"

"We ain't got no problem. You the one got a problem, boy."

"It's been a long time since I was a boy, Mister Officer."

"Never mind. What you mean tearing up the highway a while ago at eighty miles an hour?"

Reverend Purdy laughed a dry laugh. "You must be got the wrong party, Officer. This old buggy ain't done eighty miles an hour in so long, it wouldn't know what it was all about."

The other cop said, "That's that nigger preacher been raising all that hell round here, ain't it?"

The first cop said, "You must been drunk or something, driving that fast like you done lost your mind or something."

"No, sir. You got the wrong party again. Cause I'm a man of the cloth, and I don't never imbibe, although I don't hold it against a man who do."

The other cop said, "You know how to drive, boy? You, boy, you, you sitting next to the preacher."

"I know how to drive," Othello said. "And I have my driver's license."

The first cop said, "Well, we gon take you down to the lock-up, preacher, and you can tell that lie to the shaff, and see if he believes you like your flock do evey Sunday." The other cop had come and joined the first one on Reverend Purdy's side.

Reverend Purdy said, quietly, "No, sir. I have to be getting along home. I got company for supper. And being as how I ain't broke the law, I don't see what business I could possibly have with the shaff."

All during this time Chuck had a feeling of profound ambivalence. He was indignant, because he knew the cops were deliberately gunning for his pastor. In his anger he sympathized with his pastor all the way. And he hated these peckerwoods as much as anybody. At the same time, he could have kicked himself for being caught out on this lonely and deserted road. These cops could do anything they wanted with them. He and his pastor were completely helpless. The night came suddenly alive with all the sounds of night in Mississippi. Frogs croaking, crickets giggling; he even thought he heard some owls hooting. And whippoorwills. He was with the Movement all the way, but he wanted to pick his own arena for the fight, and he damn sure wouldn't pick a dark and lonely spot like this, where the only lighting was from the blinking lightning bugs.

His belly flip-flopped as he heard the first cop say, "All right, preacher, you gon come peacefully, or do I got to pull you out the car? You want us to start some rough stuff? We damn sure

[286]

can accommodate you." He put his hand on his gun which rested snugly in its holster.

Reverend Purdy reached over Othello into his glove compartment and took a gun out and placed it on his thigh. There was a slight tremor in his voice now. "You gentlemen might try to take me outa this car, and one of y'all might get me, but one of y'all ain't going to feel so good about it, cause he going to meet his Maker, 'bout the same time I do. And that's my promise. I might board the train for Glory in the next few minutes, but this is one train gon be integrated." They both had their hands on their guns now, and he had his hand on his gun, and there was that moment when the whole world hung in balance for these four men. Sweat rained from all over Chuck Othello. The policemen looked at Reverend Purdy, then at each other. Which of them would make the first move and which would live to tell the story? And be a county hero. And get a fat promotion. They looked back at Reverend Purdy. The first cop said, "All right, boy. We gon let you go this time beingst it's your first offense and seeing as you a man of God. But you better watch your step from now on in."

His pastor said simply, dryly, "Thank you, kindly."

The lawmen backed away and walked back to their car and got in and drove past them back down the road from whence they came. Reverend Purdy gazed into his rear-view mirror, then took a large colored handkerchief out of his back pocket and wiped his face. "Whew!"

Othello said, in open boyish admiration, "Reverend Purdy, you sure did stand up to them. You sure got a lot of courage! I mean to tell you. Man! You shook them to their natural chittlings!"

Reverend Purdy said, "I figured it this way. I done lived up off my knees all this time, I ain't gon do no different this late in the game. I don't git on my knees to nobody but the Good Lord up on High, and He sure don't look like none of them peckerwood policemen. Leastways I sure God hope He don't."

Othello said, "Yeah, but I mean, they had you where they wanted you way out here in the middle of nowhere. They had both of us where they wanted us."

"Well, you right about that, son. But the way I figured it, to go or not to go, the percentages was in my favor. If I had gotten

[287]

out the car they could've whipped both of our heads till their arms got weary and shot us in the back and locked our dead bodies up for resisting arrest. That's how come I figured I had nothing to lose by not gitting out the car. On the other hand, I figured that they loved their little white lives just as much as I loved my black one. I figured they might even love they lives more than they love they white supremacy or whatever you call it. And it looks like Reverend Purdy gambled rightly."

He laughed a short and angry laugh and wiped his heavy brow again and started up the car and took off slowly down the lonesome road.

Chapter

3

Othello went to church every Sunday, and some evenings he visited with Cora Mae and Bessie Mae and Little Jake. He sneaked food from the Wakefield mansion and took it to Tent City, where he saw Bessie Mae helping out a couple of times, and saw her hero-worshipping Luke Gibson. And he told himself he was not jealous. All colored folk talked about this soft-faced soft-voiced don't-care colored man who stood up every moment of his life against one of the meanest crackers in all of Mississippi. Othello wasn't jealous. Luke deserved all the adulation coming to him. Bessie Mae said, "Lawdy Claudy! John Henry musta been just like him." Cora Mae said, "Tall, black, brave and handsome! Ooh-wee! It's a good thing Brother Gibson married and got a house fulla childrens, else I would naturally run away with him."

Both Bessie Mae and Cora Mae worked in "service," that is, they worked as cooks, each in a rich white man's house. They brought other maids and cooks and general-cleaners into the Movement. They organized the Domestic Workers Committee as a part of the Wakefield County Civic Association. They got hundreds to come to town and register. With a little notice, Bessie Mae had boasted she could call three hundred cooks and maids together. They stayed in readiness for muster: the Minutewomen of Wakefield County.

Meanwhile Othello did his part. It wasn't a big thing, but every little bit helped. Like Carrie Louise, he brought food to Tent City every chance he got, and he made financial contributions from time to time to the Wakefield County Civic Association, which was the name of the organization they had formed under Reverend Purdy's chairmanship. He did not go from house to house each night like Bessie Mae and Luke Gibson, urging people to register, teaching them to fill out registration forms. He was too busy for that. Most nights he escaped into his books, getting ready for the next semester. But one night he went to see Luke Gibson. He visited the living legend. They sat out in front of the shotgun shack in the heat of the evening (there was no cool this night). They sat there, each one of them waving a fan in front of his face, stirring up the evening heat.

The kerosene lamp on the center table out in front of the Gibson shack attracted every bug in 'Sippi. It was the only light among the entire row of dilapidated shacks—except the lightning bugs, of course. Darkness lay over the plantation as if the whole wide world had gone to sleep—except, of course, the brightly lighted Big House. Luke Gibson puffed quietly on a corncob pipe. Othello tried to keep his eyes off Mrs. Gibson who was feeding the baby at her young and swollen breast. The other children were already asleep on a pallet in the shack. Luke was fifteen years older than Mrs. Gibson.

"You're sure doing a great job, Mister Luke. Everybody gives you credit."

He smiled a slight smile. "Yeah, I remember you, boy, when you won't knee-high to a hoppergrass. You always was a smart one, a real go-getter. I remember when you used to keep the fire going all night long at them Labor Day weekend barbecues over on the Wakefield plantation. All night long before the picnic, you would keep them fires burning. You would scamper from one to the other. Busy as a cat covering up shice." He laughed quietly, puffing on his corncob pipe.

Wakefield County was mosquito country and they seemed to be holding some kind of convention right in front of the Gibson shack. And the order of business at the moment seemed to be to eat alive and without cooking one Mr. Charles Othello Chaney. He was slapping at them all evening long, so much so that his hands began to smell of blood. Othello remembered the good old days, when all the hostility, as he looked back at it now, always stayed beneath the surface, and rich white folks were "kindly," and colored folks were "happy and contented." He remembered the time in the very young days of his youth when he saw no contradiction in the position of his family and himself and other colored people who made the fires and kept them going and killed the cows and killed the hogs and got them ready for the barbecue, did all the labor, happily, saw no contradiction between them and those who came gaily and merrily and prettily, and whitely, to enjoy the results of the black folks' labor. It was the way things were, and no one questioned, that is, out loud. Black folks even played the music, and smilingly, while the pretty white folks danced, carefree and also smilingly. Othello wasn't that old. It had not been that long ago. A few black grumbles here and there from the arrogant and disgruntled ones. But hardly ever anything of an overt nature. Whatever happened to those carefree days?

He stole another glance. Why didn't she take the baby inside the shack if she had to suckle it? Her breast looked so dark and brown and sweet and swollen-ripe.

"When did you make up your mind to stand up against them like you're doing, Mister Luke? I mean, it sure does take a lot of courage."

He seemed psychic, seemed to know what was bugging Chuck Othello. "You doing the right thing, Chuck Othello. Get some education up in your head. Nobody can take that away from you lessen they take away your life. What I mean, you'll mean more to the Movement when you git something up here." He tapped his own head with the tip of his index finger. "Stick with it, son. Don't let nothin' throw you off the track. When you git all you kin up there, you'll be a hundred times more important than some ignant cotton picker like the likes of me."

"But you," Othello protested, "your example of courage. You've inspired every black man in this county. You've put backbone in every colored man and woman in this neck of the 'Sippi woods."

"Ignancy is one of our main problems," Luke Gibson stated heatedly. "We fighting for voter registration, right? And we outnumber the peckerwoods three to one. That means, by God, that black folks oughta be running this county. I'm talkin about a black shaff, a black mare, a black govment. Why not? We couldn't make a worser mess of it then they been doin all this time. When the time come we got to organize a black party and take hold and make the whole dang county free, the whole doggone state. Black and white and everbody."

Othello felt a chill race up and down his spine and flutter out across his shoulders. He slapped at a flock of mosquitoes holding a caucus in front of his face. He looked around through the darkness toward the Big House standing there ablaze with light. Goddamn! This was the black revolution everyone talked so glibly about. Othello swallowed hard, deep deep into his flip-flopping belly. And what the hell had he done all summer? Run around the county and the state with Mister Charlie! And carrying stuff from the white folks' kitchen to the poor downtrodden colored people. He was doing missionary work, while Luke Gibson was a dedicated revolutionary. He, Charles Othello Chaney, was no better than that yellow-haired Wakefield gal. He felt his guilt and shame deep deep inside of him, and he struck out weakly at his hero in defense of his own piss-poor position.

"Somebody has to go to school and stay in school and get an education. It sure won't do any good for us all to grow up dumb and ignorant. I mean you're doing a good job, no doubt about it, but—" His voice trailed off—his shame before his hero choked him up. He was a first-class twenty-four-caret phony.

"That's what I mean," Luke said quietly. "We gon need educated men to rule us, to serve us, to take charge of the govment. To help free us from ignancy. I mean, I know I'm ignant, I don't make pretend."

"You are not ignorant! You are one of the most intelligent men in all of 'Sippi. You got a vision, Mister Luke, and the courage to carry it all the way through. I don't know what this county would do without you. All the universities in the United States couldn't give me what you already got. Can't give me what you've given me tonight."

Othello glanced at Luke's wife, who was rocking the baby to sleep now. Her eyes were closed. He thought she had also fallen asleep. She said, "It takes you *and* Luke and me and everybody else to win this battle with the white man." She had a voice as soft as corn silk and as sweet as sugarcane syrup.

Luke laughed softly as if to himself. "You go back to that college, son, and git yourself a education."

[291]

Later that night he lay on top of the sheets in his bed and he could not go to sleep. Luke Gibson! Luke Gibson! The soft-spoken quiet-faced man had set his heart and soul and mind afire. He felt great shame because he was doing so little and this man was doing so much. He felt justified because this man who did so much had stressed the importance of education. All right then, he would buy that. He would get as much as possible from the University and pay it back in service to his own people right here in 'Sippi. Goddamn! Don't kid yourself, Othello. You're escaping from the struggle into the University. Luke Gibson knows what you're up to, you opportunistic bastard! He's got your number. He just didn't want to embarrass you. He's the kind of man who is embarrassed by another man's embar-rassment. Education is important, goddammit! I don't care what Luke Gibson or Hoot Gibson or anybody else says. But that's what he said, old baby. Education is important. Between the mosquitoes, and Luke Gibson's vision and his own great guilt, he wasn't able to fall asleep.

The mosquitoes chased him under the sheet, and he had pulled the sheet up over his head to protect his face, and he was just about to fall asleep when something like the loudest clap of thunder he had ever heard rocked the entire countryside. It rattled the windows in the Chaney house. Had the Great Big Bomb been dropped? He leaped from his bed. He walked around in his underwear in a kind of daze. He heard his parents stirring in the front room.

"What happen, Jess? What was that great big noise? It didn't sound like thunder." His father mumbled something to his mother.

Othello hurriedly got into his trousers and threw on a shirt. He forgot to put on his shoes. But by the time he got outside of the house, many houses had already emptied and folk were run-ning toward the conflagration, which lighted up the sky as if the world were burning down. It was Luke Gibson's shack. There was no doubt in Chuck Othello's mind. Yet he was afraid to say the words aloud, even to himself. It couldn't be Luke's! It mustn't be! Men, women, children moving toward the big bright blaze.

"Lord Savior, Savior, have mercy on our souls!"

"Jesus!"

"Goddamn old rose!"

"My Lord, what a morning!"

"I thought Judgment Day'd done come!"

People poured out of their houses on the way to the big bright blaze. By the time Othello got to the shack there was only smoldering ashes. No more blaze. No more Luke Gibson. No more Gibson family. Luke, sweet-faced Miss Mamie, Miss Mamie's mama, and all the children—gone forever. Even the little baby who had sucked his mother's teats just a few hours back, when he had sat and watched them on the sly. Madonna and child. He walked around with the other people, walked around the smoking ruins. People crying, talking, cussing, swearing. Angry people. Mean, frustrated, vengeful people. Legs, arms, heads, flung all over the place, all over the plantation. Some of them would never be collected. Othello couldn't believe it. It couldn't be! How could it be? He had sat there talking with the gentle indestructible man just a few hours back that evening. The pipe, he thought, the pipe! What happened to the pipe? He found himself thinking stupidly that if he found the pipe intact there he would also find Luke Gibson. Intact. Whole. Complete. Unaltered. Alive. Speaking. Planning. Fighting! But Luke was gone and all his family gone forever. But he couldn't be gone. But he was gone and forever gone. Othello looked around him at all the weeping, moaning people. We'll weep and moan and gnash our teeth and not a goddamn thing will be done about it. About the brutal senseless murder of this great courageous man and his family. Nothing! Not a goddamn thing! It was too much.

He walked away from the multitude of weeping, helpless people, who would say, "It's a sin and a shame before the living God!" But would do nothing to give this man's life a deeper meaning, to make this man's life be the starting point of something. He could not stand his moaning, grumbling people any longer, who would shake their heads and suck their teeth but do not one damn thing in vindication of this man who lived and dared to live abundantly. And loved life enough to give his life so that other men might live life more abundantly. Deep, deep inside of him his soul cried out for vengeance. But, just like the rest of his people, he would cuss and let off steam and then do not a goddamn thing.

He walked away from the plantation, walked down the road into the night. His heart filled up and he overflowed with anguish. Great big six-foot-three black boy walking down the dark road crying like a little baby. Luke Gibson! Luke Gibson! He felt an overwhelming helplessness. How in the hell could black folk ever win, if they couldn't protect a fearless leader like Luke Gibson? Would not even avenge the leader and his family's massacre. He wiped his eyes with the back of his hand. He smiled a grim smile through his tears. Luke was finally evicted. He and his family never again would have to worry about food or clothing or shelter or the meanness of the peckerwood. Luke was a freedom fighter, and he and his family were free at last. Bitterly Chuck Othello thought: The Lord works in mysterious ways His wonders to perform.

The state, county, and city police looked high and low for the violence perpetrators, the dynamiters, the courageous bombers, but naturally came up with not a single arrest, not a single clue. It was not expected that they would. It would not have been traditional. And the good white folks of 'Sippi were true believers in tradition. Even the Government men came into the county to investigate the incident.

It was a big, a lovely funeral. All black folks in the county knew them, loved them. You heard comments like: "Even the poor little biddy innocent childrens!" And there was no widow to mourn Luke's untimely passing, no father and mother to mourn the little children. There were no relatives at the funeral. All the relatives were in the caskets. And there was very little crying at the funeral. Purdy preached a quiet sermon. He didn't want to ignite the fires of anger which were already smoldering. There was a kind of silence at the funeral which comes before a volcanic eruption or an earthquake, as when suddenly all the birds hush their singing, and the lightning bugs stop their blinking and the crickets and the bullfrogs pause awhile to listen. Reverend Purdy heard the angry silence, as did all of Wakefield County.

That morning following the dynamiting, 'Sippi Negroes had watched the news of themselves on television, had watched a national leader of the people way up yonder in New York City, had heard him call on Negroes in the Deep South and in the ghettos of the North to stick by their moral posture of nonviolence. "I know it's hard after what has just happened to our brother and his family in Mississippi, but we must not let them bring us down to their level. Our mission is to bring them up to ours."

[294]

They watched, also on television, a Black Nationalist leader talking to an audience on the streets of Harlem. "Malcolm should be here! Malcolm should be here! Brother Malcolm should be here with us tonight, black brothers and sisters. We need to march on Mississippi! The murdering peckerwood bastards!"

A young man in the crowd of black folk shouted, "It's time for us to shed some white blood now! They've killed too many of us without us fighting back!" The tears flowed down the young man's face, but he was hardly conscious of them. "Even their own Bible says, an eye for an eye, a tooth for a tooth!"

The leader shouted, "How long? How long? How long? How long—before we tear this building down?"

During those first days after the dynamiting, you could feel a tension in all the white folks' houses in which there were servants. Maybe it was the white folks' great guilt, but they seemed to sense a difference in the way their servants looked at them. The fact of the matter was, the whole county was in a state of shock. It was one thing to keep the black man in his place and to knock one over every now and then to make an example for the rest of them. But to wipe out a whole family with seven children and two women, this went against the grain of tender Southern sensibilities.

Even the *Wakefield Daily Chronicle* issued a disclaimer the morning after the dynamiting. Rab and Rogers Johnson both denounced the dynamiters.

The night after the funeral, the Domestic Workers Committee called a meeting in the basement of Mount Moriah Baptist Church. More than three hundred and fifty women showed up. Some came from neighboring counties. They argued, they screamed, they wept in anguish. Some shouted that the time had come.

"Put up or shut up!"

"How long are we going to make their beds and cook their food so they can go out and kill our folkses?"

"They trample us underneath their feet and come right home and don't even worry about the something to eat we fix them. What kind of people is we become that white folks can take us so for granted?"

"You gone too far now! You in the presence of the Lord! Remember, sisters, we in God's tabernacle!"

[295]

"Vengeance is mine, saith the Lord!"

Bessie Mae was chairman of the meeting.

A long tall sister took the floor. "I want to remind the sisters that when the crackers murdered Brother Banks, we made certain decisions. We took an oath to stand together. We likened ourselves to the house slaves and we had access to our masters. We said the next time, sisters, that we were going to strike a blow for freedom would be heard clean around the earth. We elected a committee to get the stuff to work with. Well ladies, sisters, the stuff is here, and the time is come! If we ever going to strike back, it's now or never! Not one, but ten did they strike down. One man, I mean a *real* man, a black and beautiful man! And two women and seven little innocent children!"

"Wait a minute now! You know we didn't actually mean it!"

"Shut up, Aunt Jemima!"

The long tall sister knew her parliamentary procedure. She had been a leader in the Western Star of Mississippi, the Grand Lodge of Yazoo City. She was the present president of the Willing Workers Club of Mount Moriah Baptist Church. She said, "I still got the floor, Madam Chairman. I still got the floor. Thank you. I want to make a motion that we carry through our plan on this coming Friday night at suppertime."

"No! No! No!"

"I second the motion."

"All in favor say Aye."

"Stand up and be counted!" the tall sister shouted. "Let em stand up and be counted, so there's no who-shot-John when the deal goes down." She turned and faced her sisters, and they began to get up one by one, two by two, three by three, till at least two-thirds of them were standing. Sitting and standing, most of them were weeping now. Crying unashamedly.

"It ain't too late to reconsider! We all Christians! Remember Reverend Martin Luther—"

"Shut up, Aunt Jemima!"

The tall one walked to the front of the room where a Bible lay on the table. "Each and every one of you line up and come and put your hand upon this Holy Bible and swear allegiance to each other and to our mission. This mean you won't breathe it to another living soul. Not even to your loved ones." Some sat in their seats, but most of them came up single file and solemnly placed their right hands on the Holy Book.

The vote was taken Wednesday. The way Bessie Mae figured it, more than a thousand white folk would die at their supper table on Friday night. She hardly slept a wink that night. She turned and twisted all night long, and the rare moments when she did capture sleep, she slept with nightmares. One thousand people! Human beings! It was a mighty burden to carry. And she felt that she was more responsible than anybody, because she was the first to bring the group together. She was in truth the original organizer of the Domestic Workers Committee of the Wakefield County Civic Association. She and the late Brother Willie Banks. Which was why Brother Banks's untimely death had hit the group especially hard. He had worked with them so patiently, so tenderly. But to have a thousand lives on your conscience for the rest of your days!

She worked all day the next day in Judge Marshall's home. She cooked breakfast, dinner, and supper; all day long it walked around with her. After tomorrow night, the entire world would be different. There would be blood on her hands, blood on all their hands, all the hands in the Committee. Bloodless blood. White blood. And she would live with blood all the remainder of her life, their lives, the nation's life. Blood and death and death and blood. And she was the most responsible. She watched her victims all at dinner Thursday night. The Judge, his wife, Miss Lucy, the pretty blond-haired children, Roy Junior and Essie Belle and Pamela. Wide blue eyes of innocence. They had twenty-four hours to live. The Judge was not the most hateful cracker in 'Sippi. In a way the children were entirely innocent. But then she hardened herself against them all, remembering Willie Banks and Emmett Till and Parker and Medgar Evers and Chaney and Goodman and Schwerner, and the river, which for her was the symbol of the whole white world. And Luke Gibson and his family. In her image of the river, it had swallowed up black men by the thousands. Sometimes she pictured Judgment Day as a Great Getting-Up Morning, when the river would be dredged and made to give up all its black souls. But the Judge was not the evilest cracker in Wakefield County. Had a reputation of being a pretty good peckerwood when it came to dealing with black folks. And the poor little innocent children! As she served them dinner, she felt her eyes filling up and she almost threw her arms around them to protect them from the black death they would suffer. She almost broke down into tears. She

[297]

almost blurted out the truth to the whole family, this family of good white folk.

The white-haired friendly faced Judge had watched her closely all during supper. She caught him staring at her more than a dozen times. Near supper's end, he looked up at her and asked her to come to his study after she had finished her evening chores.

Her heart beat crazily as if it would leap out of her bosom, as she walked back into the kitchen. She went to the sink and put cold water on her face. He knows! He knows! He knows! That's why he looked at me so funny all during supper. Shaking from head to foot, she somehow made it through her chores, she washed the dishes and put things away in the kitchen, she straightened up the dining room, and took a quick swallow of bourbon which almost took her breath away. She thought her throat and stomach were on fire. Back in the kitchen she sat for a moment getting herself together. She walked around putting things in place that were already in their proper places. She talked big at the meetings, and she looked beautifully mature, but she was only a twenty-year-old girl after all, and she was scared almost to death. She thought maybe she should open the back door quietly and go across the backyard and out the back gate and run and run and never stop running away from this place, away from 'Sippi, away from Dixie and never come back, never ever even take a look back southward. But something foolish in her told her that he might not know about the plot at all. Maybe he was thinking about giving her a raise. Maybe— maybe—maybe—a hundred other maybes. She must not panic. She made her way shakily through the dining room, taking another quick swallow from a bottle on the buffet, Scotch this time, she did not know the difference. Steady, Bessie Mae. Calm yourself, she told herself.

Now she stood outside the Judge's study. She raised her fist to knock. She brought it down again and breathed a deep sigh. She walked away and then came back and rapped sharply on the door. He told her to come in.

The Judge sat there in his smoking jacket puffing on a small cigar and holding a highball glass of bourbon and branch water. She said, "You wanted to see me, sir, Judge Marshall?"

He looked her up and down and through her. He knew! He knew! He knew! "How long have you been with us, Bessie?"

"One whole year come the first of next October," she answered primly, successfully hiding the fear she thought would surely overcome her.

"How do you like your job, Bessie Mae?"

"I like it right smart." Maybe he was going to give her a raise.

"Well, everybody here likes you too. Miz Marshall is very satisfied with your work. You're the best cook we've had in this house in a coon's age."

"Thank you, sir."

"But here lately something seems to be troubling you. Tonight you walked around like you were in a trance or something. What's the matter, Bessie Mae?"

"Nothing, sir. Nothing at all, I thank you." She changed her mind again. He knows! He knows! He's playing cat and mouse with me.

"How's your mama getting along these days?"

"She's right poorly, sir. You know she had a stroke last January."

"Oh, I see. That's what it is. Your mama ain't worked since January, and all them doctor bills piling up and all like that."

She said, "They piling up all right, sir." He was indeed a kindly man, but tomorrow this time he would be no more of this world, unless she—

"I expect you need a little old raise. I expect that's what's worrying you so much."

"I could stand one, sir. I really could use a raise right along in here."

The Judge got up and started to walk up and down the thick carpeting. "Well, when you got a problem, you just come and talk to the Judge about it, you hear? Ain't no reason it can't be straightened out to everybody's satisfaction."

She was overwhelmed with her good fortune. Somehow the plot against these white folks' lives had been buried somewhere beneath her consciousness. "Thank you, sir!" She felt so filled up with gratitude.

He stopped his pacing up and down. He stopped and stared at her. "I think a little old raise can be arranged. You know, Bessie Mae, I believe the nigrah has a right to live just as much as the white man. The Good Lord made us all in His own image." He paused and stared up at the ceiling, as if he thought God were up there in the chandelier. "And I have made of one blood all the nations."

Her conscience said to her, "But you are going to kill this kindly old white man and his whole family tomorrow." She felt herself filling up with grief.

He said, "Like I say, Miz Marshall is just tickled to death with you. She says you're so neat and clean. And she would trust the children with you as much as she would trust them with her own self. And the children love you almost better'n they do their parents."

Bessie could hold it in no longer. Her heart broke and she burst into tears. "Lord have mercy!"

He was also moved to great compassion at her great show of emotion. He put his arms around her shoulders, in a fatherly gesture. "There now—there now. Any time you have a problem you bring it right to the Judge."

She turned and buried her head in his chest, and she must tell him now, she must tell the Judge about the plot against his family. Against him, who was the kindest-hearted peckerwood in Wakefield County, against his young pretty sweet wife, and against those poor little innocent children who loved the ground that Bessie Mae walked on. She was choking with sobs now as the Judge caressed her shoulders and the middle of her back. "Judge, your Honor," she blurted between sobs. "Judge, there is a plot to—"

But the Judge was so wrapped up in his own magnificent compassion for this poor little helpless nigrah girl he did not even hear the word "plot." She was about to give the whole thing away, when the Judge's passion took precedence over his compassion and she felt his arm tightening around her shoulders and his hand stealing down into her brassiere, as his other hand squeezed her buttocks.

She brought her knee up viciously to his crotch and pulled away from him and her open hand went up against his face like a toy balloon exploding. She said, "You dirty lowdown peckerwood sonofabitch! The next time you start to put your hands on a black woman you'll damn sure remember Miss Bessie Mae Brazwell."

He was so stunned he stood there rocking and reeling, soundlessly. She picked up her pocketbook where she had laid it on a chair and she hit him in the head with it and he sank down into the carpeting. She turned and made her way out of the study, and for the very first time she did not leave by way of the back door but headed straight for the front entrance and the foyer with its brilliant crystal chandelier.

The enormity of what she had done and of what she had been on the verge of doing did not strike her until she was out in the hot, sticky summer night air. Then her eyes began to blear and cold chills danced across her shoulders. And she felt a queasy feeling deep down where her bowels quivered. She walked and walked and walked and she stopped walking and looked around her. Where was she? She was surely nowhere near the Bottom. She stared down the dark street, and there was something strangely familiar about this street, and then she knew that without knowing she had come to the street where her lover lived, her lover who didn't even know he was her lover. Her University lover. She needed so much love, this lovely girl, had starved for love nearly all her born days ever since her daddy died. Her mother loved her, but could not make up for the love her daddy would have lavished on her.

She found her lover alone studying for his next semester at the University. His mother and father were at some meeting or the other. She wept in his arms. He thought at first she wept for Luke Gibson, which was not too far off the target.

She said, "Let's walk in your backyard, in your garden. I'm so sorry to bother you, Othello, but I feel so terrible and I didn't know nowhere else to turn."

Maybe her mother had had another stroke!

They walked out back, hand in hand, and followed a path that ran through the rows of corn, and they stood there in the moonlight, and he turned toward her and she toward him and her head upon his chest, and she wept and wept. And he kissed away her salty tears making way for fresher tears to flow. He kissed her mouth, her lips that he had always loved before he'd ever kissed them. And she blurted it all out to him, the plot to kill a thousand white folk at their supper tables.

Shaken badly, he took her to see their pastor. When they arrived at the church, he was just about to leave. "You're just the one I want to see. I was about to go by your house just this minute," he said to Bessie Mae. "Y'all come on back in my study for a minute."

They were in his study now. He shook his head. "Lord forgive us for our transgressions."

She blurted out, "Reverend Purdy, I got to tell you something."

He said, "Never mind. I already know about it. And never mind how I got the news. It sure didn't come from you." He shook his head. "Sister Brazwell, if we going to bring these walls tumbling down we got to do it together, not one pulling this way and one the other. We can't have secrets by divisions. This is one indivisible movement."

She said, "I'm sorry, Reverend Purdy. We thought the men would be against us doing it."

"Never mind," he said, "That's water under the bridge. I just want to tell you that I've known for more than a half an hour, and I sat here wrestling with myself and the Devil. I was tempted, yes, God forgive me, I was greatly tempted, to let the whole dang thing go through. Let them die, as we have died at their white hands, I said, but I could not convince myself." He brought himself up short. "This is no time for sermonizing. Y'all got names and addresses and telephone numbers of the maids and cooks committee?"

Bessie Mae said, "Yes sir, the secretary has the list. Julia Anne Starling. And she got a telephone." They called Julia Anne and she brought the roster of the membership and they called a meeting for midnight that night by telephone and by word of mouth. About two hundred and seventy-five women showed up.

Reverend Purdy spoke in a quiet voice that was unusual for him. He spoke of the unity of purpose that the Negroes of Mississippi must work for. And unity of program. "We can't win if one group is going to go off all by itself and commit the whole community to mass murder without giving the community a chance to voice its opinion. To vote for or against it. That's one of the things we are fighting for more than anything else, the right to vote for the things that's life and death to us. We fighting against taxation without representation. And all the blacks in Mississippi woulda been taxed if y'all's plan had been carried out. I know how you feel. We been buked and we been scorned for hundreds of years in this sweet land of liberty. We been strangers in the house that we constructed. We've been murdered, lynched, raped, robbed, exploited, and how long before we fight fire with fire. I say, not yet. Not yet. The time is not come yet.

[302]

But we may have to come to this, that we will kill them in their beds! As human as we are, we may someday have to come to this. But not yet. The Good Book says, an eye for an eye and a tooth for a tooth, and we may have to come to that. But the time is not now."

"When is the time?" the tall sister shouted.

"When all else has failed. When all else has failed us, then we come to that moment." He paused. "Is it time for self-defense? Yes!" He answered his own question.

"Yes, Lord, yes!" the congregation shouted.

"You mighty right!" "Long past time!"

"And we must make preparations to defend ourselves."

"Amen!" a sister shouted.

And another: "Praise His Holy Name!"

"But self-defense is one thing and mass murder is another thing!"

"Yes!"

"And remember, the Bible says, 'Take care of the widows and the orphans.'"

"Yes, it do!"

"Pray for them that wrongfully abuse you."

"Well!"

"And he who lives by the sword shall perish by the sword."

Then he talked to them about the beauty of Luke Gibson's life, and its deepest meaning and asked them to reflect on the meaning of Luke's life and to dedicate their own lives to the principles for which he gave his life and the lives of his beloved family. There was weeping now throughout the church. He said, "How many within the sound of my voice will pledge with me to dedicate their lives to the cause of freedom in the spirit of our departed and beloved brother and his family? Whosoever will, let them stand."

And the women stood unanimously.

Then there was the practical job of notifying the women who were not in attendance, to tell them of the decision reached, to call off the Friday evening "mercy mission," as some sisters had euphemistically named it. Actually there never was a vote to overrule the mercy mission. There was just a general understanding.

Some sisters stayed at the church till three in the morning, telephoning and giving assignments to others to walk and drive miles out of their way to see those sisters who were not in attend-

[303]

ance and were not reachable by telephone. There were at least twenty-five with whom they were not able to make contact at all that night. All day long the next day, Friday, Reverend Purdy and Bessie Mae and others went to rich white folks' back doors and spoke to maids and cooks even up till five o'clock on the evening of the mercy mission. White folks ate heartily that evening, having not the vaguest notion what a close call they had had toward taking that ultimate journey to the land where they would never grow old.

Thus it was averted—the first mass murder of the Southern white folk (and quality white folk in the bargain), since that terrible billion-dollar misunderstanding, which some men called the Civil War.

Chapter
4

Since the night she came to him crying, Othello saw a lot of Bessie Mae, that summer of summers. Every moment he could steal away from work and books (which did not amount to many hours) he spent with her or with the Movement. He even helped with voter registration. Together they visited black folk all over the county up and down the countryside, sneaking onto plantations under the cover of darkness. And the moonless nights could get really dark in the 'Sippi jungle land, as if God had blacked out Mississippi in His righteous wrath, which would have made Godlike sense to Othello whose faith in Him above came and went like the seasons of the year. He was a backslider most of his nineteenth year. He sometimes went to little clapboard churches out along the byways of the countryside, deep into the bush, went with Reverend Purdy and Bessie Mae and Miss Ida Lee, who would talk to the country folk about Negro history and their African heritage. One night he was really shaken, pleasantly shaken, to hear Bessie Mae herself talk to a group of Hardshell Baptists down near the southern end of the county, speak to them articulately about voter registration and their heritage in this country and in Africa—using words like "heritage" and "identity." And the people somehow got the message.

It rained all night that night. It rained inside the little clapboard church and leaked outdoors. There were umbrellas up all over the place. A sister held an umbrella over the speakers in the pulpit. If the speaker moved around she moved with him. But Bessie Mae brought the folks the world in context, and they naturally got the message. In one year she had changed so much; she had run so far ahead of where she'd been the year before. She was clean out of sight. Othello felt proud of her, deep deep inside of him; he felt proud of her, and guilty.

So many things happened so fast and furious that summer that before he knew it, Labor Day was just around the corner. The week before Labor Day was Big Meeting time, and people came from miles around that Friday morning, converging on Mount Moriah Baptist Church from all over the state. They came in cars, they came in trucks, they came on foot, they came in horse-and-wagons. They came bringing baskets of food, all kinds of food and drink, and bushels of love and human kindness. It was the most unusual Big Meeting the folk had ever witnessed. Instead of bearing witness to Jesus, Purdy made a witness to freedom. He preached in the morning, John Lewis of the Student Nonviolent Coordinating Committee preached in the afternoon, and Martin Luther King preached that night. People wept and jumped and shouted, fell on the floor and kicked like epileptics. Red-faced white men stood around and watched and listened to the happenings, heard Purdy preach freedom all the way to the Pearly Gates, preach Old Man White Supremacy straight down into the gaping jaws of hell.

That first night, after the service, Reverend Purdy invited a few folk to his home to meet the speakers and other guests in a quieter atmosphere. It was the very first time that Othello and Bessie Mae met Martin Luther King and John Lewis, and they, like many of the others, followed the two distinguished guests around, asking questions, listening avidly, and staring at the two men, bug-eyed. John Lewis looked as if he might have been a fugitive from a college campus, he looked so young. Martin Luther King looked extremely tired that night and preoccupied, or simply overwrought. It had surely been a long hot summer: Harlem, Watts, Chicago, Cleveland, 'Sippi.

[305]

About an hour after Othello and Bessie Mae arrived, a lady came breathlessly up to Reverend Purdy. "Look out the front window, Reverend Purdy! The Ku Klux Klan! The Ku Klux Klan!"

Just at that moment a deafening explosion shook the house as if a volcano had erupted and caused an earthquake. Windows shattered, people thrown across the room and to the floor. Othello thought his time had come, thought his race was run. He stared around him at first. How long after the explosion? He looked for Bessie Mae. He saw people talking near him but heard not one word spoken by them. He saw Bessie Mae on the other side of the room. He looked for Reverend Purdy and King and Lewis, and everybody seemed intact, but the whole world had become sound-less. He made his way like others were doing to the front window just in time to see hooded men jumping into cars and taking off down the road. The lawn was lighted up like Independence Day with a giant white cross burning brightly in the performance of some kind of peculiar Christian ritual.

Othello asked Reverend Purdy where the lawn hose was. His hearing was slowly coming back to him.

"Let it burn!" Reverend Purdy said. "If Caesar wants to burn Jesus on the Cross, let it be on the Romans' consciences." Then he went around the room accounting for everybody. All were safe and sound, excepting that all of them were shell-shocked in varying degrees. A couple of people had been cut by flying glass and were being taken care of. He went to his study and returned with three rifles. "Excuse me, Reverend King, but I have a hunting license—to hunt animals—that is. Wild beasts." He handed one to Othello and one to Worth Sheppard, a deacon in his church, and he headed for the front door. They followed. Out on the front porch they saw that half of the porch had been blown away by the explosion. There was a huge crater in the ground beneath the porch. Reverend Purdy said something under his breath. The telephone rang inside the house, and somebody answered it and called Reverend Purdy to the phone. He said to Sheppard and Othello, "Y'all come on in the house. Ain't nothing you can do out here, unless you want to look at the Savior on the Cross."

Othello followed him, like a man sleepwalking, followed him into his study and watched him pick up the phone. The voice

[306]

on the other end was so loud, Othello could hear every single word, distinctly almost.

"Rev'n Purdy, this here's Shaff Carlton."

"Yes, sir."

"You know me. I'm the shaff of Wakefield County."

"Yes, sir." Carlton had been sheriff for the last twenty-nine years.

"I hear you had some trouble with the Klan, Rev'n."

"Yes, sir."

"I hear they dynamited you and they got a cross burning on your lawn."

"You heard the gospel truth."

"Purdy, I'm coming out there with some of my policemen right away to take down that cross and give you some kind of protection."

Reverend Purdy said, "Well, sir, Shaff, I don't advise it. Cause the first white face I see start 'cross my lawn he'll never see the sun come up in the morning. Cause the way I feel now, I can't tell the difference in a white man with blue uniform on from one that wears a sheet. They both cut from the same damn cloth." He hung up on the sheriff of Wakefield County. He had not raised his voice one octave during the entire conversation, but he was burning up inside with anger. Othello knew. Othello could feel his pastor's anger.

Labor Day. And the Wakefields had their annual barbecue and party. All the quality folk in the county and some from as far away as Jackson and Yazoo City were in attendance. If you were anybody and white, you made the scene at the annual Wakefield barbecue. The Old Man asked Othello to work at the party as a waiter. "Make yourself a few dollars extra before you take off for the University. Come in mighty handy."

Othello answered, "Yes, sir." To himself, he said, why not? He had no honest complaints against his Great White Father, except for the fact that he was white. And he certainly couldn't lump the Old Man together with most of the 'Sippi peckerwoods. The Old Man was different. He was cosmopolitan. He was not a "nigger-hater." Sometimes Othello actually felt a warm human feeling for Charlie Wakefield, which, being black, he actively resisted. Always fiercely fought against. Yet sometimes the feeling persisted.

[307]

It was a party that really was a party. The pits were dug and the barbecuing began the day before, and they barbecued all night long and well up into the day. All kinds of barbecue: spareribs, chickens, squabs. They had shish kebab and charcoal-broiled steaks and ham. And they had chitterlings. You could smell the barbecue for miles around. And drinks flowed like the river. Dancing outside underneath electric "Japanese" lanterns hung especially for the occasion, with a live dance band of colored musicians. Dancing, eating, drinking, laughing, petting slyly, making passes. Rich white folk really had a ball, Othello thought. They were the happiest damn people in the whole unhappy world.

As the dying day gave up the ghost out on the river, night fell upon the countryside (and you could almost hear night falling); it fell sharply, definitely. The party went on and on, got gayer, rougher all the time. Dancing cheek to cheek and belly to belly, and Frugging and variations of Watusi and the Twist and some of the dances which had to be unnamable. Men took liberties with other men's wives. Some of the genteel ladies developed wandering fluttering eyes; fickled-eyed women all over the place.

One chubby lady of middle age bounced up to Othello. He gave her a martini from his tray. She was already tipsy. "Boy, I bet you can do a buck dance that's clean out the country and nearly out the state."

Othello said, "Buck dance, m'am?" You got your drink, lady. What else do you want? His neck began to sweat.

She said, "Yeah man, the stuff is here." And popped her fingers. She thought she was imitating colored talk.

Othello said, "What stuff, m'am?" He looked around him. Somebody throw out the lifeline.

She said, "You know, *buck* dance, that's what stuff. Don't you try to pull my leg." The band was playing "Mack the Knife."

He said, "Madam, I kid you not. I don't know the buck dance. I'm really not such a good dancer."

Suddenly there was a look on the chubby lady's face of profound betrayal and confusion. The light went temporarily out of her blue eyes and they turned dark and darker. She was lost, it seemed. All at once the world had become too much for her. A colored man who couldn't dance. Then she got it. Of course. He was pulling her leg. Her face lit up with smiles.

[308]

"You naughty boy," she remonstrated. She shook her finger in his face. She burped. "Come on now, stop the teasing and do a buck dance for us."

There was an uneasiness coursing through him now. His entire body had sprung leaks of perspiration. He looked around for an escape hatch of some kind or other, and then back at the lady, who seemed to have anticipated him. She grabbed his arm. "I do not know the buck dance, m'am. Besides, Mister Wakefield would not like me dancing. I'm working as a waiter."

She said, "Come on now. It goes like this." And as he stood there, she went into her version of the buck dance. She jumped up and down and sideways, as he stood there, unbelieving.

A big white man came up and dragged her away, just as she had pulled her dress up well above her knees and was about to go to town. "Whatchoo tryna do, boy? Make a fool outa my wife?"

"No, sir," Othello answered.

As the night wore on and moved toward midnight, the party got rougher and rougher and out of hand from time to time with a few small-sized engagements in the art of fisticuffs.

"Fitz, I saw you pinch Lulu's behind."

"I tried, Lord knows I tried, Jimmie boy. I paid my respects. But she ain't got enough behind to pinch. She is as flat-assed as an ironing board."

"Jimmy, you going to let him say that about your Lulu?"

Othello stood to the side now, straight as a ramrod, watching the white folks having the time of their lives. A slim nice-looking peroxide-blond lady had taken the center of the temporary stage where the colored musicians were playing, and she went into her dance. She was kicking up her heels, showing everything she had. The other social dancers stopped to watch. She went into a bump and grind, and she pulled her dress all the way up to her backside. The musicians smiled behind their dark faces, as Miss Josie showed them everything. Her thighs were not as young as her face.

A little red-haired white man came up to Othello. "What you laughing at, black boy? What's so damn funny to you?"

"Nothing at all, sir. Not a thing. There's really nothing funny."

Congressman Johnson's voice came over loud and clear, over the sound of everything, music, laughter, talking. "Josie, will you come down off that stage and stop making a damn fool of yourself?" Josie was his second wife.

Josie said, "I'm just having a little fun. Ain't harming nothing and nobody." She kicked her legs up higher, showing sallow thighs and pea-green panties.

Some drunken vulgar bastard of a Southern gentleman shouted, "Atta girl, Josie baby! Higher! Higher! Let me see your lengeree! Let me see your lengeree!"

Othello moved off just as the Congressman walked on stage and seized his wife and dragged her away, scratching at him, crying, screaming, "Leave me alone, you whoremonger! Go grab one of your black-ass whores!" He slapped her once, twice, thrice. "Whoremonger! Whoremonger!" She was a pathetic sight, weeping, screaming "Whoremonger!" Rich white folk were the unhappiest happy people in the entire universe. Othello had rephrased his thought. White folk were so grim in their determination to enjoy themselves. The last he saw of Mrs. Johnson, the Congressman was handing her over to his oldest boy. "Take her home, son, and tell Mamie to take care of her. Your mother's just a little bit under the weather."

Earlier Othello had glimpsed the same Rogers Johnson the Third trying to hem Carrie Louise in a corner and smother her with hands and kisses. But her footwork had been too clever for him.

Along about midnight, some of the party moved indoors. And Othello moved indoors with that part of the party. Some of them gathered in the Old Man's den. Othello did not remember when he'd started to think of Charles Wakefield as the "Old Man." He thought it must have happened at the beginning of the summer, when he had noticed for the first time that even Great White Fathers grew old. Everybody went when the wagon came.

The Old Man was as high as an astronaut, as were Rogers Johnson and Judge Marshall and all the other men who had gathered in the den. The county's First Citizens. Othello took over from another man behind the bar. He served drinks and listened idly to the drunken arguments.

"It's coming, Rogers, goddammit! I don't say I like it any more than you do. All I say is we responsible men must get ready for the change and get Mississippi ready. And I say that damn rag of yours does nothing but spread ignorance throughout the land."

"That's what you say," the Congressman answered weakly.

"Yes, that's what I say. Mississippi, our beloved state, is the most backward in the Union. And we *are* in the Union you know. The Civil War's been over for a hundred years."

A smile was playing around Othello's lips without his knowledge. White folk were the natural most.

"We lost the war, sir, because of the attitude of people like you. But I swear to the Good Lord up on High, we shall not lose this present war, this holy war to hold the line on segregation. I believe in giving the nigger a fair shake. Separate but equal. That's the slogan. It must forever be our slogan!"

Othello took a quick shot of Scotch. He thought, If only Ron were here to dig this crazy discourse on the Colored Problem! His mind wandered. He thought of winter in the city, of the campus white with snow. Of Ludlow Lane and sweet Naomi Hester. The sound and smell of chicken frying in her kitchen. And the love they made together. His face flushed hot with shame and guilt, the shame and guilt of his betrayal.

"Segregation in our modern society is impractical in the long run, Jeff," he heard the Old Man saying. "It's too damn expensive. Separate but equal would mean we'd have to construct a colored law school, a colored medical school. We're already the poorest state in the whole damn Union."

"Let me straighten you out on something, Jimmy Dick. You sound like you're either naïve or a Commonist. In the long run, segregation might be more expensive for the people of Mississippi, my people out there in the backwoods, God bless them, and all the other ordinary citizens of this fair state." It was always hard for the Congressman to remember when he was off stage and not speech-making. He would have made a good Baptist preacher. "But for me and you and people like us, it is one helluva lot cheaper, if we have to build a nigger university, a nigger law school, medical school, the whole damn kit and kaboodle. The profit system in Mississippi is based on segregation. The political system in Mississippi is based on segregation. If you admit a nigger is your equal, then you got to give him equal pay for equal work. You take away the poor peckerwood's white superiority, and you got to give him some other kind of compensation. By God, you desegregate the sunny Southland and inside of a decade, the niggers and the peckerwoods will take over everything. Can you imagine how powerful the damn labor unions would be in Mississippi if niggers and peckerwoods got together? How come you think all that new industry is coming down here from out the North? It ain't 'cause they like the smell of honeysuckle. Power, I'm talking 'bout. Political power! Economic power! That's what me and you and every last one of us in this room represent."

Pink-faced, red-necked Rab Johnson, the Congressman's brother, motioned to Othello. "Come over here a minute, boy. I'm gon tell a little joke that you'll appreciate."

"Who me, sir?"

"Yeah, you—I don't see no other boys in here. You'll appreciate this one; it's a jim-dandy." He began to laugh in great anticipation.

Othello came, blank-faced, and stood nearby. Deliver him from jokesters.

"Heh-heh-heh—Haw-haw-haw—This blond-headed Swedish-American brought his friend home to see his newborn baby laying up there in bed in his mother's arms. The wife's skin was as white as sweet milk. But the damn baby was brown. The man's friend says, 'But how come the baby is so black?' The blond-headed husband says, 'It oughta to be black. I had to work like a nigger to git it!'"

The den erupted with laughter; Othello felt hot flashes in his face and shoulders as he backed away.

"Donchoo git it, boy? Donchoo git it? He had to work like a nigger to make the baby." Rab Johnson laughed until the tears streamed down his cheeks.

Othello turned and walked away.

Wakefield looked behind him for Othello but Othello had left the bar to go to the toilet for a moment to get himself together. Mr. Johnson's joke had cracked him up. He saw the Old Man looking and he paused in the doorway momentarily. The Old Man didn't see him.

"Back to the other question, let's put it this way," he heard the Old Man say. "We can't run things like we used to. The world won't stand for it. Pure, white, obvious, unadulterated power is passé. It's world power we're negotiating for now. Follow me? And we have to be more subtle, because in the first place the Negroes aren't going to stand for us doing it like we used to do

[312]

it. Secondly, the world dictates another approach. Africa, Asia. Don't shake your head, Jeff. We need markets, man. We need political influence on a world scale. And the world is colored, therefore we got to at least pretend to be fair to our colored people. Let's put it this way. The President is a Southerner. He's one of us. All he's saying to us is, we got to desegregate like the North is desegregated. In other words, make the South like the North. And niggers sure haven't got any power up there, and everybody knows it. We got to do the same thing down here. Appoint one Negro here and one over there and let the others have one great vicarious experience. It's worked beautifully in the North. That's what I'm preparing my black boy for. Why do you think I'm sending him to college?"

Othello went, perspiring, off down the hall toward the toilet. He ran into Carrie Louise coming from the opposite direction with a black-haired white boy. She stopped in front of him and pinched his cheek. "I danced with colored boys in New York!" she whispered excitedly to him, as if the white boy were not present.

"You are not in New York City now!" Othello answered in a violent whisper. Sweat dropped from his eyebrows into his eyes. He was blind with anger.

"Watch yourself around a white lady, black boy!" the black-haired white boy commanded, his pale face turning red now like a ripened tomato. He drew back as if to slap Othello.

Othello caught the white boy's arm and stopped its motion. He hissed the words. "You put your hand up side my face, white boy, I promise you, I'll be the last black boy you'll ever slap! I'll wipe up this damn corridor with you!"

Carrie Louise giggled and she hiccuped. "Goody!" She clapped her hands. "They're going to fight over me! My Iago and my Othello!"

Othello pushed the boy away from him and stood there staring at them for a moment, and when she looked up into Othello's eyes and saw the violent rage in them, his face a mask of angry hatred now, for her as well as for Iago, the smile left her face and she shuddered, as if a chill had seized her. She remembered Sherry Kingsley, and she shuddered. Othello turned and walked off down the corridor. He heard her saying as he left them, "I really don't think the feller likes us."

The white boy laughed uneasily. "I swear to God, Carrie

Louise, you have the wildest impulses. You can do the darndest things."

He stood in the servants' bathroom, trembling with rage, washing his hands and staring at himself in the mirror. He put handful after handful of cold water on his face. He was steaming with his anger. He hated every white sonofabitch who ever lived. He hated every one of them. Every lowdown man, woman, and child of them. He wished now that the cooks and maids had carried out their "mercy mission." The one thing he would not stand for is to be used by anybody as a plaything. "Don't fuck with me!" he said aloud to no one in particular, to all white folk in general. "Don't fuck with me! Don't fuck with me!"

Now he went back up the corridor almost placated by the single consolation that the time was not as long as it had been. He would be leaving for the University in a couple of weeks. He heard Congressman Johnson sounding off when he was still a distance from the den. "Underneath the whole civil rights struggle is the nigger's burning desire to marry the white man's daughter. It's just as plain as the nose on your face."

Another voice (sounded like Judge Marshall's) said, "If that's what it's all about, they sure could find a plenty of white men's daughters every Sunday at the Colored Presbyterian Church on Walnut Street. There're more Massa's chillun and grandchillun in that church than you can shake a stick at. I ain't never seen so many high-yaller nigrahs."

The den exploded with laughter again. Rab Johnson, the Congressman's brother, said, "I'm gon tell the honest truth. I like dark meat. Man, sir! A black woman is made for love. And she's so affectionate. She'll wash your drawers and drink the water."

Once more the old boys cracked up with laughter. Othello felt his body growing hot all over again. He could not go into the room now, while they enjoyed their little white man's joke. He understood at this moment more than he ever had before in all his life, the total degradation of the Southern white man, the absolutely total fakery and sickness of the myth of miscegenation. He even heard the Congressman roaring with laughter. And, yes, his Great White Father, Charles James Richard Wakefield. Their laughter was his anger as he stood there outside the door just out of their eyesight. Stood there smoldering with rage. And almost jumped out of his trousers when Carrie Louise came up behind him and pinched him on the cheek again, as she went past him into the den of laughing white men.

The Congressman laughed as if he were strangled or had asthma. "Lord have mercy, come here to your Uncle Jeffy, darling." Then he laughed some more, and then he said to Wakefield seriously, "You can sit there as smug as you please, but chickens have a way sometimes of coming home to roost. That black boy you got hanging round here all the time and sending him to college and all like that. How would you like for him to marry this precious pretty thing of yours?"

Wakefield said, almost complacently but you could hear the indignation underneath, "Water seeks its own level, Jeff. That boy knows his place. I mean he knows his superiors. He knows his betters. Don't you worry. I mean the thought wouldn't even enter his head. He knows his place because I taught it to him. And if he didn't, my Princess certainly knows her inferiors, which includes every black boy in the first place and just about every other male child in this county, in the second place. And that includes those two sons of yours. I mean those lecherous wolves that you helped bring into this world."

Othello walked back down the corridor with the sound of the good-natured white-gentlemen laughter from the den ringing in his ears and an angry heat consuming his body, as he swore vengeance on his Great White Father. He did not come back to the den that night. He kept walking out of the side entrance past the white folks still out in the now darkened yard, some of them lying together in the bushes, some of them giggling, some sighing. He walked through the moonlit 'Sippi darkness and all the way to home. And he swore vengeance on his Great White Father.

Chapter
5

His second year at the University went faster than the first, the one big difference being that he did not lag behind but always kept apace and sometimes ran way out in front. Something seemed to be forever in pursuit of him, kicking him in the backside, spurring him on and on and on. And he would never forget that summer back in the county. Bessie Mae and Uncle Bish and the "mercy mission" and Luke Gibson and Reverend Purdy, the KKK, and all the rest of it. And last of all, and maybe first of all, the Wakefield barbecue. He had grown up that night, he thought. He had lost his cherry. He had no more illusions—he thought.

There was this picture that kept unreeling itself before him on the screen of his memory. Of the Wakefield barbecue. Of the Great White Fathers in the Wakefield den that orgiastic night. The fog of cigarette smoke—the whiskeyed conversation—the stench of alcoholic breaths—the drunken laughter—the white philosophizing on the ways of black folks—and Mister Charlie Jimmy Dick, himself, the very last of the Great White Fathers, philosophizing about him, his black namesake, Charles Othello Chaney. "That's what I'm preparing my black boy for. Why do you think I'm sending him to college? That boy knows his place, because I taught it to him. He knows his betters. Don't you worry."

Othello made a promise that night. He took an oath, that some-day, sometime, somewhere, somehow, vengeance would belong to him, and he would wreak his vengeance with a hearty appetite. Shame on his victim—shame on his victim. He would bide his time. He would be cunning. He would be clever. And he would show no pity. He promised he would show no pity.

Sometimes he thought the second school year would never end, as swift as the pace was. Sometimes he thought he would quit school and head for home, but not for reasons of nostalgia and homesickness, as had been the case the first months of his fresh-man year. This time he wanted to go back home and fight. He was spoiling for a free-for-all. Sometimes he walked around feel-ing so evil he could taste it. Especially just after he had read some account in the newspaper about some white injustice, and had read some sanctimonious talk about the "free world" which of course, included Mississippi and South Africa. Accounts of Vietnam gave him the taste of gall in his mouth and a sickness in his belly. Black men dying thousands of miles from home in the name of freedom, which was denied them in their homeland of the brave and free. Along with his anger grew his facility to articulate. He learned gradually to talk that talk. Living around Ronnie Gilbert, his dialogue became a curious mixture of Mississippi Negro idiom and the jargon of a New York Negro hipster. Sometimes he sounded more New York than his Northern roommate. But when he went home that next summer he made himself understood, as he went all over the county preaching the gospel of registration.

He went to Jackson to attend a workshop on rural registration. He met young folk from all over the country up in Jackson. White and black, men and women. Some white folk with Southern accents even. Serious young folk with a missionary zeal. With a firm commitment to liberate the country. It was a kind of spirit he had never known before. And they seemed to love each other, the people in the Movement. It was an experience he would never forget. In the evening after a long day's work of endless orientation, they would gather and sing songs of the Movement and Negro spirituals and folk songs and songs of other righteous movements. It was strange to see the few white Southerners in this kind of atmosphere, acting as if for the very first time in their lives they had been completely emancipated. Not that there weren't uncomfortable moments, many of them. Not that arguments did not flare up from time to time, between the black and white. Not that some of the black young folk did not exhibit their black revolutionism, nationalism, and not that some of the white ones did not show themselves to be missionaries instead of revolutionaries. White girls sometimes went out of their way to show that they were with the black men all the way. One New York black boy told a Southern white girl to go back where she really came from. "Honeychile, you are the last of the great white missionaries!" The poor child cried the whole night through.

By the time Othello left the Jackson workshop, he believed that black and white could live and work together and maybe even love—together.

That summer Othello went to every nook and corner of the county, teaching black folk how to sign their names and how to register and vote. He saw poverty in its utter nakedness, ignorance in its purity, despair at its greatest depths. But in some eyes he saw the beams of hope and fierce determination. He saw people dying of starvation. He knocked on one door in the eastern corner of the county, about six miles into the bush, way off the beaten path, just outside of Budapest, Mississippi, and when no one answered, he pushed the door open and found the entire family lying together on a single bed. The coroner's verdict was

Death Due to Starvation. He saw people in the county so poor they couldn't afford to owe the Man for a television, which is to say they were living with privation. He saw a father so weak and emaciated, he did not have the strength to lift a pencil, so that Othello could teach him how to sign his name, or even make an X. Little Jake said, "Man, some of the people in this county so poor, their shadows done disappeared from them. I reckin they can't afford em."

Othello went to see Uncle Bish, and Uncle Bish told him about the incident in the woods with Millgate and his buddies. "For six whole months after that I was one step ahead of starvation. My old lady won't working neither, and she got evil like some yaller women get sometimes and she threaten to put me out in the cold. We was poor as Job's turkey. I mean, naked as jaybird in whistling time. And Mister Congressman Johnson saw me on the streets one day and told me, 'Uncle Bish, I heard 'bout your misfortune, and it sure was a damn shame, but I reckin that oughta to teach you to stay away from that silver rights mess.' I told him I ain't been near them silver rights. He say, 'Well, I tell you what I'm gon do. You keep your nose clean and be a good nigger and keep your eyes open and I'm gon give you a job down at the *Chronicle*. And I been working for him ever since. All the niggers round here talks against him, but he came to me at a time of need and he held a helping hand out to me."

Uncle Bish's eyes were redder than they'd ever been. "Even my own son turned against me. Little Jake called me a Uncle Tom." Tears came to Uncle Bish's eyes. "He love me though. I know he do, deep down inside. When the thing happened in the woods, he tried his best to get me to tell him who done it, but I wouldn't tell him, cause I didn't want him to get into no trouble with the white folks. He told me he would killed him some peckerwoods just as sure as gun was iron."

"He's a good man, Uncle Bish," Othello said quietly.

"I know he a good boy, and you is too, but both of y'all better be careful messing around with them there silver rights. Niggers ain't gon do right nohow."

The third year at the University went even more swiftly than the second. Before he knew it, the streets had been decorated and the shop windows in downtown Johnsonville read: FIFTEEN MORE SHOPPING DAYS TO CHRISTMAS. This year, he did not go home for the Christmas season. He went to New York with Ronnie, where they both got jobs working as extras out of a Brooklyn post office. They got special permission and went five days before school closed officially for the holidays.

All the way to New York on the bus, Ronnie kept telling Othello, "Baby, I got a little chick I want you to meet. She's going to naturally turn you on for real. She will shake you to your chitterlings, baby, I mean deep down in your small intestines! I mean, this is a stone fox, and she is elegant, she is intelligent and militant. She's fine as wine. I mean sparkling burgundy! She will shake you to your chitterlings!"

"Is she colored?"

"She is Afro, baby. I mean Afro all the way. From the crop of her hair to the tip of her tippy toes. Like Ossie Davis says: 'Ten thousand queens of Sheba!'"

Othello said, "Lead me to the slaughter."

Ronnie said, "Course you might not be her speed. You're a country boy, Little Abner, and she's city to the marrow. I mean this little lady has lived all her life in the city, I mean, *the* city. The one and only city. And then too, last summer she went to Ghana and Nigeria—Crossroads, Africa or some kind of shit like that. She's been to London and Paris. And she can come on strong on any question, anytime, anyplace."

"I would certainly like to meet the lady," Othello said, assuming as nonchalant a pose as possible.

"Then again, she might be too sophisticated for you."

"That would remain to be seen, wouldn't it?"

"Then again, old baby, you aren't as naïve as you pretend to be. I forget, sometimes, that fine cousin of yours you used to go to see every Friday night and sometimes didn't get back to the dorm till Saturday morning. You don't think you were bull-jiving me with that cousin bit, do you?" Like Old Man River, Ron went on and on and on. "That's right. She just might go for an uncool cat like you. Soft-spoken but fairly articulate, yeah. Getting more articulate by the day. Like the cat unloosened your tongue or something. Getting militant too, yeah, I noticed that. You got to be militant to make the scene with Sherry."

Chuck stared out of the window, as the bus kept heading northward every second. He was really going up-the-country. The farm country up this way was different somehow. The land looked as if it had been manicured, or painted lavishly by an artist with

[319]

great feeling for symmetry. Mile upon mile of farmland through Tennessee, through Kentucky, through Ohio. First dark dark green, then brown, then a yellow-golden landscape. Then a raging red as if the woods were burning. Farmland and farmhouses. But here, there was not the classic portrait of the 'Sippi plantation with the Big House and the cabins; big, gleaming-white farmhouses here, and further north the entire world was white with newly fallen snow. And the cities! Good Lord the cities! It seemed the further north they went the more magnificent the cities. Buildings reaching up into the clouds. Hundreds of them. Cincinnati, Pittsburgh, Philadelphia. Newark to the left of them. And then the city!

He was convinced New York was not America. It was a country in and of itself. And what a country! And he had thought Johnsonville was fast. But New York made Johnsonville seem like the age of horse-and-buggy. One evening they were walking in Manhattan near Rockefeller Center. Othello told his buddy, "Look, man. I don't care what people think. I am going to look my head off. Let them think I'm from the country, cause that's exactly where I'm from. I'm going to gawk up at these buildings till my neck gets sore."

Ronnie said, "Be my guest, old baby."

It snowed off and on the first three days he was in the city. And he had to trudge through the ice and snow with a mailbag on his back, brimming full with Christmas goodies. His poor feet felt put upon. It was not that a country boy like him was not used to walking. But pulling your feet in and out of that deep snow was something else. That first Saturday night, Ronnie took his buddy-from-the-country to a party in the city. They went to President Street in Brooklyn. To the elegant home of Senator Kingsley.

"This is the real dyed-in-the-mink-and-cashmere Big Black Bourgeoisie. These are Franklin Frazier's people," Ronnie told Othello, as they went down the walk toward the brilliantly lighted mansion.

As they reached the porch, Othello slowed down and stared in awe up at the three-storied mansion reaching majestically up into the sky. The moonlight threw soft shadows on the new snow which covered the lawn, and icicles glistened from the hanging ivy which clung to each side of the house. He looked up and

[320]

down the street. All the houses spelled affluence. Ronnie read his mind.

"That's all right, man. This *is* a colored place. You don't have to go around the back." He leaned a thumb upon the bell.

Othello laughed. "You go to hell."

Almost everybody at the party knew Ronnie. And they were the most elegant-looking colored people Othello had ever imagined. He couldn't help gawking at chandeliers and vases and lamps and carpeting, and all of it just like a story out of *Ebony* magazine. There were large paintings on the walls by Charles White and Ernest Crichlow and Jacob Lawrence and Leo Carty, by Elton Fax and Thomas Feelings. Ronnie knew them all just by glancing at the paintings. He rattled the names off. Othello told him he was "artist-dropping." And colored people acting like they were used to everything. Acting like white folk, he caught himself thinking. He felt out of place, all thumbs, ill-outfitted, ten big toes on two left feet. Ronnie had him dead to rights. He *was* a country boy. No doubt about it. And he had never heard so many proper-talking colored folk in all his days.

When he tried to recapture the whole experience later, it was like a dream-montage of movie sequences—of beautiful people; bartenders, waiters moving in and out through the gathering of people, anticipating every wish; food, drink, music; brilliant conversation.

Sometime shortly after midnight, he realized that Julian Bond and Stokely Carmichael of SNCC were there. Ronnie introduced him to them. "Backwoods of Mississippi," Ronnie boasted of his buddy and roommate, as if he were announcing that Othello was the heavyweight champion of the world. Othello wanted to go right through the floor.

But Bond and Carmichael looked at him with a new light in their eyes. "I'd like to talk with you before the party is over," Carmichael told him.

His montage-remembrance of the party included Senator Kingsley's brief introduction of Bond and Carmichael to the seemingly well-heeled group, the dyed-in-the-mink-and-cashmere colored bourgeoisie. The young men spoke briefly of SNCC's work in the South and especially in Mississippi, the voter registration drive and Fannie Hamer and the Mississippi Freedom Democratic Party. They were applauded roundly after their remarks.

"What beautiful, courageous young men," one lady hiccuped.

But the Senator said, pleasantly and firmly, "Well, of course, this is a pre-Christmas party and not a fund-raiser, but I think we ought to be able to give these young men a little practical encouragement in addition to polite applause. SNCC salaries are down beneath the bare subsistence, but money is needed to carry out this very necessary work. I mean, if we meant the applause we just gave the young men, let us put our money where our hands were."

Out of a crowd of about a hundred people, Kingsley collected one hundred and eighty-five dollars, one hundred of which he gave himself, a hundred-dollar bill to start it off. Julian Bond thanked the group kindly and politely, but Ronnie, who had by that time had too much to drink, chose that moment to tear his ass.

He walked out of the gathering and stood beside Bond and Carmichael and said, "Excuse me, Mister Bond, but what is there to thank these people for?" He turned to the gathering. Othello heard murmurs of shock and embarrassment. His own face grew warm. "Eighty-five dollars!" Ronnie's voice dripped with sarcasm. "And all you split-leveled Negroes were up in arms when E. Franklin Frazier told you where it was. Each one of you spend more than eighty-five dollars every weekend on your cocktail parties. It's like Ossie Davis said in his play, 'You're a disgrace to the Negro profession.'" Ronnie swayed from side to side. "These men and their colleagues, John Lewis, Mrs. Fan—Hamer and all, James Foremen, risk their lives in the backwoods of 'Sippi, and you sit up here in New York City on your big fat rusty-dusties and pat your feet and clap your hands and get up off of eighty-five dollars. I mean, haven't you got any self-respect? What goes on in those little brainwashed minds of yours?" Somebody pulled at his coattail.

"Ronnie!"

"I mean, look how the Jews raise money for the Jewish cause, for-for-for Zionism, for-for-for Israel. Some of you would give more if the Jewish Appeal knocked at your door. We are a messed-up people. An-an-an-and you split-leveled, dyed-in-the-mink, wall-to-wall black bourgeoisie are fucked up more than anybody else." Somebody tried to pull him away. "Turn my coattail loose." And then: "Senator Kingsley, let's take up another collection from this bunch of phonies. They can do better'n—they-they-they can do better'n better'n that."

The Senator stepped forward and cleared his throat. "Well, they do say, out of the mouths of babes and children—Ron Gilbert is no baby, he's no child either, he's a serious-minded young man, and although his remarks to you were a bit on the crude side, he spoke the truth—I mean, he told it like it was."

On the second go-around they raised two hundred and fifty-three dollars—checks, cash, pledges. Othello felt mighty proud of his audacious buddy.

In Othello's remembrance there was the time he spent downstairs in the basement where the action was—the dancing—the younger generation—his kind of people. The cool ones and the hot. Age-wise and like-wise. Dancing, talking, jiving, drinking. And he met Sherry Kingsley. Ron had not exaggerated. He felt like shouting the words he'd heard his roommate shout so many times, the words from *Purlie Victorious*: "Ten thousand queens of Sheba!" She wasn't tall, but nonetheless, she had a queenly aura about her. Her hair was dark brown, almost black, as were her wide and staring eyes. Her hair was close-cropped Afro and just the right kind of hairdo for her small face. Soft and round and brown her face was. And outrageously intelligent. She was not overly large at the bosom but she poked out and was fully rounded. She was Sherry "Lady" Kingsley and her legs seemed longer than the rest of her body, slim and rounded. Her mouth was full, her lips large shapely lips that seemed to always smile and pout, simultaneously. With all the look of majesty about her she could not be more than five-feet-three.

"This is the lady I was telling you about," Ron told him. "She is a true fox. I mean, she is really into something."

"Pay no attention to his raving," she said, as she stared up into Othello's face, as Othello stood there feeling the country bumpkin bit as never before. He felt he was standing there before her with his bare face hanging out, with his long arms dangling from his shoulders, with the sleeves of his jacket halfway up his arms. He was truly shaken to his chitterlings!

Her entire face smiled and eased the moment for him. "Welcome," she said, and held her hand toward him. And he took it and tried to say, "Thank you, m'am. Delighted to meet you." But somehow the words got stuck deep in his throat. And his own voice sounded strange to him, like an adolescent at the change. He felt miserable, and at the same time, he felt joyous. At that moment, she could have put a noose around his neck, as he did

to Missy Anne, the cow back home, and could have led him anywhere and left him anywhere, and he would have stayed put until
she came back for him, which was more than he could say for his
damn stupid cow. He put that crooked nervous smile on his face,
which, unknown to him, made him charming to the ladies. Her
eyes said she was interested. He told himself her eyes said she was
interested, particularly interested in him, and he hoped he wasn't
lying to himself.

Then his bosom buddy lowered the boom on him as he always
had a way of doing. Ron said boastfully, "My man is from the
backwoods of dear old Mississippi. I mean, the natural bush.
Alligators and rattlesnakes and all that treacherous jazz, and
crocodiles and peckerwoods." Othello wanted to hit his buddy in
his big mouth.

She looked at Ron and then back to Othello. "Really?"

He mumbled, "I was born in Mississippi," seeming to imply
he had not lived there all his life.

Her face glowed anew with interest now and she took his hand
again, and her smile made his stupid rustic heart beat faster. She
was just too rich for his blood. Too damn sophisticated. She said,
"Well, well, well—" as she led him across the room toward a
circle of boys and girls together, laughing and talking. When
they reached the group, she tapped one of the girls on the shoulder. "Honeychile, I have a landsman for you to meet, and he is
one great big beautiful hunk of landsman."

The straw-haired girl turned toward them, and the two Mississippians stood staring at each other, black boy and pink-faced
white girl, oblivious of everybody else. Both of them were speechless at first, then they both tried to speak at the same time.

She turned to Sherry. "It's him!" she said softly. "It's the boy
I told you about from back home!"

Sherry said, "What boy? Oh, no—not Tommy-boy—not Gunga
Din!"

Carrie Lou said, "Tommy-boy? Gunga Din? It's Charles
Othello Chaney." She turned to him again. "What on earth are
you doing in New York City? You haven't dropped out of college,
have you?"

Sherry said, "Down, honeychile. You are not addressing one of
your nigrahs down on the old plantation." Her wide mouth wore
an amused expression. Her eyes were smiling.

Othello got himself together quickly. And he remembered the

[324]

barbecue and her father in the den with the rest of the Great White Fathers. Her father the great expert on Negro psychology. "That boy knows his place. He knows his betters. The thought would never enter his head. . . ." Othello could hear the laughter of the drunken Southern gentlemen. He stared sarcastically at the white girl. "Why Miss Carrie Louise, what would your old pappy say if he saw you way up here in New York City socializing with your inferiors. I can just see him now a-sitting in his den with all of his old cronies, avowed peckerwoods every single one of them. 'I know the nigrah. Treat them halfway like human beings and you won't have any trouble out of them. Take my nigrahs for example.' "

Carrie Lou was a frightened little girl again, her eyes full of anguish and confusion. Just one moment before, her eyes had glowed, her heart had danced a jig at the joy of seeing Othello all the way up here in New York City. And she didn't understand him attacking her like this.

He thought, You don't understand me, hunh? How about that? And you thought you were an expert on the Southern Negro. You and your pappy. How about that? The last of the Great White Fathers. Your pappy. She looked the way he remembered her that day many years ago when they chased her crying from the cotton fields, the hurt deep in her eyes. The time she had run toward him in the cotton field and he and his buddies had turned upon her.

> *Your pappy is a pecker,*
> *Your mammy from the woods.*
> *They both got together*
> *And made a peckerwood.*
> *And you the peckerwood*
> *Yeah, you the peckerwood.*

But he felt no compassion for her this time, he told himself, as he had felt before, when he was a stupid little black boy down in the backwoods of old 'Sippi. He had gone through many changes. The soft thing in him had hardened.

She looked around her. All were listening, watching. And back into his face she looked, as if she were searching desperately for a sign from him that it was all a joke. And she didn't run this time. There was no Big House for her to run to.

She said, "I don't understand, Othello."

He said, "I'm hip. You never understood."

Sherry laughed, "Why don't you two lovebirds just kiss and make up?"

Othello heard Jimmy Dick's voice again. "That boy knows his place. And if he didn't, my Princess certainly knows her inferiors." Suddenly Othello changed his tactics. "Yeah—" he heard himself say. "Yeah—why not kiss and make up? How about that?" And he took the stunned girl in his arms and kissed her fully on the mouth, and then stepped away from her.

She stood there transfixed. Her face turned ten different shades of pinkish red and a tremor went across her shoulders. The taste of his kiss still pressed angrily against her mouth, as if he still were kissing her.

Sherry said, "Everything's cool, Desdemona. You can wash Othello's kiss off. It won't poison your bloodstream."

Then Sherry turned to the boy from 'Sippi. "Let's dance." And she was in his arms. As they danced he stared down into her face, and tried to think of something to say to this beautiful Afro-American woman who was a true fox for sure and shook him deep down in his chitterlings.

"You really do come on strong, Mister Chaney," she said mockingly, "for one so recently from the Mississippi bush."

He smiled his nervous crooked smile. "Thank you kindly, m'am."

They danced together for four or five numbers, ten or fifteen minutes. She was a talker and a listener, and she knew the art of drawing the other person out. She had him talking like a chatterbox. They talked of their families and Mississippi and New York and books and her trip to Africa with Crossroads, and the Negro middle class and Europe. And all the time she stared up into his face with her wide, deep, dark-brown eyes. She had a total impact on him, emotionally, intellectually, physically.

"Are you coming to New York after you finish college?"

"I don't think so."

She said, "How're they gonna keep them down on the farm after they've seen Pa-ree?"

He said, "The way I feel now, I'm going back home—and join up."

Her face clouded. "Join up? You mean, enough of our boys aren't dying over there already?"

"Over where?" he said. "I mean, down there. Down in 'Sippi.

[326]

That's where the revolution is going to be, if it ever happens. Right down there in the backwoods of old 'Sippi. David Woodson says——"

She said, "You read Dave Woodson? Would you like to meet him?"

Othello said, "I already met him. He was to my house for dinner right down there in Mississippi. He was born and bred not far from where I live." He heard the pride and boasting in his voice.

She said, "Really?" He could not tell whether or not she was impressed. Then she said, "The revolution is going to really erupt in *two* places. In the backwoods of 'Sippi and the black Northern ghettos like Harlem and Watts and in Chicago. Dave said that also."

As intellectual as she was, he was never for one moment entirely oblivious to the physical her, in his arms, especially when she leaned against him briefly, accidentally, as they danced. He knew a throbbing in his loins that came not from weariness. This chick isn't studying about me in that kind of way, he told himself. She's being polite and kind, and she's interested in me as a thing from Mississippi. She's amusing herself. Intellectual curiosity. "In that case," he said, shakily, "you and I both will be in the midst of the volcano when it erupts. You in New York City, and me in Mississippi."

"Me? Negative," she said. "The volcano smolders in Harlem and Bedford Stuyvesant. I live on the perimeter. Black bourgeoisie. Prep school, Wexler College, President Street. I'm a white colored lady." She laughed at the serious look on his face.

His hand pressed the middle of her back and pushed her closer up against him. "You are not!" he argued heatedly. "And you know you're not."

"Oh," she said, "don't let this glib tongue and Afro haircut fool you. Men and women are what they eat, and there hasn't been any soul food in the Kingsley house since dear old Daddykins passed the bar, and that was quite some time ago. I don't know what chitterlings and hog maw and fatback taste like, and I'm not dying to find out. I'm strictly a beef-eater. Steaks, stroganoff, shish kebab—martinis—"

He was silent for a moment, and held her up against him even more tightly than before, almost as if he thought she was trying to get away from him with words and class distinctions. And he wouldn't let her go. She would not get off so easily.

It was Joe Williams, singing the blues, as only Joe could sing them. "Every day, every day"—and when the number ended she smiled up into Othello's face which was a mask of seriousness now. And she moved slightly away from him. "Well, I'm sure I'm being a terrible hostess, depriving the other girls of your charming company. Your landswoman, Carrie Lou, must be champing at the bit."

When he danced with Carrie Lou, they had very little to say to each other, except that at the end of it, she looked up into his face and looked away again, and said, "Give me your phone number here in New York."

And he gave the girl his number.

Chapter

6

It was Brooklyn, U.S.A.—famous Bedford Stuyvesant, of the "police riots." And brownstones and churches and black folk. Black and brown and light-brown folk. Ronnie's mother and father did everything to make Othello feel at home in the Gilbert home on Dean Street near Nostrand Avenue. Ronnie's father was a post office supervisor in the main Brooklyn post office in downtown Borough Hall. His mother was a teacher in the public school system. The house was an old three-story-and-basement brownstone. It was not nearly as well appointed as the Kingsley mansion in Crown Heights, but it exuded comfort.

It was Sunday, the day after the Kingsley party. The Senior Gilberts had gone off to Siloam Presbyterian Church. Othello and Ronnie shared a large bedroom with twin beds on the second floor. Earlier, Othello had been awakened by the screams of alley cats having an orgy in the Gilbert backyard. He got shakily out of bed. He stared over at the other bed where Ronnie lay sprawled on his back, his mouth wide open, and his arms stretched out like the Savior on the Cross at Calvary. Ron was snoring so loud he couldn't possibly have heard the jamboree of cats outside. Othello smiled, shook his head, and put on his bathrobe; he made his way up the hall to the bathroom, took a leak, and took care of his ablutions, whatever ablutions were, he thought. Ablutions? He had read the damn word somewhere in a book. He was always building his vocabulary. He made his way quietly down the stairs to the basement where the kitchen was. Big and newly painted lemon-yellow and glisteningly clean. There was a note to him and Ronnie: there was pancake mix already made and in the refrigerator and eggs and bacon. Hunger stabbed Othello. His belly growled. He drank a glass of orange juice which did little or nothing for him.

"Let him sleep," he said aloud to himself. "I'm going to make me some of these pancakes." That's when the phone rang. There was an extension in the kitchen, and he picked up the receiver after the sixth or seventh ring.

"Gilbert residence."

"Hello, Ronnie?" One of Ronnie's lady friends. A sort of familiar female voice.

"I'm sorry, Ronnie's still sleeping. Can I take a message?"

"Is that you, Chuck Othello?"

"Chuck Othello?" he said, as if he had never heard the name before. Who in the hell in New York would be calling him Chuck Othello?

"This is Carrie Louise," the girl said.

"Yes m'am, Miss Carrie Louise."

"Will you stop that silly Yes-m'am business!"

"All right, Miss Carrie Louise."

She said, "Othello!" He imagined that she stamped her foot.

He said, "Yessum."

She said, "I declare you are the meanest boy I ever did meet in all my born days."

Othello said, "Whatever you say."

"Are you busy this evening?"

"No'm."

"Can you come to dinner?"

"When?"

"This evening."

"It's a distinct possibility," he said.

"I'll expect you then at seven." And gave him an address on MacDougal Street.

All day long he wondered if he would go. Why the hell should he? On the other hand, why in the hell shouldn't he? Go. No-go. Go. No-go. A-go-go. No-go-go. In the first place, why had she invited him? Had he made her feel shitty or guilty or something at the party last night? Maybe she wanted to talk him out of the kiss he had slapped upon her mouth. Maybe she hates me for it. He laughed. Maybe she'll put poison in my chow. He laughed sarcastically. Maybe she'll have some white hoods there to beat me up.

That evening he went to MacDougal Street because he was curious about this rich white girl from 'Sippi. He went, because he had a score to settle with her and her father, his Great White Father. He had promises to keep. He told himself this was the actual reason for his going. Vengeance is damn sure going to be mine if I can make it happen. She was right. He was the meanest boy she ever met. He meant to prove it.

He caught the "A" train at Nostrand Avenue and Fulton and came up out of the ground at the West Fourth stop. As cold and as windy a day as it was, the sidewalks in the Village were jammed with people, all kinds, all sizes and denominations. He sensed that half of them were from out of town, just walking around and going nowhere in particular.

He pushed the 3-B button downstairs and walked up two flights of stairs to the third floor, where she stood in the doorway waiting for him. Smiling for him. He tried to make himself smile in return, but it did not come off. She took his hand as he walked into the apartment, and she closed the door behind them. He looked around him. The living room was large and wide and high-ceilinged. It was creatively furnished with little or no regard for expense; paintings and sculpture all over the place.

"This is your place?"

"No, silly. I live uptown with Sherry Kingsley in the dormitory. This is my aunt's place."

"Oh, I see."

"And she went away to Europe for the Christmas holidays."

Well—well—well—

"Let me put some records on, while I finish with the dinner." She went toward the record player. "How about some Beethoven?"

"Anything you say."

He sat down on a sofa and almost sank clean out of sight. He

[330]

closed his eyes and let the sounds permeate his senses. Not that he really dug Beethoven. But he wasn't too bad. The cat was into something, although for the life of him, Othello couldn't tell what the cat was into. Even so, the music got to him. A teensy bit. He thought of Wakefield County, Mississippi, where both he and Carrie Louise had been born and had lived out most of their lives, and lived according to the rules of the game, which you questioned only at your peril. He thought of their parents, his and hers, and what would they think, if they knew, if they even halfway suspected. The daughter of the Great White Padre himself, making dinner for little old humble Gunga. Suddenly, he knew a great uneasiness. He got up and went to the window and pulled back the drapes and looked out on the busy street, as if he thought there might be spies outside keeping the house under surveillance. Miss Anne herself, in person, spreading the table before little black Gunga. Uncle Tom's great-grandchild. What if she had set a trap for him and lured him into it?

After dinner, after Beethoven, they sat listening to jazz records. Then they danced and after the music stopped, he deliberately continued to hold her in his arms.

She said, "Weren't you surprised to bump into me last night?"

He said, "Yeah."

"Me, of all people!" she said excitedly.

He said, "You made your point. You of all people at a colored party."

"What did you think of Sherry Kingsley?"

He said, "She is the absolutely positively most! She is the end and the beginning. She is alpha and omega."

She said, "Isn't she."

He still held her in his arms. He said, "I just said she was."

"I'm glad you liked her."

"There is no girl like her anywhere. She is *too* much. Moocho much. No girl I ever met could hold a candle to her. I would be her happy and contented slave. And I damn sure don't like slavery."

The girl said, "She's my roommate. She's my best friend in all of New York City."

The boy said, "You're a lucky so-and-so."

The girl's face blushed a pinkish red. "I guess I am at that."

The boy said, "Take my word for it." He still held her in his arms, a fact that they were both very conscious of.

[331]

She said, her voice getting more breathless by the moment, "I guess you're wondering why I invited you over." Perspiration just above her lips.

He said, "Negative. What's to wonder? I imagined it was because you wanted me to come to dinner."

She said, "You don't talk like yourself at all, like you used to talk. You don't sound like Mississippi."

He said, "Was I right?"

"Yes, of course," she said. The music had started up again.

All the time they danced, he only spoke in answer to a question from her. He stared silently down into her face. The next time the music stopped, he kept her in his arms, and took her face in his hand and kissed her lips. He deliberately and slowly kissed her.

She pulled away from him. "How dare you!" Righteous indignation. He thought, Lily-white-as-the-driven-snow righteous indignation.

He stared at her, blank-faced. "That's a damn good question. How dare I?" He looked around him and went to the closet and got his overcoat. "I expect that was a bit impertinent of me, wasn't it?"

She said, "What are you doing with your overcoat?"

He said, "When the native boy gets out of his place, it's time to show him the door. Check?" He smiled. "As you pointed out: How dare I?"

She said, "I didn't mean it that way. I wish you wouldn't go off in a huff like this. You're so damn sensitive. Let me fix you one for the road at least."

He said, "No more how-dare-me's?" He wasn't smiling.

She agreed. "No more how-dare-you's."

He put his overcoat across a chair.

She made Scotch and soda for both of them, and they sat there sipping their drinks and staring at each other like boxers sparring for an opening. She said, "What I meant was, you sort of took me by surprise."

He put his drink aside and got up and pulled her to her feet and began to dance with her again. Then he put both arms around her and drew her up against him. "Please be advised. I am going to kiss you, and I would not want to take you by surprise again." And his lips found her lips, as he pulled her heavily against him. She stood impassive in his arms with her own arms

[332]

hanging limply at her sides. And his mouth pressed so hard against hers, it hurt both of their mouths, but she gave nothing in return. He might have been kissing a corpse. She was frigid.

When he released her, she went and sat down and took a swallow of Scotch and soda. She put her head in her hands. Then she looked up at him still standing blank-faced in the middle of the room. Her eyes were full of seriousness. "This is not why I invited you for dinner. Not for this."

He sat down and began to sip his drink.

"I know what it looks like. Me inviting you to dinner in my aunt's apartment with her away for the Christmas holidays, but I didn't mean it that way at all. I was just glad to see you last night. I just thought, here we are, in New York City, from the same home town, grew up together, but separately. And here was a chance for us to know each other better. I never gave a thought to sex."

Othello said, "Sure you didn't." He yawned.

"I thought we'd get together and talk about old times. You understand, don't you, Othello?"

He changed his tactics. "Let's have one more for the road and for old time's sake." And he came toward her and could feel her tensing up, balling up into a knot. He took her glass and went to the bar and poured the drinks and came back and gave hers to her. Then he banged his glass against hers. "To friendship, for old times' sake, and all that jazz."

She said, "To friendship, for old times' sake."

He said, "Do you have Billie Holliday's 'One for the Road'?"

She said, "My aunt has just about every record Billie Holliday ever made."

She went and looked through the pile of records and found "One for the Road." She put it on the record player and came back and sat down and began to sip her drink, and listen to Lady Day. They listened in silence for a moment. Then he got up and came toward her and held out his hand and mumbled, "One more for the road."

She looked up into his face. He said, "Just one more—like for the road?"

And she got up into his arms and leaned heavily against him as they danced, their faces together, and his chest against her breathing bosom, belly to belly, thigh against thigh. He said, "Do you

[333]

remember how we used to rip and run and tear all over the Big House, up and down the stairs, front and back?"

She laughed seriously, and said, "Do I remember? How I do remember! We were terrors."

His sex was throbbing nervously against her thigh now, a fact neither of them was unmindful of. He began to laugh at the remembrances of their childhood, lost forever, but his laughter was much more nervous than it was genuine and hearty. Her eyes were gone somewhere, lost in reverie of the gone-by days. Her reverie contained no ugliness.

He said, "You remember the time up in the guest room when we played Mama and Papa?"

Her face burned down to her neck and further. "How could I ever forget?" She shook her head. "Mama and Papa!"

"My mother beat the hell out of me." The laughter left his face now. "My mother whipped me but you got no whipping."

The record had changed now, and Lady Day was singing "Ain't Nobody's Business If I Do." "I was five years old and my own mother accused me of raping you. And beat me for it!" He held her so tightly now she thought the middle of her back would break. "And held you in her arms and made you feel good about the whole damn thing."

"I'm sorry, Othello. It was all my fault. I'm truly sorry." She reached her hand up and she touched his scowling face.

He said, "To hell with it. Do you remember the time we chased you out of the cotton field?"

She said, "Do I remember? Good Lord, that was a trauma."

He said, "I'm not sorry. Like shame on you."

"I went home and cried and cried and cried. I hated myself, I hated my color. I wanted to be black and brown like you and the rest."

He said, "Sure you did."

Carrie Lou said, "Honestly."

"Do you remember that summer day when you gave me mouth-to-mouth resuscitation?"

"Good Lord, yes!"

He said, "We've had a lot of happenings together. We share gobs of memories."

"Yes," she said, her eyes her face aglow with a kind of happy melancholy. "So many many memories."

The boy said, "I'm afraid I'm going to kiss you again."

[334]

The girl said, "I'm not afraid." Her eyes said she was scared to death.

And his head moved downward, his mouth to catch her mouth. Her trembling lips did not try to escape his lips this time. And his tongue began to pry, and her mouth opened to take his kisses, and her tongue rose to the challenge, and they waged a desperate struggle tongue to tongue, mouth to mouth, belly to belly; his hand seized a cheek of her roundish backside and tried to pull her even closer to him. For a pure sweet moment he had been lost with her in the passion of the moment, but now he remembered who she was, the Princess and he, the untouchable, and he would have it out with her, take his great spite out on her, in her. He, Chuck Othello, nineteen years of age, black, Afro, country bumpkin, Lil Abner, was the deliberate seducer, for a sadistic kind of kicks. He led her to the couch and they sat down and went into each other's arms again. She said, "I don't want this! I did not invite you here for this!"

He said, "I know, darling." He was an expert by now, this boy, who was still boyish in so many ways. But in this, he was an expert, he was beyond his years in this, the art of making love. He knew the keys to turn a woman on. Miss Naomi had given him many lessons. Therefore his fingers did not fumble like a novice with the buttons on her blouse. They were possessed of unusual intelligence and profound dexterity.

"Please! Please, Othello! Please. Goddammit, no!"

"Yes, Desdemona!"

He dispossessed her of her bra, and now his hand cupped her breast, so ripe and taut and bursting with the passion of the now moment, his other hand hard at work zipping down her slacks. The dear girl was defenseless in the hands of such an expert. So pure and white as the driven snow was she. His mouth was on her breast now, as the girl wrestled hopelessly and aimlessly against her own desire. Her arms around his neck, his tongue playing tricks with the brownish nipples of her pinkish breast and she was going crazy with a passion she sought to fight with all her ammunition, which was like a popgun against a hydrogen bomb. Her slacks off now, his hand, the talented explorer, caressing her thighs and then and then and then in between her legs moving aside the crotch of her dampened panties.

"Othello! Please, Othello!"

"Desdemona—baby!"

His knowledgeable fingers played with her quivering sex now. Explored the tunnel of her sex. He knew it took a woman time to get ready. Miss Naomi had taught him. He knew better than "Wham! Bam! Thank you m'am." He played with the tender lips of her sex, all humid now. Played with her and played with her. Her eyes closed, her face losing color. Then he took her hand and put it on his hardening sex, rude and arrogant and black, and held it there, but when he finally took his hand away, she withdrew hers, so he placed it there again and held it there, and when he took his hand away the second time, she still held his arrogant sex, and squeezed it. He took her by the hand and carried her to the bedroom and laid her on the bed and got quickly out of his trousers and pulled her panties down and off her legs and got into bed with Carrie Louise, Mister Charlie's only child. And they made love together.

She was tight at first, scared, though very very wet, but as he penetrated deeper, she gave way before the onslaught. She cried softly into his ears at first. "You're hurting me! You're hurting me!" At that point he couldn't have helped her if he had wanted to, which he didn't. He lunged deeper and deeper and viciously into her as he laid siege to her in the undeclared war—for cherries. After awhile the girl forgot the great hurt, caught up as she was in the war and in the excitement of the battle; she began to moan and groan, and her roundish backside moved from side to side and thrusting ever upward toward him, ever upward. Spiraling and ever upward. "Oh my darling! Oh my darling! Oh my darling!" She began to shake in spasms, and he knew the time had come for both of them. And so they came together. He was an expert in these things. He told himself he was an expert. There was no sense in being overly modest.

Talk! Talk! Talk! he thought to himself, as he lay naked beside her. Talk a hole in my head.

"I reckon I always was in love with you, Othello. Even when I was a little biddy girl, it was Othello this, Othello that. My mother told me one day, 'You better get that little nigger boy off your mind.' But somehow or other I never did. I used to think about you a long time after I found I wasn't supposed to."

Yeah, yeah, yeah, Othello thought. Don't talk me to death, cause I ain't ready to die. He thought, if Mama Wakefield could see her little girl now. Not to mention Jimmy Dick, the old philosopher on the Color Question. The old cunt-chasing whore-monger.

"When I read Shakespeare, I told myself, he's Othello and I'm his Desdemona."

"Shee-itt!"

"My father always thought of you and your daddy as Gunga Din, his favorite black character. I knew you were not Gunga Din."

He said, "Actually!"

"I love you, Othello. I don't care who knows it. Mama, Daddy, everybody, anybody."

Down girl, he thought. Take it easy, greasy. You got a long ways to slide.

"I mean it, I don't care who knows about it."

Let us not get carried away.

The brrriiinng of the telephone exploded in the room, catapulting them out of a sweet lethargic nostalgia, the after-effects of the love they'd made together. She leaped naked from the bed and started toward the phone, as he watched her jiggling, jouncing buttocks. She remembered she was naked and said "Oh!" And she turned toward the bed again and he idly watched the front of her with the yellowish straw that made a triangle above the sanctuary of her love. "Oh!" And she pulled the sheet from atop him, leaving him exposed and now limply naked, and she draped it around her body and moved hurriedly toward the telephone, which had brrunnng six or seven times, and by now was getting damn impatient.

"Hello," the girl said. Out of breath. She was bleeding perspiration.

"Long distance calling Miss Daphne Wakefield."

"She is not here, Operator."

"Do you expect her shortly?"

"No, Operator."

"Miss Wakefield is not in, sir. Shall I——"

"Is that you, Carrie Louise?"

"Daddy!"

"Put the call through, Operator. I'll speak to the party who is there."

Othello got up and walked naked toward Carrie Louise.

Charles Wakefield said, "I really wanted to talk to *you*. I called

[337]

you at the college and no one could locate you or your roommate, so I thought your aunt might know where you were."

"Is anything the matter?"

She felt Othello's tongue, thrust into her other ear. She tried to push him away.

"No, honey. Everything is fine. I just missed you and wanted to talk with you, and find out what plane you were coming in on, for Christmas, so I could come and meet you at the airport."

Othello opened up the sheet and exposed her nakedness, and she could feel his lips on the tightening nipple of her nervous breast. She could not help from breathing loud and labored.

"I don't know which plane I'm taking yet, Daddy. I'll call you tomorrow evening. I'll probably leave here sometime Tuesday morning." Stop it!

His hands roamed tenderly all over her now, and it was terribly upsetting, and she was sure that somehow her father could see the whole thing via the telephone and knew what they were up to. His hands had come to rest on the straw-colored moss above her sex. And it was awfully upsetting. He plaited the straw between her legs.

"All right then, your mother is doing as well as could be expected, and sends you her love, of course."

He took her free hand and put it on his naked sex, and she stared fascinated as she watched it actually grow underneath her touch. The hair around his sex was black-on-black. Gleaming black. Her pale hand on his black sex. It was the blackest part of his entire body. She thought, my white hand holds his terrible throbbing black thing. Or is it my pulse throbbing?

She said absentmindedly, "Give Mother my love, my daddy."

Her father said, "Are you alone? You sound distracted. Are you having a party or something?"

Othello kissed her, tongued her. She had to pull away. Perspiration on her forehead now, and moisture just above her lips.

"I'm by myself, Daddy. I just wanted to get away from the college, so I came down here to do some studying and thinking."

"You're sure?"

His fingers were inside her now and she was squirming terribly, her whole body growing warm and warmer. She shivered as if a chill had seized her.

"Of course I am, Daddy."

[338]

"All right then. I'll look to hear from you tomorrow. Goodbye now."

"Goodbye, Daddy."

She put the receiver back in place. Her blue-green eyes flashed with anger at him. "What were you trying to do? Let him know you were here with me? He probably already knows you're in New York. If anybody in Wakefield County knows, you can bet he does."

He was smiling as he picked her up and carried her toward the bed. "I thought you didn't care who knew about your great love for Othello." He mimicked, "Mama, Daddy, anybody, everybody."

"I didn't say I was ready to hit him in the face with the good news, or to broadcast it on television. I meant, all in due time."

"You are a fake, that's what you are. A dyed-in-the-cotton Southern-type phony." He laughed softly at her.

She kicked and scrambled in his arms. She shouted, "Let me down! Let me down!"

He said, "Be my guest." And dropped her without warning plop on her back on the bed, and stood above her staring arrogantly at her in her reddening nakedness as she pulled the bedcovers over her.

"Please go into the next room while I put something on," she ordered him, like the true Princess she was and had always been.

He said, "Anything you say." And started toward the living room.

She said, "And take your clothes with you and put them on!"

He said, "Anything you say, Miss Carrie Louise." And took his clothes and made it toward the other room.

Just as he was tying his shoe, she came back into the living room in a flowing hostess gown. She said, "My aunt and I, we wear the same sizes. This material is pure Japanese silk."

He said, absently, "How about that?"

"She bought it in Japan herself on one of her visits. She brought it back with her. Isn't it stunning? Isn't it simply beautiful?" She made one complete rotation, as if she were modeling it for him.

His answer, simply: "Yeah."

She said, "Will you have a cup of coffee before you go?"

His answer, simply: "Why not?"

They sat sipping coffee now, sat opposite each other, he on a couch and she in a club chair, her face anxious, as he put on a bored expression. "I don't want you to think I'm like that way at all," she said.

"What way?"

"I mean, I'm not that kind of a girl. I didn't invite you here for that. I could never be promiscuous. Sex is never that important in a lady's life. I mean, in a true lady—I mean, after all——"

He said, "Especially a Southern white lady. Right? But then what other kind of ladies are there?"

She said, "Southern white? I didn't mean to cast asper——"

He said, "If the fine upstanding Southern white gentlemen stopped chasing black women long enough to catch their breaths, and did their homework, you wouldn't be so everlastingly virtuous. You wouldn't be so damn frustrated."

She said, "I *am not* frustrated."

He laughed. "And you are not virtuous, lover. You *are not* a virgin. Check? And you were not a virgin when I got here this evening."

She said, "There was only one boy before, about three years ago. It was a night in Paris. It meant nothing, nothing at all."

He said, "And what am I supposed to do? Be thankful for what I have just received?"

She said, "It doesn't mean what you think it means."

"It means nothing at all. Check? Just like that other night in Paris. That's fine with me. *C'est bon!*"

She said, "But it *must* mean something. I just don't go around giving myself to anybody and everybody. I'm not like that. I'm not like that at all."

He said, "Neither am I. I'm a Southern gentleman. I'm not a man of easy virtue." He laughed at her. "I'm very particular about who I sleep with."

Her face lost color. "I can have the cream of the crop. I can marry any boy I choose in the entire State of Mississippi. They all run after me. The best—the cream—"

He knew what she said was true about the boys running after her. He'd seen them chase her all summer long. He stood up and stared down at her. "*I'm* the cream of the crop, little Mississippi lady, and you damn sure can't marry me. And to set the record straight, I did not run after you. I have never run after you. Remember?"

She stared at him. He remembered the time in the cotton field. Her blue eyes had the same lost, scared look. "I don't understand." She was used to having her way with anybody and everybody. She was used to having her say—the last word, no matter what. And she didn't understand.

He said, "I'll break it down for you."

"I'm a lady," she reminded him. "I'm a lady—I'm a Wakefield lady. That's important for you to understand."

"You're a lady," he agreed. "And one day you just might grow up to be a woman, you know?" He went for his overcoat and slipped his rangy body into it.

"But you can't leave like this. I can't let you leave it just like that. I am a lady. You must understand that. I felt sorry for you. In this city all by yourself. I knew you wanted me, and needed me, or thought you did. And I felt compassion for you, that's all. You mustn't think about it ever. You must not let it be a trauma for you. You must get it out of your mind, as if it never happened. It can never happen again."

He stood there with an arrogant smile on his face, as he heard her out. "What the hell's the big deal, lady? You were fucked, that's all, by a good black man. You want me to forget it? Sure, why not? It wasn't that sensational. I've had better women," he boasted, as if he had sampled dozens of them. In reality, she was the third woman he'd ever been with in all his young life: the other two—Cora Lee once, when the two of them were still kids, and Miss Naomi. "The thing is, can you forget it, little big lady? That is the question." He moved toward the door.

"But-but-but you can't leave it like this!"

He turned. "How else can we leave it?"

She was coming apart now—at the seams. Her face was as white as biscuit dough. "You have no humility at all. I-I-I-I gave you everything."

He stared at her, smiling contemptuously. He looked up at the ceiling and back at her. He said, "Shee-itt!"

She grew more desperate by the briefest moment. "I gave you my pure white body, and you're entirely ungrateful about it. I mean, I even overlooked the fact that you were black. I mean, what more do you want me to do?"

"Nothing. Not a goddamn thing. I gave you my pure black body. Fair exchange? Maybe I got cheated in the deal."

"I proved to you I wasn't prejudiced." She rose from the chair.

"Why in the hell do you keep talking about it then? Like you say, why don't we just forget it?" His voice hardened, his smile widened. Since college, he had developed a kind of sophistication which brought a smile on his face without him really smiling. Smiling only in his widening eyes and in the crinkled corners of his mouth. "Let me put it crudely, little mama. You were a pretty good piece of ass. Nothing more, nothing less. So like it will be no great chore for me to forget it."

Her face grew even whiter; her knees buckled, as if Muhammad Ali had thrown his Sunday punch. Her mouth worked, but no words came forth.

He went to the door and opened it. "Goodnight, my pure white Southern Princess."

She stomped her foot. She found her voice again. "Come back here! I have not dismissed you. I have not finished with you!" She tried to look officious, but she looked pathetic. Yet he would not let himself feel compassion for this wilted flower of Southern womanhood.

"That's what you think," he said, and kept going out of the door. He did not even bother to shut it after him. He had had his sweet revenge on her and Jimmy Dick and all the Great White Fathers and all the Southern Womanhoods.

And yet the taste was bitter in his mouth.

Chapter

7

When he came in from work at four-thirty the next evening, she had already called him three times and was on the phone a fourth time as he walked in the door.

Could he come to dinner tonight?

No. He could not come to dinner tonight. He had other things to do. Like he was tired and very sleepy. He lied. "I have a very important appointment."

But it would be her last chance to get him and Sherry Kingsley together. She had invited Sherry to dinner also.

Othello said, "Oh. Well, possibly I can postpone my other engagement."

She said, "Swell! My boyfriend is coming to dinner too, and I'd love for you to meet him."

All the way to the Village, he stared at people getting off and on the subway, glanced from face to face at the people seated across from him, wondering who they were and why they were, as the great train thundered underneath the city. Most of all, he thought of meeting Sherry Kingsley again, and wondered how the evening would go. How would Carrie Louise carry it off with Sherry there and Carrie Louise's boyfriend, and this thing between her and him, this thing that happened yesterday? How would Othello carry it off? Would they give themselves away? Mostly, he thought of Sherry Kingsley. She was the everlasting most. She was everything Ronnie had said she'd be, and more, much much more. He licked his lips and swallowed his saliva.

Othello was the first to arrive at Carrie Louise's dinner party. They sipped Scotch and soda as she bounced back and forth to and from the kitchen seeing to the dinner.

"I woke up this morning thinking about you," the girl told Othello, "and I've been thinking about you all day long."

He answered, "Really?" And wondered how long it would be before Sherry Kingsley made her entrance. He did not feel like rehashing last night's opening performance, especially the conversation afterward. The rationalization. He'd been down that road before. It was a deadly dead end.

"Oops, I forgot to—" she exclaimed, and ran off toward the kitchen. She operated on a very high wire of extreme tension. She had become the kind of person who seemed to run everywhere she went. He could not relate the girl she had become to the easygoing Southern way of life from whence she came. But she had always been in a hell of a hurry as long as he remembered.

She came back and sat and sipped. She stared into her glass, as if she sought the answer to whatever it was that was troubling her, would find it right there in her glass of Cutty Sark and soda. She looked up and across at him and then back into the glass, and then she said, "I wanted you to know—that is—I mean—what happened last night was just one of those things."

Othello used his best New York idiom on the lady. "Yeah—right. Like just one of those things."

She said, "I didn't want you to think, I mean, that I was a

[343]

part, I mean, of the sexual revolution going on on all the campuses."

Othello said, "I wouldn't think of thinking such a thing. So don't you worry about it."

She bounced off to the kitchen again. And where in the hell was Sherry Kingsley?

She came back and sat and sipped. "It's so easy to be misunderstood, Othello. To get the wrong impression. I surely wouldn't want you to get the wrong impression."

He said, "What time were you expecting Miss Kingsley? And your boyfriend?"

She said, "Oh, I meant to tell you—they're not coming."

He said, "They're not coming?" Heat collecting in his collar. Anger filling up his face.

She said, "I'm sorry, Othello. I know I should've called you, but by that time it was too late. I figured you were already on your way. Sherry called me about five-thirty and said she couldn't make it. To give you her best regards. She was truly sorry she couldn't make it. And my boyfriend called a few minutes later and asked me could he take a raincheck."

Othello did not try to hide his disappointment.

She said, "I'm truly sorry, Othello. I'm really sorry that you have to be put through the boredom of another evening with just little old insignificant Carrie Louise Wakefield."

He stared blankly at her. No comment.

"I want you to know I didn't plan it this way. Neither did I plan the way things happened yesterday. You just seemed to need me so much. I felt so much compassion for you."

He said, "Bullshit!"

She was startled. "Othello!"

"I planned it," he told her. "I planned the whole damn thing. And like you better believe it."

"You didn't!"

"I promised myself one thing after I overheard the little old summit meeting in the den summer before last after the Great Feast, the all-night barbecue. All of you were in there philosophizing about the black man. And the black woman. Check? I mean you should've heard those Great White Fathers boasting about their exploits in the darker sections of town. And then your father, the natural-born last of the Great White Fathers." Othello mimicked Jimmy Dick Wakefield. "Water seeks its own level, Jeff. That boy knows his place because I taught him. I mean the thought would never enter his head. And if he did forget his place, my Princess certainly would remind him. She knows her inferiors." He stared an angry smile at her. "I mean you heard the whole thing, Desdemona. You laughed along with the rest of them. It was a real funny bit. I just don't have a sense of humor for that type of thing."

She got up and came over to him. She put her arms around his neck. "I didn't laugh, Othello, sugar. I swear before the Lord I didn't." Her eyes were filling.

He stood up and pushed her away from him. "Don't waste no tears on me, baby. I promised myself that night that one day I was going to make a liar out of Jimmy Dick. I was going to get into his daughter's drawers. And he didn't have to worry about me marrying her, even if she was of a mind to, because it takes two to tango, and when I tango for keeps, it's going to be with a black woman. Believe me when I say so. I planned the whole thing, you follow? I seduced you, old broad. I seduced you, just for the hell of it."

"You're making it up!" she shouted. "You're lying! You're making it all up. You're horrid and I hate you! I hate you! Hate you! Hate you! Hate you! You black——"

He put his hand hard across her mouth. It was not a slap, more push than slap. "I'm Othello," he said sarcastically. "Your black shining prince." He paused. "And now that the truth is out between us, shall I also take a raincheck on your dinner? I mean, like the others did, Miss Kingsley and your boyfriend?"

"No—no—no—please stay," she said. "It's my fault more than anybody else's." Then she said, "The dinner! Oh, dear!" And she ran toward the kitchen filled with smoke and smells, which now had reached them in the living room.

After dinner, they sat listening to the record player. They sat across the room from each other, in silence most of the time. He closed his eyes and let the sounds flow through him. He thought he was floating along on wave after wave of sound, and he lost contact with time and space and even place. He was not here in this place, he was not there, he was just floating, and letting whatever happened happen.

She brought him back with: "We must work this thing out between us—talk it out and get it over with. It must have some meaning when a lady like me—I mean——"

[345]

"Check this out," he said, wearily. "You invited me over to seduce me. I came over to seduce you. We both won, or lost, however you want to look at it. So what's the big mystery?" His voice deliberately hardened. Sometimes you had to put up guide posts when you insulted white folks, or else they would not admit it to themselves. "Let me spell it out for you. We fucked each other. Right? I mean, just like millions of people are doing at this moment all over the world. I mean, you're pretty good in bed. Neither the best nor the worst. What the hell are you complaining about? You think you got shortchanged?"

She sobbed, "No! No! It must have had more meaning than that! You're just hurt and angry—that's why you talk like this. It's a defense mechanism. You're just hurt and angry, and it's all my fault! It's all my fault!" She was sobbing now without restraint.

He started to laugh at this crazy hysterical woman, and she got up and came toward him, and she knelt at his feet and put her arms around his legs, her face losing color completely now. She was as white as bathroom enamel. Even her ruby lips were white. I read you, bitch, he thought to himself. You want this black boy to feel grateful to the great white lady for making the supreme sacrifice.

"All right," he said, "I'm deeply thankful, O Great White Priestess, for the sacrifice you made to nourish my perishing body when you gave to me the most sacred of gifts, your great white, pure white, virginal body. For I was on a vast desert of black loneliness, and I was dying of thirst and you gave me a drink, and I was starving and you fed me of your glorious body. For we did fuck each other to our hearts' content."

She was whimpering like a little puppy at his feet now, and he tried to steel himself, because he wanted to feel no compassion for her. The phone rang four or five times before she heard it.

Ultimately she went and picked it up. "Hello."

Then she muttered, "Sherry!"

Then she looked quickly away toward Othello and back to the phone again. "Oh nothing. I'm not doing anything."

After a moment she said, "Not tonight, darling. I'm really exhausted." After a moment, she said, "Besides, I would have to bathe and get dressed and all that mess, and I am just completely bushed. Maybe we could have lunch tomorrow." After a moment she said, "*Ciao,* darling." And hung up.

She looked at him. "That was Sherry."

He said, "I'm hip." And stood up. "Why didn't you tell her to come over here? Why didn't you tell her I was here?"

She said, "I—I—I——"

He said, "You didn't invite her in the first place, did you?"

She shook her head from side to side. "No——"

"You didn't invite your boyfriend either?"

She came to him and leaned against him. "The whole thing was a pack of lies. I'm a bitch, a whoring bitch." She thought he would dispute her word.

But he said, "Of course you are. You just wanted to get me over here to do a whole lot of talking and fucking, didn't you?"

She said, sobbingly, "You have no feeling for me at all. You don't give another human being any area for dignity. You just strip them of everything. You leave them nothing, not even self-respect."

He said sarcastically, "Isn't that what you want me to do? To strip you naked and fuck you?"

"Please! No! Please!"

He said, "Do you want to fuck or don't you?"

She said, "Please! Please!"

He said, "Please what? Please fuck you?"

She almost lost her voice, but he heard her hoarsely whisper, "Please fuck me—" And she leaned upon his chest and wept tears upon his jacket.

They went together to the bedroom, and they undressed, and they got together on the bed, and she was shivering with chills of heat. Heat wave after heat wave moving over her and through her trembling body.

He said, "Let's have a drink to calm you down a bit."

They drank together and then made love. Maybe it was loveless love they made. But she was more relaxed this time than she'd been the night before.

And he was the expert, the veteran. He knew better than she did that you must prepare a woman. He thought he knew better than she did. So he kissed her mouth, her eyes, her ears, he tongued her tongue, her ears; meanwhile his intelligent hand explored her body, the private secret parts that were sure to turn her on and on and on. It might have been loveless love at that, but he was the kind of lad that took pride in his work, whatever it was. His mouth was on the nipples of her breasts now, from one nipple to the other, his fingers playing with the wet lips of her sex. She was leapingly alive. She took his hard sex in her hand and tried to shove it into her.

He said, softly, "Not yet. Not yet. I'll tell you when."

She murmured, "All right, sugar."

He said, "You haven't relaxed enough yet."

"All right, sugar-pie."

He said, "Take it easy, greasy. You got a long ways to slide. Everything's going to be real cool, if you just relax and take it easy. Daddy's going to see to it that you reach the city."

With his fingers he reached deep inside of her, as with his mouth he tongued her nipples. Her body was quivering now from head to foot, and not from fear this time, but from excitement. She tongued his ear and whispered, "I'm ready, sugar. I'm relaxed and ready. I'm so ready I can't stand it."

He agreed with her. "You're really ready, baby." And he put his hard thing in her hand, and she guided it to the tunnel of her sex; he missed the mark the first time, but then she moved and shifted and finally she contained him, and proudly did she hold him captive. They started slowly at the beginning, her eyes closed, her pink face gaining color; as the red blood flooded through her face, her cheeks seemed newly freshly rouged. Red, red, redder, flaming.

He said, "Open your eyes. Relax and have yourself a ball. It's just me and you fucking, that's all. It's happened a million billion times before. You close your eyes like that and you lose sight on the whole damn world."

She opened her eyes. She was shy at first to watch the action. She stole glances at the action and looked away again. Then she couldn't keep her eyes away. She said, "Our bodies go so well together. Look how our colors match so beautifully."

He thought, Yeah, yeah, yeah. Don't talk me to death, cause I ain't ready to die. As he lunged deeper and deeper into her up to the hilt and back and forth and back and forth with the rhythm of a pom-pom gun.

"Oh, sugar-pie!" she cried in hoarse whispers. "Oh, darling, how beautiful we are together! Look how the hair contrasts! Your black curly hair entwined in my yellow straight hair! Isn't it simply marvelous?"

He said, dryly, "Check. And my black cock in your pink pussy."

She shouted, "Yes! Yes! Yes! Your black cock in my pink pussy!

[348]

Your black cock in my pink pussy!" And she closed her eyes again and began to work her backside in a kind of frenzy as if Judgment Day had come, as he lunged deeper and deeper, pounding away like a trip-hammer, as if he were trying to come out on the other side. Then she began to thrust her buttocks upward, ever upward, violently upward, as if she would throw him from the saddle, but he rode her straight home like a champ.

Her body took off into orbit, went into spasm after spasm. Her mouth was open wide now and her face losing color again. And she gave out with shouted cries. "I'm going to reach the city, sugar! I'm going to reach the city! I'm going to reach the city! Now! Now! Now! Now!" Her body was completely seized with spasms now. She reached the city ahead of him. This time he came a moment later.

She lay there now beside him, breathing laboredly, the color returning slowly to her cheeks.

"Do you love me, sugar-pie?" she asked him.

He turned it over in his mind. Tell her you love her. Why not? What the hell? You're supposed to tell any woman you love her after you get through making love to her. Even a whore. If she asked you. It would be no skin off of his ass to tell Missy Anne he loved her. Besides, she wasn't that bad. He had to admit he enjoyed screwing her. He told her, "Nope—I do not love you." You're a mean Black Nationalist bastard, he told himself, and laughed out loud at himself. You're fulla shit, that's what you are, he told himself.

She reached for his hand and took it in hers. "It was good, wasn't it, sugar? It was so good. It was perfect. Tell me it was perfect."

He said dryly, "It was pretty good. I mean, it was fair-de-middling. But I damn sure wouldn't write home about it." And he laughed at his own pun, which he had not intended. "I wouldn't write old Jimmy Dick about it."

She said, almost wistfully, "You are the meanest boy I've ever known in all my born days." Her greedy mouth was open and happy and complacent. She felt like she'd just had a sumptuous meal and was curled up by the fire.

He said, "What do you want me to do? Write a poem about it?"

She squeezed his hand. "Let's be friends forever, my Othello."

[349]

He said severely, "Let's get one thing straight. Two things. I am not a boy. And I am not your Othello. I am *my* own man. And you'd better believe me when I say so."

She changed the subject. She smiled complacently, luxuriating in an ocean of good feelings. Smells, touch, tastes. Horns blowing down on the street. "Ever since I can remember, I always got whatever I wanted. And I wanted you, and I got you. You think you seduced me. That's all right. Have it your way. Nevertheless I got what I wanted all the same." She laughed softly to herself—at him.

He turned it over in his mind. Had he really been had—as she said he had? Had she really turned the tables on him? Who had sacrificed what? Who had had whom? After all of his deliberateness, he did not want to feel, to even think, that he had lost something of value in this place; that he had not wrought his sacred vengeance, that he had not emerged triumphant. He did not, would not let himself believe that White Southern Womanhood had won again. He said, "You got what you wanted all right, but you didn't get me, baby. You got fucked, that's what you got. And believe me, baby, that's all you got. And that's all you're ever going to get from *me*. And believe me, baby, as Ronnie would say, you can make book on it."

She was quiet for a moment. And he was restless there beside her. Finally she said, "I can have your friendship, can't I?"

He said, "Why would a black man want to be friendly with a white woman in the State of Mississippi? Or in any other state for that matter."

She said, "I mean real friendship."

He said, "What the hell you think I'm talking about? In Mississippi, we are sworn enemies. You got the whole world in your hands and I aim to take it away from you. It's as simple as that." It was never clearer to him than at this very moment.

"Nothing is that simple," she said. "I'm on your side. I've always been on your side."

He laughed at her, contemptuously. "Bullshit! You're on your own side. Your father's side. The white man's side."

"But my father, he's on your side too. He's not like the others, else why would he send you off to school."

He got up and went for whiskey, talking as he went. "I thought you'd get around to that sooner or later."

"Well, why did he pay for your education if he's so much against you? Answer me that?"

He gave her her drink and stood above her as she lay naked on the bed. "The question puzzled me at first, I'll admit. But now I know the answer. College taught me a few things your father hadn't counted on. Your father thought if he paid for my education, I would be eternally grateful to him and be his head house nigger, his educated Gunga Din, and stand between him and the field Negroes when they start to move in Wakefield County. My first loyalty was supposed to be to Old Master. He had it all planned out, since the day I came into this world."

She sat up in bed and took a drink. She shook her head. "I feel sorry for you. I really do. You are so sick. You are paranoid. Oh, God! What have we done to you people? You are so sick and suspicious, you can't even accept a true hand of friendship. You even suspect my father! You, Othello, of all people!"

He drank deeply. "Wanna know something? I suspect *you*, of all people. If I remember correctly, baby, you told me just yesterday that your father looked upon me as a Gunga Din. And I heard him say what amounted to the same thing that night at the great all-night barbecue."

She sighed. "If my father is against you, then I'm against my father." She reached out and touched his sex. His terrible black sex. Limp as a dishrag at the moment. She caressed it. He pulled away from her angrily.

She said, "Do you believe in nonviolence?"

"I do not believe in pure nonviolence." It was the first time he had spoken against nonviolence even to himself. "But what the hell has that got to do with the price of Mississippi cotton?"

She reached for him again, and he backed away. She said, "I believe in nonviolence. Believe in it devoutly. If we can't settle this thing between us with love and nonviolence, what is the human race coming to?" There was worry in her face now.

"To violence," Chuck Othello said.

"But I don't feel violent at all," Carrie Louise said. A smile relaxed her face now as she reached for him again and this time seized his sex and held it. "I just want to love the entire human race, and especially my Othello." She squeezed it. "I want my Othello to love me and at this very moment, and never ever think of violence again."

He said, "I know, baby. You want to sheathe my terrible swift

[351]

sword, and keep it sheathed forevermore. Yes, I know you, baby, just like I know Jimmy Dick." He took her hand deliberately from him. He went to the bathroom and got under the shower. She got underneath the shower with him. He kept talking as he went about his business. "Your plan is part of the same plan as your daddy's. You just go about it differently. It's the same damn goal. He just believes in straight hard power-plays right down the middle, and you believe in fakes and end-runs and the old Statue of Liberty. Both of you are trying to steal the game from me. Both of you want my manhood. But, lover, that's one thing you'll never get. And that's what you want most of all."

"You got me all wrong—you got me all wrong. I want to join the Movement. I told Sherry I——"

"Sure you want to join the Movement. You've got nothing else to do. You never had to hit a lick at a snake in all your worthless life. I mean, you're a parasite, lover. Most people work because they have to, but you don't have to do a damn thing, right? You don't know a damn thing worth dying to get, because you already got everything worth dying for, worth trying for. That's what you think. That's why you can bullshit your life away from one thing to the other. And this time it's civil rights and the year to be nice to black folks."

He was dressed now, and she sat motionless on the couch in the living room naked to the world. She looked numbed and shattered, speechless. He had lowered the boom on her, her very own Othello had.

He said, "In the words of Godfrey Cambridge—bye, baby."

She said, "No, no, no, you're all wrong. You're so very very wrong."

"Am I, Desdemona?"

"Yes. Yes. You are. You are. I feel so sad and sorry for you."

He said, "Bye, baby."

Chapter
8

He did not see her again in New York City. But he saw an awful lot of Sherry Kingsley. And she saw to it that he saw an awful lot of New York City. The Village teeming with people and Café Wha and Au Go Go and The Village Gate and teen-agers thronging Bleecker Street and Thompson and MacDougal; the bookshops on West Eighth. Bearded youngsters, bearded oldsters, beatniks, and well-groomed people, natives and foreigners. He was overwhelmed by New York accents, various and varied. People crowding off the sidewalks into the narrow streets calmly stopping traffic. There were more people on two or three streets in the Village than there were in all of Wakefield County. One day he went to meet her at the fountain in Washington Square. Suddenly, three days before, the people had exploded into the streets. The weather had warmed up and it was like the very first day of spring, even though it was December. He got off the "A" train at the West Fourth stop and came up at West Eighth and walked up Eighth to MacDougal, through hordes of strolling, standing, staring, lolligagging humanity. He turned into Mac-Dougal and headed toward the Square. A bum walked up to him.

"Buddy, could you lend me a dime? I ain't had a drink all day."

Othello gave the blond-haired bum a dime.

As he entered the northwestern end of the park, three teen-agers, white girls, were seated on a bench. One of them accosted him.

"Hey, handsome, could you spare a quarter?" Startled, Othello stopped and stared at the girl, wide-eyed and arrogant and green-eyed, and somehow he knew that, despite her dungarees and her scraggly hair and her unwashed face, she needed to be hustling quarters in the Square about as badly as a fish needed to be on a desert.

"What about it, baby?"

It was as if they all had wallowed in dirt and deliberately smeared it on their faces, like children do. But somehow he was unimpressed. Beneath the grime, somehow he knew that they were frightened middle-class children in flight from their own reality. He thought of Carrie Louise. They were all in the self-same bag. Rebels with an empty cause.

Another of the girls said, "How about a half a dollar, pretty baby?" Dark-haired, dark-eyed, she got up and started toward him.

"Some other time," he answered, and walked away from them toward the fountain.

That night, he and Sherry had dinner in a quaint little restaurant in the Village. The waiters were dark-haired and blond-haired, mostly worn in bangs, and they were very pretty fellows and very very happy ones, flittering and fluttering around the place. They served the best shrimp curry in town. Sherry suggested both the restaurant and the shrimp curry. That night he was the last of the big spenders. They held hands in a movie as they watched *Good Times, Wonderful Times*. They saw Odetta at the Village Gate. She took him backstage and introduced him to the great and gracious beautiful one.

Later she told him, as they sat long after midnight listening to the sounds of Randy Weston at the Top Of The Gate, "Next time we go out together, you don't have to spend your money like you have a money tree."

He said, with slight indignation, "It's my money, isn't it? I work to earn it. One sure thing, I can't take it with me." Somehow he thought of Uncle Bish.

She said, "You can take some of it back to school with you, which was probably your reason for coming up here to work in the first place, instead of going home for Christmas."

He said, "I like you, and I like to do things with you." His voice had grown strangely husky.

She stared into his eyes. "I love you too. And I love you without the big-spending bit."

Somehow he knew she used the word "love" too loosely. And yet to hear her say it just like that started bees to buzzing in his belly. She lived at home in Brooklyn during the Christmas season. He wanted to take her home by cab, but she insisted on the subway. He didn't know whether to be pleased or insulted. He didn't know whether she was putting him in his place or showing tremendous understanding. She slept most of the way home with her head on his happy nervous shoulder. And now they stood at her front door on President Street.

[354]

The old expert made a clumsy effort to take her into his arms, but she just reached up and pecked him briefly, but full on the mouth, and said, "Goodnight. I really had a lovely time."

Again he tried to take her into his arms, but she eluded him. He said, "What's the matter?" Pouting.

She told him, "What on earth would Carrie Louise think?" She laughed softly at his face which looked like it belonged to a little boy who had been caught with his hand in the cookie jar.

He said, "But there's nothing between me and Carrie Louise. How could there be?"

"Do me a favor," she said. "Please explain it to my roommate." She laughed quietly at him. "Don't take it so seriously. Everything will work itself out—one way or the other."

He said, "When will I see you again?"

She said, "Friday night?"

Friday night they made it up to the Times Square neighborhood. Forty-Second Street—Seventh Avenue—Forty-Fourth Street. Rockefeller Center. People everywhere. Thousands of them. Buildings and people. The buildings stared down at the people and the people gawked up at the buildings.

Tuesday night, Thursday night, Friday night—Harlem. People. Black, brown, and light-brown people. West Indian accents. Southern drawls. Afro-Americanese. Talk that talk. Tell it like it is. Take the "A" train and drop me off uptown. They went to the Apollo, Jimmy Witherspoon, Wilt Small's Paradise. Street-corner meetings in the wintertime with black men mounted on platforms talking about Whitey to crowds of black people with the American flag flapping paradoxically in the Harlem breeze. Brother Malcolm's name was still magic and every speaker made sure to mention him. It was a guarantee for spontaneous responses from the folks. It seemed Sherry knew everybody, integrationists, conservatives, Black Nationalists alike. Othello met Richard Moore at his Frederick Douglass Bookstore, met Micheaux at his bookstore on Seventh Avenue. He met the Prime Minister of Harlem of the government-in-exile. He met the Yorubas and the Queen Mother. He thought there were more Black Nationalists in Harlem than there were people in all of 'Sippi. A couple of nights they sat almost all night long in the Dialogue Restaurant, drinking coffee and talking literature and revolution. He met LeRoi Jones, Bill Branch, Loften Mitchell,

[355]

Larry Neal, Bill Kelley. His poor head would be buzzing with words by the time he got home each night or early morning. This lady knew where the action was. He would work all day the next day in a near daze, and later wonder how he made it through the day with his mind totally absorbed in nothing related to his work. He met Paule Marshall at a party. He fell helplessly in love with Sherry, and he thought she loved him—he hoped, else why spend so much of her precious time with him? Why did she saturate him with her city? But at the end of each evening, when he took her to the door, it was always the same happening. A friendly sisterly peck on the cheek. Or on the mouth.

One evening he took her roughly into his arms, and she went limp and lifeless. His mouth tried desperately to find her mouth, and when he found it, he found that she had made her own mouth disappear. She had folded her lips inside of her mouth, and all his lips found were outer edges, not even that.

"Do you hate me that much?" he asked huskily. He sounded unsophisticated, even to himself. Corny but sincere.

Her face was serious for a moment. Her eyes were full of trouble. "Dear Othello, I do not hate you. And you know I do not hate you." Her voice was as soft as the yellow moonlight.

"But why—then why—I mean—" He was stammering like an idiot, like the country bumpkin that he was. Him, Othello, the great lover. The man who had a way with women.

She said, "I just—I mean—when I fall in love—it'll be all the way. I act sophisticated, but I'm terribly mid-Victorian and bourgeois and unimaginative when it comes to that. I'm not the emancipated woman I pretend to be, Othello. I'm terribly serious about love and sex and all that jazz."

He almost lost his voice. "I am too, Sherry."

"And besides, I don't have an aunt on vacation in Europe with an apartment in the Village." She laughed at the silly look on his face, but it was not a good laugh. Then she reached up and kissed him full on the mouth this time; she held his lips with her own soft lips for the briefest moment.

Then—"Goodnight, dearest Othello."

And left him standing where she left him.

She put her key in the great storm door, and then she turned toward him again, her small face wearing the slightest hint of a serious smile. "I had lunch with your beloved landswoman the

[356]

day she left for down-below-the-border. You ought to know, Honeychile cried all through lunch about her wonderful Othello. I hope you know that I'm not overly concerned with white folk's tender sensitivities. I'm not being moralistic, I don't think I am, but like she's a real serious chick. She's so serious sometimes she is a natural drag, sometimes. And I ought to know. I mean, I put her through the paces, baby. I found out the hard way how serious was our Honeychile. And she gets tore up something terrible. She told me all about the happenings between you and her on MacDougal Street. So if you're not serious about her, and I assume that you are not, then drop her lightly, softly, but firmly and decisively. After all, she is a human being, even if she is a Mississippi peckerwood, which probably sounds to you like a contradiction of terms. To be a human peckerwood takes quite a bit of being."

His face was a mask of seriousness, a nervous perspiration on his troubled brow. "How in the hell could I be serious about a Mississippi peckerwood?" Knowing full well it was not that simple. Nothing ever was, goddammit.

The sweet-faced brown-faced girl of Brooklyn put her soft hand up against his face. "Let her fall gently, dear, brave, and gentle blackamoor. The quality of mercy and all that other jazz—"

And left him standing where she left him.

And there was the time he had dinner with David Woodson, who showed him letters threatening his life.

David told him, "I talk tough, Othello, but sometimes I think of the essential goodness of our people, our black people, how much they have given to this country, and how this country has repaid them with denial and alienation. I don't mean Ralph Bunche and Belafonte and Poitier and Jackie Robinson. I don't even mean you and me. I mean the people, the black people in the middle of Harlem, on the West Side of Chicago, standing ten deep in the cotton fields of 'Sippi. When I think of their denial, I wish I believed there was a God so I could curse Him." David's eyes were filling now. "Goddammit, Othello, I mean folk like your mother and father. They deserve everything and get not a goddamn thing!"

They had dinner down on Forty-Seventh Street, and all during the meal, fancy-dressed white folk would come over to them.

[357]

"Mister Woodson, I just want to shake your hand. You're doing an excellent job. . . ." "Mister Woodson, may I bother you for an autograph for my wife and children. Mrs. Dawson thinks you're God's gift to American letters. . . ." "Mister Woodson, we ladies are from Miami, Florida, up here to a convention, and you would make our trip complete if you would be kind enough to give each and every one of us your autograph." Another one of the ladies giggled, a blondish one on the chubby side. "I can't believe it! I can't believe! When I tell them about it when I get back home, they won't believe it either." Othello was bursting open with the pride he felt for his famous friend. When he mentioned it to him later, David said soberly, "I used to flatter myself that all this white-bestowed celebrity meant something, I mean, more than just grist to the mill of my insatiable ego. But now I understand that it's all fake, Othello. Sham from the git-go. What counts is staying in touch with the dues-paying club members. I mean members of the black brotherhood from Watts to Mississippi. I'm talking about people like your mama and daddy."

Othello stared at his famous friend with bewildered admiration. David said, "Don't get me wrong. There are some tremendous white folk in the Movement—dedicated unto death—and we must use their dedication. But, baby, the main thrust must come from the black and disinherited. Black union is the ship; all else is the open sea!"

Chapter

9

He was twenty-one in the late spring of his junior year at the University. And he went out on the town (what there was of it in comparison with New York City), and he really hung one on. Went out all by his lonesome. Bought himself a bottle of cheap whiskey and went to a joint in town and had dinner and drank his bad booze silently and then he sat in a park and finished most of it off and sat in a movie and slept it off and woke up still drunk, when the usher told him they were closing for the night. He walked around the town like he was in a daze, holding the bottle to him like a sleeping baby. Even walked through a fancy white neighborhood, the kind of neighborhood where police prowl cars are on the perpetual prowl for prowlers, especially colored prowlers. He was like a man sleepwalking. Oblivious to danger.

"I'm twenty-one," he kept saying to himself. "I'm twenty-one and still a schoolboy while the whole damn world around me is going to pot. I'm twenty-one and still being put through school by my beloved great goddamn White Father. I need to get outa here and make me some money too. Take care of my own self. Do something for my daddy and mama—my people."

He'd met Stokely Carmichael again on the University campus. The great debate in the civil rights movement was raging between nonviolence and the right of self-defense. Carmichael talked about Black Power. Black Power! Black Power! David Woodson had written a thing on self-defense in a national magazine. At first Chuck was confused by the whole thing. His great admiration for the Reverend Martin Luther King was very much a part of his growing up, a part of his inspiration for being, a part of his understanding of the meaning of heroic struggle. King had been his childhood patron saint. In the beginning there were 'Sippi peckerwoods, and then there was the word, and the word was Martin Luther King. Deep down where it mattered there was still this admiration for this righteous man from Georgia. Othello loved this man like a boy who loved his father and yet could criticize him. But Carmichael was closer to his age, a part of his generation, closer to his disposition, his psychological need. Black Power! And David Woodson—Othello liked to think of him as his most distinguished friend and colleague. His big brother. "Wait till I get outa this damn University. I'll show them all about Black Power. Right down there in 'Sippi!" Othello seemed to be addressing his remarks to the whiskey bottle.

He got letters regularly from Sherry Kingsley, all of them very social and sisterly and very very political and very very platonic. Words like "historical perspective," the "objective reality," the "subjective situation" were in every other sentence. "Objective reality," "objective reality," "objective reality!" . . . "The real world," "the real world," "objective reality!" Her letters were so political and platonic that the "black revolution" was coming out of his ears. Black Power! Black Power! He finally decided that she regarded him as a country cousin, no more, no less. He might have been a eunuch as far as she was concerned, despite the fact that she ended all of her letters with: "Much love, Sherry." Sometimes he let a letter from her lie around for several days without opening it. To hell with her and her New York arrogance. She might need a brother, but be damned if he was looking for a sister. And he was about to puke his guts on her "objective reality." Her real goddamn world!

That week he'd gotten a letter from home. Most of the letters from home were full of information about the Movement. Who got beaten up, who got run out of town, who got fired off his job, who got shot by peckerwoods. Either that, or it was a grim tabulation of vital statistics—who got married, who was born, and who up and kicked the bucket. The Lord giveth and the Good Lord taketh away. His last letter was not a happy one. Bessie Mae's mother suffered another stroke and this time she passed on. Uncle Bish took a shotgun and put it in his mouth and blew his head clean off his body.

On this moonless and this starless night of the great date of his birth, he was lonesome and felt bitterly unwanted and unloved. And he did not give a good goddamn whether anybody loved him or not. He told himself he did not care. Who in the hell needed it? He thought of Bessie Mae and told himself that he wished he had gone to Wakefield County last Christmastime. Uncle Bish and Miss Ella Mae—he would see them never again. Bessie Mae was the one girl who loved him and would always love him. And she was beautiful and he loved her and he should have told her he loved her many many times and years ago. He had not written her in several months and finally her letters to him had tapered off and then had stopped completely. And he didn't blame her, but he knew she still loved him. His mind conjured pictures of his childhood with Bessie Mae Moocho and Little Jake. Sharp vivid scenes of the house out in the Bottom. Bessie Mae's mother in the front room watching television, and he and Bessie Mae in the backyard of a summer evening, holding hot and desperate hands, slyly, shyly, lightning bugs blinking off and on, frogs honking, crickets screeching, giggling, an old owl hooting. Maybe Bessie Mae didn't love him anymore. Maybe she never really loved him. Maybe she and Jake had fallen in love— his best buddy and his best girl. He had his goddamn nerve expecting her to wait forever, while he chased all over the world and New York City.

It was as if his feet had an intelligence separate and apart from him and anticipated his wants before he knew them himself. Walk up the steps, across the porch, knock on the door. Knock once, twice, three times, each time harder than the other.

Finally from the other side of the door: "Who's knocking on my door this time of night?" Sleepily. Aggressively.

"It's—it's me, Bessie Mae. It's Chuck Othello."

"Who?" Wide-awake.

"It's me. Othello."

She unlocked the door and stood there staring at him in disbelief.

He said, "Aren't you at least going to invite me in?"

Naomi said, "At this time of night? I'm a married woman."

He said stupidly, "So you married Little Jake after all. You married my best buddy."

She said, "I didn't marry your best buddy no sucha thing. But come on in for a moment. Let me get you a cup of coffee. You oughta be ashamed of yourself. Drunk as a cooter!"

He said, "Bessie Mae——"

She said, "You got your women mixed. I'm Naomi—Mizzes Naomi Donaldson." She took him by the hand and inside the house and closed the door and led him to the kitchen and sat him down at the kitchen table and fixed coffee for him. And sat across from him watching him drink three cups of it.

He looked up from the coffee and gratefully into her face. Her face had changed very little, if at all; maybe it was rounder, maybe warmer, even kinder. More relaxed. Her eyes were warm and darkly bright even with the sleep still in them, and he could see the breathing outlines of her youthful fully rounded breast beneath her nightgown. He said, "You're married—"

"Yes, I'm married. That's the first thing you got straight since you got here."

He looked around him uneasily and looked behind him toward the bedroom. "Where's your husband?"

"My husband works on the railroad. He's out on his regular run. Won't be back till tomorrow evening."

Othello stared down at the cup half-filled with coffee. "I'm sorry, Naomi. I mean I'm very glad for you."

"You don't need to be sorry for me. He's a real man, a real

[361]

black man, a railroadman. And he loves me and he takes care of me. I don't general-clean no more. He don't allow it."

He took a swallow of the coffee which was cold and bitter to him now. "What I meant was, I'm sorry about the way I treated you, the way I acted. I took advantage of you. I exploited you. I—" He thought of the time he'd had dinner with David Woodson in New York. Naomi was one of the honest-to-goodness dues-paying members of the brotherhood.

"Don't worry about the mule going blind," she told him. "We took advantage of each other. I got as much out of it as you did. Believe me when I say so, little boy. In some ways, I used you more than you used me. Believe it."

He wondered if it were true what she'd just said. He wondered if it were always true. Did people always use each other to their advantage? Did real lovers always exploit each other? "But every time I thought of you, I was so ashamed of myself. Ashamed of me being ashamed of you. I should have been proud of you. You are good and beautiful and honest and strong. I mean you're—" He stared at her through the fog of his drunkenness and loneliness, and she looked more beautiful to him than any other woman ever looked throughout the centuries of man's existence on this earth. "But I was brainwashed with bourgeois snobbishness, and you were all right to meet with under the cover of darkness, to eat your food and partake of your body, but not to appear with in public, oh no, especially not at the University. I was a goddamn fool, Naomi, and I'm ashamed of myself, and I'm so glad you got yourself a good husband. I wasn't good enough to kiss your feet. It's a thing I'll be ashamed of all the days of my life."

She just stared across the table at him and listened to his ravings. "What's your husband named, Naomi?"

"John Henry Donaldson."

"A railroad man. Big and strong and healthy and manful. John Henry—John Henry Donaldson. He's older than I am?"

She said, "He's old enough to be your daddy—maybe your granddaddy."

He said, "I'm sorry. I didn't know——"

"Ain't nothing to be sorry about. He's very much a man."

Othello said, "Today is my birthday, and I'm very much a man."

Naomi stood up. "All right, Mister Man, I'll give you a kiss for your birthday and then you best be getting on your way. After all, I'm a married woman."

He got to his feet and she came toward him and put her arms around his neck and pecked him briefly on the mouth, and, "Happy birthday, baby." She'd always called him baby. Her baby.

He smelled the pungent odor of her body, musty-sweet, and awakened from a deep deep sleep, and his arms tightened around her waist and he drew her up against him, and his mouth found her mouth again and tasted of her sour-sweetish sleepiness, a cold-damp taste, and he said, "I'm still your baby, and you know I am." And held her even closer to him and he felt his manhood growing up against her. And he said, "And you're my baby too. You know good and well you are." His mouth found her mouth again, and this time her mouth parted, her lips seized his lips hungrily, desperately, and her tongue engaged his tongue. Her knees buckled, she dissolved in his arms. He took her toward the front room which was also the bedroom. He laid her on the bed and lay beside her, his hand was beneath her nightgown now, caressing her plump warm thighs as she squirmed beneath his touch, her body flaming now and very much awakened. And then his nimble fingers explored the wonderfully tangled moss between her legs.

"I'm still your baby, and you know damn well I am."

She said, "Yes! Yes! Yes! You're still my baby! Still my baby! Still my baby!"

He felt a great exhilaration. He took her hand and put it on his sex, and she caressed it and she squeezed it. But when he tried deftly to unzip his fly, suddenly she seemed to change into another woman. "Don't! Don't, Othello! Please don't do it, darling! Please have mercy!"

His trousers unzipped now, he tried to guide her hands inside, but she suddenly pulled away from him. "Get up outa my bed, you sonofabitch, and get the hell out of my house. I'm a married woman. If my husband caught you here he would kill you dead as you got to die."

She had vaulted out of bed and was standing on the other side.

"But, Naomi——"

"You got your damn nerve, college boy. I ain't seen or heard of you in I don't know how long and you think you can just come in here any time of the night and just throw me on the bed and my legs spread open."

He got up and he walked toward her. "You know better than that, Naomi. I'm sorry. I didn't mean—I just—I mean, it was my birthday and I started to drinking and feeling lonesome and I wanted to be with the person in this town that I care about more than anybody else."

She said, "Get outa here. I don't wanna hear no more of that crap."

He kept coming toward her and she went to her dresser and pulled a drawer out, and when she turned toward him again, she had a gun in her hand. "Now get out! Get outa here, else I'll blow you all the way to hell and back!"

He stopped and stared at her with the gun aimed at him. Somehow it held no terror for him, held in her hand like that. He could not imagine her pulling the trigger on him. He thought of Bessie Mae out in the Bottom the day the insurance man had pulled his gun on them. That had been real terror, humiliating fear. He moved toward her again, smiling.

She said, "Stay away from me, I mean it, goddammit. My husband bought me this to protect myself whilst he's on the road, and I'll damn sure use it, cause I ain't like Martin Luther King. I ain't nonviolent."

He still came, smiling, and took the gun from her and put it on the dresser, and took her into his arms, and she wept upon his chest. "You knew I couldn't shoot you, baby! You knew I couldn't shoot my baby! You knew I couldn't shoot my baby!"

He said, "Yes, I knew. Yes, I knew." And massaged her back and shoulders with his fingers. "I love you, Naomi," he said. "I never really knew it before until this very moment. This moment when you stood there with the gun aimed at me. I knew I loved you, truly loved you. I don't even know what kind of love it is, but I know I truly love you. I love you, because you're a great truly wonderful woman."

She was bleary-eyed and sniffling. "You make me feel so happy, baby. You make me feel so wonderful and happy."

"Because you *are* wonderful, and I'm glad, and I feel happy too."

"I told Mister Donaldson all about you. I——"

"You mean your husband? You didn't! I mean you told him

what a bastard I was—how I took advantage of you? You told him what a snob I was? Well, I don't blame you—"

She moved away from him and looked up into his eager face.

She said, "I told him what a sweet boy you was and how we took advantage of each other. I was as big a snob as you was. I looked at you and I said to myself, Here's a young pretty college boy, and it made me feel I was better than most general cleaning women, cause I had me a young pretty college boy."

Othello said, "Naw—come on—you're just being generous like you always are. I was the bastard all the way."

She smiled, she wiped her eyes with the back of her fingers. "Baby, I'm a hard, grown woman, ten years older than you is. I knew what I was doing. I saw you, I wanted you, and I had you for a season. I knew it couldn't last forever. I reckin I wanted to make a man out of you, and I b'lieve that I succeeded."

He took her into his arms again. "Thank you, dear Naomi. Thank you, thank you, thank you!"

She said, "And you'll have mercy on me tonight, won't you, baby? You'll leave me alone tonight, cause I'm a married woman, and I ain't never been with another man since I married Mister Donaldson. I ain't two-timed him and I don't want to ever two-time him. I been honest with him and that's the way I always want to be. I don't want to do nothing I have to lie to him about. So please be kind to your Naomi and stay out of Mister Donaldson's bed."

He said, "Yes. I'll leave you alone tonight, and every night, because you're a married lady and because I love you, and you're a great friend and I love you and respect you and I love you as a friend and respect your marriage and your dignity, and I love you because I love you and I will never betray our love and friendship."

She was weeping now, weeping almost silently. "And you'll come to see me sometime, and meet my husband?" Her eyes were brimming full of tears of happiness.

He turned it over in his mind. "Yes," he said, "and meet your husband."

She said, laughingly and bleary-eyed, "All right then, we'll kiss goodnight."

And so the lovers kissed goodnight.

PART FOUR

Chapter 1

It was the hottest summer on record throughout the entire nation, and nowhere was it hotter than in the backwood jungles of old 'Sippi. Everything in Wakefield County slowed down to a walk, except voter registration, which did not contribute to the cooling off of white folks' dispositions. Hens stopped cackling, grasshoppers stopped hopping, birds stopped flying, lizards stopped scampering. Sometimes even birds stopped singing. Black and white, rich and poor, nobody escaped the heat, even those who lived with air-cooled housing, because air-conditioning units broke down in face of the omnipresent heat, which hovered day and night in the neighborhood of one hundred Fahrenheit all summer long. Nevertheless, black folks in the town still sat on their porches in the heat of day (more and more of them with no work to put their hands to), and some waved paper fans before their faces. And said, "Evening, Othello." Even though it was only one o'clock in the afternoon.

And he said, "Evening, Miss Billie Lee."

"Jes' tolable, son. Ain't nothing to brag about. Just here by being careful."

And strangers said good morning when they met you on the street. When Othello was in New York, he found himself saying good morning to people on the street who looked at him as if they thought he was out of his cotton-picking mind.

In Bedford Stuyvesant, he said, "How are you?" to one soul sister, and she said, "None of your goddamn business."

Every living human in the county sweated that summer, rich and poor, black and white. And along with the heat, the tension between the races mounted. The tension and the fear. In Wakefield County, Othello could feel the fear, the tension, could taste it in his mouth, read it in the people's faces. Fear was in the air you breathed, mixed and stirred together with heat and the fragrance of magnolias and honeysuckle and hyacinths and pine cones, and everything in a color-drenched rage of growth and beauty. Green grass and cypress trees all heavy with their dazzling greenness. Everything grew in such outrageous abundance during that summer in Othello's county. Heat and shrubbery and fear and tension, clashing and blending, made a sweetish sickish kind of smell like the fragrance of a funeral in Mount Moriah Baptist Church. It was a smell that put a queer taste in your mouth and made your stomach queasy. It was anywhere and everywhere. A smell Othello never remembered smelling in his county in his lifetime.

He worked for the Old Man, Jimmy Dick Wakefield, during the day, and worked for voter registration late into the night. Worked with people from the civil rights organizations from out of the county and out of the state, and with people he had known all of his life right there in Wakefield County. Jake and Bessie Mae and Cora, who had married meanwhile, and Miss Ida Lee and Josh Hemlock and Reverend Purdy and so many other Wakefield County brothers and sisters. White folks got meaner. Some black folks got bolder. Other black folks got more scared than ever.

One Thursday evening in late June, Othello and Bessie Mae did some voter registration visitations together. It was the practice for canvassers to go in pairs, especially after dark. They had made two or three visits before night fell, but then night had fallen, and when night fell in the 'Sippi backwoods, it fell suddenly and definitely. It fell so quickly and so abruptly you could hear it falling. And suddenly the nighttime orchestra went into its usual jam session, a symphony of sounds, of frogs and crickets and owls and whippoorwills. And yet there was a fearsome quiet about the 'Sippi nighttime, especially in parts of it like Wakefield County, where there was a sharp feeling that night had cut you off from the rest of the world. The county was deep deep in the 'Sippi jungles. To Othello, from the University, it felt like a million miles from nowhere, as he went with Bessie Mae through the total blackness that blanketed the countryside, especially that part where black folks lived their lives out. There were no street lights in the Bottom. When he had grown up there in the county, he had not felt this total isolation from the remainder of humanity. His whole world had been the county, but now the county was the end of the world for him. It was the abyss into which men toppled. Sometimes he was almost overcome by such

[370]

a lonely feeling in this place which used to be the world to him. Sometimes the county seemed as lonely as a deserted bird nest in the middle of the winter. Lonesome and isolated.

Some evenings, after night fell, they would be followed from house to house by a car full of armed white hecklers. A couple of canvassers had been beaten by white men. One canvasser had been shot—dead. Some nights, like this Thursday night, scared black folk would shut the door in the canvassers' faces. It happened to Othello and Bessie Mae on more than one occasion.

"Git away from here! I ain't innerested in that reddishing mess!"

Some nights, as had happened this night, black folk would see him and Bessie Mae coming and pull down the shades and turn off the lights and lock the doors and pretend not to be at home. Since night fell, they had made five visits before they visited the Lumpkins.

Deacon Lumpkin told them before they got started. "I know all about it, and I'm against this reddishing mess. Ain't gon do nothing but cause a great disturbance." He was angry with Othello and Bessie Mae before they even got started. It was as if he had known they were coming and had worked himself up into a righteous wrath before they got there. And everybody knew that Jeff Lumpkin was usually a mild-mannered man.

They sat on the front porch waving at their faces with paper fans from the Hoskins Colored Funeral Home, stirring up the still heat and the very active mosquitoes. Miss Mary just rocked back and forth and nodded her approval.

Othello said, "But Deacon Lump, sometimes there has to be disturbance in order for there to be progress."

"The Bood Book don't say that," the deacon argued angrily. "It say, blessed is the peacemakers."

Miss Mary rocked, and said, "Aah Lord."

Othello glanced at Bessie Mae. She was as sweet-faced as she'd ever been. Her face was a little rounder. Her mouth as sweet as ever but larger, fuller than he remembered, and more set and determined. He wondered what had gotten the deacon so "het up" before they had begun to make their pitch, to do their number. Maybe Bessie Mae knew the answer. But she just sat there staring at him. He got distracted for a moment. He wanted to walk over to her and kiss her. She was that lovely in the moonlight.

He looked back at the deacon. "But, Deacon Lump, even Jesus Himself caused a disturbance. That's how come the Romans got rid of him. And remember how He disturbed the Pharisees? And remember how He chased the moneychangers out of the temple with a buggy whip?"

The deacon was about fifty-five years old. He was coal-black and his eyes were small and dark, and angry at the moment; his skin beginning to wrinkle ever so slightly. He went to the edge of the porch and spat tobacco juice into the great black nothing-ness. He came back and sat down again. "Even if what you say is true, which I don't necessarily agree it is, but even so, Christ didn't have to deal with no Mississippi peckerwoods. And things was different then."

His wife said, "Amen, Deacon Lump," as if she were shouting softly from the mourners bench. She called him Deacon Lump, as did everybody in Wakefield County.

Deacon Lump stared fiercely out into the blackness. "Fairysees was Fairysees and Romans was Romans, but these here pecker-woods in 'Sippi is another breed of monkeys altogether."

Somehow Othello felt like laughing, even though he knew the deacon's statement had been made in deadly earnest. "I got to agree with you to that extent. They are a different species."

"Course they is. Fact of the business, they the meanest thing the Good Lord ever put on this earth in His own image. Espe-cially when they dandruff's up. And it ain't gon be nothing but violence coming out of all this reddishing and all that Black Power whatchamacallit."

"It's the truth so help me," Miss Mary mumbled.

Othello stared out into the great black void, as he waved the paper fan in front of his face. He wondered why so many black folk preferred to call it "reddishing" instead of "registration." He'd heard so many Negroes in the county say, and proudly, "I'm gon reddish if it's the last damn thing I do before I die." He'd heard others say, "I ain't studying about that reddishing mess." Did he say "reddish" before he entered the University? Maybe it was a sarcastic joke his folk played deliberately on the English language. They sure didn't owe the English language anything. It had been used against them ever since they were brought here to this place. Othello batted his eyes. There was nothing out there in the night but blackness, except for lightning bugs which kept blinking off and on like neon signs in Times Square, as he remembered it. New York City seemed a million miles away in time and space. He should have gone there and forgotten 'Sippi. And should have taken Bessie Mae with him. He slapped the side of his face and killed a lazy mosquito. Felt the fresh blood on his hand and cheek. His ears strained, alerted now, as he thought he heard an automobile coming up the dusty road.

He said uneasily to the deacon, "But Jesus Himself was kind of non-nonviolent, wasn't He? I mean, with that buggy whip at the temple."

The headlights of the car stabbed long slices into the blackness now, and Othello stared across the porch at Bessie Mae and wondered if it were the same car which had followed them ever since they began their visits earlier that night.

"Ne'er mind that," the deacon argued. "I done told you Jesus was dealing with Fairysees and Romans. We dealing with Mississippi peckerwoods."

Flashlights from the car dipped from one porch to the other of the houses on the street, coming closer to the deacon's house. Othello felt the perspiration now pouring from his armpits and his crotch, his entire body leaking perspiration, as they continued the conversation on the porch as if nothing at all out of the ordinary was happening or about to happen. He felt a cold fear in his mouth and a griping in his stomach as if a school of crabs were staging an orgy. He should have talked with them inside the house. What a fool he'd been!

"You believe in taxation without representation?" Othello asked the deacon. He should say to the deacon right now, "Let's go inside and shut the door." But he couldn't and the deacon couldn't.

"I believe in dealing with 'Sippi crackers as little as possible. That's what I believe in." Fear was on the porch now. Othello could taste it, smell it, as fear waged a pitched battle with dignity and pride.

The cars were three doors away now, the floodlight made a stream of light from car to porch three houses down from them.

A loud voice broke the stillness. "Where them voter redistration niggers?" Cracker voice and cracker laughter.

"If all the black folk registered who are eligible, we could outvote the white man three to one," Othello said, more loudly than he usually spoke.

"That's right," Bessie Mae said. "We could elect a county sheriff."

Two doors away now the floodlight played its beam upon the house. Othello could see now that rifles were pointing out of windows of the car, as it crawled slowly up the road. The floodlight's beam was on the house next door now, as even the lightning bugs stopped blinking and the crickets hushed their racket. A funny thing happened as the floodlight reached the side of the deacon's house. Suddenly the car lit up like daytime, as flashlights from the vicinity of the yard on both sides of the deacon's house began to play upon the car.

From the car came: "Turn them goddamn lights off!"

From the blackness came only silence, black and terrible silence. Only silence and great beams of light.

The car stopped now in front of the deacon's house. The floodlight's beam from the car caught the faces on the porch.

"All right, you niggers, turn off them goddamn lights! Ain' gon give y'all but one more minute!" Rifles pointed toward the porch. "One more minute and we shoot up the goddamn place!"

The floodlight from the automobile dipped from the porch and began to search the yard. "Hold it, men!" somebody shouted from the automobile. "Them sonuvabitches got rifles too!" The floodlight dipped all over the yard now. Next to every black man holding a flashlight was a grim-faced black man with a Winchester taking aim at the crackers in the car. One of them was Othello's buddy, Little Jake Carson, who was anything but little. He was the head man of the Elders of Protection and Defense, which was the name of the Wakefield County organization patterned after the famous Deacons of Bogalusa.

"All right now, goddammit, drop them Winchesters." From the car.

Nought but silence from the black men in the yard. Silence and great beams of light that cut the darkness.

"I'm gon count to three and y'all better drop them rifles or——"

"Aw, shit, Sam Rawlins, let's git the hell outa this Bottom and leave these niggers alone. It ain't no fun if niggers don't cooperate."

"Whatchoo mean fun? We didn't come out here for fun. When I come way out here I mean business."

"Yeah, but they mean business too."

[374]

The car started up again and pulled off down the road, and finally out of sight. The Elders remained in the blackness of the yard, except for Jake, who came up to pay his respects to the people on the porch.

"Everything copacetic?"

"Swinging," Othello answered, as the tension flowed out of him now, like air out of an inner tube.

Jake disappeared down into the blackness of the yard again.

"We could elect our own county sheriff," Bessie Mae repeated, as if the last few minutes had not happened. Othello stared at her with open admiration. Had he dreamed the last few minutes? The crackers in the car, the Elders in the yard? Was this 'Sippi? Was this Wakefield County?

Deacon Lump said, "I don't know about that. That'd be carrying the thing too far. The Bible tells you, in all things let there be moderation." He looked toward his wife, Miss Mary, but she did not say Amen this time. She just stared back at her husband.

Othello wiped his sweating forehead with a handkerchief. "What do you mean too far? If we had a black sheriff he would protect us from these peckerwoods. Then we wouldn't need the Elders."

"That's right," he thought he heard Miss Mary mumble.

"Peckerwoods wouldn't like it eee-tall," the deacon stated. "They'd kill him fore he served a week."

Othello said, "The Elders would protect him from the crackers just like they protected us a while ago."

"That's right," he heard Miss Mary mumble.

"You just said if we had a colored shaff, we wouldn't need no Elders. Now you disputing your own words."

Othello said, "The Elders will be with us until we teach these crackers the true meaning of nonviolence and get them to change their violent ways. The Elders would be necessary till we got everybody in the nonviolent mood."

"You sure do talk pretty." Miss Mary was speaking clearly now.

"I don't know. I just don't know. I just can't see it thataway." The deacon shook his head from side to side.

"You mean to say, if Reverend Purdy ran for Mayor of Wakefield City, you wouldn't register and vote for him?"

Miss Mary laughed softly. "Aah Lord. You got him that time. You sure Lord got him."

"All right—all right. You win," the deacon said. "Me and the

Missus will be down to reddish next Wednesday morning. Which it's not that Reverend Purdy ain't got no better sense than to run for Mayor of Wakefield City, but just to get you out of my hair." He was as bald as Reverend Purdy. "Which I know good and well Reverend Purdy got better sense than to stick his head in that kind of noose."

Othello answered, "I'll bet my bottom dollar Reverend Purdy's got no better sense than to run for Mayor of Wakefield City, and I'm betting that you and I and Miss Mary and Bessie Mae haven't got any better sense than to work for him to get elected."

Deacon Lump smiled for the very first time that night. "Ne'er mind Reverend Purdy and all lacka that. We're reddishing next Wednesday just to git ourself a little peace from Chuck Othello Chaney."

"A little peace and freedom." Othello laughed. "You can't have one without the other."

They left the Lumpkins in great spirits as they began the long journey to Bessie Mae's home out in the Bottom. They walked the dark and dusty roads, hand in hand, and he remembered the many times in his childhood, which seemed so remote now, a million years ago, he had carried her books and walked this sweet child home from school. Sometimes they would walk paths close to the river, and, despite the fact that she hated the river, even hated it symbolically, she nevertheless enjoyed the walks he walked with her. He knew she did.

Oh my Great God, how sweet it had been to walk with her down by the riverside, with the sunlight bouncing off the river's surface like a thousand jeweled devils dancing. He remembered the black-necked stilt, a handsome but ungainly bird, with its funny, long, and skinny legs, wading in the marshes, looking for his dinner. Remembered the cypress trees. And the weeping willows hanging heavy with their shawls of silvery Spanish moss. When Bessie Mae and Othello had walked together, the longest way around had always been the best way home. But this night they took the shortest route, which was still a long walk through the darkness.

He remembered the marsh hawks squatting quietly in the tall wet grass. Remembered vividly the winter of the heaviest snow in Wakefield County's history, and he had walked with Bessie Mae. Remembered all the sun-kissed days of spring and summer with everything come alive and sounding off, with birds singing and bees buzzing and hummingbirds and grasshoppers zooting through the green grass and flowers blooming, and new smells and new feelings and new words and brand-new conversation. And she and he had grown together, and then had grown apart, and now had come together again.

They walked silently along this moonlit night. Out this way there were no street lights. Your feet had to have good memories and had to make their way across the ruts and ditches, relying on their own intelligence. He remembered Uncle Bish's song.

> *Way down yonder where the moon shine bright*
> *Folks don't need no 'lectric light.*
> *Pharaoh's army got drownded*
> *Oh, Mary, doncha weep—*

He smiled. He did not need to look sideways at her; he knew her face by heart now. Her face which was to him beloved of all faces. He knew every inch of her sweet face. His mind was like skillful fingers etching out the blessed contours. He felt like crying, laughing, dancing, singing. Her wide, deep dark-black eyes shaped like almonds; her full-mouthed, heart-shaped lips the blue-red color of wild grapes and sweeter than the wildest grapes. He felt so good he felt uneasy. He never remembered ever feeling so romantic. They walked in silence, lost in one another's thoughts. And felt no need for conversation. This was where it was, he thought. This was *home*. She had always been where it was *at*. It was he who had gone through so many different changes. She had always been so close to him, he could not see for looking.

He hoped nobody would bother them this night. Sometimes it was safer to come the longer route along the paths down near the river and take your chances with the wilder things that scooted through the bushes than to come this route they walked tonight and take your chances with the night riders, the goddamn peckerwoods, who were getting meaner by the minute. He felt good, and he hoped the peckerwoods had gone home by now and called it a night like they had some sense up in their heads. He hoped no one came along to spoil the mood they shared so quietly. He squeezed her hand unknowingly. He heard a car coming up behind him. He would not let his body grow tense, even as he felt the hot glare on his back, felt the glare on both their backs. He

[377]

would walk relaxed. He was with his woman, and he would be a man, and if it were his night to die, then he would die like men must die when die they must. He would not crawl.

But he could not prevent his body warming and sweat pouring from his armpits. There was this moment when the headlights held them directly in their beams. Again he squeezed her hand unknowingly, as they kept walking up the road.

A voice from the automobile said, "Hey, you lovebirds, why don'chall get out the middle of the road?" Then the same familiar voice said, "Well I be doggone, the Devil! Chuck Othello and Bessie Mae—Whatchall doing out here this time of darkness? I betchall been registrating."

"You would win an easy bet," Othello said, as Lester Primrose brought his struggle-buggy to a choking-spitting-coughing stop. Lester had come into the Movement halfheartedly, but had gradually become one of the mainstays among the canvassers. He drove them all the way to Bessie Mae's and left them.

Now they stood alone and close together with the moonlight spilling upon the porch, and the rose bush and the honeysuckle making shadows and filling the air with a sweet perfume. He took her into his arms and took her lips to his happy lips and held them for a long sweet spell. And when she came up for air, she said, "Mister Chuck Othello Chaney!" With pretended indignation. But there was so much happiness in her voice he could hardly stand it.

She said, "How about let's making a little lemonade to cool things off a little bit?"

They must have both remembered the time, years before, when she had asked the selfsame question, because they both laughed together at the memory of it. Laughed at a time of their young lives gone forever, laughed at the day of their magnificent frustration. "We were too much!" he said huskily.

She laughed. "You ain't whistling 'John Brown's Body.'"

They walked now together through the front room to the kitchen. They made lemonade and they sat at the wooden table taking it into their overheated bodies. There seemed to be here in this room the same fragrance as before, the other time they made lemonade together. Her body smelling of newly roasted peanuts and fresh coffee cooking. He thought of burning leaves in autumn time. He stood and came toward her and saw the fear in her dark eyes that was there for one brief moment. He reached out and pulled her to her feet and into his arms and up against him, his mouth tenderly against her mouth, tongue to hungry, eager tongue, his chest against her deeply breathing breasts, taut and tightly nippled, his thighs hard against her thighs, his hand dug into her roundish buttocks, tight and tender to the touch.

"I love you," he said in a strange and froggy voice.

She said, "Chuck Othello, I've been waiting for you to say those words to me ever since I can remember."

He said, "I'm saying it, and I love you. Want me to say it again? I love you—I love you—I love you!"

And he took her in his arms again, and they kissed a feverish kiss again. Then he led her to the other room and laid her on the bed. She was trembling with excitement. He undressed her, and he kissed her on her lips again and nibbled at her swelling breasts. Then he hurriedly undressed and went to bed with her. This time he forgot he was the great expert. When he took her naked in his arms, he was an unsure anxious boy again. He didn't make love at her or to her, as so often is the case with men and women, boys and girls. But they made tender love together; they made love, the lovers, with each other.

They lay luxuriating now in the sweet afterglow of the love they'd made together. He said, "I want to marry you, little missy." He lay beside her naked, staring at the dark ceiling. He had never had such a feeling of complete contentment. He put his hand on her tightly swollen breast.

She said, "You don't have to say that, Othello." He felt her heart beating a mile a minute.

He said, "I know damn well I don't have to say it."

She said, "I mean, don't say it 'less you mean it. Don't say it just to make me feel good, or just cause you had a good time with me."

He said, "I'll say it if I want to, and because I want to and anytime I want to." He raised his voice. "I love you and I want to marry you. I love you and I want to marry you!" He got up out of the bed and went and flung the front door open and stood there naked, shouting: "I love you and I want to marry you! I love you and I want to marry you!" She leaped out of bed and ran laughing toward him. There was so much happiness in her laughter, he couldn't bear to listen to it. So much love and rapture in her face.

[379]

"Get out of that door naked, you crazy thing. You'll disgrace me with the neighbors!" She shut the door, and he gathered her into his arms. She felt him hard again, and fluttering against her.

"Will you marry me, woman, or won't you?" he whispered in a froggy voice. And for a brief and stupid moment he thought possibly there was someone else. Possibly he had waited too long to ask the sixty-four-thousand-dollar question. He said, "Don't you want to?"

She said, "Othello! Othello! If I ever wanted to do anything more than I want to marry you, I can't remember what it was."

"What's the matter then? What's the holdback?"

"I thought, I mean, I thought you just said it, just to be saying something after what we just did together. I mean I just couldn't bear for you to play with me about something like this. I mean, if I found out you were playing me for a good thing, I mean, I just don't know what I *wouldn't* do."

He said, "I want to marry you, and if you want to marry me, well then, that settles it. All we have to do is name the date."

She said, "Othello, we will wait until you finish at the University."

He said, "I don't want to wait that long. Let's get it over with next week."

She said, "When you get married, you don't get it over with, you just begin it."

He said, "Baby, you know what I mean. Let's get the ceremony over with, so we can begin the marriage. I'm just dying to be married to you, with you."

They talked about it late into the night as they lay beside each other on her bed. She told him she had bided her time for all these years (she was only twenty-two). She could wait another ten months. She told him how she had tried to keep up with him by reading every book that she could beg, steal, or borrow. She wanted him to be proud of her. But she wanted to do nothing to stand in his way of a University education. They argued quietly about it.

But she was adamant.

Chapter
2

Fear and tension stalked the bayous, stalked the Delta and the lowlands, like creatures in a deadly jungle. Stalked the bush of Mississippi. In Wakefield County, men walked with fear, lived with fear, ate with fear and tension. Fear stalked them like their own shadows, stuck as close to them as their summer drawers. And now and then fear and tension collided and erupted into violence. Even as most black and responsible leaders preached nonviolence, white violence exploded in their faces.

"Love your enemies!"

Preach the gospel, brother!

"Pray for him who spitefully abuse you!"

Yes! Yes! Yes!

One evening a few of the brothers and sisters met in the back of Josh Hemlock's store with all the shades pulled down. Before they could get into a discussion of ways and means of stepping up voter registration, Josh Hemlock told them he had something to say to them before the meeting began. He had written his statement down on a little piece of paper.

Even with an electric fan hanging from the ceiling and going a mile a minute, his forehead bubbled with perspiration before he began to speak, and the hand in which he held the paper was trembling. His light-brown face was a terror-stricken mask. He swallowed his spittle and cleared his throat.

He said, "All of you have known me all my life. Fact of the business, some of you have known me longer than I've known my own self. And which I want you to know that I'm with you all the way. And which the race must stick together, and when one of us progress the rest of us progress. When one of us is discriminated, all of us suffer discrimination. We all of us in this thing together, swim or sink, through thick and thin."

He pulled a white handkerchief out of his back pocket and

wiped his face where the sweat was pouring now. Both armpits of his white shirt were stained with sweat.

Reverend Purdy said, "We know you with us, brother."

Hemlock continued. "I'm with you every step of the way, except when it comes to this new thing, this violence and Black Power."

Reverend Purdy said, "What is your problem, brother? We are a nonviolent organization."

Hemlock's face was paler than it had ever been. His hand shook so, he held the paper down to his side. "But the Elders for Protection," he mumbled.

"This is a meeting of the Wakefield County Civic Association, Brother Hemlock, and we pursue a policy of nonviolence. It's in our Constitution."

"Nevertheless," Hemlock said heatedly, "I see some Elders here this evening, and——"

Reverend Purdy said, "We do not bar Elders from our membership. Yet and still, the fact of their membership does not change the Association into a non-violent organization, any more than a few black folk joining the Wakefield Democratic Party would change it into a black political organization."

"I can't help that, Reverend Purdy," Hemlock insisted. "Will you please let me finish my statement?"

"My pleasure, Brother Hemlock."

Hemlock's hands shook so, he had to hold the paper in both of them. "Due to the constant threats on the lives of me and my family, due to the threatened boycott of me by many of the wholesale dealers in the state, I, Joshua Hemlock, do herewith resign from membership in the Wakefield County Civic Association and request that its members never meet in my store again." He mumbled the rest of it. "Signed, Joshua Harry Hemlock." And he turned to Reverend Purdy and handed him the paper.

There were shouts of "Uncle Tom!" and "handkerchief-head," but Reverend Purdy brought them to order again. Then he said to Hemlock, "I truly wish you would think this over carefully, and maybe recon——"

"I have already thought it over carefully, Reverend." Hemlock was smiling now, as if a great burden had been lifted from his slender shoulders, as perspiration of relief flooded down his face, and maybe he was crying too. Maybe tears were spilling from his eyes.

"Maybe you would want a little time to talk it over with your God?"

"I have already talked it over." He spoke in such a whisper now, they could hardly hear him. Yet they clearly heard him. "I wish you good people would leave the premises immediately, and please find it in your hearts to forgive me my trespasses."

"All right, brothers and sisters, let us forgive our brother, even as the Great Nazarene would have us forgive our enemies."

"Amen, Reverend Purdy!"

"Yes, my Lord!"

But one man mumbled, "A nigger ain't shit!"

Reverend Purdy said, "I'll entertain a motion to adjourn and reconvene tomorrow night at the Mount Moriah Baptist Church."

Somebody mumbled as they walked out of the store, "We oughta boycott the shit-colored bastard!"

Another agreed. "You mighty right! You can't trust them half-white ones no shape, form, or fashion!"

Another said, "He worried about the white man boycotting him. We'll show him what a boycott is!"

But they never got an opportunity to show Hemlock what a boycott was. Mr. Millgate saw black folk filing out of Hemlock's and got in touch with other white men. Mr. Millgate was a white insurance agent who collected mostly from a colored debit. And later that night about eleven o'clock, while Hemlock worked late with inventory, an automobile of courageous white men drove past the store and tossed a bomb and blew Joshua Harry Hemlock to that Land beyond the River that men called the Sweet Forever, that land where he would never be afraid again.

In his sermon the following Sunday, Purdy called on Negroes to defend themselves. "I am not preaching violence. I am not preaching hatred. But I am preaching self-defense." And the congregation said Amen. "I'm telling you, if you say you love your enemy who spitefully use you, and you don't love your brothers and your sisters and your loved ones and your own self, you're a liar and the truth is not in you." The congregation said Amen. "Hear me now. Hear me clearly. A man can't love nobody unless he's able to love himself. Hear me now. Hear me clearly. I'm preaching love, not hatred. And I'm telling you that love, like charity, must begin at home."

[383]

A sister shouted, "Preach it, Purdy! Preach it!"

"How'm I going to love Eastland, if I don't love Purdy?"

"Preach it!"

"How'm I going to love Mack Brady if I don't love Purdy?"

"All right, Reverend Purdy!"

"I'm preaching love. I'm preaching love so strong that it will settle for nothing short of love in return. I'm preaching total love."

"Yes!"

"Eternal love!"

"Yes, Purdy, preach it, darling!"

"Love everlasting!"

"Tell it all, Purdy! Don't hold nothing back!"

"But I'm not preaching unrequited love."

"Yes!"

"Because unrequited love is not total love."

"Preach!"

"Unrequited love is not love everlasting."

"Yes."

"Unrequited love is one-sided."

"Preach Christ, Reverend Purdy! And Him crucified!"

"And the Scripture tells us, love ye one another. And that's the kind of love I'm preaching this morning."

"Go ahead and preach it then!"

"I want you to love yourself so much you don't have to hate the other feller! I want you to love yourself so much that you're willing to lay down your life to save yourself. I'm talking about self-defense, not violence."

And the congregation said Amen.

Monday morning. The *Chronicle*'s leading editorial attacked the pastor of Mount Moriah Baptist Church for preaching violence and race hatred. Called on the good black folk of the county to continue to work in the old tradition for racial harmony and to reject this man, this black pretender. For he did not represent the teachings of the Lord and Savior. He was the Devil's delegate.

At the meeting of the Civic Association, Reverend Purdy told the brothers and sisters they must redouble their efforts to register the black folk of the county. "We must now begin to think in terms of running our own candidates."

[384]

Worried faces. Anxious faces. Faces glowing with agreement. Fear. Doubt. Hope. Faith. Did they dare to think in these terms? In Wakefield County? In Mississippi? They looked around at each other, then back at Purdy. Was he carrying things too fast? Four hundred years of bowing and scraping, of leaving white things up to white people (and politics was definitely white) could not be transcended overnight. It was a river that took years and years to navigate, if ever. First you had to work up enough courage and imagination to even think of trying to navigate it. And you kept such thinking to yourself. Then you had to figure out how deep the river was, how strong the current, how far away the other shore.

One brother said, "That's gon be a pretty tough row to hoe, Reverend Purdy."

"White folks ain't gon like it." Another brother shook his head.

Reverend Purdy said, "Did you think all this fighting and struggling over voter registration was just to keep the white man happy? Did you think all this sacrificing was to keep white folks in power? Is that why Luke Gibson gave up his precious blood? Black Power means love of our black selves. It means pushing our black selves up the ladder."

"I don't know. I just don't know."

"Are we a people sunk so low that we don't think we capable of running our own affairs? We got to always leave it up to white folks?"

"Black Power!" Jake Carson shouted like he'd just got new religion.

"Is there anyone here who think the black folks of Wakefield County couldn't put up a candidate for shaff better than the poor excuse we got now?"

Silence.

"Is there anybody here who thinks us black folk can't put forward a candidate for mayor better'n Mack Brady?"

A brother said, "That's still gon be a mighty tough row to hoe."

Before he knew it, Othello got to his feet and heard himself talking as if he knew what he was talking about. "Of course it's going to be a tough row to hoe. But we've been hoeing other people's rows all this time, it's time we hoed some of our own and for our own." Sweat pouring from all over him now. His voice was trembling. But he felt good talking with his people.

[385]

"The fields are fertile," he said. "The time is ripe right now to plant the seeds, if we ever intend to reap the harvest." He heard a few Amens now and Yes-my-Lords. "All this time we've been sowing for other men to reap. It's time now for us to lay in a crop of our own and plan ourselves to reap this harvest."

"Black Power!" Little Jake shouted.

Somebody took up the chant.

"Black Power!"

"Black Power!"

"Black Power!"

Some faces were frightened even as they shouted Black Power, as if they uttered blasphemy, and perhaps they did. One brother got carried away and started shouting "Black powder! Black powder! Black powder!"

Another brother poked him in the ribs. "The slogan is Black Power, not black powder."

The other brother answered, "You gon need some black powder to back up Black Power, mean as these crackers is round here."

Joe Lumpkin raised his hand and got the floor. "I don't know about this Black Power to-do. We oughta give it a heapa studying before we jump into the water and find that old river too dog-gone deep. Mister Charlie Wakefield jest told me the other day. He said he didn't have nothing to do with it, but he thought we oughta take it a little easy with that there Black Power politic thing. And all of us know he the Negro's friend."

He sat down. There were many worried faces now. Even Wakefield was against it, and that was power, that was *the* white power. And Wakefield was not an ignorant peckerwood. He was the black man's friend.

Deacon Jimson got slowly to his feet. "I been studying this thing for more'n eighty years, and I done finally figured it out this way. The only way the black race can prosper is to listen carefully to what the white man say we oughta do, then head hell-bent cross the cotton patch in the opposite direction."

The meeting almost broke up with the laughter of agreement.

Chapter
3

The tension built quietly, steadily, in Wakefield County. Fear was as naked as the morning sunlight. White folk no longer looked black folk in the face when they met on the street. If an automobile backfired downtown in Wakefield City, people rushed out of the shops into the streets. Those who were already in the streets ran for cover. Black folk did not go into town unless they had definite business to attend to. Some white folk stared at Negroes, as if they were just seeing them for the very first time. Are these *our* Negroes, who were once so happy and contented? They look like our Negroes, but they sure don't act like them anymore. They don't talk like our Negroes. They don't even walk like them anymore.

It was a Thursday morning in July. At eleven-thirty, the temperature reached one hundred and five at the corner of Lee Boulevard and Jackson Street. The streets were empty except for a few white farmers who had come into town for one kind of business or the other. Some of them stood around at the street corners, as if waiting for something to happen. Not a black man was in sight, except Charles Othello Chaney. He had driven into town to take care of some business for Charlie Wakefield at the courthouse. He had parked the long steel-gray Cadillac in the courthouse square and had walked to the courthouse very much aware of the white scowls on the faces of the men he passed. Now as he walked down Rob Lee Boulevard heading for Douglass Avenue, where the colored businesses were located, he felt like a stranger in a hostile country. This is my town! he told himself. I was born here! Grew up here! There is nothing for me to fear here in this town. I know these people. These people know my people. They know me. This dialogue with himself did not kill the fear in him, the deep feeling of aloneness and isolation. He was a soldier in enemy territory. As he walked down

Lee toward Jackson, he saw the group of white and overalled farmers gathered at the corner. Somehow he felt a tension building up inside of him. His body seemed to have a mind of its own. Without him willing it, he felt his body stretching itself taller than before, and found himself walking straighter with his shoulders back like a soldier marching off to war. He was a half a block from them when he thought he heard the words "Black Power." He kept walking toward them with the perspiration pouring from all over him. When he had almost reached them, one of them spat the words out clearly and contemptuously.

"Black Power!" And he spat tobacco juice in front of Othello, missing him by inches. Othello did not slow up his pace. He kept walking past them, shaking with anger now, but glad the spit had not landed on him, because he knew that he would have died there in the 'Sippi sunlight in the blazing heat of morning.

In the barber shop on Douglass Avenue, he sat in one of the barber chairs and stretched his long hot body and sighed a deep and lasting sigh, and felt the tension oozing out of him. He listened to the buzzing of the electric clippers and almost fell asleep, except that he was too awake to fall asleep. His barber and his preacher was the selfsame man. Reverend Purdy. Besides preaching, Reverend Purdy was a businessman, one of the few black businessmen in Wakefield City. He ran a combination barber shop and shoe repair business. And he cut hair in the first chair of his barber shop.

Reverend Purdy was giving him a haircut and talking to him about college. "Son, they sure made a man outa you. And, what I mean, a good man. And I mean, we need some educated Negroes down here like old folks need soft shoes in the middle of the wintertime."

Othello felt humble and at the same time felt important. Damned important. "We need good men all right," he said. "I don't know whether I fit the bill or not."

Reverend Purdy said, "Yes sir, I know your mama and daddy proud of you, cause I'm so proud of you my own self. I just hope you don't put us down after you get educated and all that. I hope you stay with us and stand by us. But I wouldn't blame you if you told old 'Sippi goodbye and fare-you-well. I declare I wouldn't."

Othello thought of Sherry Kingsley and New York City so

many million miles away and years ago, it seemed. He started to say to his pastor that he would never leave the county, for good, that is. This was where his struggle was. He didn't get his speech together, because at that moment a white man came into the shop carrying a briefcase.

"Morning, preacher," the white man said, pleasantly and friendly-like.

"Morning. I don't b'lieve I need anything today," Reverend Purdy said.

"But I got something real special to show you," the salesman said, opening his briefcase and taking out a bottle.

"I don't believe I need a thing today," Reverend Purdy repeated.

"This is some brand-new slickum stuff. Make the boys irresistible to the womenfolks."

"Not today. I don't b'lieve I need a thing today." Spoken calmly.

"Whatchoo mean you don't need none today? You ain't never seen this stuff before. I know these boys like to have their hair nice and slick and straight. This stuff will make their's straight as mine is."

"Not today." Still calmly.

"Now come on. What yaller gal can resist a straight-haired black boy?"

Othello could hear the smoldering anger in his pastor's voice. The white man was about thirty-five years old and moustached and skinny-mouthed and getting terribly red in the face.

Reverend Purdy repeated, "Not today."

"All right then, I got here some new skin lightener. 'High Yaller' is the name for it."

"No 'High Yaller' today. No indeed. No 'High Yaller,' no 'Slickums,' no nothing. Not today."

"No hard feelings," the salesman said. "I be back to see you Thursday after next. I reckon with all this talk about Black Power, y'all don't want to be white folks no more." He laughed aloud. "Speaking of Black Power, my nephew was driving out on Route Forty-Five the other day. He won't doing over seventy miles a hour, when one of these promotion-happy speed cops hailed him down and gave him a long talking to and then had the nerve to give him a ticket. Can you beat it? What is this world coming to? Put them in a uniform and they think they over God Almighty. I reckin that's white power, ain't it? Now what do you think of that? And my own nephew!"

Reverend Purdy said, "Well I just declare." And let it go at that.

After the man had gone, Reverend Purdy said, "Ain't this a shame before the Lord. White folks are the most. It's getting harder and harder to be polite to them people. He expects me to sympathize with his nephew cause the police give him a ticket. What if I'da had a nephew and the cop had caught him doing seventy miles an hour. Probably woulda give him seventy days. Reminds me of the story of the backwoods preacher when the cycloon had done hit the town. Blew everything every which-away. He preached about it. He told the congregation, 'Y'all better git down on your knees and pray. Cause if a sow-coon could cause this much destruction, just imagine how much hell a boar-coon would've raised!' "

The barber shop exploded with laughter.

It was a hundred and six all day long and along about evening it cooled off and down to about an even one hundred. Hot. Sticky. Mosquitoes. A million different kinds of bugs. That night, at a meeting called by the White Citizens Council in the park in the grove by the river, the good, simple, God-fearing white folks of Wakefield County were on their feet and cheering wildly as Rab Johnson shouted the precious words at them. "It's been over a hundred years, but we'll never give up the struggle till old Jeff Davis and Rob Lee are vindicated! We will not let them Commonize the Southland. Our niggers don't want it nohow! And we'll starve their black bellies to death if they get any Northern notions!" The good people were on their feet now, and cheering wildly, men, women and children, waving miniature flags of the proud Confederacy. And rebel yells and singing, as the band played good old "Dixie" loud and strong.

Later that same evening close to midnight, the same voice is speaking hoarsely, telling a chosen few, the elite of Wakefield County that they were all sworn to secrecy. By the blood of Jesus which is the symbol of the Christian world. By the blood of the men who laid down their lives that the Southland might be free. This backroom of the Finley Hardware Store is dimly lighted by a lantern, and none of the fifteen gathered there can see each other's face clearly. They put their hands out toward each other in a ritualistic handshake.

Rab Johnson speaks slowly and precisely. "We've raised the two-thousand-dollar kitty, and now it's time to draw the straws." He looks from face to silhouetted face. "If anybody within the sound of my voice wants to chicken out at this last minute, I wantchoo to put your tail between your legs and run off right now, or forever hold your peace. Just get up and walk and keep your mouth shut tight, and no hard feelings." He stares again at them from face to face, and most of them seem calm to him from what he can see of their dimly lighted faces. However, there are at least two sweaty foreheads—very very sweaty foreheads.

"Are you ready?" Rab Johnson asks them in a husky voice.

Yes, they are ready.

Now he repeats what they already knew. "The one that draws the shortest straw gets the honor of liquidating the preaching nigger."

The straws are handed out. Johnson keeps one for himself. Each man holds up his straw for the group's examination. One of the sweaty foreheads has drawn the shortest straw. And now sweat drains from all over him. Sweat stains the armpits of his white shirt. He wipes sweat from his forehead, but it remains as wet as ever. His name is Ross Ludlow and he is a small plantation owner and runs a hardware store of medium proportions. He is not a political man, and doesn't feel strongly enough about the colored question to go through all the changes required. He had refused to join the Citizens Council at first, but through cajoling and sweet-talk and threats from some of his best friends, he had run out of words to express the reasons for not joining. Rab Johnson told him once (jokingly, of course), "Man, you so chicken-hearted, you wouldn't harm a nigger if you caught him raping your only daughter." In any event, he had made a choice. He had finally joined the Council and gradually had become a part of its inner circle.

He stands up and looks down and around at the others. They stare back at him, relief on all of their faces now. He is *it*. He has no stomach for this kind of business, and they know it. "I didn't count on murder when I joined the Council," he says quietly. "I didn't count on that at all. That ain't in our Constitution."

Johnson and a couple of others laugh at him. "Two thousand

dollars'll get you in the black, you lucky dog!" Ross Ludlow's comrades roar with laughter.

Much later that night, early morning, three-thirtyish, the telephone rang in the darkened house of Reverend Purdy. He got out of bed and was immediately wide-awake. He picked up the phone. "You damn no-gut peckerwood, I'll meet you anytime anyplace, you got something you want to say to me." He had been getting phone calls like this off and on for six months now, calls threatening his life, and uttering all kinds of obscenities to him or his wife or whoever happened to answer the phone.

The froggy voice on the other end belonged to Ross Ludlow. "This is Mister Ludlow, Reverend Purdy, and I want you to meet me in back of Johnson's Warehouse in about twenty-five or thirty minutes."

"What in the devil you calling me this time of night for?" Purdy asked him.

"I just got to see you, Purdy, and this is the only way that I can do it." His voice was quiet desperation.

Purdy said, "You must be done lost your mind, or you must think I have."

Ludlow pleaded. "It's a matter of life and death. And it just can't wait. It's just got to be tonight."

Thoughts leapt around in Reverend Purdy's mind like grasshoppers in the hot sunlight. "And another thing, you must come all by your own self. Don't bring nobody with you."

The city was a complete blackout as he drove toward the business district. When he got to Johnson's Warehouse, he got out of the car and looked around him. As he turned and walked toward the area behind the warehouse, ominous shadows of other men followed him, closed slowly in on Reverend Purdy. When he reached the back of the warehouse, Ludlow walked out of the shadows toward him, as Reverend Purdy stood his ground, tentatively poised for action to defend himself.

Ludlow was talking as he walked up to Reverend Purdy. Talking scared. "You just got to stop stirring up these nigrahs, Reverend Purdy. And you better stay out of this voting mess. Best thing for you to do is to leave Wakefield County tomorrow. You in big trouble."

Reverend Purdy stared at the white man unbelievingly.

The man went on and on. "I'm just going outa my way to give

[392]

you a friendly warning. Git outa town and git while the gitting is good!"

Purdy would not believe what he was hearing. He could not be in this place this time of night. It was a scene he'd conjured in one of his nightmares. He had had a few lately. But the man was here and his voice was real. "Is this what you got me outa my bed this time of night for?"

"Yes, and for this." And Ludlow reached into his pocket and took the straw out and haltingly told Reverend Purdy about the plot against his life. Reverend Purdy stared at the little soft-faced white man, speechless for a moment. Then he felt relief pour through him like ice-cold lemonade. Finally he said softly, "Thank you, Mister Ludlow. God will bless you."

Ludlow said, "Don't trust any white man in this town. Don't care who he is."

Reverend Purdy smiled at the little white man. Ironically. "That sounds like some mighty good advice, Mister Ludlow."

Ludlow said, "Fact of the matter, you were a damn fool, if you'll pardon me, for coming out here this time of night to meet a white man all by your own self."

The preacher laughed at the white man softly. "Fact of the business, you mean, I *would've* been a fool to come out here all by my lonesome." He waved his hand toward the darkness, and it was like Moses waving his staff at the Red Sea. Black men walked toward them out of the shadows.

A few nights later, Ludlow locked up his store and went around the back to his car. He reached for the car door, but never reached it. Because hands reached out for him. White hands in the black dark. They beat him up with a baseball bat and pistol-whipped him and told him he'd better not let next Thursday's sun go down with him still in Wakefield County.

He did not wait till the next Thursday.

Chapter
4

One morning the Old Man had a heart-to-heart talk with Othello, seated in Wakefield's office in the business wing of the new Big House. "Take my advice, Othello, and stay away from it. It's heading into a real blowup. And someone is going to get hurt real bad."

"I don't know what you're talking about, sir."

"You think I don't know what you're up to, boy? I know every single move you make."

Othello's body grew hot all over. "I still don't know what you're talking about."

"I'm talking about politics. I'm talking about all this Black Power business. Stay out of it, I tell you. Forget about it. And go back and finish your last year in college."

"If you're talking about voter registration, sir, I——"

The Old Man slapped his desk with the palm of his hand. "I'm talking about the whole damn mess! You stay out of it, you hear me? I'm telling you for your own benefit. You think these white peckerwoods are going to stand around and let you people elect a black mayor and a black sheriff?"

"It isn't a matter of what they'll stand for," Othello told him. "It's a matter of majority rule. A matter of who gets legally elected. That's supposed to stand for something in a democracy."

"Now you listen to me, boy. I didn't want to interfere with your activities, although I knew you were going off half-cocked. I sat back and watched you, thinking you would finally come to some conclusions all by your own self. But time has just about run out."

Othello started to interrupt, but Wakefield waved his hand. "Oh naw, you just hold your water a second and listen to me. I've been in this world a little longer than you, Othello. I look upon you almost like you were my very own son."

[394]

Othello said quietly, "I have a father, sir." He smiled sarcastically.

The Old Man said, sentimentally, "I've known your daddy all my life. We grew up together in this very county. He's always been like one of the family."

The image of his father passed before Othello. He stared at Wakefield incredulously, suddenly understanding that Wakefield actually believed at least half of the crap he was putting down. He laughed at the "one of the family bit," remembering a book he'd read last semester written by Alice Childress. Like one of the family. Yeah. Like one of the goddamn family.

"Go ahead and laugh, Othello," Wakefield said. "I know you young people have outlawed sentimentality, but it used to be important. There used to be good feelings between white and black right down here in Wakefield County. And in a house like this we were always just as close as kinfolks. Black and white, it didn't seem to make much difference in those days." The Old Man took a handkerchief out of his pocket and wiped his eyes and blew his nose.

Othello wanted to howl with laughter. He thought, an Oscar performance. The Old Man could have made it in the movies. He was a natural-born actor. But was the Old Man really acting? Could he possibly be for real? "It didn't make much difference to you, sir, because white was always on top and black was on the bottom, but when black folks begin to say, get off my back, white folks, I'm tired of carrying you, then white folks get all shook up. And that's what Black Power is all about. Nothing else. To get white folks off our backs. We don't want to be like one of the family. We want to uplift our own families."

The Old Man spoke hardly above a whisper now. "All right," he said, "Negroes have a right to achieve everything you say. There's no doubt in my mind about it. But we have to give these ignorant peckerwoods time to get used to the idea, so they can make an honorable retreat. We got to educate them gradually. It takes time. That's all I'm saying."

"Time has run out already, Mister Charles."

As if he had not heard Othello, Wakefield said, "You think I care a damn about these poor-ass ignorant peckerwoods? There's a whole heap of colored folk I think more of than this white trash in this neck of the woods. I didn't send one of them to college, did I?"

[395]

"Thank you kindly," Othello said.

"All this crap about would you want one of them to marry your daughter. Well, let me tell you one thing, the blackest boy in Mississippi has as much chance of marrying my daughter as one of them has."

Othello smiled sarcastically, remembering the apartment in the Village in the city and the old man's precious darling daughter. He started to say, "I don't want to marry your daughter, pops." He said, instead, "Marrying the white man's daughter is not a part of the Black Power program."

"I know," he said. "That's my point. But you can't convince the ignorant peckerwood. All I'm saying is, I'm with the colored people all the way. But I'm saying, go slow. I'm saying, let the idea sink in first. I'm saying it's a bitter pill. Give them time to swallow it, digest it. Give them time to come to think it was their idea in the first place."

Othello shook his head from side to side. "Black folks today are in no mood to humor white folks. We have no patience any longer. You have no right to ask such patience of us. We will not wait another hundred years."

"Willie Faulkner was a friend of mine. He used to visit at the other house. All I'm saying is what he advocated. Take it easy right along in here, or else even if you win, there'll be bitterness for centuries. Even Lillian Smith——"

Othello said "There's already been bitterness for centuries, but all of it's been in the black man's mouth." He thought to himself, Why am I here trying to convince this white man? A total waste of energy. A criminal waste!

"Will you listen to me, boy? Your Black Power doesn't frighten me, or threaten me. The only reason I'm wasting my time trying to talk some sense into your head is because of my concern for you and your family. Let me say it plainly. A group of white men came to see me yesterday and told me that if you people didn't let up there would be bloodshed."

Othello laughed bitterly. "You mean there's been no bloodshed up till now?"

"They asked me specifically to speak to you. And here is a chance you have to serve your people and all the people of Mississippi and the nation. Tell them to let up on this voter registration and this Black Power business. Let's have a moratorium, a cooling-off period."

"In the first place, I don't have any such power to change black folks' minds in the county. Second, if I did have it, I wouldn't use it to placate peckerwoods, who are never going to be placated anyhow."

The Old Man was perspiring now in his chilly air-conditioned office, and he was aging by the second. "I sent you through college. That ought to count for something. I sent you, because I wanted you to be better than the common run of blacks around here. I wanted you to be a good influence on them, a moderating influence."

"Thanks a lot," Othello said. "That's why I'm not going back next year." He had never said it out loud to himself before. That if he went back to his final year in college, it would be because he could pay his own way. It would be on his own terms, under his own steam.

"You've changed," the Old Man shouted. "You have no humility whatever."

"That's your reward for sending me to college. Right? I changed. That's what colleges are for, isn't it?"

"I had such high hopes for you," the Old Man said hoarsely. "I wanted you to lead your people away from the ways of these radicals who've taken over. I wanted you to lead them on the peaceful road to freedom. They told me you wouldn't appreciate what I was trying to do. They told me, 'Educate a nigger and he'll show his black ass every time.' They told me, but I told them you were different. I've even been called a nigger-lover. And this is the reward I get. This is the way you show your gratitude."

The Old Man was on the verge of tears. Othello was angry and embarrassed. He stood. "There's some business I have to take care of, Mister Wakefield," he said absently.

"Martin King is absolutely right. If black men imitate these ignorant peckerwoods and sow the seeds of hate and violence, all of us will reap a bitter crop for generations yet unborn. King is a saint sent by God to save all of us Southerners from ourselves. Sent to save the entire nation. We're at the abyss, Othello. There is a famine of love in the land. What if Gandhi had preached hatred? Where would India be today? Don't laugh, boy. What we plant now in the field of human relations, we will reap for a hundred years and more. Can't you see it, boy? Martin Luther

[397]

King is the last clear chance for the entire human race. And as far as Black Power is concerned, it's just as immoral, just as un-Christian as white power. You can't have your cake and eat it too." The Old Man had run out of breath.

Othello said heatedly, "I don't have to stand here and listen to you blaspheme the name of Martin Luther King. Whatever disagreements I might have with him, he is still blood of my blood and flesh of my black flesh. And he is my brother; he *is not* your nigger. He is not your Gunga Din." In the bygone days of his youth, in the days of hopelessness of his childhood, Martin Luther King had been the first voice in that vast wilderness to reach him way down in the cotton fields of 'Sippi, as his heart and soul remembered it. For there had been a famine of hope and inspiration, and the name of Martin Luther King had brought them Good Hope—faith. Martin had been, and still was, his patron saint, and he would not hand him over to the white establishment.

The Old Man said, "Have compassion for the poor-ass pecker-woods, son. Forgive them, for they know not what they do."

Othello laughed openly at Wakefield. He could not restrain himself. He stopped and stared at him. "You got to be joking." But he knew the man was serious.

The Old Man shouted, "Don't you see, you fool? There's going to be shooting in the streets of Wakefield City and all along the dark roads. All over Mississippi. Shooting and killing. And the blood will be on your hands. And probably your own blood——"

"Don't talk to me about it, Mister Wakefield. Go talk to your poor-ass peckerwoods. They're the ones that always start it. And when they do, we ain't about to forgive them, cause they know damn well what they're doing. And if they don't, we'll damn sure teach them."

"Nothing can stop it, unless you slow up on this Black Power! This spreading racial hatred!"

"You'd better tell them, Mister Wakefield; black folks got a hunting license too."

The Old Man said, "Just when we're on the verge of arriving at some understanding, just when we're about to get the average Mississippian to accept the inevitability of integration, here you-all come with something different, Black Power! I'm with

[398]

you, son, you know that, but Black Power is another peck of peas altogether. Tell them for me, son. Tell the black folks of the county I'm working for them day and night. But they simply must not rock the boat."

It was one of the rarest moments of great clarity for Othello. He smiled at the Old Man sarcastically. "Rocking the boat—why should we black folk be worried about rocking the goddamn boat, when we're not even in the boat, but drowning in the open sea? Our job is to capsize the boat—and build another one with accommodations for everybody."

The Old Man was standing now. His face was ashen. "But can't you see, if it comes to that, I'll have to join up with the peckerwoods and shoot down Negroes on the streets of Wakefield City."

"At last we understand each other," Othello told him grimly, almost happily. He felt the Old Man had at long last emancipated him. Thank you, Massa. Now there need be no subtleties between us. We both know where our basic loyalties are. "Thank you for drawing the demarcation lines so clearly. You with yours and I with mine."

The Old Man said, "Don't fool yourself, boy. Willie Faulkner was right. My own Negroes will join up with me and kill other Negroes. All I got to say is, 'Come on boys, pick up your guns and follow me.' "

Othello laughed at Wakefield angrily. "You'd better say you reckon, Jimmy Dick."

It was the hottest night in the memory of anybody living in the county. His mother and father were seated in the backyard trying desperately to keep cool and to keep from being eaten alive. A thousand mosquitoes must have had the same idea (keeping cool, that is), except that they apparently meant to keep cool on the warm blood of his mother and father. Othello stood tall and naked in a washtub in the darkness of the kitchen, which still functioned as his bath-and-bedroom. He soaped himself down from head to foot and thought about the voter registration meeting at the church. One day, goddammit, he would have a bathroom with a real bathtub and shower. He reached for a pitcher of cold water and poured it slowly down his body from top to bottom. It was his second bath in a single day. His mother had said laughingly, "Boy, you gon wash yourself away you don't

[399]

mind out." There was a time when people in the county bathed once a week, Saturday nights only. He smiled. He remembered. Through the week you just washed your face and neck and ears and underneath your arms. He laughed quietly, remembering a joke his father used to tell about an old lady who got sick and sent for the doctor. The doctor sniffed at the lady as she lay in bed and asked her, "Have you bathed recently, Madam? The old lady said, "This morning I washed down as far as possible and I washed up as far as possible." The doctor sniffed at her again and told her, "Next time, Madam, please make sure that you wash *possible*."

The cold water splashed down Othello's long and lanky body and rivulets of coolness spread out across his back and shoulders and down his thighs and long legs, wave after wave. His entire body tingled. His mind recapitulated his scene that day with Jimmy Dick. Somehow he was glad it had happened. Grimly happy that everything was out in the open now. He stepped out of the tub and wiped himself down with a large white towel and began to sweat all over again. The more he wiped, the more he perspired. It was an exercise in frustration. He heard an automobile pull up to the front of his house and stop. And heard his heart begin to pound. He jumped into his trousers and ran into the front room and pulled the shade aside and stared out at the darkness. He felt a great relief as he watched a woman get out of the car and walk toward the house. He was getting too jumpy here of late. He had to calm down a little, or he wouldn't make it through the long hot summer. Take it easy, Greasy. You got a helluva long ways to slide. He wondered absently who the woman was. There was something familiar about her walk. Like she owned the earth she walked upon. Then as she entered the yard, his heart began to pound again, and new sweat broke out all over him. What the hell was a white woman doing coming to his house this time of night? Probably somebody to see his mother. Sometimes white folks got his mother to do a little sewing for them. But then he thought his heart had stopped beating completely, and the bottom had dropped out of his stomach, when he recognized the walk and face, as she came up on the porch. What in the hell was Carrie Louise doing at his house this time of night? He retreated to the kitchen and put on his shirt and stood there in the dark listening to her knocking at the front door.

[400]

His mother called from the backyard. "You gon answer the door, Othello? You through taking your bath?"

"Yes m'am." He walked back into the front room and pulled a string that switched on the light of the single bulb that hung from the ceiling. He opened the door and let the white girl in.

"Good evening, Othello."

"Good evening!" He closed the door behind her and turned to face her. "What in the hell you want?"

"Aren't you going to offer me a sitdown?" she said with a frightened smile on her face.

"You want to see my mother about something?" he asked angrily.

"No," she said with a nervous giggle. "I came to see Mister Charles Othello Chaney." She was scared to death and trying to cover it up with smiling. Like whistling in a lonesome graveyard.

He spat the words at her. "Miss Carrie Louise Wakefield, you just do me one big favor, honeychild, and take your white backside back where you belong!"

She said, "Thanks for offering me a chair, Mister Chaney." She sat. And she carefully sat carelessly, her dress well above her knees, halfway up her thighs. With all the heat and tension in the county, this was all he needed.

He said, "Lady, you are definitely not welcome. Like please go quietly in a great big hurry."

"I want to help your people," she said. "I want to join the Movement."

"What old movement?" he asked. "I don't know anything about any movement you might want to join."

"I want to help with voter registration," the girl said.

"The only way you can help me or the Movement is to stay the hell away from me and to stay the hell away from the Movement."

She shook her yellow head at him. "You don't understand me at all. After all these years, you don't understand me. I want to help. I honestly and truly want to help. Black Power doesn't scare me away. I feel it's my mission in life to help the poor downtrodden——"

"You want to do missionary work?" he said. "You really do want to do missionary work, right? Okay. Go among the savages and spread the light. I mean, amongst the poor-ass peckerwoods. Open their eyes—teach them which side their bread is buttered

[401]

on. Go to the rich white folks too. That's the real contribution you white missionaries could make to the Movement—to Christianize the white savages, the poor-ass peckerwoods, and the rich ones. Preach Christ to them, and *Him,* black and beautiful, and *crucified!*"

She hadn't understood a word he'd said.

"I know," she said. "I understand." She got up and started toward him. "You do care about me, Othello. You want to protect me from myself. You think if I join the Movement I'll be hurt in the crossfire. But I don't want to be protected. That's the trouble now—I've been sheltered all my life."

He almost laughed out loud at the crazy girl. Shee-itt! White folks were the everlasting most. They still clung desperately to the notion that black folks loved them better than they did themselves. He would have laughed, had she not come so close to him, had he not suddenly realized she meant to put her head on his shoulders, in Wakefield County in the backwoods of old 'Sippi!

He shoved her violently away from him. "You got to be out of your mind!" His voice was a shouted whisper. His body shook with fear and anger. "Get the hell out of here and don't come back!" He heard the motor of another car coming closer every second. What if some no-good cracker came smelling around and saw the Jaguar outside and recognized it, and found this white girl in the house with him, this rich white girl, this purest of all symbols of Southern Womanhood? He could not hear the car any longer. Had it stopped outside, or had it gone about its business?

His mother's voice almost made him jump out of his skin. "Who that in there with you, Othello?"

Before he could answer, his mother and father were coming through the kitchen. When they came into the room, his mother exclaimed, "What in Jesus's name is you doing here, child?"

And Carrie Louise said, "Aunt Carrie!" and ran into his mother's arms. "Aunt Carrie! Aunt Carrie! Aunt Carrie! Aunt Carrie!"

His mother said, "What's the matter, child? Something happened at the house?"

The white girl blurted words out now, incoherent, all mixed up with sobbing. He watched her rooting herself into his mother's arms, weeping like a baby on his mother's breast. He almost felt compassion for her. Straw-haired white girl weeping in his mother's arms.

"What's the matter, child?" he heard his mother say, stroking the white girl's head gently. He almost felt compassion, but then he remembered another time a hundred years ago it seemed, yet somehow just like yesterday. A black boy and a white girl, five or six years old. "Let's play Mama and Papa." Upstairs in a guest room in the old Big House. His mother pulling him from atop the white girl. Stripping him naked and whipping him till the blood came. He remembered later the same day, the white girl came running to his mother. Weeping in her arms, on her black breast, just as now. "There now, child. There now, baby!" It was as if nothing had changed. As if time had somehow passed and yet stood still. He remembered the little black boy's feeling of jealousy and anguish and even hatred toward his mother and the straw-haired white gal.

He heard his mother now, as if he were coming out of a deep sleep which had lasted all of fifteen or sixteen years. "There now, baby. There now, child." When he was five, he had softly shouted, "I'm your baby! I'm your child! Not that old white gal!" But his mother hadn't listened to him.

This time his mother heard him. This time he said, "Turn her loose, Mama, and let her get the hell outa here. You are not her mammy anymore!"

His mother looked at him, as she massaged the white girl's head with her black muscle-bound hands, gently stroked the white girl's head. "You ain't never spoke like that to your mother, Othello. Is that what they teached you at the University?"

His voice trembled with his anger. And he demanded anger from his mother against this goddamn sick white world. His heart, his soul, demanded anger from her. But his mother had a face that was never ever really harsh. Of late, she seemed to live in tender shadows and soft reflective meditations.

"Mama, you have to make a choice this very moment. You are either my mother or her mammy. You can't be both any longer."

Her face did not change expression. It was a face above which storm clouds always hovered. The torrents in her life had through the years constructed trenches in her cheeks down to the corners of her mouth. Her heart had lived with stormy

[403]

weather, all the more reason for demanding anger from her. She was old. She was his mother but she was of the ancient ages. She said quietly, "There ain't no cause for you to act disrespectful to your mother. Don't care how big you done growed, you ain't grown yet. And even if you is grown, I can still slap you down a peg or two."

"Mama, you have not answered my question. Are you going to be my mother, or are you going to suckle this white wench at your black breast?"

She pushed the sobbing girl from her, gently, and moved toward her son and drew back her hand to slap him, but the blow never landed, because Jesse Chaney grabbed her arm. And now his thunder filled the room.

"Othello is a man, and you ain't gon treat him like a boy no more. And I'm waiting just like he is to hear the answer to his question."

She looked up into her husband's face, a face that had been conditioned through the years, had learned painfully never to show his inner feeling. Yet she felt his anger now, like a slap in her face. She felt both of her men's anger. And she didn't understand it and had not the strength to do battle with it. Somehow she saw, or felt, the deep truth of their anger.

"I still wants to know whether you Othello's mama, or *her* mammy. I also wants to know whether you my wife or her auntie. You damn sure can't be both, cause I don't reckon to be married to no woman that got white folks in they family."

Carrie Chaney looked from Jesse to Othello and back to Jesse again. She knew the truth they spoke between them, felt it sharply in the depths of her, cutting her loose forever from every mooring of the past. If you grew up in Mississippi, certain things were fixed forever. Black and white were fixed forever. And here came this new generation with this new thing and everything was changed forever. She was in the swampland of a Mississippi bayou, and the bayou was there and had always been there and would always be there, only suddenly it had turned to sinking sand. She had a choice. To sink forever or to reach the high ground where her two men stood with their hands reached out toward her to haul her in. But she had to make the effort. They would not leap into the quicksand with her. She had to move toward them and they would haul her in. She turned toward the weeping white girl.

[404]

The girl started toward her. "Aunt Carrie——"

"I ain't your auntie, honey. I don't have no white kinfolks. You better get on home where you belong. God bless you. Heaven help you."

The straw-haired girl turned wearily away from Mama Carrie. She stared at Jesse Senior, then helplessly at Othello. Her pink face, losing color, was really white now, not unlike the white enamel of a white bathroom. She moved across the room toward the front door like a decrepit old woman. Frustrated, disappointed, defeated. She was like someone sleepwalking.

Othello fought violently against the compassion which he somehow felt for this straw-haired Princess from the Big House. Goddamn his softhearted time! That was the trouble with his people. Pity always bubbled in their bosoms. They were too goddamn softhearted, which, in the final analysis, made them softheaded too. Well he'd be goddamned if he would be softhearted, or softheaded. Get the hell out of my face, honeychile. Get further and smell better. He laughed harshly at the girl. He thought, Miss Rich Bitch, like let the doorknob hit you, where the bad dog bit you. He laughed again.

"She's a serious chick." He could hear the clear articulate voice of Sherry Kingsley. "Like she's so serious, sometimes she's a natural drag. Let her down gently, dear brave and gentle blackamoor—After all, she is a human peckerwood—contradictions and all that jazz—" was the way he remembered Sherry, standing at the great storm door on President Street in the Borough of Brooklyn in the County of the Kings.

Honeychile was at the front door, and she was a natural drag for real. Against his will he heard himself say hoarsely, "Carrie Louise—"

The sleepwalker turned toward him. She opened her mouth and worked her white lips but not a sound came out of them. The words clogged in her throat like a New York traffic jam.

He said, irritably, "Have a sitdown. Take the load off for a minute." He hated this soft thing inside of him.

It seemed the whole world was too much, was too confusing for the girl. Her mouth, her eyes expressed her wonder and her gratitude, but wordlessly. She sank into the nearest chair.

He said, "Sit down, Daddy and Mama Carrie. I mean, please, m'am—and please, sir."

They sat and stared at their Othello. He was their boy, grown

[405]

into full manhood, and he was in the driver's seat. All right, boy. Take charge, Mister Charles Othello Chaney. Teach us old heads how to do it.

Othello looked upon the pale-faced straw-haired girl. Against his will, he felt no need to beat her to the ground—and kick her. He wished he felt the way he thought he should have felt. Kick her in her natural ass! But she was already whipped. All of her haughtiness, all of her sophistication, all of her superior airs were gone like a puff of summer breeze down by the river-side. She looked like a whipped puppy about to lick her master's hand. He shook his angry head. Don't give me that pitiful routine, Miss Rich Bitch. You still got the world in a jug and the stopper in your hand. You look whipped now, but tomorrow morning when you wake up in the Big House, this will be just another episode in your holy quest for kicks. What could he tell her any-damn-how? What did he know?

He said, "Let's say you're serious, okay? Let's say you're the sincerest of them all. So what? What the hell's that got to do with the price of cotton or Black Power in the Mississippi bush? Okay, so your heart's in the right place. Every living's heart's in the right place, or else they wouldn't be living."

She searched Othello's face. "But you don't understand—I mean, I don't understand. I mean——"

He wanted to be patient, but there was a great heat in his voice. "All right, I know you don't understand. That's the big hang-up. No understanding whatsoever. But you're sincere, right? Like one of the family and all that jazz, right? That's why I'm going to try to break it down for you."

"You don't hate all white folks, do you Othello?"

"How could I hate you?" he said sarcastically. "After all your Great White Father has done for me? If I actually hated you, I wouldn't go to all this trouble trying to break it down for you, now would I?"

"You don't believe in collective guilt, do you, Othello? I mean, I've never done anything against your people."

He was losing patience. "I'm going to try to break it down for you, if you let me, but you're going to have to stop interrupting, cause I haven't much time. I have a very important engagement."

"All right, Othello."

"At this juncture in Operation Free 'Sippi, there must be a

division of labor. Sincerity, good intentions, trustworthiness have nothing to do with anything. When it comes to the question of Black Power, it is up to black people and only black people to organize their own. Right?"

The white girl whispered, "Right."

"Which means, for one thing, we do not need you to help in things like black folks' voter registration. Right?"

He could hardly hear her answer: "Right."

"It also means that white folks, who are really serious, will work with their own kind. Which means that here in Wakefield County to try at least to neutralize some of these peckerwoods. Right?"

The girl said, "I don't know—I just don't know."

"You say you believe in David Woodson, right?"

"Yes." A whisper. "He's an angel."

"Well, the last time I saw him, he told me he wished some of his white missionary friends would go and work amongst the white folks, who, after it's all said and done, are really the ones that need the civilizing—Christianizing, if you please. I mean, take Congressman Jefferson Davis Johnson for example. A throwback to the Neanderthal man, and there's not a damn white man or woman in the country who'll stand up against him and that ignorance-spreading rag of his, the *Chronicle*. Am I right or wrong?"

The girl squirmed around in the chair, as if bugs were in her underthings. "Yes—yes—you're right," she whispered. "Except perhaps my father maybe—" Her voice trailed off and he could hardly hear her.

"Your father? You got to be kidding. I mean I thought we were having a serious discussion. I mean, I saw your father and his cronies at the great big barbecue. Remember? I mean, talk about a den of thieves. And, Honeychile, they *were* as thick as thieves."

"Okay, you're right. There's nobody really standing up against Jeff Johnson and his *Chronicle*. Maybe that's what I can do. My father said once I could have my own newspaper. Maybe—" She was almost mumbling to herself.

He didn't hear the "Maybe that's what I can do" part, or the rest of it. He said, "You really want to contribute to Operation Free 'Sippi, right? Then go amongst the peckerwoods. Try to

[407]

neutralize the Klan, the White Citizens Council. Take civilization to the poor white trash."

The heat was heavy in the room now. Outside the symphony of night was well into its overture. Frogs, crickets, hooting owls. The girl was drenched with perspiration.

"But I can't work with those people. I despise the peckerwoods. I love your people, and I hate the Klan and all it stands for." She searched his face. She felt a great human warmth, as she remembered the profound warmth she had shared with him in New York in her aunt's apartment. How could he speak to her as if she were the enemy? Had it really meant so little to him?

She heard him, vaguely heard him say, "Love—hate—what's that got to do with anything? A total irrelevance in this fight to change the country. The thing is, it's both our country although it never belonged to me. Still it's mine, goddammit. It's our country, and you have your job and I have mine. Your job is with your people, and my job is with mine. Your job is to help get your people ready for this new world we're going to build, whether they like it or not. You don't expect me to do your work for you, do you? The only way a black man can educate a white man is to beat some sense into his head. That's the only thing he understands. Power—strength—violence."

"But they're not my people. Can't you see. They are not my people. I deny them! I despise them! You're my people. You, Aunt Carrie and Uncle——"

His mother said in a clear strong voice, "I ain't you auntie, sugar-pie."

She looked around at Mama Carrie. She looked up into Othello's face again. Her eyes in desperation begged him to give her some little indication that he remembered the things they had shared together, to give her some sign that he believed in her, believed there was some goodness in her somewhere beneath the whiteness of her skin. She said, "All right, Othello. All right. I reckon I know by now just how I stand with you and your family. You have poisoned them against me. I know how I stand with all the black folks in the county." She stood up wearily and turned toward the door. "I don't blame you. Why should you trust a mean ignorant cracker like me? I mean, a Mississippi peckerwood?"

He made his voice harden with sarcasm. "That's right. Go

home feeling sorry for yourself, you poor, poor, miserable Mississippi peckerwood. Go home and cry your poor little self to sleep in that twenty-three-room mansion. But every time I see you from now on, I'm going to ask you—what're you going to do with your own people, I mean the Mississippi peckerwoods."

She turned toward him again. "What do you want me to do? How shall I go about it?"

He said, "That's your problem, baby. They're your people. I got my hands full mobilizing my own. I mean I got no alternative but to mobilize my folks. But you—you can just go home to the Big House and forget it. And blame it on Black Power and the White Backlash."

She said, "My memory is not as shallow as you might imagine."

"What can I tell you?" he said. "You're a good kid. You mean well. Now go home and forget it."

She said, "My memory's not as short as you might think, Othello."

"All right," he said. "I don't blame you. I wouldn't want to be a white man in Mississippi either, or anywhere else. But what can you do? You're stuck with what you got. Every living human is. So you make the best of it. Like I say, you got alternatives. Like you can just plain forget it; you can join your kind against my kind, or you can work at humanizing your kind."

She looked down at the floor and back up into his face again, and all at once her face broke down, as suddenly she overflowed with anguish, and the dam broke loose and the tears flowed now in flood tide. "I don't know—I just don't know!" Crying, sobbing, talking, interchangeably. "I try so hard! I want to be a part! I want to understand! Lord knows I want to understand. This terrible hate you have for me and all white folks and especially for me—" Wiping her eyes now and blowing her nose. The tears still cascading down her face. "How can you keep me out like this? How can you hate me so? I'm not just any old white woman. I'm me, Carrie Louise Mariah Wakefield, your mother's namesake, whom you've known all your life. And the things we've done together—and you know I've always loved you—I mean, never hated you or any black folks."

He tried to shout above her hysteria. "I do not hate you, goddammit! Excuse me, Mama Carrie and Daddy. How many times do I have to say it? Love and hate haven't got a damn thing to do with it!"

Sobs still shook her entire body. "What's happened to everybody? I attended the Freedom School up in Jackson last summer, and each night we all joined hands together and sang, black and white together—we shall not be moved—we shouted, black and white, unite and fight. We worked together, black and white. We lived together like brothers and sisters. But what has happened to us now?"

He said, "Well—now it's time, way past time, for you to go into the white community with those songs and slogans and see how long you last."

She said, "Othello! Othello! Othello! What's the use? What's the use? If love is irrelevant, what's the use of anything?"

His voice hardened. "Collect yourself a group of well-meaning sincere-type white folks with a missionary zeal and go into the peckerwood neighborhoods and sing those songs and shout those slogans. I mean that black-and-white-together-jazz. And see how long you last. That'll be the test of its validity. And even if I loved you more than anything and anybody in all the world, I would still tell you the same damn thing. Understand?"

She had stopped crying now. She looked Othello in the face. The fog seemed to be slowly lifting in the swamp of her confusion, but the reality beyond the fog was hard for her to take. She said, "I don't know—maybe so—I mean—"

His voice filled with compassion now. "I truly think you're a great gal, I mean really a tremendous, I mean wonderful person, but it doesn't change a goddamn thing. The objective reality remains the same. I mean the real world is still out there in the cotton patches, in the Delta and the swamps and in the ghettos of the cities. The real world is still white, and it's white against the black. Ask your daddy, you don't believe me." His voice softened. "Sure there's room for white folks in the Movement. There's a job for you to do. But your job is with your people, giving them the word, spreading the light amongst the white folks. Understand?"

She looked into his face and away again. "I thought you'd thrown us out of the Movement. I thought we had no function anymore. I thought the Movement hated white folk now."

"But now you understand," he stated softly.

She whispered, "Yes—I think I understand. And thank you,

[410]

Othello, for your generous indulgence, I really mean it. And you too, Aunt, I mean Miss, Carrie, and Uncle, I mean, Mister Jess."

Othello answered, "It was nothing."

Jesse Senior said, "Don't mention it."

Mama Carrie said, "God bless you."

Chapter

5

They had come from all over the state to hear him, this black son of Mississippi. Had come to Oculmugee, Mississippi. Deep deep in the 'Sippi backwoods. Oculmugee's sole claim to fame was its famous son, David Woodson. Notwithstanding, white Oculmugeeans took a dim view of the fact that nobody had ever heard of the place before Dave Woodson told the whole world he had come from there. Born and raised up in the little factory town of sawmills and lumberyards. Compared to Oculmugee, even Wakefield City was a thriving metropolis.

The church was jam-packed. People standing in the aisles, all along the sides of the church and in the back. The church was a panorama of black and brown and light-brown faces, and even a few white faces, sprinkled like salt in the midst of all that pepper. And paper fans of all colors and descriptions waving back and forth. They had come from all over the state and even from beyond its borders. They had come to hear David Woodson. And now he stood before them in the pulpit. He was talking to his people.

"There is a rising storm throughout this land that will leave this nation a different place, when ultimately it blows out to sea."

"All right!" the black girl with the red hair shouted from the middle aisle. She was a student at Alcorn College.

Young folks, old folks, middle ages. Students, workers, cotton pickers, menfolks, womenfolks. Little children, babies.

"There is arising in this land, a renaissance of black consciousness."

[411]

"Have mercy!" the redheaded black girl shouted.

"The challenge to our generation is to lead the pilgrimage back to blackness."

A "sophisticated" black girl turned to a straw-haired white girl seated next to her. "Why does he insist on using the word 'black' so much?"

They had come to hear him, out of varying and varied motivations. Some came to hear the gospel according to Saint David. Some came out of curiosity. Some came to hear and see a famous Man, a celebrity, in much the way they would have showed up for the President of the United States.

"It's been almost four hundred years of alienation and self-hatred and denial. And now it is time to begin the journey home."

"Yes!"

Othello had driven from Wakefield City the day before with a group of Wakefieldians. He had spent most of last night talking with David Woodson over beer and a little corn whiskey. And soul food in a little eating joint about as big as one of the bathrooms in Jimmy Dick's house. It had been a memorable evening. Dave felt more like a brother to him than anything else. A big and famous wonderful brother. Othello's face beamed with pride and admiration as he listened to his "brother." A well-dressed young man seated next to Othello leaned toward him and whispered, "They couldn't get me back to Africa even if they drew a pistol on me. I ain't lost a damn thing in the jungle."

As if he overheard the young man, Dave Woodson said, "I am not at the moment talking about going back to Africa. Physically, that is. There are many ways to go back to Africa, other than on an ocean liner or by jet airplane. The question is—are we ready to make the trip back to the old country in our hearts and souls and minds? Are we ready to identify?"

Othello heard Little Jake shouting from the other side of the church. "Tell it all! Don't hold back nothing!"

Somebody yelled, "Little David, play on your harp!"

Last night in the "Nitty Gritty" (the name they gave the little soul café where they had supper and corn whiskey and reminiscence), they talked far into the night about the South, about 'Sippi, about Oculmugee where Dave had spent his childhood. He talked about the raging beauty of the Delta; he spoke of beautiful incidents of his childhood when no one but the "crazy"

[412]

questioned anything, when everything was settled forever in terms of black and white relations. He said it was like a tacit understanding between a husband and a wife. The husband went out and grew and developed and prospered and the woman's place was in the home. He said in the Southern situation the black man was cast in the role of the woman, who must always know her place and stay forever in it.

"Are we ready to go back to the old country of our black manhood and womanhood and self-esteem? This is the pilgrimage to Mecca that black folk must begin, or else we are a people lost forever."

Othello heard his roommate from the University shout, "Educate! Educate! Educate the people!" Ronnie and Sherry Kingsley had come down from Jackson with a cavalcade of black and white students. They had been working out of Jackson all summer in the registration drive.

"Just as Jesus of Nazareth was the Messiah to the ancient Hebrew children, Brother Malcolm was our black Messiah. He lived among us as a pimp, a hustler, a dope peddler, a jailbird. He knew our pain, our black pain, our degradation, our deprivation, because he was a black American who lived all of the deprivations black folks have experienced. Malcolm reached the lower depths of this sick society. But then he was converted."

"Educate! Educate! Educate!" From Othello's roommate.

Dave Woodson paused and stared at the audience. Eager faces, frightened, prideful, anxious, puzzled faces. Some scowls on a few white faces. David smiled. His face glowed, blackly glowed. Glowed blackly, as if he had been touched with inspiration. He was of medium height, slim, black, handsome, full-mouth, thick and shapely lips. Broad nostrils slightly turned up at the tip. Large eyes, the shape of almonds. Black and deep as a bottomless pit. His smile was like the white keys on a black piano.

He continued. "I have decided that in my writing and in other means of expressing myself, to stop this talking and writing in riddles and in pretty precious subtleties, going off into beautiful exercises of rhetorical ecstasies to say something that can be stated very simply. I have decided to speak so I can be understood by my own people, primarily. I mean, black people. There used to be a slogan in Harlem. 'Think black! Buy black! Vote black!' Well I have reached the decision to *talk black*."

"Talk black then, baby! Talk that black talk!"

Some sophisticated black folk stared back at Ronnie. Why did he insist on such vulgar outbursts? Did he think he was at one of those nigger camp meetings?

Dave Woodson said, "So when you hear me say that Brother Malcolm was converted, you know I mean that he was born again."

There was laughter and applause.

"He was born again, and he was preparing himself to lead us black folks out of the wilderness of self-hatred into the Promised Land of self-esteem. And so the Romans thought that here was a very dangerous man. Teaching niggers they aren't niggers. Teaching niggers to love themselves."

"Yes!"

"Teaching them not to love their enemies, but themselves."

"Yes!"

"Educate!"

"Teaching them not to love them who spit on them, but to love themselves."

The audience was stirred now, deeply stirred. Emotions were a fog of thickness like a mist hanging over the Delta. Applause interrupted him at the end of every sentence.

"Not to love those who practiced genocide against us but ourselves." He paused. "Our beautiful black wonderful—sometimes terrible—selves."

"Our beautiful black wonderful—sometimes terrible—selves," somebody in the audience repeated. And the audience erupted into laughing, crying, feet patting, hand clapping.

"Brother Malcolm didn't preach hate. He preached love. He was a great lover. But he believed that love, like charity, should begin at home. Must begin at home. He taught Negroes to love themselves, and he knew that if they loved themselves they would have no need to hate Mister Charlie, or any other people, as a people. And so the Romans evaluated the situation and concluded, 'This man is dangerous. He's teaching niggers to love themselves, and if they follow his teachings, they won't be niggers anymore. We must get rid of him. He's a true black revolutionary.' And so they gave the sign to Judas to destroy the black Messiah. And Brother Malcolm lies a-moldering in the grave, but his truth is marching on."

"Have mercy!"

"Educate!"

[414]

They applauded for two or three minutes, and Othello saw a black priest with a white inverted collar wipe his dark eyes with a large white handkerchief. Some were sobbing now, unashamedly, and some were blowing nostrils.

After the café last night they had driven out into the countryside, out into the 'Sippi bush. It was so dark out there in places and the bush so thick the full moon could not penetrate it. It had been an irresponsible thing for them to do, to go out there isolated from everybody. They even sneaked off from the Elders and they could have been waylaid and murdered and thrown into the swamp and might never have been found for years to come. As Ronnie and Bessie Mae and Sherry and Othello and Woodson had driven through the swampy bush, the hot humid mosquito-infested bush, chill after chill would spread across Othello's shoulders as he thought of legendary martyrs like Emmett Till and Parker and Chaney and Evers and Goodman and Schwerner, and further back, Willie McGee and all the rest. Many thousands gone. And Willie Banks and Luke Gibson. Even as he thought these thoughts, he listened to this great man, who had been born in this place, and "This is the place where my grandfather was born, and this is the birthplace of my mother and we used to have a ball-playing ball right in that field over there. And one time I was playing ten-ten-double-ten and I hid in the well, my body hanging down in the well, holding on by the fingertips, and everybody was found but me, and the one who was *it* came over near the well, and when she came too close I knew she would surely see my fingers holding on at the top of the well, and so I pulled my fingers in and fell *splash* all the way to the bottom. I wasn't going to let that girl find me. Of course I damn near drowned." They laughed as they drove through the Delta night, they laughed like it was the last laugh they would have together.

"We are not talking about hate this afternoon," Oculmugee's favorite son said. "We are talking about love. At this juncture, at this fork in the road of black and white relations, the questions of love and hate are total irrelevances. Whether I love or hate Mister Charles has nothing to do with anything. As we bring our black cause before the court of reparation, *love* for Charles is immaterial. But there is this strange sick need on the part of many white folk. They demand that black folk either love them or hate them, as long as, God should forbid, we never ever ignore them, as long as we continue to be obsessed with them. As long as we are not indifferent to them. But a slave cannot love his master unless that slave is out of his cotton-picking mind."

"If he do, he's out of his cotton-picking mind," echoed an old man in the audience.

Outside, black and white stood sweating in the churchyard, some of the women with multicolored parasols to shield them from the sun. Somebody said it was a hundred and seven in the shade. Policemen ringed the church. Policemen with rifles and shotguns and big, nervous, vicious dogs, each one straining at the leash. White peckerwood backwoodsmen standing on the other side of the dusty road. Black folk had started filling up the church since seven-thirty in the morning. By ten o'clock they were overflowing into the churchyard. Five persons had already passed out from the heat. They came from deep in the Delta, came from Jackson, came from Yazoo, came from Hattiesburg and Natchez, from the piney woods and the black prairie. Came to get the word from their favorite and most famous son. It was Big Meeting time and they came to the Great Big Meeting. Since the Big Meeting was to be held this time in Good Hope Baptist Church of Oculmugee, the church in which the famous son grew up, it was decided to bring him home and let him preach the lay sermon. And he had chosen his text, one brother said jokingly, from the gospel according to Saint Malcolm. The Brotherhood of Blackness was his theme. Many of these black folk knew Dave Woodson personally, had broken bread with him in their shacks at their humble tables. For he had come back home time and time again. Had talked with them and walked with them and shared their lodgings for a night. He had come back time and time again to the source. The Brotherhood of Blackness! It had a sound to it that left a good taste in your mouth, made your heart begin to beat wildly, proudly, in your chest. It frightened you, even as it lifted you. It was audacious, it was fearsome. Most of the white folks hated 'Sippi's famous son, most of the black folks loved him. Nobody was indifferent to him. Some black folks loved him, not because they had read his books or heard him speak. Some would never have heard of him had the white folks played it smart and cool. They were his best publicity agents.

On a cotton plantation deep in the Delta:

"What do you think of that Woodson nigger, Jeremiah?"

"I ain't never been to Woodson, Boss."

[416]

"I mean that nigger, David Woodson."

"Who he, Boss?"

"That foreign nigger stirring up all that trouble twixt the races?"

"I ain't never heard tell of him, boss sir, but ain't he from round these parts?"

"He bet not come down here no more if he knows what's good for him. We'll have him running like a suck-ass dog done got caught in a old hen's nest."

"We will?"

"I ain't whistling 'Dixie!' "

"You sure ain't whistling 'Dixie.' No-sir-ree-bob!"

"He gon be on that interview television show tonight coming out of New York City, New York. Don't you waste your good time looking at it, you hear me, Jeremiah?"

Jeremiah answers, "Boss, you sure ain't just whistling 'Dixie.' " Thinking to himself, "That there David Woodson sure do upset these peckerwoods. I'm gon see what he putting down this evening if I live and nothing don't happen."

At a turpentine camp in piney woods:

"You going to the Big Meeting this year, Jim?"

"What kinda big meeting, Cap'n."

"You know what kinda big meeting, you black sly bastard." Good-naturedly.

"The only way I'm gon know about it is if you gon be telling me about it, Cap'n."

"It was over in Hattiesburg last year and you outwhooped and hollered everybody else."

"Oh—you mean *that* Big Meeting."

"What other kind Big Meeting is there?"

"I ain't heard tell of no other kind."

"Well—you going or aincha?"

"No sir—not this year. I don't b'lieve I will."

"It's a good thing too, cause it ain't gon be nothing but a whole heapa mess with that Northern David Woodson nigger preaching hatred 'tween the races."

Jim Diddly scratches his head even though it doesn't itch. "Well I declare." Meaning: Thank you, Cap'n, for telling me all about it. Maybe I'll make the Big Meeting after all.

And so they came to the Big Meeting from all over.

"Call it Black Power," David said to the fan-waving, perspiring audience. "Call it black love, call it black consciousness, call it anything you like. Sometimes I like to call it the Brotherhood of Blackness. We must learn to love and trust each other. We must learn to love and trust each other so much that we would trust our lives in each other's hands. Love each other so deeply that we would put our destinies in each other's hands. Our destinies have been in white hands all these centuries and it has left us empty-handed. Yet some of us right here in this church are still mumbling about, 'I don't know nothing about no black sheriff, no black mayor, no black governor. That might be carrying it a little too far.' But our love must be strong enough to overcome distrust of each other. You mean to tell me you would rather have Sheriff Digby Adams and his deputies whipping your heads, than to have a black sheriff, elected by you and responsible to you, to protect your heads from being whipped?"

"No!"

"No!"

"Have mercy!"

"Will you register?"

"Yes!"

"Will you vote black?"

"Yes!"

"Vote black, Jesus!"

"This is the meaning of Black Power, brothers and sisters. It means a new day for Mississippi. It means black love."

"Yes!"

"Black love!"

"It means black dignity."

"Black dignity!"

"Yes, Jesus!"

"Is Black Power against black businessmen?"

"Is it?"

"Tell us, Little David."

"Black Power stands for black economic power, therefore it is not against black business."

"Talk about it, Brother David."

"Black Power means black freedom," David Woodson said.

"It truly do mean black freedom!"

"It means one man, one vote."

"One man, one vote is all it means," the colored lady shouted.

Dave asked, "Does black freedom mean white slavery?"

[418]

"No!" a young man answered.

"Do it?" An old man wasn't too sure.

Dave said, "It does not mean white slavery. Our fight as black people for Black Power does not threaten the poor white folks. They don't have any power to begin with. In Mississippi, they're about as poor as poor can be."

The laughter of agreement.

"They are not threatened by us, because they don't have anything we want. The only thing they have we don't have is their whiteness, and that is the one thing we do not want. Right? We want our blackness. We affirm the beauty of our blackness. White poor folks have everything to gain from our struggle for Black Power, because one of our aims is to fight a last-ditch struggle with poverty. One of our slogans will be 'Death to poverty.' "

"Death to poverty!" they repeated.

"Not death to poor folks," he explained. "But death to poverty."

"Death to poverty."

"Death to black poverty."

"Yeah!"

"Death to white poverty."

"Yeah." Not quite as enthusiastic.

"When the poor white folks understand deep deep inside of them what we are up to they will join hands with us maybe." He paused. "But we ain't waiting for no days like that."

The audience erupted with applause and laughter.

"In our thrust for Black Power, we *do* pose a threat to the white power structure. We cannot create power out of nothing. So when we say we're fighting for Black Power, that means it has to come from somewhere, which means it has to come from the white power structure. Right? Which means we have to take it. From Mister Charlie Rich-Man."

"Do Jesus!"

"From Mister Charlie Politician."

"Yeah!"

"From Rankin and from Eastland."

"Have mercy!"

"And from Rogers Jefferson Davis Johnson."

"Yesssss!"

"And from Charles James Richard Wakefield."

The decision to have David Woodson speak at the Big Meeting

[419]

had not been a unanimous one. There were some black preachers who felt as threatened as most white folk did at the very mention of Woodson's name. Some claimed he advocated violence. Some claimed he taught race hatred. Some claimed everything the big white folk claimed about this famous son of 'Sippi. But the more some of the black preachers declared against him the more some others wanted to see for themselves.

One brother got the floor and said, "This David Woodson must be the second coming of the Devil, and beingst as how I ain't never heard tell of no black Devil before, I'm gon vote for him to come before us. And see what a black Devil looks like, and see what a black Devil walks like, and see what a black Devil talks like. I'm gon certainly look forward to it."

When the vote was taken, it was thirty-five to seven for him to be invited. Then came the pressure from big white folks to rescind the invitation. The day before the Big Meeting, the Big Meeting Committee met with a group of Elders for Protection, and got a promise from them that they would not show up at the church. If they were determined to protect Brother Woodson, then they would have to agree to accompany him to within a block of the church, at which time he would be met by church-men and escorted to the church. When the meeting ended, they could take up their armed protection of him, when he was again a block away from the church. Either this was agreed to, or the meeting would be called off or another speaker would be sub-stituted. The Elders grudgingly and nervously agreed. There would be no black guns within a block of the church.

"The Bible says, 'The wages of sin is death.' But we must also understand that the wages of life can likewise be death, and sometimes some men must die to live, must die so that their brothers and sisters might live, and more abundantly. This is the meaning of black consciousness. We must sacrifice for each other in this Brotherhood of Blackness."

"Yes, little David!"

Woodson had come into town yesterday morning. The large snow-white wooden-frame church was on the southern edge of town, sitting off the road in an amphitheater of bright green clear-ing amidst a grove of pine trees that glistened like icicles as the sunlight danced upon them. Othello had arrived shortly after noon of the day before, and he and Dave had spent every waking hour together ever since.

[420]

It was Big Meeting time, and folks had come from all over everywhere. Country people and town people. Farmers, croppers, day workers, domestics, factory workers, a dribble here and there of middle-class black folk, schoolteachers, preachers, one or two doctors. Businessmen. Students. Many students. Every family brought a basket. Scores of long wooden tables on both sides of the church, and behind the church all the way to the woods, loaded with food. And everybody seemed to know David Woodson.

"Come here, boy, and let me look at you and hug you. Knowed you since you was knee-high to a hoppergrass!"

Old women, young women, all of them hugged and kissed him.

"Great big little old Davey Woodson. You don't remember me, boy. What's my name?"

"Of course I remember you, Mister Ben. You gave me the first real job I ever had. When I was seven years old I worked as your helper on the parcel delivery wagon during the Christmas season."

Mr. Ben threw back his grizzled old head and howled with laughter. "Boy, you really is a mess! After all that famosity you done got all over the world you still remember old triflin' Ben Evans!"

The tables were piled high with home-cooking. Fried chicken, potato salad, black-eyed peas, ham, chitterlings. Barrels of ice-cold lemonade all over the place.

One man walked up to David and threw his arms around his shoulders. "Just keep on keeping on, Davey boy. Give them peckerwoods heapa hell. Give 'em down-the-country."

Othello noticed that every now and then some of the men would wander off into the woods behind the church, and come back with a livelier walk and a different look about them. Some eyes were getting redder and redder, some breaths were strong enough to knock you down. This not being Othello's first Big Meeting, he suspected there was a place in the woods where the drinks were stronger than lemonade.

Once David turned to Othello. "These are the people, Othello. These are the folks that count." David's eyes were misty. His voice was strangely gruff. "These are the people and don't you ever forget it! I forgot it for a couple of years. I thought the most important people were my liberal white friends in New York. I can't tell you how many hours I spent with them, being flattered

[421]

and admired by them, sipping cocktails with them, learning to laugh and talk with them—like them. I had become a white man in a black skin, and I thought I was free—free at last. But it was nothing, Othello. It was a fake! It was pure sham! I thought it was everything, but it was pure sham from the git-go! I don't blame my white liberal friends. They meant well, or didn't mean well. It doesn't matter. It was me! Me! In flight from myself! In flight from all the Great Big Meetings! I thought I was in flight from Mister Charlie, but I was running from my blackness, from my blessed negritude. Everybody in that other world called me Mister, treated me respectfully, like a brother sometimes, but I was nothing but a modern Uncle Tom, a slicked-up Gunga Din, even as I gave forth with my militant pronouncements. I thought my job then was to scare hell out of white folks, or at least to titillate them."

Othello was embarrassed for his great friend, by this sudden great outpouring. This self-criticism. He started to protest. "But you couldn't, I mean——"

"Oh yes I did. Yes I was. I was lost, because I had lost all this —all my Big Meetings were behind me. I had lost my soul in this place. But I'm home, Othello! I'm home, baby! And I'll never leave home again, even if I go around the world a million times. Even if I never return to Oculmugee again in all my life, I'll never leave my negritude. I mean the fellowship of my blackness!" David wiped his face with a large white handkerchief and slyly dabbed his eyes. "You understand, Othello?" His voice choked off.

Othello was deeply moved also. He could only say, "Yes! Yes! I understand!"

"I mean a black man must first find freedom amongst his own folks, or everything else is unadulterated bee-ess, sounding brass and tinkling symbol, signifying nothing." He laughed. "I was lost but now I'm found—was blind but now I see."

All that day they laughed and talked and ate and drank with the folks. "This day, I have taken far more than I have given," David told Othello that night. "Taken enough love and fellowship and belonging and soul to last a lifetime. Brother, I have drunk deeply from the fountain of soul."

They even went with a few brothers into the woods a couple of times and drank from the fountain of country corn.

Chapter
6

And now 'Sippi's favorite black son stood in the pulpit wiping his wide forehead. He had been speaking for more than half an hour in all that Mississippi heat and not a brother or sister had moved out of the church.

"One of the gravest dangers facing the Movement is the alienation, the drawing away of the black middle class from the black impoverished masses. The new thing is that where there used to be token integration, the establishment, the white power structure, may be ready now to buy off the entire Negro middle class and separate them forever from the black poor folk. And most of our people are black and poor and uninfluential."

"Yes they is! Lord knows they is!"

"Teachers, preachers, doctors, lawyers, economists, civil servants. Integrate them. Buy them off. Even let them marry your daughters. But never have the slightest intention of integrating the Negro masses. The danger is the black middle class will buy this alienation. Will allow themselves to be estranged from their black roots and their black culture. The danger is that the black bourgeoisie hates itself enough to become white men in black skins and think they got the better of the bargain. Think they put something over on Mister Charlie, the shrewdest con man of them all."

A man in the front row shouted, "Little David, play on your harp!"

David smiled. "When I was a child, I spake as a child, I understood as a child, I thought as a child. But when I became a man, I put away childish things."

"Amen!" the congregation shouted.

"Lord have mercy!"

"Tell the truth and spite the Devil!"

Woodson continued. "And if we're serious about this business of freedom for black people, brothers and sisters, we must put away childish things."

"Yes!"

"He said, put away childish things!"

"Educate! Educate! Educate the people!"

"We must put away this childish notion that we're going to love the Man into giving us freedom."

A brother in the third row shouted, "Put away childish things."

Woodson said, "We must also put away this notion that we're going to hate the Man into giving us freedom."

"Yes!" ... "Yes!" ... "All right!"

"Some of our so-called militants seem to think we can titillate the white man by calling him bad names, dirty names, and in that way, we'll be able to cuss him into granting our freedom."

"Put away childish things!"

"We must put away this childish notion that the Man is going to *give* us freedom on any basis."

"Yes!"

"We must also put away the childish notion that the Man is going to give us power."

"Educate!" an old lady shouted.

"Frederick Douglass said over a hundred years ago: 'Find out how much a man will take and that is exactly what you give him.'"

"God bless old Fred Douglass!"

"We black folk will take only as much power, we will take only as much freedom, as we're strong enough to take."

"Tell everything, Brother Woodson! Don't hold nothing back!"

David wiped the perspiration from his face. "Black Power means black strength. The pooling of black strength to take some power from Captain Charlie, power that he had no business with in the first place. But he had enough white strength to take it from us and keep it. And now it's time for us to take it back. What is the Brotherhood of Blackness?"

"Tell us what it is!"

As Othello listened, he basked, as it were, in the sunlight of his own complacency. He bathed in the glowing warmth of his great friend's profound friendship. He thought of the hours, the days, the months, the years ahead for both of them. The times that they would share together, as men, exchanging words and feelings, concepts, ideas, actions, that would shake the earth's foundations. Sometimes, in the deep deep swampy delta of his lonely isolation, he had known a helpless feeling that there was no time left in all the world for anything. Judgment Day was just around the bend of the River. But today, he felt a certain timelessness and endlessness of everything. And everything was possible. And everything was probable. For he had all the time there was and all the time there ever would be. David and he would change the world. They were young and they were friends and together they would change the world.

"The Brotherhood of Blackness means we must pool together all our mutual black experiences in this place and the experiences of black folk everywhere. We must pool our mutual sufferings, our triumphs and defeats, our love for each other, our self-respect, our confidence in each other, our consciousness of ourselves and of each other. When we do all this, then we will be able to join black hands together and truly sing 'We shall overcome,' not someday—but today—now—this very moment!"

Outside the church the people stood around, quietly attentive, as if they could hear what went on inside the church. Police with police dogs still held forth on the perimeter of the gathering. Peckerwoods stood across the road. Elders stood with rifles at the ready a block away from the church at the eastern and western approaches to the block in which the church stood on Chickasaw Road. The 'Sippi sun beat down on everything, the road, the houses, the cars, the people. Its intention seemed to be to set the world on fire. The stained glass windows of the church blinked back at the unrelenting sun. Inside, the people had begun to sing "We Shall Overcome Some Day." Outside, the people joined hands and swayed back and forth, and sang, "We Shall Overcome Some Day." Their faces shone with perspiration, their faces shone with the dignity of determination. Some eyes were filled with weeping, silent weeping, as they sang "We Shall Overcome Some Day." Deep in their hearts. From deep deep in their hearts they sang. Deep deep in their hearts and souls.

The church was emptying now. Black folks milled restlessly around the church grounds, especially around the entrance. Some, who were unable to get inside the church, strained to get one glimpse of 'Sippi's famous son. One woman sighed, "If I could just touch the hem of his garment."

Inside, David Woodson and Othello and Little Jake and Bessie Mae and a couple of others around David had to fight their way

[425]

to the front of the church. Young people wanted autographs, and David, though whipped by the heat, refused to refuse them autographs. Old folks and middle-aged ones threw their arms around him, smiling, crying, laughing, hugging him and kissing him. "God bless you honey!" "God go with you and stand by you!" Earlier, Othello had introduced Little Jake as the chief elder of the Elders for Protection and Defense of Wakefield County. David had shaken Jake's hand warmly, and said, "May your tribes increase." Old men, young men shook hands.

"We with you every step the way!"

Despite all the words he had written in magazines and books and all the speeches he had made on the question of self-defense, ironically enough, David did not like to be overprotected. He had been all over the Southland in the recent past, and he always went out of his way to avoid overprotection. Every chance he got he would give his bodyguards the slip. In Birmingham—in New Orleans—in Jacksonville.

Finally they reached the back of the church and stepped out into the sunlight. And the crowd outside surged toward them. And the hugging and the kissing and handshaking and the pulling at David began all over again. Meanwhile a big black Oldsmobile sedan loaded with white men had parked on Chickasaw Road three long country blocks away.

In the churchyard they were literally pulling their famous son apart. It was as if they meant to tear him apart and each keep a tiny part of him as a souvenir. The native son kept smiling. He was having the greatest time of his life. But he was tiring. He was only human. Othello saw the tiredness in his great friend's eyes.

When Woodson stumbled and almost fell, Reverend Bullock, the pastor of the Good Hope Baptist Church, bellowed in his good strong country Baptist voice. "All right! All right! Let's show our brother we love him enough to give him just a little ree-spite. Just a little ree-spite. He'll be back this afternoon to see the baseball game, and he'll be back to tend tonight's Big Meeting." The crowd still pulled at David Woodson.

"I just want to shake his hand one time!"

"Carry Jesus with you, Davey Woodson!"

"I just want to touch him one little time!"

They ripped his jacket. Reverend Bullock pleaded with them, begged them, cajoled them, told them God wouldn't bless them the way they were acting, told them to have a little mercy and

[426]

show a little compassion for their brother. "He'll be back. I told you he'd be back. He'll be back to the ball game and to tonight's meeting. I heard him preach today. Now he gon have to listen to me preach tonight." The crowd grudgingly, laughingly, complainingly, gave ground.

And finally Woodson, flanked by Othello and Reverend Bullock and Little Jake and Bessie Mae, moved down Chickasaw Road in an easterly direction toward the Elders standing at the ready. Two of the peckerwoods across the way began to whoop and holler and gave out with their rebel yells.

"Yi—hoooo!"

"Yi—hoooo!"

It startled Othello and the group at first. They stopped momentarily and stared across the way at the howling peckerwoods. Then they started toward the Elders again, who started toward them, keeping an eye on the place where the peckerwoods whooped and hollered. Alerted for trouble. Forgotten was their pledge to stay at least a block from the church. It was not the place they should have watched though. The whooping was the signal; it was also the diversion.

A white man got unnoticed out of the parked car three blocks away and climbed quickly atop of it and took cold aim with his high-powered rifle. He took cold quick aim and pulled the trigger once. He jumped down off the top of the car and leaped inside, and the car did a sweeping U-turn and sped away in a whirlwind of dust back up Chickasaw Road.

Othello's body hit the earth, it seemed, almost before the shot rang out. Gunned down in broad daylight? He felt a wetness on his forehead, and his hand went up exploring. When he took his hand away, instead of blood he stared at perspiration. He laughed at first; he couldn't help it. It felt so good to be alive. Alive! Unharmed! Then he thought guiltily of David Woodson. He raised himself and looked anxiously about him; his heart beat like summer thunder. He saw his friend stretched out as if in slumber. And felt a great shame at the recent laughter which had slipped from him involuntarily, and at the gladness he could not help feeling that he was still alive—breathing, sweating, crying.

For David Woodson lay dead in the middle of the road in front of the Good Hope Baptist Church. He lay dead in the blistering sunlight that danced off the stained-glass windows. He lay

[427]

dead now in the arms of his weeping friend and brother, Charles Othello Chaney. It had happened so quickly, Othello thought that maybe this was one of those dreams he sometimes dreamed. He was a boy who had dreamed every night of his life. Surely this was one of his horrible nightmares. And he would wake up any minute and be glad that he'd been dreaming, and go out on the back porch and get himself a drink of water. It had worked for him like that so many times before. He stared down at David, as if he expected to find the answer in his great friend's face, as if he expected David to open his eyes and wink one of them at him, and the whole thing would be one great big colossal joke. But David's eyes did not wink at him, his face did not break into a smile for his buddy, Chuck Othello Chaney. His face was relaxed, weary but relaxed. Tired, but relaxed and happy. It had happened so quickly and the sniper's aim had been so accurate, David had not even had time for his face to change expression. He had died relaxed and happy.

As he stared at his great friend, Othello remembered words his friend had spoken just minutes ago inside the church.

"The wages of sin is death, and sometimes men must die to live. A man, who has nothing he would die for, is a man who has nothing to live for."

He shook his head from side to side. "No! No! No!" He wept.

When the shot first rang out, the black folk outside the church were startled into a state of complete immobility for a moment. As the whole world stood still right there in Mississippi in Oculmugee on Chickasaw Road in front of the Good Hope Baptist Church.

Then someone said, "He's dead! He's dead! David Woodson is dead!"

"They killed him!"

"They killed him!"

"Lord Jesus have mercy!"

"Keep calm!" a preacher said excitedly. "Be Christian ever step the way!"

It was as if he had said, "Get em! Get the goddamn peckerwoods!" For they went immediately into motion. Some of them moved toward the group around the body. Others moved toward the white folk on the other side of the road, who should have had sense enough to have moved off more quickly. Enraged black folk set upon the few white folk and beat them about their heads and kicked them and knocked them down and stomped them into the dark gray earth, blood splattering all over the earth, slowly turning it red. And they surely would have torn them limb from limb had not the police moved in quickly with their guns and nightsticks and their police dogs. There were police cars in evidence, but not a single one of them drove off after the black Oldsmobile. By the time the Elders took off after it, it was already out of sight.

EPILOGUE

Within an hour the news went out around the world. Riots broke out in all the major cities of the United States. Black American soldiers deserted all across the earth. Some of the black leaders went on national television, looking as if they were in a state of sustained shock, as they undoubtedly were, and called on all black Americans to stick by their dedication to the Christian principle of nonviolence. "Don't let your white brother bring you down to his level. Don't let him make you hate him. Love your enemy. Pray for him who spitefully abuses you." A black brother spoke these pious words at a street meeting in Harlem, and the riot squad of New York's Finest had to move speedily to save his life at the hands of his black brothers.

Othello vaguely heard the sound of sirens as the ambulance drove up Chickasaw Road more than a half an hour after his great buddy fell. He looked toward the ambulance as it sped toward him, making enough noise to wake up the dead. But it could never waken David Woodson. He was dead, forever dead. Othello laid his friend's head gently now upon the dark earth and got to his feet. Bessie Mae stood beside him, weeping unashamedly. He put his arms around her to tell her not to cry, but his voice choked off and he felt helpless tears spill down his own face. The police had cleared the streets a few moments before, but hundreds of black folk had collected again. Othello stared through his tears at Ronnie and Sherry making their way through the crowd of black folk toward him and Bessie Mae and Jake and Reverend Bullock and a few other black folk who were standing resolutely near their fallen brother. Between the little group near the body and the crowd that thronged the streets and churchyard was a ring of white policemen. Protecting whom? From whom?

Jake was mumbling to himself. "I just can't believe it! I just can't believe it! How come we let it happen? How come we let it happen? It'll never happen again, I swear to God, it ain't gonna be like this again. This time we gon teach the whole damn world a lesson!"

The cops would not let Ron and Sherry into the inner circle. They stood there just on the other side. Ron now with his hands dangling helplessly at his side and Sherry's head against his chest. Othello could hear her screaming, "What're we going to do? What're we going to do?" This girl who was possessed of such magnificent poise and sophistication. "What're we going to do?" Ron would not try to answer, knowing full well the question was rhetorical, and that he had no answer for her. "Lord have mercy!" Sherry shouted. "Lord have mercy!" Somehow Othello was surprised to hear her call on the Lord for mercy. She, who did not believe in God. He knew it was just a saying with her, coming to the surface from the depths of her background, from her fellowship of blackness. Yet he wanted to shout back at her: "No need to ask God for His mercy. If there is a God, He damn sure must be white!" But he stood there saying nothing, feeling nothing, numbed and feeling nothing, except that he should be feeling something.

All over the world in every corner of the earth, American Embassies were stoned and set afire. London, Moscow, Paris, Rio, Buenos Aires. Outraged demonstrations everywhere, especially in the colored nations of black Africa and brown Asia. Pitched battles between black and white Americans in the rice paddies of Vietnam. The President expressed his sense of outrage and great loss at the incident in Oculmugee and called upon the nation to be calm in this hour of great stress. One of the "big six" colored leaders called for a pilgrimage to attend the funeral of our "fallen comrade-in-arms." Another leader followed suit. "Let us march on Mississippi in the spirit of nonviolence!"

Woodson's body lay "in state" for five days in the Good Hope Baptist Church. From morning till late at night when the church closed, the people came, black folks from all walks of life. A long line of blackness that stretched around the church and up the road for ten long blocks. Quiet people, angry people. They came to stare briefly upon his face, and go away perhaps changed forevermore. From his death they hoped to gather strength to live. They made pledges to themselves that he should not have died in vain. The spectacle of the long never-ending line of black folks scared the hell out of the courageous men of the white establishment of the great Magnolia State.

On the second morning after Woodson fell, a middle-aged colored lady, on her way to make life easy for a rich white family, passed the white First Baptist Church of Oculmugee. It was early in the morning, in the cool of early morning, as the rich white folks still slumbered like newborn babies without consciences. By the time "her white family" arose from slumber, their breakfast would be ready for them. All that was required of them was a hearty appetite. As she walked along, lost in thought, she almost stumbled over the object. She stopped and stared down at the white man lying dead and bloody just in front of her. She smiled. It was a smile all mixed up with compassion and a funny sense of great fulfillment. "Aah Lord," Sister Jamison mumbled to herself. "He sure do work mysterious ways." And went on about her business. She said nothing to a soul about it. Later that morning a white man discovered the body and pushed the panic button. All day long, Sister Jamison went around the white folks' house doing her chores, and she couldn't get that Bible quotation out of her mind to save her life. Sometimes she even said it aloud. "A eye for a eye. A tooth for a tooth." The Lord sure do work mysterious ways.

Back in the rest of the world, the pilgrimage had started. The pilgrimage gathered momentum, even at that very moment, as Othello and Jake and Bessie Mae and Sherry and Ron stood with thousands of others in the line that led to the church where David Woodson lay so beautifully, so dignifiedly "in state," with Elders standing stiffly at attention on both sides of the casket. They were the honor guard, and they did themselves great honor. They stood guard in shifts, and they never left their fallen brother unguarded for a single moment day or night. He was a soldier fallen in battle. He was a martyr of the black revolution. And possibly the revolution had finally begun. For real this time.

Even as Othello stood there now staring down into the casket at his swollen-faced buddy, his brother of the brotherhood, black folk were converging by the hundreds of thousands from all over the nation. Some flew in from Europe, Africa, and Asia. All roads led to Mississippi to the Delta to Oculmugee to the Good Hope

Baptist Church. They came on foot, came in buses, by air, by train, some rode the rails, hoboed, hitchhiked. They came from churches, came from lodges and associations, they came, they walked off their jobs and headed southward, they came angry, proud, defiant, singing, cussing, threatening. Some came with a terrible vengeance in their hearts; others came nonviolently. Came from SNCC, from SCLC, NAACP, the Urban League, CORE, NNLC, came from the Council of Negro Women, from the Federation of Colored Women's Clubs. The Muslims and Christians came. Jews came. Even infidels. The Deacons and the Elders came with their arms and ammunition. Men came from the labor movement. Came from the Willing Workers Club of Harlem, the Busy Bees, the Shining Lights, the Yorubas, the Climbers, the Ebonites, the Elks, the Masons. Some white groups threatened to pull out of the pilgrimage unless they got certain assurances as to how the funeral would be conducted, and unless the "big six" could hold down the number of people coming. The first call had been for twenty thousand marchers, but things had gotten out of hand almost immediately. Out of about a million people clogging the highways and the train stations and the airports all over the country, five hundred of them were noncolored. Most noncolored friends of the Movement went into temporary hiding. The President called out the National Guard and converted them into Federal troops, and dispatched fifteen regiments of infantry to Oculmugee and other places in the state.

Each morning of the remaining three days that David Woodson lay in state, some sleepy, early-bird Oculmugeean came suddenly and startlingly alive, as he stumbled upon a different white man, in front of a different church, lying on his back staring at the rising sun with sightless eyes, lying so peacefully in death with the sunlight on his face and a bullet in his chest. Each mother's son lay piously and primly in a lovely section of the white, inviolate community.

By the evening of the third day, hundreds of thousands of pilgrims had already reached the State of 'Sippi and were pitching tents in any field they found on every approach to Oculmugee. Some sensitive Oculmugeeans thought that a black army was laying siege to their fair city. It didn't help them at all to get rid of their insomnia. Black folk pitched tents in the cotton fields, they trampled on the corn. The "kindly" white plantation owners did not order the trespassers from the land, as might very

[433]

well have been expected. It was a curious thing, a thing unprecedented, the way the Governor of 'Sippi and the 'Sippi KKK and the White Citizens Council, with one clear and united voice, called upon the good Christian-hearted people of the great Magnolia State, regardless of race, creed, or color, to "Love ye one another. Let nonviolence be the watchword, in the spirit of the brotherhood of all men and the fatherhood of our Lord and Savior." Some black folk couldn't believe their ears. And kept their rifles at the ready. Hundreds of thousands were already at points around Oculmugee and hundreds of thousands were on the way, even as Othello stared at his fallen buddy, his friend and comrade so relaxed in death. Othello's eyes and ears played tricks on him. He thought he saw David's swollen lips move and thought he heard him say, as clear as summer sunlight:

"The wages of life is death, my brother. Sometimes some men must die to live, so that other men might live and more abundantly, and die more naturally."

As he moved away from the open casket, an old black woman lifted her two- and three-year-old grandchildren so that they could look upon the remains of David Woodson.

"Place your hand on his face, both of y'all," the old lady told them in a strange fierce voice, "and swear in the name of Great God Almighty, that as soon as each one of y'all is strong enough to lift a rifle, the first thing you will do is to register to vote and the next thing is to join up with the Elders."

Othello turned back toward the casket. He felt a wetness in his eyes again, as cold-hot chills spread over his back and shoulders like live electric currents. Then his eyes cleared. His mind cleared. His body, firm, no longer shivered. It was not the time for shivering. And the crying time was over. He placed his right hand on his buddy's forehead, even as the children drew their hands away. He was barely twenty-one, but it was time to join the Elders. He thought grimly, there was no time not to join the Elders.

He thought: *When I was a child, I spake as a child, I understood as a child, I thought as a child: but when I became a man, I put away childish things.*